# WHERE ELEPHANTS FOUGHT

## THE MURDER OF CONFEDERATE GENERAL EARL VAN DORN

BRIDGET H. SMITH

*Bridget Smith*

MILFORD HOUSE

an imprint of Sunbury Press, Inc.
Mechanicsburg, PA USA

**MILFORD HOUSE**

an imprint of Sunbury Press, Inc.
Mechanicsburg, PA USA

ISBN: 978-1-62006-598-3 (Trade Paperback)
ISBN: 978-1-62006-599-0 (eBook)

Library of Congress Control Number: 2015941725

FIRST MILFORD HOUSE PRESS EDITION: March 2018

Product of the United States of America
0 1 1 2 3 5 8 13 21 34 55

Set in Bookman Old Style
Designed by Crystal Devine
Cover by Lawrence Knorr
Edited by Amanda Shrawder

*Continue the Enlightenment!*

# Acknowledgements

Special thanks to my husband Ray for his incredible eye for detail and endless encouragement, and to my children Hays, Madison, Jackson, and Audrey Anne, for their love and support throughout the long years of research and writing.

To my mother Lunette Harris who went out of her way to read and edit anytime of the day or night, who helped me sort through the maze of research, and supported me every step of the way.

To Bonnie McBee Bak, my dearest friend and the inspiration I needed to write this book.

And to Nate Lenow who shared my dream.

*What is history but a fable agreed upon.*
—Napoleon Bonaparte

# AUTHOR'S NOTE

When I was a child, I spent a great deal of time daydreaming—not of dragons and castles, though. My dreams were often set within the cold, lifeless walls of the antebellum homes that dotted the lush hills surrounding my hometown; places like the Rectory of the Athenaeum School, and St. John's Church; Rippavilla, and Rattle and Snap, to name a few. These dreams were long and sweeping like the landscapes of their settings, rich as the ground beneath those opulent mansions, timeless stories of love and sacrifice, their characters aristocratic and fair-haired. And so I floated through warm summer nights in a bedroom whose open windows hosted cricket symphonies in perfect sync with the flicker of lightning bugs, and there I dreamed of long silk skirts and buggy rides, handsome generals and gray, tin-typed soldiers. These were the characters most dear to my heart and thus the heroes and heroines of my childish fantasies. It is only natural that the story of the beautiful Jessie Peters and the dashing General Van Dorn would catch my fancy and haunt me for nearly a quarter century—haunt me until I at last uncovered the truth.

Perhaps it was a voice from the grave—Jessie or Earl, Medora or Clara—that compelled me to search through countless records and manuscripts, diaries and biographies, to trudge on until I found a living Peters relative in search of the same answers, a Memphis private investigator named Nate Lenow, a burly man with a cop's sixth sense, the perfect research companion, a man who was not only enchanted by the story of his ancestors, but who also shared my idea that historians had perpetuated a long-held lie about the circumstances surrounding the general's murder—a lie whose initial purpose had been to protect an innocent girl—the daughter of the murderer himself.

Over the course of several months, Nate and I shared our research and our theories, and after collecting overwhelming evidence, we were elated to find our search had not been in vain. The facts as they were presented some 150 years ago were skewed; some were even outright lies. If not for advances in research, and the mere passing of time, it is likely that this secret would have remained buried under the layers of love and betrayal that had kept it hidden for so long.

This is the story of one tragedy during the dark days of our American Civil War. The names and places mentioned herein are real, with the exception of a few minor characters created only when research failed to name them, the motivations of the characters deduced through exhaustive research and human intuition. The evidence will speak for itself.

My only hope is that the truth might find acceptance if only in the pages of this book.

# FOREWORD

By January of 1863, General Earl Van Dorn had become one of the more controversial characters in the Confederate Army. Known for his youthful good looks and sophistication, he carried himself with the pomp and circumstance of a king, though his personal reputation was tainted by rumors of ungentlemanly conduct, and his military record was dotted with battlefield losses. He was charming and intelligent, a talented musician and painter, who never failed to disappoint his superior officers in the field, and almost always managed to raise an eyebrow (or skirt) in the social arena.

A graduate of West Point and a decorated soldier in the U.S. Army, he was a career military man whose desire for fame far outweighed his devotion to his wife and children; in fact, after nearly twenty years of marriage, he had never provided a permanent home for his family.

So it was when General Van Dorn made his way into Tennessee that winter, his foul reputation far preceded him. Though he had just conducted a very successful raid in Holly Springs, Mississippi, in which he burned over a million dollars worth of General Grant's supplies, he still suffered under the weight of Corinth and the subsequent court martial hearing. His own home state of Mississippi had even turned against him, the once bright star of Jeff Davis and the Confederate Army was now despised, his name synonymous with that of a lecher, a drunk, and an insubordinate—a failure in every instance.

Yet, General Van Dorn held out hope that the lush Tennessee Valley would save him, would offer a new opportunity for the glory he so hoped to attain. He was confident, eager, and undaunted by public opinion. And in the sleepy village of Spring Hill, a quiet hamlet of churches and rich farmland, the townsfolk were eager as well, ripe for some excitement, maybe even a little scandal, especially the beautiful Jessie McKissack Peters. In this, the dashing Van Dorn would not disappoint.

*General Earl Van Dorn, CSA*
*(Courtesy of Mississippi Department of Archives and History)*

### Where Elephants Fought

*The gigantic beasts disengage,*
*Back slowly away,*
*Seemingly satisfied they stagger in opposite directions,*
*A scarred hide,*
*A marred tusk,*
*Nothing of consequence —*
*But the ground,*
*As if plowed,*
*Chips of wood like a sawmill floor*
*And vegetation ground into a green powder.*
*An acre of devastation*
*This hole in the jungle to endure for hundreds of years*
*Where elephants fought.*

*From the Diary of Jessie Peters*

*Monday, January 22, 1863*

 *Today is absolutely dreadful, as the rain has fallen since midday without cease. But I have just received the most exciting news. The Athenaeum will host a benefit concert in the next few weeks. It seems the rumor that fresh troops were coming is true after all. It will be simply grand having all those handsome officers around. Why, my insides are burning with excitement! If the newspapers are correct, the leader of these men is none other than that handsome General Van Dorn I met in Holly Springs last summer. So full of charm and wit—why, he's positively perfection. If he is indeed coming, I expect this will be a spring like none other!*

# CHAPTER 1

# INTO TENNESSEE

*"Cavalry knows no danger—knows no failure; what it is ordered to do, it must do."*
—GENERAL EARL VAN DORN (GENERAL ORDER NO. 5; FEBRUARY 1863)

**February 20, 1863**

General Van Dorn roused in his tent to the sound of cracking limbs. He moved slowly in the bitter cold and peered out the canvas doorway as a large, yellow moon lit the ground below. His men had made crude beds in the adjacent open field, away from the thick grove, but close enough to camp to avoid capture. He had retired before sundown since they would need to rise very early if they were to make Columbia before nightfall next day. An icy rain had covered the ancient pines, and the weighty branches snapped under pressure, falling like the very cones they held. He looked up at the limbs just above his tent and satisfied himself that he was in no danger and then returned to his cot and pulled the woolen blanket to his chin. His fevers had subsided over the last few weeks, but even the slightest chill could cause a recurrence and knock him off his feet again. This bout had left him frail, his mind mottled. He had work to do in Tennessee. No time for weakness.

The general peeked through a hole in his tent and watched as the angry cook cussed his damp fire and threw a load of kindling on top of the wet twigs. A cloud of smoke shot up and over toward a group of men swapping letters from home. They waved their hands and coughed and cussed back at the old cook. One soldier, propped against a tree listening as his friend read aloud from some local paper, threw a handful of acorns at the old man. But the cook took no notice of him.

The general closed his eyes again and tried to concentrate on the morning's route. He must move cautiously, must avoid the enemy at all cost. His men needed a break from the fighting. He needed a break from the bad press. The only hope now was for some great victory to come his way.

A tune drifted in from some lonely campfire and he hummed along, relishing every soothing sound. Eventually he drifted off to sleep, traveling back in time to Holly Springs, and endless supply trains, the smoke of burning buildings, and smiling beauties in sleeping dresses shouting from their open windows, "Hoorah for Van Dorn!" and "Long live the Confederacy!"

A sudden noise startled him awake and he rolled onto his side.

"Umph, um... excuse me, sir," Clement whispered. He came just inside the doorway and halted. "I hate to wake you, but I have a message here from General Wheeler." He ventured further into the dark tent and placed the message on a large stack of maps. "I can just leave it for you to read, or I can wait if you prefer, Uncle—uh, General, sir."

Van Dorn smiled. Clement took his role seriously and wanted respect, and begged his uncle to keep the familial ties a secret with the men. Van Dorn had been impressed with this and treated Clement as he did the other men. This arrangement had worked well thus far, at least no one had ever complained.

Van Dorn inched from the small wooden cot he had placed strategically in the middle of the tent—a habit he picked up during the Indian Wars when one of his men was stabbed through the burlap as he slept. He walked to his desk and read the message over twice, scratching his head and rubbing his eyes. He sat down, lit a candle, and wrote the following response:

*General Wheeler,*

*I am now, sir, here with my whole command and will be ready to make any movement you may desire. I have recently asked General Johnston to make me part of the picket of this army, as I feel I can better serve in this capacity. My men and I are proud of being cavalry and desire to win distinction under this title. I will eagerly await your orders. Rations are sufficient but thinning out and the men could use a rest once we arrive in Columbia tomorrow. Expect to acquire fresh horses upon arrival. We will move out at first light.*

*I am Sir very respectfully your obedient servant,*
*Major General Earl Van Dorn*

He folded the letter and rose from his chair on weak, shaky legs, fatigued from the long day's ride.

"You fared quite well today, I think," Clement remarked. "Will you be riding again tomorrow, sir?"

The general stood motionless for a moment, unsure how to respond. His health was much improved now, but for the last few months he had been relegated to an ambulance and out of his saddle more times than he liked to remember. His symptoms had relapsed once already when he and his men were caught out in a freezing rain for the better part of three days, but he was much improved now. His grand plans for Tennessee required a full recovery and to lead his men he must be seen as strong, unconquerable—a Lee or a Jackson. He nodded. "Yes, I'll be riding."

"Very good, sir," Clement said, as he turned to leave. "I'll see everything is prepared."

"Wait, Clement. One question." Van Dorn motioned his nephew back to the desk. "The men—uh, they are in good spirits?"

"Why, yes sir. Good spirits indeed. Not a deserter in this bunch."

"Good, then. I have high hopes for Tennessee. I want to make a mark there, you understand."

"These are good men, sir," Clement said. "They'll do the job."

Van Dorn nodded to his nephew. "You're a good soldier, Clem. I trust you are right."

Clement walked out as the general leaned back on the cot and closed his eyes once again. He envisioned a lush Tennessee valley and a victor's crown resting just atop a distant hill. In his dream he reached out for it, stretched across miles of rutted, smoky fields of battle, while outside the freezing rain fell like fine pieces of glass against the burlap tent.

***

The soldiers lay down a section of split-rail fence for use in repairing the Duck River Bridge and tied the rails end to end behind an old mule. When the mule got stuck in the frozen muddy road leading to Columbia, they walked on the planks to avoid the flooded roadbed, balancing themselves on the beams like delicate ballerinas. They avoided getting wet at all costs. They understood frostbite. Just keep out of the water was all a fellow had to do. The camp doctor had preached this ever since a bunch of them showed up with black toes after the last march from Ripley.

Crossing the washed-out road had taken more time than anticipated. Most of them were exhausted by the time they reached dry ground, and though he was eager to reach Columbia by evening, General Van Dorn announced they would rest there till morning. They had but a few hours' march remaining, but complaints had been rumbling up the line since morning. The general knew well the repercussions of pushing the men beyond their limits. The train of men and horses stopped abruptly as orders were sent down the line. A few men grumbled from within the ranks about wasting time now with such a short distance remaining, but Van Dorn ignored them. Better listen to the ones who moaned and complained. Better to stop the procession. Corinth taught him that.

A handful of men from Company E, Third Texas Infantry, warmed their hands by the fire near a grove of trees at the far corner of an old cornfield. General Van Dorn floated from campfire to campfire, making small talk with the men. He stopped just as he reached Private James

Thomas who sat at the base of a large elm tree. The private propped his journal against the mass of bark, pulled a pencil from his coat pocket, and scribbled across the top line of the page.

"Private?" Van Dorn smiled at him and leaned forward.

"Yes, sir!" Thomas shot up off the ground and saluted his commander. His face turned red with embarrassment.

"At ease, soldier." The general leaned against the trunk of the tree. He picked at a blade of grass as he spoke. "About your brother," he said in a whisper. "He was a fine soldier, son. I want you to know that."

Private Thomas looked away and nodded. "Yes, sir. Will was a fine soldier indeed. Mighty nice of you to say so."

Van Dorn put a hand on his shoulder. "You can tell your mama, too. In that letter you're writing."

Thomas turned to the general and smiled. "Yes, sir. I'll tell her. He was mighty fond of you, sir, I'll tell you that."

"Thank you, soldier. It's not often I hear—" But he stopped there. "Give your mother my condolences if you will."

The private smiled. "Yes sir. I'll do that right now." He picked up the notebook and finished the letter as the general walked away toward another group of soldiers.

*February 21, 1863*
*Last night we had some biscuits cooked at a house close to our camp. Consequently we fared finely today... The railroad is close to a town named Columbia. This is the place where General Pillow lives who built the fortifications at Fort Pillow on the Mississippi. M. D. Cooper and D. Frierson & Company also reside here. There is a large female Academy in town. We traveled all day in a very hard rain. The water run in my boots. The weather got very cold and I came very near freezing. The Yankee pickets are in fifteen miles of our camp.*

*General Van Dorn has just spent a private moment with me to let me know his sorrow over poor Will's passing. He bids me tell my dear mother what a fine soldier Will was. I believe he is the finest soldier and man in the whole of the Confederate army.*

*From your loving son,*
*Jimmie*

Next morning, they crossed the river at Bowden's Ferry. Columbia was just over the ridge now. The soldiers were wide-eyed with excitement at the prospects of a warm fire and a good home-cooked meal, and the once slow moving procession now gained momentum as it moved like a great gray elephant over the ridge top. The valley below shone golden as the morning sun beat its way through the milky Tennessee sky. And from somewhere in the back of the infinite stream of horses came a crude rendition of "The Bonny Blue Flag."

# CHAPTER 2

# CLARA MEETS THE GENERAL

*Van Dorn with his light, graceful figure, florid face, light waving hair, and bright blue eyes, seemed made for love and war.*

—DABNEY MAURY

## Columbia Athenaeum Benefit
## February 27, 1863

She scooped up her skirts and held them tightly as the heavy rain blew in horizontal sheets across the lawn of the Athenaeum, the girls' seminary in Columbia. A young man with dark brown hair and eyes like two large walnuts stood awkwardly balanced between the middle step and the muddy walk and offered a hand as each girl ascended the brick steps to the school rectory.

"Miss Clara Peters, is it?"

A sudden gust of wind caught her cape and sent her falling into the young man's arms. He smiled sheepishly as he set her back on her feet and picked up her soaked bonnet that now rested in a small puddle of water next to his feet. He rubbed it against his wool pants, scraping the dirt from the light gray silk ribbon that hung from the sides. She placed it back on her head, but it soon slipped down, and they both giggled slightly, agreeing that she was quite a sight in her disheveled dress and bonnet.

"Thank you, Frank," Clara said, blushing slightly with embarrassment.

Frank was the youngest son of Reverend Franklin Gillette Smith, the director of the Athenaeum and a prominent minister in the town. Frank, Jr. was a charismatic young man, not quite sixteen, unusually comfortable around strangers, especially those of high social standing. Unlike other boys his age, who avoided nearly all social gatherings, Frank was drawn to these events like a moth to a flame. Entranced it seemed by the lamplight of parlors, the music, and laughter. And he was an excellent host. So good, in fact, that his father had placed him at the helm of many of the school's social events. Tonight's benefit concert was his largest yet and had attracted quite a crowd with its prestigious guest list of Confederate generals. All but a few patrons of the school had arranged to attend, several of whom sent hefty donations to the wounded-soldier fund days before. To date, this event had brought in more money than all the past benefits combined, and young Frank strutted around campus like a banty rooster.

The rain fell hard as a crash of thunder boomed across the columned front porch of the rectory. Frank, Jr. took Clara's hand. "Might I be so bold as to say you look especially lovely tonight, Miss Clara." He blushed slightly and bowed to her at the top of the stairs.

Clara turned nervously away and rolled her eyes. Out of nowhere, a red-faced girl rushed past them into the open door leading to the music room and Clara tried to fall in behind her, but Frank grabbed her hand again and pulled her toward him.

He held her tightly and whispered, "Will we have the honor of hearing your sweet voice tonight?"

"Oh, how very kind of you," she stammered. "Yes, I'll be singing. Actually, several girls in the upper-school choir will perform." She spoke quickly, avoiding eye contact, but he only stepped closer.

"Has anyone ever told you your eyes are remarkably Egyptian?" he asked.

Again she looked away. He was overbearing and presumptuous, just like his father, and if he cornered her, he would torture her with one of his self-serving ramblings. Clara had fallen victim to him on a few occasions, but tonight she refused to let anything get in her way. This benefit was unlike any other. Tonight she was to sing for the most heroic men in the country and her heart soared at the very thought of it. She had spent hours telling herself she would not be scared, that she would sing like she had never done before. She wasn't about to let someone like Frank ruin it.

As predicted, young Frank launched into his opinions on the war and Clara made a move toward the hallway. The front gate suddenly opened and several ladies rushed in. Their small parasols whipped as the chilly rain blew parallel and soaked their cloaks. They rushed the stairs like a frightened herd of buffalo as a clap of thunder rang out overhead.

Frank turned to meet them. "Let me assist you ladies," he bellowed from the top step. "Watch the steps! They're very slick!"

As he stepped down to help a buxom young girl in blue velvet, Clara slid into the choir room and disappeared into a sea of silk and taffeta. She had escaped him for now.

By now, the West 7th Street entrance to the school was inundated with buggies that clogged the entrance to the rectory and forced several patrons to trudge across the flooded yard. A group of young boys cheered loudly as a Confederate officer made his way inside. "Long live the Confederacy!" and "God bless the South!" rang from the porches and windows of the rectory.

Reverend Smith entered the packed room and stood behind a makeshift podium. He was dressed in a black coat with a high starched white collar. His silk tie, a rich red and gold stripe, rested neatly above the top button of his overcoat. In his right hand he carried his leather bound Bible. In his left he gripped an ornate walking stick. He ascended the pulpit and cleared his throat.

"Let us come together tonight," he began, "with full hearts as we thank the good Lord above for the generosity represented in this room. To the wounded soldier we offer up our utmost gratitude. And to the families of these wounded men, we send up prayers of healing and strength. May God shine a blessing on each of them as they work each day to overcome the afflictions they have received from this terrible, however necessary, war..."

***

As the reverend's voice trailed off, Jessie Peters squirmed like a child on the front row as she searched the room for a familiar face. Her gray velvet gown was damp and uncomfortable and her shoes dripped onto the red carpet that covered the floor of the rectory. She shivered slightly and looked about her as Reverend Smith continued reading a lengthy list of supplies needed at the local hospital.

"The fine nurses have informed me they are desperately in need of cloth for bandages, spare sheets, and metal pots..."

The list was endless it seemed, and Jessie could no longer listen. She sighed loudly, and woke the old man sleeping next to her.

He gave her a bewildered look. "Wha... what?" he asked.

"Oh, nothing Mr. Odom, you go on back to sleep now." She smiled and patted him on the hand. He drifted off again, lightly snoring beside her. Jessie held a soft spot for Mr. Odom who had been her neighbor when she was a young girl. He had no children of his own, so he and Mrs. Odom had always treated her like a daughter. When Jessie's father William McKissack died, and the family began to squabble over the will, Mr. Odom stood beside her and offered his full support, even going up against her brother-in-law Nathaniel Cheairs on one occasion. Jessie was quite impressed by the old man. When his wife passed away, she found herself looking after her old neighbor with the same fervent devotion.

Reverend Smith droned on as a petite lady approached the pew and sat directly behind Jessie. She was attractive, with light yellow hair and sky blue eyes, and in her form-fitting silk dress she caught the attention of every man in the room. Even Jessie strained to get a good look at her as she pushed and shoved her way between two elderly men.

"Why the nerve," Jessie muttered, turning sideways in the pew and glancing casually back at the noisy latecomer. The ruckus even caught the attention of the reverend and he paused briefly as the young girl finally settled into her seat.

It was Elizabeth Daniel! Jessie watched gleefully as sweat poured down the reverend's face. She wondered if he still held a grudge. After all, when the choir director caught them in the vestry, half-naked and in a rather compromising position, Elizabeth had nearly ruined him with all sorts of wild accusations of sordid rendezvous and midnight trysts—all forced upon her, of course. Had it not been for her already soiled reputation, the patrons of the school may have strung him up right there in his own rectory. But that had been years ago. Maybe he had searched his Christian heart and found it in him to forgive her. Either way, this was going to be interesting.

Jessie turned in her seat and pretended to be surprised. "Why, Elizabeth Daniel! What on earth brings you here?"

Elizabeth batted her gorgeous blue eyes. "Wouldn't miss this for the world! It's not every day a girl gets the chance to see this many handsome faces in one room!"

Jessie giggled. "And make a preacher blush! You're going to be the death of that man yet, Elizabeth!"

As Reverend Smith concluded his long-winded speech, the sound of chatter came from behind the closed double doors of the rectory. A group of girls emerged from the dark hallway and filled two rows of chairs directly behind the reverend. The girls had been hand-picked for this benefit by Reverend Smith himself. Of course, Fannie Smith was first to perform. She was Reverend Smith's eldest daughter and a graduate of the Athenaeum. She entered, nose pointed up, chest out, regal as a queen. Tonight she would play the harp. After weeks of practice, she took her place at the helm of the instrument as Mrs. Leigh the choir director took her position on the left of the harp. Their voices were in perfect harmony as they sang their first piece, the beautiful "Vivre." When the song ended, the entire room exploded in cheers and three new girls joined the pair.

Mr. Odom was awakened by all the noise and jumped in his seat. He looked up at the processional of girls entering from the side door and poked Jessie with his cane. "Isn't that Clara?" he asked.

Clara looked stunning in her flowing white dress. Her dark hair was fastened neatly at the nape of her neck with pink silk ribbons. The soft colors of her ensemble made her chestnut eyes black as coal, and gave her olive skin a dewy radiance. She stepped up and stood alongside Mrs. Leigh while another young girl took a place at the piano. Fannie struck the harp and they began singing Handel's "Hallelujah." In perfect step, the remaining choir members walked slowly up until the entire coterie had joined in the singing. The scene was quite lovely, each girl attired in the most admirable taste and with much extravagance.

Jessie was most impressed as she watched a pretty auburn-haired girl in the front of the group. "Is that Anna?" She asked Lillian Branham who was seated behind her. "I do swear she is an angel in that white gown."

"And that Clara," Miss Lillian replied. "She's just a picture of heaven itself, and has such a lovely voice. She is an absolute songbird!"

"Why, thank you, Miss Lillian," Jessie answered, shocked by the rare compliment. Miss Lillian was a tough woman who found fault with everyone. "Dr. Peters is very proud indeed, as am I," Jessie said with a hint of arrogance.

A half hour later the concert concluded with a dramatic parade of wounded soldiers, who dragged their bandaged bodies down the long aisle of the rectory as the shocked congregation gasped at the pitiful spectacle. When the last soldier reached the end of the aisle, Reverend Smith sent the offering plate around for one final collection. Shallow pockets became suddenly deep as every man plunged his hand in and came out with piece after piece of silver for the wooden plate. The generals smiled as they rose and bowed to the congregation.

"Give them that," Mr. Odom demanded as he dropped in a bank note for one hundred Confederate dollars and rose from the pew. As the crowd began moving toward the door, he pulled on Jessie's arm and whispered, "Walk with me outside to meet the Generals. But be quiet about it, we don't want to draw all these hens out there."

Jessie giggled and took his arm. They moved quickly through the rows of people and out the door. The rain had stopped, and now most of the men moved out onto the porches to have a smoke. Mr. Odom led Jessie into the sea of men, but he knew she would not complain. No man had ever intimidated Jessie, not even a Confederate general.

"Mr. Odom," Reverend Smith bellowed from the far end of the rain soaked porch. "Join us down here, won't you! I'd like you to meet our distinguished guests."

Jessie frowned at Mr. Odom. "You know how I despise talking with that man. He goes on and on and all about nothing! Makes my poor head ache!"

"I know you do." He laughed, squeezing her hand tightly. "But you'll do it for me."

The porch was covered with soldiers leaning out over the railings, their pipes lit, smoke trailing out over the misty lawn like a fog.

General W. H. Jackson, who stood like a tree trunk against the porch post was first to speak. "Your school is a fine example of the Southern culture and what we are fighting to preserve."

Reverend Smith smiled and gave a long, dramatic bow before replying, "And we, kind sir, are forever indebted to the service of our great Confederate Army."

Jessie rolled her eyes. The very sound of his voice made her skin crawl. Always so melodramatic. Besides, she wasn't here to listen to him. She was in the midst of a veritable goldmine of handsome faces!

General Nathan Bedford Forrest caught her eye first. He stood to the right of General Jackson and spat profusely into a holly bush planted beside the steps. He spent several minutes wiping his mouth on his coat sleeve and scraping his muddy boots against the spindles of the porch railing until the reverend finally asked him what he thought of the concert.

"Well, I'll jest tell ya, Reverend," Forrest said. "Got yourself a fine lot of Southern ladies here." He grinned broadly, revealing a set of straight white teeth.

"If you'll allow me, sir," came an eloquent voice from within the crowd. "I might add that your ladies' voices are as beguiling as their lovely faces."

Jessie stopped in her tracks at the sound of the familiar voice. Could it be? She stretched high on her tiptoes until she could just see General Van Dorn standing hat cocked, a riding crop in his left hand. He winked at her and walked to where she stood on the opposite side of the porch.

"As I have said," he continued, wetting his lips. "Columbia is certainly blessed with some of the South's most beautiful ladies." He kissed Jessie's hand lightly. "Mrs. Peters. It is a pleasure to see you looking so well."

Reverend Smith's eyes shot open. "Why, General Van Dorn! I didn't know you had made the acquaintance of Mrs. Peters. And so soon, I might add."

Jessie glared at him. "As a matter of fact, Reverend Smith, we met just last winter while I was visiting my brother Alexander in Holly Springs. You do remember Holly Springs, don't you Reverend?"

"Of course I remember," Reverend Smith said, his face flushing red. "Why who could forget! Quite impressive indeed."

General Jackson nodded. "One of the best damned raids I heard speak of. Burned near all Grant's stores to the ground!"

"Damn right!" General Frank Armstrong added, punching his gloved hand in the air. "I'd like to do the same to Schofield! Burn him right out'a Nashville!"

The porch erupted in wild cheers. Hats were thrown high in the air as a group of wounded soldiers treated the crowd to an ear-piercing rebel yell. The patrons all poured from the rectory onto the porch and formed a line to shake the hands of their generals. Even the little old ladies who never spoke above a whisper joined in the shouting of love and support for their brave Southern boys.

"Why they've gone crazy," Jessie said to Mr. Odom. "Just listen to them!"

"It's God's will, no doubt about it," he said. "Even God hates a Yankee!"

Jessie nodded though she wasn't convinced this war was God's will at all. As she caught sight of a one-legged soldier in the bunch—his bandages soiled red—she thought the war might even be a curse. So much death and destruction. "Come with me," she whispered as she led Mr. Odom back into the rectory where Clara now sat at the piano. A group of younger girls circled her and joined in singing the "Bonny Blue Flag."

General Van Dorn slowly made his way into the room and stood beside Jessie. They were soon joined by Clement Sulivane and the rest of the young soldiers who stood mesmerized as Clara played and sang. Her voice was perfect in pitch and tone, her flowing white dress spilled delicately over the sides of the piano bench like a billowy cloud.

The general clapped his hands and sang along. "She is quite impressive!" he shouted above the noise. "It's rare to see such talent these days!"

"Oh, do you think so?" Jessie shouted back, her voice irritated. "Well, she is my step-daughter," she quickly added. "Of course she's talented!" She tried desperately to conceal her jealousy, but the tone of her voice told the truth. "She's a strange girl, though, quite studious and not at all social. Trust me," she said lightly touching his hand. "You'd find her quite dull."

Van Dorn laughed. "Why, I can't imagine any lady in your home being anything but the loveliest, most exciting creature in the South."

"Well, she's nothing like me," Jessie said as she repositioned her bodice. She stroked his arm lightly and smiled. "Or you, for that matter."

The general turned to face her. "And just what are we like?" he asked with a smile. "Sounds scandalous, Mrs. Peters."

"Well, let's just say she lacks passion—for life, that is." She raised her eyebrow and laughed, but the general had not taken his eyes off Clara.

"You surely remember meeting Clara last fall at my brother's plantation. In Coldwater, remember? She was there for nearly a week. Right after I arrived, I believe it was." She daubed her forehead with her silk handkerchief and stared intently at the general, trying hard to appear confident. "Remember, Earl?" she asked with an unusual gentleness in her voice.

"Oh, yes," he answered. "I believe I do recall that now."

He turned to glance back at Clara when Jessie reached up and gently touched his cheek. She smiled slyly, her lips quivering with nervous anticipation. "Well, let's talk about the present, shall we?" She wanted to remind him of those few weeks in Coldwater, the buggy rides and grand balls, their private walks...

"No, I dare say if I had heard that voice before now, I would certainly recall," the general replied. "And how could I forget such a lovely face?" He stared at Clara, his eyes set firm like an animal on its prey.

Jessie clinched her teeth. "Did you not hear a word I said, Earl?" She wanted to scream at the top of her lungs, to tear out his eyes! How could he ignore her like this? How could he talk this way, and about Clara! She moved closer and in a sensual voice asked, "Those were the most wonderful days. Were they not, General Van Dorn?"

At last he snapped out of the spell and moved in closer. "Yes, of course, Mrs. Peters," he said in a low voice. "They were wonderful days indeed." He took her arm and lightly caressed her delicate wrist. "Perhaps we will find time to reminisce about those days. Say, this evening?"

Jessie lifted a fan to her hot face. "Well, of course, Earl," she said in a giddy voice. "I never turn down a handsome caller."

They walked toward the entrance of the rectory where a large group of men leaned casually against the massive arched doorway. "Mrs. Peters, you remember my nephew Clement, don't you?" Van Dorn asked.

Jessie whirled around, her mouth agape. "Why, Clement! Of course, how could I forget?" She had hoped the general would be alone.

"Mrs. Peters has asked us to be her guests this evening," Van Dorn announced.

Clement smiled and gave a quick bow. "How could anyone refuse such lovely company?"

"Well, certainly," Jessie said. "You must join us." She returned the smile, though the tone of her voice cut like ice. She had not expected additional company, had no desire to share the general.

"My pleasure indeed," Clement said. "Shall I bring up the carriage?"

"Why, yes," Jessie replied. "I, uh..." She was just about to suggest that he take her carriage, when she was suddenly interrupted by several students pushing their way down the aisle toward Clara and the other girls.

Without warning, Van Dorn took Jessie by the hand and wheeled her around to face him.

Her heart fluttered! "Yes, Earl," she said softly, eagerly.

"You must introduce me to that stepdaughter of yours," he said.

Jessie opened her mouth to speak when a young man shouted, "God Bless the Confederacy!" and the entire crowd erupted.

Van Dorn released his grip and joined in the cheering, as he and Clement moved past the crowd and toward the piano while the other guests walked slowly to the door, shaking hands with Reverend Smith and his family. Young Frank bolted in the direction of the piano as well but was pushed aside by General Van Dorn. "Move on, son," he said threateningly.

Jessie watched as Clara turned to the general and batted her black glossy eyes. He bowed to her and held out a gloved hand. Clara smiled shyly and rose slowly from the piano bench, her eyes entranced, hypnotized as she wrapped her arm in his. The pair walked slowly toward the door.

"Hurry up, Clara!" Jessie shouted over the noise. She stood arms crossed, jaw set, waiting impatiently, her jealousy seething from her pores. They approached the door slowly, as if they were floating on clouds. "Thank you, General Van Dorn," Jessie said as she grabbed Clara by the arm. "I can take her from here."

"Jessie!" Clara squealed in pain, but Jessie only pulled harder as she dragged her out the door.

"We must be going," Jessie growled. "Stop your whining!"

"Wait, Mrs. Peters!" Van Dorn yelled as he pushed his way through the packed doorway. "May I have the honor of walking you two beautiful ladies to your carriage?" He took Jessie's arm and tugged at it until she released her hold on Clara. Clement then took Clara's arm in his and the four of them walked down the steps to their carriage.

Jessie turned her head away from the general. "Honestly, General!" she huffed. "Must you indulge every young girl?"

He smiled and stroked her hand. "Now, Mrs. Peters," he said laughingly. "You're not jealous are you?"

Jessie jerked her arm away and poked her lips out as a child pouting. She rushed to the carriage and jumped inside, but when she turned to see the generals' reaction, he was no longer there. She stepped back out to look for him as Clement approached with Clara.

"Get in," Jessie said, pushing Clara inside. "Home, Alexander!" she yelled.

The driver cracked his whip and the carriage lurched forward. The two rode in a strained silence until several minutes later when Clara turned to her and asked sheepishly, "Is this the same General Van Dorn we met in Holly Springs?"

Jessie rolled her eyes and glared at the girl. "You don't need to worry yourself with the general. Do you hear me?" Her voice was cold and threatening. "You tend to that charming nephew of his and stay out of my way!"

Clara lowered her head and dared not say a word the rest of the way home. But when they arrived, they were quite surprised to see General Van Dorn was already there, sitting at the piano.

"There you are," he said flashing a brilliant smile as Jessie and Clara entered the parlor. "You must play one more song for me, Clara."

"Oh, I'm sure Clara's exhausted from all that singing," Jessie said in a commanding voice. "I think perhaps she should join Mr. Sulivane—"

But the general cut her off and got up from the piano bench. He took Clara's hand and stared into her eyes. "I beg you, Miss Peters, just one more song and I will be satisfied."

Clara glanced nervously at Jessie. "Well, I suppose I could play just one more. If it's ok with you, of course."

Jessie was speechless. And when the general and Clara took their places side by side at the piano, Jessie walked over to young Clement and offered him a glass of brandy. "Shall we," she said in a flirtatious voice. "Come sit with me and you can bore me as long as you like with all that war talk."

Clement sat beside her on the large brocade sofa and for the rest of the evening Jessie pretended to listen to his battle stories as Clara played the piano for the starry eyed general. By the time they left, she had made up her mind. Clara must go.

## From the Diary of Jessie Peters

*February 1863*

*O, be still my heart! The Devil take us all, but I simply must say it—Earl Van Dorn is the handsomest man in the entire Confederacy! I suppose I should feel like a wretched sinner for saying such, but I don't care! And he is intelligent too! But not like some men who are too smart for their own good. No, the general has quite the clever tongue. I've come to the conclusion that he is perhaps the most entertaining guest a person could possibly have. He has the voice of a songbird and plays the piano as well as anyone I've ever heard! Why, it's incredible! And literature—well he practically recited an entire Shakespearean play. And all of this in the short time after the Benefit last night. Oh, what a wonderful time! But of course, there is always that one person who comes along and ruins the evening—Clara! That girl does amaze me. She's absolutely dull in my opinion. I don't see any of the usual femininity of so many charming young ladies her age. Why, it's as if she's no girl at all. The way she dresses—in that Puritan frock. It's enough to send a blind man running! (And to think I had so many beaus by her age.) George says she's modest as a well-heeled lady should be—well, he may call it whatever he likes. But I say she is priggish, ha!*

*The news in town is quite hopeful as of late. The general's presence has given everyone a renewed sense of esprit de corps! The newspapers have yet to catch the bug, however. All they care to speak of are our losses—particularly Corinth, which is a nasty jab at the general. I believe those reporters ought to be made to trade their pen for a gun and they might not be so quick to criticize. Still no word from George. Perhaps he'll stay away for another year. I don't mind really. The children are well and I rather enjoy the peace and quiet—not to mention, I find it quite exciting to run my own affairs. Papa always said I was as tough as any man and I suppose he was right. I've done well enough with Alexander on the place—better than most families around here. Perhaps George is truly not meant to return—and this is God's way of preparing me for something... Oh, if only Papa were here!*

It is nearly midnight now and I must get to sleep but I'm afraid I may never calm down—I'm absolutely beside myself with excitement. I had the most delightful surprise this evening! General Van Dorn and his officers were out scouting, or something of the sort, and they stopped to visit. He says there will be a grand parade tomorrow and we are all to come out and cheer them on. He even offered to send a carriage for me and I accepted. He is so kind and handsome! Well, off to bed now—tomorrow promises to be quite a day indeed!

# CHAPTER 3

# A FINAL BATTLE AT
# THOMPSON'S STATION

*"Wait for the wagons boys, and we'll take a ride."*
—GENERAL EARL VAN DORN UPON HEARING OF COBURN'S WAGON TRAIN
(MARCH 4, 1863)

The soldier lay on the cold ground, death having come to him in the form of a splintered, misshapen mini ball. Van Dorn looked closely at the prostrate frame; face up, ghostly white, the bullet having entered with an unnatural accuracy in the exact center of the forehead. He considered the odds of shooting with such precision. It had to be mere chance that the bullet entered so perfectly, lodging somewhere in the brain, no exit wound, not one mark of violence except for the tiny black hole. He leaned down and touched the dead man's head, a habit since his days in Mexico. He said a prayer and forced the lids shut and then he scribbled in his journal: "Private D. R. Gurley, killed, shot through the head."

The battle was a grand one at Thompson's Station, a quaint village nine miles south of Franklin, wedged in a valley between two ranges of hills. The train station lay on the Nashville and Decatur Railroad line and had been the site of constant annoyance for Van Dorn's cavalry since their arrival. General Granger had teased the Confederate cavalry on a regular basis until the morning of March 4, when Colonel Coburn of the 33rd Indiana accidentally ran up on a portion of Van Dorn's men and the fight was on. After five hours of heavy skirmishing—attack and repulse, attack and repulse—General Armstrong's brigade finally joined forces with General Forrest, and taking cover behind the stone fences of the train station they opened fire on Coburn's men. When the enemy retreated into a cedar brake, Forrest fired on their rear, and having no alternative, they were forced to throw down their guns and surrender. At final count, the enemy had sustained losses of 1446, with 1151 of those having been captured.

An ecstatic Van Dorn and his men arrived in Spring Hill later that evening and were greeted by hundreds of men, women, and children who lined the streets for nearly a mile to watch the procession of Yankee prisoners, some of whom were bootless, victims of the spoils of war. The battle was a grand victory for the recently tarnished Van Dorn, who met the cheering crowd with the air of a gallant knight, his regal black mare stepping high and deliberate to the beat of drums as their small band led the parade. He turned in his saddle and waved his hat in the air as a crowd of young boys chanted, "Hoorah for Van Dorn!" and ran alongside him to the end of the street.

The revelry lasted until well after dark when a weary General Van Dorn lay on the small bed in his room at headquarters. Here he closed his eyes and replayed the last three days of fighting as he drifted off to sleep. In his dream he rode back through the smoke-filled valleys and crossed the icy waters of the Duck River, his battle flag flying behind him as he floated past blue coats and bayonets. He passed whole forests of oaks and pines and green grass as far as the eye could see. He turned in the saddle to see small dark-eyed children with dirty faces and bare feet following behind him, their hands stretched out. Then suddenly the trees were gone and before him lay a flat ground with clay houses and miles of sand and cactus. He was in Mexico, back when he was a hero and the world was his to own.

"Gen'rl."

The voice shattered his quiet ride and he bolted up in bed. "What?" he shouted breathlessly.

Standing before him was Milton who looked down at him with those white wide-set eyes. He held out a clean white shirt and a bottle of whiskey. "Doc say bring you this," Milton said as he laid the bottle on the bed. "Say some Yankee colonel give it to him for diggin' a bullet out'n his leg." He walked to the general's desk and draped the clean shirt across the back of the chair. "Doc says he don't drink none."

Van Dorn lifted the bottle and smiled. "Indeed." He laughed. Headquarters was now in the home of Dr. Aaron White, a quiet, religious man, and a teetotaler. "Very good indeed. Well, you tell Dr. White I'm much obliged."

"Yassir," Milton said, turning to leave.

"Milton," Van Dorn said as he rose from the bed. "You could probably use a little yourself. Join me, won't you?"

Milton smiled and looked at the floor. "You knows Fanny sho be hard on me if she fount out. Sides, I ain't a drinkin' man."

Van Dorn laughed as he poured the two glasses of whiskey. "No, Milton," he said smiling. "You ain't a drinkin' man until you've got something to drink." He held his glass high in the air and said, "Here! Here!"

Milton took the glass and quickly drank it down. The general poured them another.

"You're a good soul, Milton." Van Dorn slapped him on the back. Milton was like an old friend to him, loyal and dependable. He wasn't just property like the others, and the general wouldn't think of giving him up.

"Well, I reckon it ain't hurtin' nothin'," he answered in his deep drawl. "Mighty obliged, sir." He took a swig and smiled. "Yassir, mighty obliged indeed."

They were toasting their second drink when Captain Brooks suddenly entered. He gave them both a hard look and Milton quickly took his glass and left, but not before the general filled it again. Brooks was a strict Methodist, uptight and unfriendly, a self-serving soldier who spoke out against the general at Corinth. Van Dorn hated the man.

"At ease, Captain." Van Dorn laughed. "You act like you've never seen a victory party before."

"Well, of course," he said, in an agitated voice. "I just— uh, well, sir, here's a telegram from Bragg." He put the paper on the desk and turned to leave.

"Today was a good day. Wouldn't you say, Captain?"

"Certainly was," Brooks said, forcing a smile. "A good day indeed."

Van Dorn smiled at the red-faced captain. "Say, won't you have a drink, Captain?"

Brooks' nostrils flared in anger. He had shown his own dislike for the general by asking nearly every week for a transfer to Polk's division. "No thank you," he said coldly.

"Very well, then, I'll just drink one for you, Captain Brooks," he said with a laugh. "You may go now. And close the door behind you."

The captain turned and stormed toward the door. "Goodnight, sir."

Van Dorn laughed and fell back on the small bed. He loved nothing better than jabbing at hypocrites like Brooks. They were great pretenders all of them—quick to point out every last error in his life, while their own sins lay hidden under layers of pretension. They too would fall from grace, just as he had. He only hoped he would be there to watch it when it happened.

He closed his eyes and tried to relax, tried to let the whiskey warm his body. He must keep his spirits high, must not focus on the negative around him. In the morning, he would lead the boys of the Third Texas in a grand parade through Spring Hill, while every damned newspaper in the South wrote about his recent glory. He felt hope again. Thompson's Station was just the beginning.

## From the Diary of Jessie Peters

*March 10, 1863*

*The sun is shining much brighter this morning though my soul has yet to feel its warmth. I wish I knew the cause of my unrest—but it is nevertheless there, gnawing away at my nerves, an undeniable uneasiness in the pit of my stomach. At times I believe I am suffering nothing more than fatigue since these last few weeks have been a whirlwind of parties and benefits. But even after I've rested, the feeling comes over me again. I declare, if I could only have a moment's peace then I'm sure I could resolve my distemper —but given my sister's early morning visit, peace seems nowhere in the stars, at least not for me. Poor Susan, poor, poor Susan. How I would love to get my hands around her tiny little neck! She amazes me more as each day passes— how positively naïve she is, to go about doing the Devil's bidding. And just when I thought we had put that dreadful incident forever in our past—that nasty letter written by her nasty husband—Major Cheairs. The nerve! To ask me for money for a few miserable months spent at his home when Papa died. Payment? For what? For cold mornings with little firewood—and what little I did acquire was purchased by me! The insult is really too much to bear—or so I thought— but the Lord was not done with me yet. No, indeed! Not only am I to bear unthinkable insults from my own family, but I am to bear them alone. But of course! Who would ever expect George Peters to defend me—he is far too weak. But that's quite alright! As I always say, "Vengeance is mine sayeth the Lord!"*

*Yet, my heart tells me I must forgive Susan. I suppose it's only right. She is so needy, so dependent on a man. She will never see the Major for what he really is—a greedy, selfish tyrant. But, I'm no fool—I would never lie to conceal my own poor judgment—yet, Susan will go to the ends of the earth, will swear on the graves of her children that she married that man for love. If she only knew the truth— whom he really loved... Well, that is something I shall never tell! Oh, the scandal indeed! I will take it to the grave for her; after all, she is my sister.*

*8 p. m. — There is much to be said for a quiet moment
and now that I have had mine I feel much better about
everything. I have given it considerable thought and feel
quite content with my life—I'm no fool, as I always say. I'm
smart enough to know that a husband must be a man who
measures his worth by his wealth—for that is a man who
will shower his wife with luxuries! Give me that man over
some insufferable dictator! As for a lover—well that is a
different animal altogether...*

# CHAPTER 4

# THOMAS PETERS – A LEAVE OF ABSENCE

**Shelbyville, Tennessee**
**March 20, 1863**

In camp, the men held their coats tight to their bodies as a bitter wind blew in from the north, chilling all hopes of spring. Winter was forever in the Tennessee valley. Though the milky sky flashed an occasional ray of sunlight, no morning warmth broke through. A group of soldiers stood huddled around a fire they built on the north end of the camp, while others sat on the hard ground and wrote letters home or read the latest newspapers aloud.

Thomas Peters rubbed his head and walked quickly by a group of soldiers, trying desperately to avoid eye contact. He had hoped to slip out of camp without asking, but he had not possessed the courage to abandon his post and risk arrest. He was a lieutenant now. No matter if the position had been handed to him by General Leonidas Polk, his commanding officer and distant cousin. He had no intentions of giving it up.

The general's tent stood at the far end of the camp within a few feet of a muddy path. General Polk was often seen walking this path to the tobacco fields that lay a safe distance from the Union lines. Out of the public view, he would kneel in the lone field and pray for the safety of his men and success for the Confederacy. Many of his men had expressed doubt that an Episcopalian minister would kill another man, even if it was for the good of the country. But he had proven them wrong and was regarded as a very capable soldier, bravely entering every battle, fearless of death or the damnation he may face.

Thomas stopped outside the tent and addressed a soldier standing guard. "Is the General in?"

"Yea," the soldier replied insolently.

Thomas cleared his throat and looked at the ground. "I need to see him, if possible."

The guard just eyed him with suspicion. Thomas Peters was no favorite of the regular soldier, the soldier without patronage. He was protected, kept out of harm's way by his family's relations, and in turn loathed by his comrades.

"It's personal," Thomas added in a low voice, his forehead glistening with sweat. He watched a group of soldiers huddled by a tent and shuffled his feet on the frozen ground.

"General Polk's busy," the soldier explained. "Nobody's to disturb him."

"It's, uh—" he stammered. "It's very important. I assure you," all but pleading. "Tell him Lieutenant Peters needs to see him." His patience was wearing thin. "Look, tell him I'm here. I'm going in no matter."

The soldier laughed and shook his head. "Yea, yea, real tough guy. Go ahead if you got it in you." He was a strapping young man, tall and wide shouldered, a good foot taller than Thomas. "I don't think you want to fight me, now do ya?"

Thomas had enough. "Look, I've told you once. I'm going in, so you might as well..."

"Calm down, Peters," the soldier said smiling. "Don't get your feathers all ruffled now." He walked to General Polk's tent and leaned in the doorway. "Little Tom Peters requests a word with you, sir," he said smiling back at Thomas. "What should I tell him?"

Thomas bowed out his chest and shoved the soldier hard. "Out of my way!" he yelled.

The soldier stumbled back a few steps and pretended to fall as a group of soldiers standing close by mocked him. "Outa my way," they crowed in unison. "Move or I'll tell my daddy."

Thomas glared at the scraggly soldiers and clinched his jaw. He wanted to bash their skulls in with a log from their fire, but there was nothing he could do now, not while his body was all but falling to pieces. He walked past them and into the tent, which was dark except for a small candle on the general's writing desk. An adjutant stood just inside the tent door like a stone statue at a Roman temple.

General Polk rose from his chair. "Tom," he said, holding out his hand. "What's on your mind, son?"

Thomas looked at the ground, more eager to run than anything. "General, sir," he began, his eyes still focused on the ground, beads of sweat formed on his upper lip. "Sir, if I might be granted leave, uh, for medical purposes," he stuttered, his voice shaking as he struggled to find the words. "I am not well, sir," he went on. "I'd like to go to Memphis. Father is there, you know."

"Memphis?" the General asked. "Why not see the doctor on staff in Tullahoma? He's a fine physician. I can vouch for him myself."

"It's not that, sir," he looked at the adjutant. "Could I speak with you alone?"

Polk turned toward the stone soldier and nodded. Seconds later they were alone. "All right, Tom," he said. "What's this all about?"

Thomas's face was flushed, his lips quivered. "It's very hard to explain, you see." He twisted his hat in his hands and shook his head. "I'm miserable, sir," he said tugging at his pants. "You see, I was with this girl back in Grenada and—"

The general held his hand up to him. "I see," he said with a frown. "And you've gotten some treatment?"

Thomas wrenched his hat until it was a twisted mass of wool. This was the worst part, worse than the pain itself. He was angry with himself and bitterly resentful that he must bear his soul, his demons, and to a minister. He cleared his throat again and thought how best to say it. "The treatments didn't work, sir. I plan to write my father and have him come to Memphis. Right now, he's at Council Bend."

Polk walked to his desk and sat down. "This is quite a request, Tom," he said, rubbing his chin. "So many out as it is, you know."

Thomas dropped his head in shame and shuffled his feet again, trying to relieve the excruciating pain that shot down both legs. He had to find a better treatment than the stingy surgeon in Tullahoma had given him. With so many cases and little medication, most were forced to suffer through the symptoms with nothing but a little whiskey to dull the pain.

The general looked him over. "You are telling me the truth, boy?" His voice had a God-like quality. "Well?"

Thomas glanced his way for a moment but quickly looked at his feet. He felt like a scolded ten-year-old boy, would rather take a beating than stand there in his shame. "Of course I'm telling the truth, sir."

"All right, then," the general said. "Have your father send word as soon as he looks at you." He picked up his pen and took a piece of paper from the desk drawer. "Will thirty days be sufficient?"

The beads of sweat now dropped from Thomas' brow. "Yes, I think so, sir." His voice sounded hollow. "I'll be back as soon as I'm able." But Thomas knew that was a lie. He was tired of the war now, was tired of the pain and humiliation. He doubted he would ever return.

"Very well," Polk said. "Take this to Major Falconer. He'll write the papers." He paused a moment then spoke authoritatively. "You've been absent more than any other soldier in this company, Tom. You must try to get well and return as soon as possible."

A young woman entered the tent carrying the general's freshly washed coat. She moved quickly past them and placed the coat on the back of the desk chair, the crisp white shirt on the foot of the bed. Thomas stood quietly by as she rushed around him, picking up a plate and a cup, moving the general's boots to the side of the tent. She was hauntingly familiar to him though he never laid eyes on her in his life till now. Then suddenly it hit him. She looked just like the other girls, the girls in Grenada, and Memphis...

Thomas looked away.

"Just get well, Tom," the general said softly. "Go take care of yourself and get back here. The army needs you."

***

At three o'clock that afternoon, Thomas rode to the depot at Tullahoma. He sat beside a wounded soldier on the bench outside the station and waited for the train. The young soldier had fiery red hair and a bloody bandage wrapped tightly around his left shoulder.

"Shot clean through," he said proudly. "At Thompson's Station last week."

Thomas nodded and crossed his arms, trying hard to sit still. He needed to relieve himself but he did not think he could bear the pain. He tried desperately to put it out of his mind. A chill rose up his body and he shook involuntarily for a moment. The young soldier droned on about the battle, his voice excited and animated. He got his wound, he said, when General Van Dorn's horse got shot out from under him.

"This bullet came whizzing by, you see," he said. "And next thing I know, this black horse comes racing by and sitting up there is none other than the big man himself." He waved his right hand excitedly and got up from the bench. "So I stop to salute him when gunfire broke out and me and that black horse fell. Bam! All at once, like we was one living being!" He slapped his hand hard on the bench and stared at Thomas. "Now," he laughed, "I bet you ain't ever heard a story like that one, huh?"

Thomas groaned a little and repositioned himself on the bench. "Nope," he finally answered. "Never heard that one before."

The soldier ran his free hand through his red hair, smoothing the fiery strays sticking up like the crown of a giant woodpecker. "Well, no matter." He laughed. "Van Dorn come out of it whole, not a scratch on his head. Course, he may not come out so lucky when that rich doctor fellow gets a hold on him!" He slapped his thigh and laughed again. "She's a looker, though! Might be worth dying for!"

Thomas smiled at the boy, thought this was quite funny, but then the words registered in his brain and he leaped from the bench. "What did you say?" Thomas grabbed the soldier by his good shoulder and pulled him close. "Did you say a doctor's wife?"

The smile disappeared from the soldier's face. "Yea," he said in a shaky voice. "A real looker, young—"

"What's her name?"

He looked up at Thomas whose hand still gripped his lapel. "Peters or Peterson, I think it was. Say, you gonna let go?"

Thomas's face went white and he released his grip. He was suddenly exhausted; his knees trembled beneath him.

The soldier got up and moved quickly to the loading platform. "You're crazy! You know that?" he yelled back. "You ought to get your head checked!"

But Thomas paid no attention. The knot in his stomach had grown and now he felt certain he would vomit. When the whistle blew, he handed his pass to the commanding officer and boarded the train. He found a window seat near the back and crawled into it. The pain in his groin throbbed and he wished he had taken the time to relieve himself. The train held only a handful of passengers, civilians as far as he could tell and when the conductor walked past, he asked about their first stop.

"Not far," the conductor answered. "Loading supplies just a few miles south of here, at Decherd."

"Good," he said, sinking down in the seat. He closed his eyes. When they stopped, he would force himself to take the pain. Then he could rest.

A young boy seated beside him jerked away from his mother's grip and shot him a hard elbow to the ribs. Thomas winced in pain and opened his eyes. Sweat beaded on his brow and above his trembling lips.

The young mother pulled the boy onto her lap and turned her body to face the aisle of the train. "Be still," she said, shaking her finger in the little boy's round face. She held him tightly and rocked him back and forth, humming softly until the boy settled down.

The train lurched forward and he struggled to stay seated. By the time they stopped at Decherd, the pain was so excruciating that he feared he would not be able to walk. He looked around him at the few passengers, most of whom were asleep, and decided to give it a try. With the first step, he stumbled into the seat behind him.

The young mother caught him by the arm and asked, "Can I help you to the platform?"

"Thank you," Thomas whispered.

She smiled shyly and took him by the arm. "You favor my Jacob, you know. Your curly hair and all."

But Thomas had no time for talking. He just nodded and hurried to the door where an attendant took his arm and led him down the steps. The depot was only a few yards away. If he could just make it there, he felt sure he could take the remainder of the ride to Memphis.

When he boarded again, he took his seat and smiled at the young woman. She was pretty. Might even be a widow, Thomas thought as her thin body moved down the aisle to where her child lay sleeping.

"You should see a doctor," she said as she passed. "It's not good to let such things go."

"Yes, I know," he answered, the shame of his sin burning red on his cheeks. He sat quietly and watched her as she sat next to the young boy and stroked his brown curly hair. He thought to tell her how nice it was to watch her. How his own dear mother had loved him as much and that he missed her terribly.

But his thoughts soon returned to the redheaded boy at the station. If this story was true then it must be Jessie. It sounded just like her. But this was real trouble—a general. His father could not turn a blind eye this time. But Thomas knew too well. Jessie would just lie and his father would fall for it, just as he had countless times before. He would have to convince his father that he must go to Spring Hill, must see for himself. There was no time to waste, not when a man like Van Dorn was involved.

The train whistle blew again and Thomas settled back in his seat. The pain had subsided enough for him to breathe a little easier, perhaps he could even bear the bumpy track. He closed his eyes and took in the sounds of the young mother's soothing lullaby.

## From the Diary of Jessie Peters

*March 13, 1863*

*A dreadful rain began to fall this morning and I find myself a prisoner in this dreary house. Little Lucy suffered a cough for most of last night and I've had only a few hours sleep. If not for some remnants of Paregoric, I think the child would have coughed herself into a fit. I suppose poor William thought he better join her or miss out on the attention and so developed a digestive problem around sunrise. I had hoped for some magic potion to cure them both, but Virethia has yet to find a remedy.*

*I find myself with so much to think about today that my head is positively spinning. I keep reciting a favorite line of mine and it simply will not get out of my head. "Love sought is good, but given unsought, is better." O how true! My handsome general accompanied me on a long buggy ride yesterday, and we rode all the way to just above Columbia and back again. And every minute was blissful! Just to hear his voice—*

*But alas—as with all good things, I fear this too shall also come to an end. I suppose I should expect a dark cloud whenever I hear from anyone with the last name Peters, and what did I get late this evening but a telegram from George's brother Tom. It was quite disheartening to say the least. It seems Thomas is not well and has taken leave. Apparently he has gone to Memphis so that George might doctor him. I do wish Tom was more forthcoming with such news—I'm still unsure what ails the poor boy. I suppose I should try to help him though I don't think I could offer much nursing with all the sick babies in this house. No, he will be better off if he goes to Memphis. If George cannot tend him, then he will surely send him to a doctor who can look after him. Poor Thomas. He is a handsome boy, but he has a weak constitution—certainly nothing like a McKissack. I'm sure his sickness is no worse than all the other soldiers have to endure—but Thomas is not like them, as I've said. He lacks the fire of a real man. I remember when he was at the university in Mississippi and he fell ill. He was home for nearly a month before we found out his sickness was*

*nothing more than love sickness. Who knows, maybe he's*
*fallen again...*

    *I will nevertheless say a prayer for poor Thomas to make*
*a full recovery—and soon. If not, his sickness may bring*
*George home. With Thomas' unit in Shelbyville, George may*
*think to come here and nurse him once he returns. Oh, I*
*pray that doesn't happen!*

# CHAPTER 5

# A FOOL'S PARADISE: SPRING, 1863

*"As Van Dorn rode along the column after the strife had ceased, cheer upon cheer greeted him from the enthusiastic soldiers, who under his daring directions had achieved the victory, and he is undoubtedly high at the present moment in the estimation of his forces..."*
—MOBILE ADVERTISER AND REGISTER, MARCH 20, 1863.

## Spring Hill, Tennessee

General Earl Van Dorn sat at his mahogany desk, his inkwell dry. He read over the letter quietly. Carey would like this very much... *I fought a battle near here a few days ago and won it. It was a beautiful affair. All in sight in an open plain. I took four regiments prisoners. Have had a rough time, but satisfactory to everybody. I am surrounded continually by a crowd and cannot write. I am well, and stand well with my troops. All cheer and serenade me. Children to change with every change of fortune!*

He stuffed the letter in his coat pocket. No couriers were present and it would be at least another week before one returned. He glanced at the papers spread haphazardly across the top of the secretary. He frowned and shook his head, loathing the paperwork. The battlefield was where he felt most comfortable. He sat back in his chair and closed his eyes while a gentle breeze blew outside and the music of a wind chime rang in the distance. In the back yard, a dog barked redundant and shrill as the chickens were shooed from the grounds, fussing and spurring as a tattered shirt flew about their heads.

"Git on," chanted Percy, the White's yard boy. "Shoo! You chickins!"

Van Dorn pulled the curtain aside in his upstairs office window and watched as Dr. White mounted his horse and set out on his morning visits. "They say he's a fine doctor," Major Kimmel had said when Van Dorn accepted the White home as his headquarters. Dr. Aaron White was known as the hardest working physician in all of Tennessee and tended his patients like no other doctor. Since the war had come he had more patients than ever, especially in the army hospital that now occupied the small hotel in downtown Spring Hill. He sat with them for hours, or even days if needed, until they had strength enough to ask for water or a blanket on their own. Dying soldiers sent for him in the middle of the night to confess their darkest sins as if salvation could be had in his salves and poultices. Yet, with all the soldiers to tend, the doctor still had his civilian patients to consider, and this morning he was off to deliver the third child of Henry and Lula Hill, a poor family who lived between Carter's Creek and Sleepy Hollow. The roads leading out to the Hill place were nearly impassable even during dry months, and with the flooding rains lately, Dr. White said it was best to allow extra time in case he had to finish the last mile of the trip on foot. It was not quite 5 A.M. when he mounted his horse.

Van Dorn stood a long time at the window. His thoughts raced ahead to the morning's parade. He hoped for a grand show, like the one a few weeks earlier when they arrived and the fine citizens of Spring Hill came out in force with gifts of clothing, guns, and boots for their soldiers. He glanced across the bed at his freshly cleaned and pressed uniform. He had not known such a luxury in months. His shirt showed some wear, but not enough to warrant a new one just yet. He would see to that in his next letter to his sister Emily. She was a fine seamstress and always mindful of his every request, usually sending two of whatever he needed and always with an apology for not thinking of it herself. Emily adored her baby brother, her dear Earl, as did his older sister Octavia. They were his greatest admirers.

He dressed in the dim light of dawn, smoothing his pants and coat with his hands. His leather boots were polished to a blinding sheen, thanks to Milton who came in the General's room and bowed like an English courtier. Van Dorn smiled at this and played along.

"It's a fine day, Gen'ral. If I might say so. I's done brung yo' horse up to the door, Sir. He's ready when you is ready."

"Thank you, Milton," Van Dorn chuckled. "Always one step ahead of me."

Milton smiled wide, his front teeth gapped like a picked-through cotton row. "Yassir," he said.

Milton held the door while the dashing Van Dorn tucked his riding crop under his left arm and strolled down the long hallway. He struck quite a pose in his grey tunic and gold epaulets, his light brown curls bouncing at the collar. At the base of the stairs, Van Dorn stopped, bowed slightly, and spoke as Mrs. White and her daughter stood whispering in the foyer. "It looks to be a fine day for you ladies to venture out and see the gallant army of the Confederacy in its finest," he bellowed as he exited the front door.

"Yes, indeed, General Van Dorn," Mrs. White said, feigning a smile. She quickly pushed her daughter into the dining room and bolted in behind her.

The general laughed. He could not imagine what he had done to cause that woman such constant fright. Since their first meeting, she had yet to say more than a few words to him. Funny, he often had that affect on women.

Van Dorn mounted a gray horse and rode west toward camp. Many of the soldiers had continued their celebration well into the morning and moved sleepily from their tents, forming crooked lines on the parade ground. The staff officers screamed orders and rode anxiously from line to line, corralling the men into place. Today's parade was expected to draw hundreds of spectators. There was no room for error.

A swarm of local ladies, all giggles and fluttering eyes, descended on the parade ground despite the early hour. Dressed in their Sunday finest, they held up parasols to block the impending morning sun, while a few old men claimed the shady front porch of a dry-goods store. A reporter posted nearby, leaned against an old oak tree and prepared his pen for the show. He made his money writing about the less serious side of the war. Grand balls and parades mostly. In late winter, he asked the general if he might ride along with his unit. Flattered, Van Dorn granted permission, but on condition that he be allowed to edit each piece before it went out. The reporter eagerly agreed to the arrangement. The general was a hot commodity for any young writer.

Today was sure to be memorable in light of Forrest's recent victory. He captured nearly 800 Yankees, their cache of weapons, and all their supplies at a garrison just outside Brentwood. They even confiscated the officers' expensive horses and saddles. Forrest's men were as excited as they were on the first day of the war, and that morning they marched proudly, arrogantly with their spit-shined boots and slicked-back dirty hair hidden neatly under fine Yankee hats.

When the crowd parted, several young girls shrieked, their eyes wide with excitement, as the soldiers held their hats high in the air for the approaching generals. The young reporter leaned back against the tree to avoid the cloud of dust that rose up as the officers rode up to the long line of soldiers. When the dust settled, every man fell silent and readied for inspection.

The smiling boys marched in high spirit, the horses danced, the guns gleamed, and the sabers glittered in the morning sun. General Van Dorn led a staff of regally attired officers and together they bolted onto the parade ground in lightning fashion toward General Forrest and his staff. The officers then lined up and rode gallantly down the line of soldiers, and when the inspection was complete, the crowd erupted in cheers. Then the party of officers dashed at a running gallop to the end of the column and threw their hats into the air.

The inspection and parade ended and Jessie spotted the scandalous reporter who called himself N'Importe. She watched with delight as he walked to the edge of the parade ground, a near-barren field about 500 yards long, nestled between two rows of old oaks. A group of elegantly dressed ladies sat perched in a black buggy, like birds in a cage, and waved to the reporter, but he did not stop. Jessie clapped her hands. He was walking toward her! She smiled and smoothed the ruffles of her green silk skirt, and when he was within a few steps, she turned in her seat and cracked the whip. The front wheel lunged a little forward.

"Wait, ma'am!" the reporter yelled, frantically jumping into the grass. "What did you think of the show?"

Jessie laughed and tugged at the reigns, jerking the buggy back onto the dirt path.

The reporter waved wildly and shouted, "Hello there! Could I have a moment of your time, please miss?"

Jessie giggled as she slowed her buggy. "You're in a very dangerous area, sir," she said, grinning slyly. "Why, just yesterday a young reporter like yourself was struck and severely injured on these very grounds." She looked him over closely. "Of course, he was a Yankee reporter. But you don't look one bit like a filthy scoundrel."

His cheeks turned red. "No ma'am. I'm not like that at all." He stuttered, "Uh, surely you remember me—the other day—in town?"

"Yes," Jessie said, holding out her gloved hand to him. "I do believe we met. But, for the life of me, I can't remember your name."

The reporter leaned in tentatively. "Why, I'm the reporter they call N'Importe," he said, kissing her hand.

"Well, aren't you the gallant knight," Jessie said, leaning back in the seat. She bit her lower lip and asked seductively, "And what is it you would like from me today, kind sir?"

The reporter stumbled back from the buggy. "Please don't misunderstand me, Mrs. Peters," he stuttered. "I only meant to ask you a few questions about the parade is all." He fumbled in his pockets till he found his pencil. "See," he said holding the pencil up.

Jessie laughed. "Well, ask me quickly. I'm a very busy woman, you know."

He looked nervously through his journal till he came across a blank page. He scribbled something down and asked, "Yes, my question to you is about the soldiers camped on your property. Would you say you feel safer with them there, or would you prefer to have them set up camp further down the road?"

Jessie laughed again. "Is that really what you wanted to ask me?"

"Why, yes ma'am," he said dropping his pencil under the carriage wheel. He looked like a child who had lost his toy. He pretended to laugh as he fumbled in his pocket again for another pencil.

Jessie watched his every move. He was a handsome young man. "Well," she said. "I am a loyal supporter of our Confederate Army and would do anything I could to help our great Cause, even if it means giving up my own home." She paused a moment and looked curiously at him. "Well, what are you waiting for? Aren't you going to write down what I've said? I wouldn't want you to write it incorrectly."

"Why, yes," he said, scribbling on the paper. "And one more thing..."

The sound of music drifted down from the parade ground and Jessie sat up straight in the seat. "I really must be going. It was very nice talking with you!" she shouted as her carriage rolled back onto the road. She cracked the whip and fell in behind an ambulance filled with giggling young girls as it raced toward the parade ground.

"Wait!" the reporter yelled as he ran to catch her. "What about the general?"

Jessie pulled the reigns hard and the reporter nearly collided with the rear of her carriage.

"The general," he continued. "Is it true General Van Dorn will occupy your place as well?"

Jessie whipped her head around. "And where on earth did you hear such a thing?"

"Why, from the general himself," he said. "Is it true that you'll allow it?"

Jessie's heart nearly leaped from her chest. "Well," she said, laughing. "I couldn't exactly say no to a general, now could I?" Then, with a crack of the whip, she bolted forward and continued down the dusty road.

The crowd had dispersed by the time she made her way back to the parade ground. For several minutes she waited until the general at last emerged from a crowd of soldiers.

He tipped his hat and stepped into her buggy. "Hello, Mrs. Peters," he said softly. "You're looking exceptionally lovely today." He leaned over and kissed her on the neck.

"Oh, General," Jessie whispered. "Why don't we take a ride?"

"My thoughts exactly, Mrs. Peters," he said, his dark eyes like onyx. "My thoughts exactly."

They rode in the direction of Columbia, a thick trail of dust concealing the buggy as it turned onto the Peters property. Jessie's heart fluttered. Not a soul was in sight. *Perfect.*

# CHAPTER 6

# THE EYE OF THE STORM

**April 1863**

The carriage rolled slowly down the bumpy dirt road. Purple and white irises, dandelions and faded yellow jonquils dotted the roadside, while remnants of last year's corn crop rotted in the adjacent field. With pickets posted on most of the rural paths in Spring Hill, folks kept to the main roads when they ventured out. This path was nearly invisible, just off Kedron Road, a main thoroughfare running easterly out of Spring Hill and up to the back entrance of the Peters' place, a well-maintained manor built in the 1850s by Jessie's father William McKissack. When Jessie and George married in June of 1858, they moved into this home even though Jessie preferred her father's stately mansion on Main Street. Country life offered little excitement, she explained, but George knew his precocious bride all too well.

His distrust stemmed from an unfortunate incident a few months after they were married. An old beau came to town and heard of her marriage to the doctor. He showed up drunk that night at the Peters' home and threw himself at Jessie, begging her to reconsider, to leave her loveless marriage. George soon entered the room and sent the drunken lover away. A few weeks later, the young man was found face down in a shallow pond. Heartbroken, Jessie vowed to ruin her husband one man at a time.

Jessie pulled at the reigns and General Van Dorn gave a startled jump in his seat. It had been days since the

Confederate Army had any rest and the rocking motion of the carriage had lulled him to sleep.

"What?" he shouted, flailing his arms wildly. "What is it?" He rubbed his eyes and stared at Jessie.

"My, you are tired," she said softly. "I didn't mean to frighten you."

He winked at her and moved closer. "No, you didn't frighten me," he said taking her gloved hand in his. "I'm sorry for falling asleep in such lovely company." He removed the glove and kissed her hand.

"Now, General," she whispered. "You know I'm a married woman." She giggled and leaned in to kiss him. His lips were rough like his hands, cracked and dry from long days in the saddle. He kissed her cheek and then her neck. She squirmed a little and laughed as his whiskers tickled her ear. "Earl," she said teasingly. "You must stop. Why, anyone could see us here."

He pulled her tight against him and kissed her hard on the lips. He let go of her hand, and she wrapped her arm around his neck and stroked his hair. They kissed for several long minutes and the general asked, "Will you take me to your cabin, ma'am?"

She laughed and wrapped both arms around his neck. "Oh, Earl," she whispered. "You are a devil!"

"You know you can't refuse me," he said, kissing her again. "I must have you, Jessie."

She fell into his arms once again and kissed him passionately. "You do love me, don't you? Tell me you love me."

He stroked her cheek and looked into her eyes. "You are beautiful, Jessie," he whispered to her. "There's no other woman like you in the world."

"But, Earl," she said, breathlessly. "You must love me or else..."

He pressed his finger to her lips. "But, I do," he said. "I do, and after this damned war, I will show you just how much."

He took the reins and Jessie leaned back in the seat. "To your cabin, my dear?" he asked.

She moved closer to him and kissed his cheek. The general whistled loudly for the horses to move forward and

Jessie took his hand and held it tightly as they rode in quiet down the deserted path. The back entrance to the Peters' property lay a short distance away; it was marked by a split-rail fence and a large iron gate, shaded by a monstrous sycamore. The tree was covered with ivy that trailed from the ground and up the tree to the topmost branch. "Turn here," Jessie whispered.

She pointed toward a cornfield situated in the northernmost corner of the property where a cabin lay nestled between a grove of pine trees and a thicket of blackberry and muscadine vine. A small creek ran snake-like through the pines and disappeared into a lush valley of sweet grass. The main house lay just over the rise of the hill so he stopped the carriage on the far side of the cabin, completely out of view. The general craned his neck, trying to catch a glimpse of the troops, but their campsite was hidden at the base of the hill. Not a soldier was in sight.

Jessie smiled. "We're all alone, Earl."

The cabin was clean and sparsely decorated with a small bed in one corner and a desk against the back wall. A large fireplace with a crude, timber mantel that held two polished pewter candlesticks occupied the main wall. Jessie lit one candle and placed it on the desk and reached inside the drawer. "I had this sent down for your arrival tomorrow," she said holding up a bottle of brandy. "It certainly won't hurt to celebrate a little early." She took two glasses from the washstand beside the bed and filled them half full.

"You never cease to amaze me, Mrs. Peters," he said smiling. "I wonder what else you have planned for me."

Jessie laughed and sat on the edge of the bed and untied her green velvet bodice. "Well, general," she said in a sultry voice. "You'll just have to see for yourself."

# CHAPTER 7

# AN INCIDENT AT
# WHITE HALL

**April 1863**

Jessie rested her head on the general's chest. "We've been here nearly an hour, Earl," she whispered. "Better not risk it. We should go now."

General Van Dorn pulled her close and lightly stroked the small of her back. "I know," he said. "Can't be too careful."

They dressed quickly, and Jessie drove the general down the same bumpy road and up to the front gate of White Hall. Van Dorn had offered to borrow her carriage and drive back to headquarters alone but Jessie insisted she take him there herself. "Better to do everything in the open," she explained. "They expect us sinners to hide and shrink from their sight. We'll give them nothing." She laughed.

"You are wicked." He turned and gave her a wink then strolled casually up the porch and into White Hall.

Jessie sat for a moment fighting the urge to run after him, to tell him she didn't want to wait till the damn war was over. But now she was unsure. Did he love her, or was she just another fool? What if the rumors were true about the other women, a second wife, and children in Texas?

She cracked her whip and drove toward Main Street. On Saturdays, the town converged on the tiny square to shop and visit—and gossip. Jessie pulled her carriage to the side of Main Street, directly in front of the mayor's office and Odom's Dry Goods. She stepped from her buggy with the assistance of Odom's stock boy and glided gracefully onto the walk and into the store.

The building was narrow and long with several aisles of shelves all of which were loaded with more goods than the town of Spring Hill had seen in months. Local blockade-runners had been quite successful lately, stocking the shelves with scarcities like coffee and sugar. Jessie glanced around the store and sauntered down the first aisle. A wide variety of hatpins were laid out on a silk shawl and above this was an assortment of handkerchiefs stacked high on a long wooden shelf. A group of young girls was stopped in front of her talking and giggling, and trying on every pair of gloves in the store. She strained to hear what they said but could only make out a word or two.

The store clerk yelled from across the room. "Could I help you with something, Mrs. Peters?" He was a short man with a beard that resembled a mountain goat.

She nodded. "Why yes, James. I believe I could use some help."

He stepped from behind the counter and motioned for her to walk ahead of him. "Why, I must say you look lovely as ever, Miss Jessie," he said in a shaky voice. He was remarkably shy and horribly unattractive. His back was nearly broken in a riding accident when he was a child and it was this injury that kept him out of the War and behind the counter of his uncle's store. Jessie felt sorry for the poor fellow and made it a point to ask for him specifically every time she came in to shop. For this, he adored her and would trail behind her for hours, ignoring every other customer in the store. Though the attention was truly an annoyance, she would allow him the luxury of showing her around today.

She took his arm and they made their way down the second aisle. When they reached the end, Jessie steered him to the corner where two young ladies stood talking beside a table of cotton cloth. She recognized one lady as Sally Lawson, an attractive recently widowed gossip. After just three months of marriage, and only twenty-one years old, poor Sally became a widow, forced to trade her youthful dress for mourning garb. Her young husband died at Fort Donelson the previous spring. Rumor spread that he was killed while retreating. It was a cruel blow but Sally had taken it remarkably well, too well some said. Everyone in town knew she had refused to marry the poor fellow for several months until he was awarded his uncle's vast estate in the rolling hills above Franklin. Then she most graciously accepted his proposal and married him three weeks later. The honeymoon lasted a mere two days when he was summoned back to his unit. Three months later he was dead and Sally was left quite wealthy. For some reason, Jessie liked her immensely.

Jessie approached the table and picked up a long piece of checkered fabric. She held it to the light and studied the quality of the weave and placed it back on the table. She sifted through several more pieces when the store clerk excused himself to help an elderly man who needed twine. He promised to return momentarily. "Wait here, Miss Jessie," he said politely.

Jessie tossed up another large piece of fabric and caught Sally's attention. "Why, Jessie Peters!" Sally screamed. "Don't I always say you look just splendid in that green velvet? Well, I'm absolutely sick with envy!"

Jessie laughed and put her finger to her mouth. "Hush Sally! You're horrible!"

Sally giggled and whispered in Jessie's ear, "Well, to think I'm expected to wear black till next winter! Why, it's just awful!"

Jessie cocked her head and laughed. "From the looks of that ball gown you're wearing, I can see you've decided against following the standard rule of social decorum."

Sally twirled around and lifted the train of her pink silk dress and laughed. The neckline was scandalously low for day wear and the sleeves were off the shoulder, resting right above the elbow. "I wore this to the parade this morning and my poor old mama nearly died! I tell you, it was absolutely grand!"

Sally's friend giggled and covered her mouth shamefully. Jessie laughed along though she was not at all interested in their girlish antics. She wanted gossip. Sally's family lived in town within walking distance of the general's headquarters. The Lawson's heard everything days before anyone else.

"I don't believe we've met," Jessie said to Sally's companion, a large girl with unwieldy curly brown hair and a pasty white complexion. Her fat face made it difficult to determine her age, but Jessie guessed her to be around twenty.

Sally apologized profusely. "Why, this is Miss Martin from Charlotte, a distant cousin on my mother's side."

"It's so nice to make your acquaintance," Jessie lied.

"Oh, Sally! Tell Mrs. Peters about that handsome general!" Miss Martin exclaimed clapping her hands. "Go on, tell her!"

Jessie perked up. "What general, Sally? Do tell!"

"Why, General Van Dorn, of course! He's staying across from our house!" Miss Martin clapped loudly again and jumped up and down like a small child. A pair of plain-dressed ladies turned in their direction and rolled their eyes.

"Calm down, Minerva!" Sally said. She shook her finger at her, grabbed her arm, and scolded the poor girl the entire length of the aisle. Jessie followed close behind, pretending to shop. When they were out of earshot of the other customers, Sally grabbed Jessie by the hand. "Now, you must promise not to tell this, Jessie," she warned. "You must promise to keep this all to yourself!"

Jessie frowned. "Well, of course I won't tell, Sally. Haven't you confided in me before?"

"Of course, Jessie!" Sally took her by the hand and pulled Jessie close. "Well, you see before the parade this morning my cousin and I were sitting in our carriage when this chubby fellow, a sergeant I believe, approached and asked if we would mind very much if he commandeered our carriage for official army business." She paused a moment and looked around for eavesdroppers.

"Go on."

"Well, I could tell right away that he was flirting with me. After all, I have been married even if it was for only three months, unlike Minerva here." She laughed mockingly. "I can tell a man's intentions, you know," she said, glancing at her reflection in the store window. She was shapely, though a bit on the large side. "Well, just then another man, handsome and lean and wearing a fancier uniform, approached the chubby sergeant and sent him on his way. And would you believe it was General Van Dorn!" She gulped some air and continued, "Well, can you believe it! The *general* himself! And such a handsome, strong man!"

Jessie fanned herself as the heat rose up her neck. For a moment she thought she would faint.

"He approached our carriage, took off his hat, bowed gracefully and apologized for the sergeant's rude behavior. He said, 'you ladies must excuse Sergeant Neal, he forgets himself in the presence of such lovely creatures. Please accept my apologies.'"

"Tell her what he said next!" Miss Martin squealed. She jumped up and down, her bosoms bouncing wildly. "Oh, he is so awfully handsome! Go on, go on," she said, poking Sally with her chubby white finger.

"I'm telling it as fast as I can, Minerva," Sally snapped. "Well," she said, smiling from ear to ear. "I hear that General Van Dorn is quite a lady's man." She giggled again and lifted her chin. "I told him plainly, that, although I was much younger than he and probably should not say such, that I strongly felt it was in his best interest to leave the women alone till the war is over." Her eyes widened. "To which he responded, 'My God, Madam! I cannot do that, for it is all I am fighting for. I hate all men, and were it not for the women, I should not fight at all. Besides, if I accepted your advice, I would not be speaking to you.'"

Jessie forced a smile and mumbled, "Oh, my."

Sally and Miss Martin clasped hands like two young girls. "Then he kissed Sally's hand," Miss Martin said, "and asked her if she would like to go riding with him this afternoon!"

Jessie's mouth flew open, her composure suddenly lost in the sacks of flour that dotted the floor. "*You* and the general?"

"And I'm going along too!" Miss Martin squealed.

"Hush, Minerva!" Sally said. "Someone might hear you!"

Jessie stared coldly at the two. "Well, I'll be sure to inform General Van Dorn that you are a widow," she said in a flat voice. "I'm sure he had no idea that you were in mourning."

"But, Jessie," Sally said. "You won't really tell him that, will you? I mean, he will certainly never call on me if you tell him that."

"Sally! Why that's not proper!" Miss Martin shouted, grabbing Sally by the arm. "Your mama's right! You do talk too much!"

Jessie watched the girls hurry out the door and walked to the counter at the front of the store.

The clerk stood smiling, an eager look on his face. "Mrs. Peters, would you look at that?" he asked, pointing to a large painting propped against the front wall. "Looks just like him, wouldn't you say?"

Jessie took a deep breath and fanned her face. She was desperate to see where Sally and Minerva were going. "What did you say, James?" she asked, turning back toward the clerk who stood staring at the painting. "I apologize, but I didn't hear—"

"Uncanny likeness, isn't it?" James said.

The painting depicted a man on horseback, an amateur work at best. A sabre hung by the rider's side; his cloak was thrown negligently across his shoulders, and his broad brimmed hat was turned up on one side with an enormous gold lace bow knotted at the back. At his feet were three maidens draped in silk. The caption read: "Ye gray Dragoon on ye black mare. General Earl Van Dorn C.S.A."

"Oh!" Jessie screamed. "Why, it's General Van Dorn!"

"Yes," James said proudly. "Came in this morning. From Atlanta, I believe. Do you think he'll like it? I mean, you do know him, right?" James' face flushed red and he averted his eyes. "I meant no disrespect, ma'am. I just heard he was quite fond of your family is all."

"Yes," Jessie mumbled through clinched teeth. "I'm quite sure he'll approve, James."

She listened intently as James read the note attached to the frame: "To one of the finest general's the South has ever known. Warmest regards, Lucinda Wilkinson."

Jessie snatched the note from his hand. "And who would this Miss Wilkinson be, pray tell?"

"Why, I don't have any idea, Mrs. Peters," James replied, his voice shaky. "But I'm sure she's a nice enough lady to just paint a man's portrait..."

"Indeed!" Jessie turned on her heels and stormed out the door, slamming it behind her.

"But, I don't understand," James said. "I didn't mean to upset you, Mrs. Peters."

But she was gone, and worse, she had slammed the door with such force that the painting fell forward and crashed against a stack of firewood. James bent over to pick it up and let out a faint cry. The face of the man was gone, torn away by the rough edge of the wood. "It's ruined," the clerk said to Mr. Odom who had come running from the back room. "The painting's ruined, and I may never see Jessie Peters again."

***

White Hall lay a short distance from the town center, a few minutes ride for Jessie. The fine swept yard and scattered beds of wildflowers framed the stark white two-story home as gracefully as an artist's brush on canvas. It was a grand home, one of the finest in Spring Hill, and its proximity to Franklin Pike made it the perfect location for Van Dorn and a few members of his staff who now occupied the entire second story of the home.

Jessie raced there, sitting straight against the back of the carriage seat, her head spinning from the morning's events. First the parade, and... the cabin. She smiled. Of course the general loved *her*. Sally Lawson was a liar, a desperate, bitter girl. And as for Miss Wilkinson—well, she was most likely some little old lady who loved to paint. She held the horses to a slow trot as she entered Depot Street, stopping her carriage at the front gate of White Hall. She marched to the door with confidence. Mrs. White had never liked Jessie and could make all sorts of trouble for her, but today Jessie didn't care what the old witch thought about her.

She reached the front door and knocked twice. A large woman of Creole descent, dressed in yellow silk, her hair tied neatly in a chignon at the nape of her neck, appeared directly and led her to the front parlor to wait for Mrs. White. Jessie shuffled her feet and wrung her hands. She had hoped to just slip in to see the general but the Creole woman reappeared to say Mrs. White would be in directly. She poured Jessie a cup of tea and left her alone in the parlor where she sat for several minutes, admiring the rich drapes and fine stitching on the parlor chairs. She had always heard Sarah White had good taste. But the truth was Jessie's home was still leagues above White Hall. She smiled at this fact.

When the clock struck the hour, a voice boomed from an upstairs room. Then a high-pitched laugh echoed down the long hallway. A *woman's* voice! And in the general's room! Jessie stood and stretched her neck for a view of the upstairs landing, but it was no use. She could not see past the enormous grandfather clock that stood outside the parlor door. The laughter came again and she leaped from the settee and ran into the foyer.

"Oh, my!" Mrs. White said as she jumped out of Jessie's way. "What on earth is the matter, Mrs. Peters?"

But Jessie rushed by her, oblivious to her presence, and stormed up the staircase.

"Mrs. Peters!" Mrs. White yelled. "Is there something I can assist you with? The general is—"

"No, Sarah," Jessie waved her hand in the air dismissively, "I can take care of this myself. You go on and don't worry a bit about me. I can see myself up."

"But, I must insist!" Mrs. White yelled as she trailed close behind.

Jessie approached the general's office and knocked. A young officer cracked the door and peered outside. "One moment, please," he whispered.

Jessie gave him a scornful look and replied, "I will not wait! Get out of my way!" She pushed past the young officer and stormed into the room.

"Ma'am!" the officer yelled. "You must wait outside."

Jessie flew into the room and stomped over to the general's desk. Standing in front of him was an old woman who turned around, startled at the uproar.

"Mrs. Wilbanks," Jessie said, biting her lip. "Why, I didn't know it was you in here."

"Well, Jessie Peters!" Mrs. Wilbanks said shaking her finger. "Explain yourself at once! What in the world is going on?" Mrs. Wilbanks was a half-witted, old widow who was known for her outlandish appearance and outrageous flirting. She had been through seven husbands and had yet to tire of the opposite sex. She hovered about the general, eyes wide, lips painted red, fanning herself as she was known to do in the presence of handsome men. She turned to Jessie and scowled.

Jessie glared back, her teeth set to bite. "Well," Jessie said. Her voice was shaky. "I have an important matter to discuss with the general and didn't know—"

"Why, don't tell me that, Jessie Peters!" Mrs. Wilbanks cut her off. "You knew good and well that I was in here!"

General Van Dorn jumped from his chair. "Uh, I'm sure Mrs. Peters has a very good explanation for her intrusion." He put his arm around the old lady and turned her toward the door. "Now, you were telling me, sweet Mrs. Wilbanks, that I have been remiss in my duties as a gentleman."

"Well." She giggled. "You have been a stranger," she said in a low, seductive voice, shaking that same bony finger in the general's face. "And, you know I told you specifically when to bring your officers over for supper."

He gave her a pat on the hand, and in a gentle voice said, "You are right, Mrs. Wilbanks. You must forgive me. What day would you like me to make it up to you?" He kissed her hand and smiled.

She fanned herself violently now. "Why, General," she replied in a schoolgirl voice. "You may come anytime you like. You are always welcome in my home." She gave Jessie a scornful look and whipped her head around. "Tonight, perhaps?"

The young officer opened the door and Sarah White ran in. "Mrs. Wilbanks," she said, taking the old lady by the arm. "I'm awfully sorry for—well, you know we must not let the actions of others upset us!"

"That Jessie Peters has some nerve coming up to the General's office so rudely," Mrs. Wilbanks snorted. "I tell you, Sarah, that woman is a—" Her voice cracked. "Well, she has no business carrying on this way! I never!"

Mrs. White led the old lady into the hallway. "You know Jessie Peters," she said loud enough for everyone to hear. "She's never been one for social graces."

Jessie started for the door but General Van Dorn grabbed her by the arm. "Good day, Mrs. Wilbanks," he said. "Look for a visit from me very soon."

"Oh, I certainly will," Mrs.Wilbanks said, smiling broadly, her eyebrow arched in a perfect half moon. "I certainly will."

***

General Van Dorn closed the door and turned the key. Downstairs, Sarah White called from the foyer. "Mrs. Peters! Please come down at once!"

But Jessie ignored her and approached the wild-eyed Van Dorn. "So, Earl," she said twisting her purse strings into a knot. "What is this I hear about you and Sally Lawson?"

The general cocked his head and glared at her. "I don't know what on earth you're up to Jessie, but this has to stop! You must get control of yourself before you ruin us both!"

"Oh, Earl," Jessie said. "You know perfectly well that I —uh, well I care most deeply for you, and—" She broke into uncontrollable sobs and fell into his arms. "You do love me, don't you, Earl? Oh, you must tell me you love me!"

"Jessie! Calm yourself!" He pinned her against the wall and grabbed her by the shoulders. "Calm down, I say!"

Jessie was shocked. Never once had the general shown any aggression toward her, but now it was as though she was staring at a total stranger, a mad man. "I won't calm down till you tell me the truth!" she hissed. "I know that the whole town's been talking, gossiping about you since the day you arrived! And, well it must be true!"

"Jessie," he said in a gentle voice. "What on earth are you talking about? What gossip? Have I not given you every moment of my spare time since I've been in Spring Hill?"

"Oh, you've been quite free with your spare time, or so I've been told!" She drew her hand back to hit him, but he caught her by the wrist.

"You wouldn't hit a general, now would you?"

He leaned in to kiss her and she melted immediately. "Oh, Earl," she said sweetly. "I do have a temper, don't I? But I can't stand it! You must tell me the truth! Sally Lawson said—"

He put his finger to her lips and shook his head. "No, Jessie," he said. "I've fought more gossip than Yankees these past few months."

Jessie forced a smile. "I know, Earl. Forgive me?" she whispered in his ear.

"You really don't care about some silly girl, do you?" he asked with a laugh.

She felt suddenly embarrassed, her confidence all but gone. "Well, of course I don't! She's just some silly girl—like all the rest!"

"Of course she is," he said smiling. "But what about the silly ladies downstairs? Poor old Mrs. Wilbanks—and Mrs. White—well, that woman is no doubt pacing the floor worried sick that there is an unescorted woman in my bedroom."

She tore away from him and stomped to the window. "Honestly! Why am I always the focus of that woman's hate? She is so insanely jealous of me!"

Van Dorn laughed and followed her to the window. "Well, she may be jealous, but right now you *are* an unescorted lady in an officer's quarters." He took her by the hand. "Haven't we given them enough ammunition for one day?" He kissed her and led her to the door. "Poor Mrs. White may not live through this one."

"Oh, she infuriates me!" Jessie replied. "Walking around with her self-righteous smile, trying her best to destroy my good name at every turn!"

General Van Dorn took a piece of paper from his desk and handed it to Jessie. "Here, tell her you got a pass from me. That ought to satisfy her for now." He opened the door and led her into the hallway. "Just smile at her. She'll have to smile back. Her position as a lady demands it, after all."

Jessie frowned. "Well, aren't you going to see me out?" she asked sweetly. "You wouldn't let me face her wrath alone would you?"

He stood silently by the opened door, reluctant to entangle himself in the affairs of women.

"Well?" She waved her hand in front of his face to get his attention. "Are you just going to stand there, Earl? Did you hear me?"

The smile was gone from his face, replaced with deep worry lines carved into the corners of his mouth. "Very well," he said, following her out the door. "But I do think it best that we meet far away from headquarters. These public encounters may cause us more grief than we know."

He was right, and though she hated to admit it, they had better keep up appearances. So, to keep the peace, she followed his lead and walked a few steps ahead of him until they reached the foyer. "Get the door for me, General Van Dorn?" she asked teasingly. "Or are you forbidden to walk me out as well?"

"Oh, Jessie," he said mockingly. "You truly have no fear, do you?" He smiled but there was worry in his eyes. He opened the door and walked behind her to her carriage. He had forgotten to put on his jacket and his once crisp white shirt was now wrinkled and disheveled. Even Jessie's green velvet dress dragged lazily along the damp brick walk as if she no longer had any care for appearances.

When they reached the carriage Jessie turned to him. "Don't worry, Earl," she said reassuringly, "about Sarah White, I mean. She's really harmless. Remember, you have a war to win. You don't have time to fight gossip circles."

"I suppose you're right," he said.

"Trust me, Earl." Jessie spoke with confidence though she had already seen Mrs. White watching them from behind the parlor curtain. "I know what I'm talking about when it comes to delicate women. She doesn't have the nerve to say a word."

And so he lingered awhile talking in the dim light of dusk, his foot propped casually on the step of the carriage as Jessie pretended not to notice the nearly imperceptible movement of the silk curtain in the parlor window.

## From the Diary of Jessie Peters

*April 13, 1863*

*I am truly suffering a bout of self-pity this morning as I sit alone in this dreary study. I can't understand why life is always so hard—why everything enjoyable must be doled out a drop at a time, why hardships are heaped upon us. It seems that just when I think I see a ray of sunshine on the horizon, I encounter nothing but difficulties. If I could only be granted the freedom to pursue my own happiness, then I should never be miserable again—O what a life mine would be!*

*I suppose I wouldn't feel so anxious if I had an idea what tomorrow held for me, but every day seems a complete mystery. There is still no news from George and this is perhaps more distressing than anything else. To wake each day not knowing if he will walk through that door—why, the suspense keeps me in a state of perpetual anxiety. If I could only live peacefully with George around, then I wouldn't wish for his absence so much. But he is so insanely jealous that he will hardly leave me alone for one moment. And dare I even speak of parties or picnics or parades—he wouldn't even consider it! Why I would be a frumpy old woman in a matter of hours—sitting there across from George, knitting a pair of socks, watching my hair turn gray and my waist grow large. Never!*

*But, I must not dwell on it—I must think happy thoughts or I will carve permanent worry lines in my brow. I truly believe if I could spend just one long, glorious day with my general, if I could tell him how much happiness he brings to my dark days here, then I think I would be satisfied. But lately, it seems even my dear Earl has an uneasiness looming over his spirit. He tells me I'm not the cause, but at times I am unsure. I believe it may be that General Forrest who keeps Earl so angry—he does dislike that man. Bedford, as he is referred, is a brute, not at all refined like Earl. Though I must admit he is a handsome man and it is rumored he is quite a successful businessman, his uncivilized ways make him undesirable to gentry folk. I'm certain it is this difference in class that causes such discord with Earl. But, then I wonder if it is Forrest at all who has*

*Earl so shaken. Perhaps he is still angry over that incident with Mrs. White. I shudder to think. The very nerve of that woman—to create such a stir over a little misunderstanding. She is a hypocrite and a do-gooder, I say! I should like to see what she really does behind those lily-white doors of her bedroom—or read her mind when a handsome man is in her presence. I dare say it would make me blush—Southern ladies and their pretense! Humph!*

*Well, that's quite enough ranting for one day. I should drive myself mad with all this negativity and worry. I should make a vow to start each day with morning prayers so I can clear my mind of nasty thoughts. I will focus on only those things that give me joy in life. It certainly can't hurt. So I will begin today with a prayer for my dear Earl. For all others previously mentioned, I pray that God may grant them the wisdom to know the errors of their ways. Amen.*

CHAPTER 8

# VAN DORN AND BEDFORD FORREST: A NEAR DUEL

**Around April 23, 1863**

General Van Dorn steadied his horse on the rutty path that ran along the northern side of Jessie Peters' property. Clement rode ahead, instructing a small detachment of soldiers. A reluctant engineer, not much older than the boys he commanded, spoke to them in a voice that was more like a Viking warlord than a redheaded boy from North Georgia. For days now Van Dorn had considered the likelihood of retaliation from the same Union line he and Forrest had pushed back toward Franklin several times in the past few weeks. He had determined an attack was certain now, and in order to win, he must not lose this advantageous position.

Van Dorn sent word to General Leonidas Polk for some engineers from his command to dig entrenchments for the inevitable attack from Rosecrans. Polk obliged him with a motley crew unlike any the general had seen before. He soon began to doubt their abilities to handle the job, and frustrated, he sent a note back to Polk with the promise to shoot any of the men who caused him trouble. Polk had yet to respond.

The entrenchment would serve as protection on the eastern side of Spring Hill. Van Dorn had no worries about his position on the Columbia Pike, but feared the Union line could slip through this eastern side with little or no problem. He watched with disdain as the young engineer attempted to steer the ragtag group to their proper positions. Polk would pay if these sons of bitches did not come through.

The ground where they worked was no good for digging. The bumpy earth was covered in gray rocks that jutted up out of the hard soil. It was a wonder anything grew on this place. With the exception of a large field dotted with dried corn stalks from the last harvest, the ground offered little beyond an occasional sprig of sweet grass and cockleburs. Van Dorn's native Mississippi was all mud and swamp, fertile enough to grow anything that fell on its surface. The crop here was tobacco, and Tennesseans took advantage of it, leaving the cotton to their southern neighbors.

The general walked off the area for digging and marked it with pieces of old brick. He placed the entrenchment near camp, which lay a hundred yards from the Peters' back pasture. This location also allowed him a good view from his new headquarters in the Peters' log cabin on the adjacent side of the field. The general caused quite a stir among his staff when he told them he had accepted Mrs. Peters' kind offer to use the cabin. Major Kimmell confronted Van Dorn and told him he thought it was a bad idea to set up camp at the home of a beautiful woman whose husband was nowhere to be found. Even his nephew Clement spoke out against the move. But the general argued his decision fervently. The location was perfect for housing the rowdy soldiers and it was a suitable distance to the main headquarters. The close proximity of the Peters' ladies was irrelevant.

The engineer bellowed from across the field and Clement rode off in his direction. Van Dorn left his nephew in charge. With luck they would get the trench finished by the end of the day. He motioned for Major Kimmell and they rode back to headquarters to meet the incoming supply train.

When Van Dorn and the major arrived at White Hall, General Forrest was waiting in his office. Forrest was a man of few words and greeted them with his usual coldness. He had railed against Van Dorn since the two were thrown together under Bragg's command, calling him a dandy and an undisciplined commander. Van Dorn laughed when he heard what Forrest said. In his opinion, the ill-bred Forrest carried no weight in the area of public opinion. After all, he was a man with no heritage, a slave-trader, an ill-tempered ruffian.

Still, General Forrest's presence invariably unnerved Van Dorn, and he fumbled with his hat and coat before placing them on a small corner shelf. He took a seat at his desk and Forrest followed, head held high. His scruffy beard poked out several inches from his chin, his coal black eyes set.

"General Forrest," Van Dorn began. "What brings you here today? Any movement?"

Forrest glowered, his lips pursed tight. "No, General, there hasn't been no troops moving." He cleared his throat and continued, "I'm here to clear up a matter that was brought to my attention a few days past."

Van Dorn smiled slightly. He knew where this was going. "And what matter would that be, General?"

Forrest's eyes grew redder. "Seems there's some confusion going 'round about Thompson's Station and I aim to get it all straight right now."

Van Dorn leaned back in his chair and casually ran his fingers through his thick hair.

Forrest slammed his fist on the table. "With regards to the property we confiscated at Thompson's Station. I don't know one item kept by my men, and I didn't have nothing to do with that Yankee reporter writing that I took sole credit for the win."

Van Dorn smiled and replied, "Well, General, in the words of Shakespeare, it seems you do 'protest too much.'"

Forrest rose from his chair, his cheeks burned red. He clinched his fists and hit the desk again, this time with such force the wooden legs bowed. "General, I demand an apology at once!"

"You may demand whatever you like, General Forrest," Van Dorn laughed. "But you have either erred in your report to me or your command has possession of this property. Now, which one is it?"

Forrest stepped around the desk as Van Dorn rose from his chair. The two stood locked in a cold stare. Van Dorn glanced at his sword, which rested on a wall mount on the opposite side of the room.

Forrest slid his hand across the sheath of his own sword, stopping to hook his forefinger in the brass hilt. "I don't much take to your tone of voice, General or not," he remarked in a cold, detached voice, his hand now firmly grasping the handle of his sword.

The two stood frozen, locked in a match of stubborn wills. "Well, let's not let my rank interfere. Sir, you may challenge me at any time."

General Van Dorn stepped from behind his desk, but Major Kimmel stepped between them and pushed Forrest back. "General Forrest, I beg you—" Kimmel stammered.

"No need to worry, Major," Forrest said, his fierce eyes softening. "I have no plans to fight General Van Dorn." He rubbed his forehead and took a deep breath. "My God, we have too much to do fighting the Yankees to take up fighting each other."

Van Dorn turned to Major Kimmel and nodded, his face still twisted in anger. "You are right, General Forrest, and I'm certain no man here would doubt your fighting abilities."

Forrest lowered his head, sweat beading on his brow. He dug his feet into the rug like a horse at the starting gate.

"But, you do understand," Van Dorn said in a condescending tone. "My orders will be followed while you are under my command. I'll expect that report."

Anger rose once again in Forrest's cheeks. "Of course, sir." His voice cracked.

Van Dorn returned to his chair. "I have a more important mission for you, General Forrest, more important than a petty clash of personalities." He motioned for Forrest to take a seat in front of him and laid out a map on which he detailed his latest plan. Forrest would move into Alabama and intercept a raiding column of 2,000 Yankees led by Colonel Abel D. Streight of Rosecrans's command.

"Any questions?" Van Dorn asked.

Forrest rose and saluted his commander. "Just one," he said, towering over the petite general. "Was you really gonna fight me?"

Van Dorn frowned and clinched his teeth. "Now, see here, General Forrest—"

"Just curious, sir," Forrest said with a crooked smile. "No offense intended."

Van Dorn rose in a fury and knocked his chair to the floor. "I'd have you remember your position," he said, his voice cracking. "There can only be one leader."

Kimmell jumped up and moved toward the desk, his pistol drawn.

But the general put his hand up. "No need for that, Major."

Forrest stood steady as an old oak, staring blank-faced at the general.

"No offense taken, General Forrest," Van Dorn said in a serious tone. "Let's put this matter behind us."

Forrest shook his hand and forced a smile. "Good then," he said. "You'll get that report soon as I get back." He walked to the door and waved his hand in the air. "You boys have a nice evenin.'"

***

Later that night, Van Dorn and his staff rode out to the Peters place. The entrenchments were nearly ready but the threat of rain that loomed over the valley was certain to delay completion, so the general demanded the engineers stay on longer.

"Polk expects them back tomorrow," Kimmell explained.

"He'll just have to wait until they've done the job right," Van Dorn said, his voice agitated. The fight with Forrest had hurt his pride and put him on the defensive once again so that he spent the evening storming through the camp yelling orders and handing out discipline.

"That man is unfit for command," Van Dorn said when he arrived back at White Hall. "He's undisciplined and crude. An embarrassment if you ask me."

Clement listened quietly to his uncle's complaints, just as he had done for him after Corinth. "Yes," he said. "He's rough all right, but I suppose he's nonetheless necessary."

Van Dorn spat. "He's no general." He reached in his desk and pulled out a bottle of whiskey. He poured a glass and held it out to Clement. "Here, join me, won't you?"

Clement took the glass and offered a toast. "Very well," he said taking the glass. "To Thompson's Station!"

"Here, here," Van Dorn replied. "And to Franklin! To hell with Granger!"

They drank the whiskey and the general poured another round and sank down in his chair. Clement sat on the edge of the bed and sipped his whiskey while the general droned on about Polk's worthless engineers. They weren't very skilled but they were warm bodies and at this point that meant a lot, Clement explained. But Van Dorn refused to listen and damned the whole lot of Polk's command for their incompetence. He poured another drink when a knock came at the door. "You expecting somebody?" he asked.

"No," Clement answered in a whisper, "not that I know of."

Van Dorn cleared his throat. "Uh, come in." His chair still faced the window where the orange glow of the evening sun settled on his face and hands. He didn't bother turning around to see who had come to call. He didn't care. His mind was lost in the argument with Forrest and the incompetent engineers.

"General Van Dorn."

"Yeah," he said, turning abruptly in his chair. "What d'ya want?" The whiskey had dulled his senses and he had not recognized the voice as that of Dr. White. He leaped from his chair and shook the man's hand. "Oh, forgive me, Dr. White. I thought you were someone else."

Dr. White grinned and rolled his eyes. "That's quite all right," he said. "Could I speak with you in private, sir?"

Clement quickly rose from his chair. "I'll just wait out here."

"Won't you sit?" Van Dorn asked politely. "Care for a drink?"

"No thank you," the doctor said. "I will only take a moment of your time." He moved his glasses to the tip of his nose and looked the general in the eye. "This is a personal matter, General Van Dorn. Uh, it's my wife, you see." He looked around the room and nervously scratched his head. "She's in a delicate way, and well," he stammered. "Her health is beginning to suffer. Her nerves, you see."

Van Dorn rubbed his whiskers and tilted his head sideways, dizzy from the whiskey. His first instinct was to tell the good doctor to take the door, but that would only cause trouble. Besides, he needed to know what Dr. White had up his sleeve. It was always the same with these families. They wanted to help the Cause as long as it didn't cost them anything. "Go on," he said in a kind voice. "Is there something I can do to help?"

He blinked and cleared his throat. "It's the soldiers and the noise, she says. I fear your presence here may prove detrimental to her condition. To be perfectly honest, my wife needs peace and quiet and has asked me to talk with you about finding another home for your headquarters." The words shot from his mouth. "We feel sure there's another family willing to take you in."

"I see," Van Dorn said. "Well, of course. I would never —"

"I knew you would understand," Dr. White said. "I'll tell Mrs. White at once." He shook the general's hand and walked quickly toward the door.

"Well, wait a minute! Just where would this new headquarters be?"

Dr. White turned quickly at the door. "Why, Martin Cheairs, of course. He has a fine home right on the Pike out here. He told me he'd be more than happy to have you."

"Very well," Van Dorn said. "But, I would ask that you send my sincerest apologies to Mrs. White." Though he didn't know for what he was apologizing.

"That's quite all right, General. Won't be necessary at all," Dr. White said. Then as if running from a fire, he tipped his hat and raced out the door.

"Now, what do you suppose that's all about?" asked a bewildered Clement Sulivane as he came back into the room.

Van Dorn walked over to the window and watched as Dr. and Mrs. White got into a carriage and rode out the main gate. "Don't know," he said in a strange tone. "She looks healthy enough to me." He scratched his chin and poured another glass of whiskey. "Jessie Peters shook'em up, that's all." He laughed. "She is something."

Clement frowned. "This could be trouble for you, sir."

The general sat back and propped his boots on the desk. "Oh, it'll be trouble all right," he laughed. "Jessie Peters will be the death of me yet."

# CHAPTER 9

# DR. GEORGE PETERS: A PASS TO TENNESSEE

**April 4, 1863**
**Memphis, Tennessee**

The ferry lurched into the slip as the cold waters of the Mississippi lapped over the sides and onto the feet of its passengers. Dr. George Peters kicked at the water as if he could somehow force it back into its dank and muddy origins. He pulled the brim of his wool hat down below his eyes and squinted at the sun that glowed fiercely against the robin's-egg blue sky. The wind blew fiercely from the north. Spring would not come for several weeks, not here, not while the muddy waters overflowed with the floods of its icy northern tributaries. Yankee bile spit into the pristine waters of the river so that when it reached Memphis its crystal clearness resembled a vast tarn, the black entrance to hell itself.

The horn blew twice for passengers to disembark and the small group of men and women slowly rose and ambled toward the dock. Some held large satchels fashioned out of multi-colored twills and heavy cotton canvas adorned with rich leather straps and buckles, while those less fortunate carried what few items they possessed wrapped tightly in a dirty cloth sack thrown carelessly across their backs. The younger passengers smiled shyly but no one spoke as the ferry operator schooled them in a gruff, leaden voice of the perils of stepping off a boat. One young lady slipped on the slimy wooden planking landing perfectly in the arms of a scruffy toothless fellow who gently lifted her and set her back in line. She thanked him kindly while his band of ruffians teased from the back of the boat, "Oh, thankee kind sir, thankee!" His dirty face twisted in anger as he jeered back at his comrades.

"Any passengers needin' a coach step right, please," called a voice from the far end of the lengthy pier.

George Peters, two large bags in hand, walked in the direction and quickly secured a driver. A stumpy black man accompanied him, pulling an oversized trunk by its worn leather straps.

"Put that trunk there, Mose," the doctor directed. "And hold onto these bags for me. Can't take any chances."

The old black man lifted the heavy trunk, which was more than half his size, and leaped into the back of the coach like a cat. He grabbed the two canvas bags and tucked them under each arm and squatted there, perched like a black gargoyle on the top of the large trunk, and traveled the road into Memphis to the Union Army Headquarters of General U. S. Grant. From the back of the coach, he chanted, rocking back and forth on the rutty dirt road. "I sho do like Memphis," he repeated. "Sho nuff, sho nuff."

"Yeah, right, Mose," the doctor smiled mockingly. "You just like being away from any work. That's all."

Mose flashed a smile like pearls in a sea of cocoa; his white eyes glowed through the crowd of people.

"Now, you sit quiet back there," Dr. Peters warned as Mose tilted his head to see a plump young black girl bend over to pick up a basket of clothes. "And keep your eyes on the road. I don't have time to get you out of trouble like last time we came to Memphis."

Mose smiled. "Yassir. Ain't getting' in no trouble. Not one bit'n."

They rode on for an hour or so when the driver stopped in front of a beautiful two-story columned brick mansion. The random screech of an owl frightened the horses and they bucked high in the air, nearly tossing Mose into the street.

A soldier wearing a finely tailored overcoat shook his head and laughed. "Better watch it old man," he said to

Mose. He held the gate open as Dr. Peters exited the carriage, then tipped his hat and marched up the brick path to the front door.

When the doctor reached the door of the ornate mansion, a middle-aged black man came out bearing a tray of bread and sliced meat. He walked around the porch to a set of French doors and quickly disappeared.

Inside, Dr. Peters shook hands with the commanding officer. He handed over his papers and was instructed to sit in the parlor till his identity could be verified.

"A Pass to Bolivar, Tennessee?" the adjutant asked, reading from the paper.

"Yes," the doctor said. "For me and my man Mose." He rose slightly from his chair and peeked out the window at Mose who was still perched in the back of the buggy, his hat pulled down over his face.

"Well, your papers ain't much good here since we never saw you take no oath in person." The adjutant bowed his chest and held back a grin, obviously enjoying this little game he played with the Union sympathizing Southerners.

"I will be happy to oblige in whatever necessary, sir. I have been away from my family for near a year now and—"

"All right. I ain't interested in your excuses. Just repeat after me."

He read quickly, almost inaudibly as Dr. Peters repeated the words, his right hand held high in the air. No Bible this time. Peters bent over the desk and signed his name. When he finished, he scanned the room for familiar faces, paranoid that he might be seen. He had no intention of making his personal business public.

"Here," the adjutant grunted, his gaze fixed on the next man in line, a sallow little fellow with a passel of children not one of whom looked to be over three years of age. White trash eager to get what they could out of the army.

Dr. Peters leaned over the large oak desk and signed the oath, then pass in hand, walked out the door of the fine brick mansion and resumed his seat in the carriage. Bolivar was a two days' ride at best. First stop would be his town home. His sister had moved in after Jessie and the children left for Spring Hill last summer. He hoped to find it in good condition, but since the Union occupation, most of the homes had suffered from pillaging Yankee soldiers in search of food or forage for their horses. But now that he had papers of his Union loyalty, he was confident he could cut some deal with the local authorities. General Brannan was in charge of the Yankees currently holding the town and was known as a fair-minded man. The doctor felt certain he had something to offer, and Brannan was just shrewd enough in business to take the bait. This maneuver had worked well in Arkansas, and Peters was able to reacquire his properties in full. Bolivar should be a cinch.

He leaned back and relaxed in his seat. He must play smart with the Yankees; beat them at their own game. Once his money and property were secure, he would strike a deal with the commanders who did not object to making a little on the side. All that remained was securing a pass and traveling without incident. Once he was in Spring Hill, he would make the same offer to his old friends. Poverty was no option for Dr. George Peters. Let the rest of them cling to idealistic loyalties; let them give away every ounce of wealth to the Cause. He was no fool. Money was there to be made. All a man had to do was find a fence-ridin' Missourian—a survivor—a man like himself. He smiled. His plan was perfect.

## From the Diary of Jessie Peters

*April 23, 1863*

　　*Today is a black, black day for my poor soul. I had so hoped to get through the month of April with a light heart and a shred of hope for the future. But, alas! That is not to be. George is coming home. I could tear the very words from the page! The letter came this morning and I have shed more tears since its arrival than ever I did even at my poor Papa's grave. O misery! What am I to do? What I would give for the pages of this book to come alive and give me some shred of hope, but I fear it cannot be. My prayer is that he is only coming for a short time, that he has business in Memphis that will require him to leave as soon as possible. In the meantime, I must get word to the general. We must conduct ourselves with caution. George would be furious if Earl paid me a visit—even if he is a major general. O, what I would give for wings to fly far away from my home!*

# CHAPTER 10

# THE DOCTOR COMES HOME

*"...I arrived at home on the 12th of April and was alarmed at the distressing rumors which prevailed in the neighborhood in relation to the attentions paid by General Van Dorn to my wife..."*

—Dr. George B. Peters, Voluntary Statement

The carriage was ancient, cracked in the center with a hard wooden seat that tilted to the left. Peters had argued vehemently for the one with shiny black leather seats and new wheels. It sat in the adjacent yard next to an old water trough where chickens scuttled across the hard clay, kicking up dust, clucking in unison at this sudden invasion of their domain.

"Take it or leave it," snorted the large bearded man as he ran his hand along the buggy's splintered side rail. "She's all I got now. Can't give you no driver though. Have to buy it if you want to use it."

Peters eyed the dirty man with suspicion. He knew his kind. They could smell money, even through the stench of chicken droppings. Like a lion, they would circle their prey until it cowered and surrendered. These rural outposts had been known for taking a man's entire pocketbook without so much as firing a single shot. The fear tactics they used made them successful, and Peters knew this lion had a number of victims notched on his belt. Still, these men were imbeciles and he could beat them with a few tricks of his own.

"I have a driver there," Peters said, pointing at Mose who had resumed his crouched position beside a giant oak. Mose didn't look up, but sat humming in a low melodic voice, a habit he had anytime the doctor got into arguments.

"Don't matter none," the man said, shoving his hands deeper in the pockets of his patched-together pants. "Ain't got nobody to bring it back. Ain't messing with it. Pay me or walk on."

Mose stood up from the tree and kicked a rock across the red clay roadbed. Dr. Peters rubbed his chin and yelled from across the yard, "Mose, bring my saddle bag here."

Mose grabbed the bag from beneath the tree and slowly, as if dragging a lead weight, he scooted across the dirt road. He kept his head down until he reached the doctor and looked up just long enough to hand him the bag, then turned and dragged himself back to the tree.

Peters stepped closer to the bearded man. "I'll be needing a buggy and driver. I can pay ten dollars—no paper. I won't be buying it. I have no use for it, so you'll need someone to drive it back."

The bearded man started to speak, when Peters held out a velvet pouch and motioned for him to look inside. "It's yours for use of the buggy and your man to drive her back."

He stared at Peters with a blank face and poured the gold coins into his hand. "All right, then," he mumbled as he turned and walked back toward the barn. Minutes later a gangly light-skinned man approached the doctor and led him to the yard where a new buggy sat. They climbed on the front seat and rolled over to the old oak where Mose was propped resting.

"Load the bags, Mose," the doctor said.

Mose stood up and stretched his long arms. "Yassir," he said at last and tossed the first bag into the back of the buggy and took a spot behind the seat where he settled down next to a large trunk. When they rounded the barn and headed toward the road, Mose began humming that old familiar song, his traveling hymn he called it. In time, the skinny driver joined in, while the doctor drifted slowly off to sleep, his head bobbing as they rolled down the bumpy road toward Spring Hill.

***

Jessie stood sideways in the mirror, admiring her thin silhouette. The babies had brought little change to her figure. Her waist was still small even without a corset and her breasts had grown fuller, spilling over the lace trim of her dress. She lit the table lamp and studied the faint lines around her eyes. Outside, daylight waned and with night would come the constant drone of men's voices from the nearby camp. The soldiers located first in the northernmost section of her property, but from sheer number alone they gradually moved closer to the main house so that at night their fires were heard crackling through the open window. Jessie smoothed out her silk skirt and fluffed the ruffles of her low-cut neckline. No light had yet shown in the windows of the carriage house, so he must have been delayed. She placed the lamp back on the table. She would ride down to the gate and wait for him.

George's letter stared back at her from the dressing table. He was coming home. She grew sick at the thought of him. He had been gone for nearly a year now and she had enjoyed every minute of it, had managed just fine without him, handled every matter of business that crossed her desk, and had even made a little money. She had proven herself quite savvy, had shown everyone she could survive very well without George. But she knew he must return—after all, she and the children belonged to him—like a home, or land.

She hadn't given much thought to scandal when General Van Dorn inquired about the troops bivouacking on the property, and though he had insisted that she get permission from her husband, she told him boldly, "The plantation is mine, not my husband's. I run this while he takes care of his patients." Then she went a step further, insisting that the general use Alexander's cabin as well. "You may use it at your pleasure," she said and sent a reluctant Alexander to point out its location. Within a few days the cabin boasted of a fine bed and mattress, a desk, and other necessities until the general had everything he needed to set up headquarters. "When you and your officers can find the time, come and visit me," she insisted. "My cellar is well stocked."

Van Dorn and his men had taken her up on the offer more than a few times over the last few weeks of their stay, and with this had come the gossip. Though Jessie cared little for the townspeople, she shuddered at such news reaching George. She had taken great care to safeguard her reputation, assisting with the War effort, making bandages, and tending to the wounded in town. But once the rumors surfaced about the general and the lone buggy rides, her neighbors began to talk. With each passing day, the rumors grew into flagrant lies until she felt sure George would hear of the entire affair. Now she was worried.

She peered out the window. Still no sign of him. She threw her shawl around her and tied her hat. The night air was pleasant enough, and since she often took an evening ride when the weather allowed, she was certain she would not arouse suspicion. The stars and moon were in full concert tonight, giving her just the right amount of light. She must find the general. She must warn him of George's impending arrival.

Alexander brought up her horse and she sauntered down her long drive. It was nearly a half-mile in length from where it began at Kedron Road to the front porch steps. A narrow bridge provided safe passage over the creek that snaked through the full length of the property to the main road. Before the bridge, the drive was often impassable in the spring when the creek rose, often catching an unwary cow in its swift-moving stream only to spit out its stiff corpse miles downstream.

Jessie was proud of her bridge, had demanded George have it built after she was forced to spend nearly two weeks stranded the previous year. But when she sent word to her brother-in-law Major Nat Cheairs to send some Negroes, he flat refused to share them. Said they might escape and never return if he let them out of his sight. So she used her own resources, and with only a few hands still on the place, built the bridge in just under a month.

When it was ready, she had the same Negroes ride across in her carriage to test its durability, and when convinced of its safety she drove straight over to Major Cheairs' place and gave him a piece of her mind while her sister stood wide-eyed and speechless. The major immediately wrote to Peters, calling Jessie a tempest. Peters laughed but Jessie refused to let it go and wrote her brother-in-law a scathing letter in which she warned him to "weigh well and tread lightly for your hand is in the lion's mouth." Cheairs did just that and never approached Jessie again.

Jessie neared the gate and turned to see Alexander walking at a distance behind her. He smiled at her, embarrassed at being caught. He went to great pains to protect Miss Jessie, as did the other Negroes on the place. She always treated them kindly, but with Alexander she was different. He had been with her family for nearly twenty years and now that her own father was gone, he had assumed that role. She smiled back at him reassuringly.

Alexander reached the gate first and lit the oil lamps. He turned and walked back up the drive to a sprawling magnolia where he sat down and lit his pipe. He would stay just within earshot.

At the gate, Jessie heard the faint sound of horses and men's voices. Dogs barked in the distance as the horses' hooves grew louder and louder, their silhouettes bursting forth in a giant cloud of dust through a row of sycamores. The horse in front was black as night, its coat tinged with silver under the glow of the full moon. Van Dorn's horse. As he approached he smacked the horse's flank sending her into a full gallop toward the gate. Jessie held her breath.

"Mrs. Peters," he said removing his hat, a faint smile on his face. "And to what do we owe this pleasure?" His dark eyes twinkled in the moonlight as he dismounted and tied his horse to the gatepost. He stood before her and bowed regally. "I do hope you are well this evening."

"Oh, yes, General Van Dorn," she said, nervously looking about her. "I only came down to let you know that Dr. Peters will be arriving shortly."

She wrung her hands, but the general seemed unmoved by the news. He placed his hat on his head and walked to the gatepost where he remounted his horse and turned to face her. "Good," he said in a serious tone. "Then you will send him when he arrives. I should like to thank him for the use of his property."

"But, you don't understand," she whispered. "George is not—well, he'll not be happy. I can assure you that."

He tipped his hat once again and kicked up a trail of dust.

"But, Earl! You must listen." Jessie reached out for him to stop. "There could be trouble."

The General looked back at her and smiled. "Oh, there may be trouble alright, but not for me." He laughed aloud as he bolted toward where his men were camped, their fires lighting up the countryside like a million fireflies. The other officers followed close behind in a stampede of hooves.

Jessie stood amazed, shocked that he would ignore her warning. And when the dust settled, she mounted her horse and rode back toward the house. Alexander started ahead of her, his heavy boots dragging clumsily along. When he reached the house he walked left and down to the carriage house where he had slept some months now. Jessie wanted him close to the main house since she was there alone with the children. She felt safer that way. From the front window of the carriage house he could watch every movement on the place.

She went to the parlor, removed the crystal decanter from the sideboard, and poured a small glass of brandy. She sat on the piano bench and stared intently out the window and down the drive. George would likely arrive in the night, traveling under the cover of darkness, a habit he had acquired since early 1862, when he signed an oath to the Union army, or *crossed over* as Jessie liked to call it. He defended his actions, almost convincing his own family that he had to give the Yankees the lie or risk losing everything. But she laughed and called him a traitor. Later that spring when he left Bolivar for Memphis, he sent her and the little ones back to Spring Hill. And there she had lived miserably—until Van Dorn arrived.

She took the last sip and poured another glass. When her eyes grew heavy, she moved to the velvet settee in the corner by the window and lay back, recalling that last conversation with George before they left Bolivar. He was heartless, a dictator, a man with little passion but for money, and she loathed him. She thought back a few years before when rumors spread about Jessie and another man. George allowed the gossip to run rampant through the town, and when she begged him to put an end to the vicious talk, he laughed and told her she must learn a hard lesson, even if it cost him his reputation. He accomplished both of these. By the time Jessie arrived back in Spring Hill, she had not one friend remaining.

She drank the last bit of brandy and prayed for an end to the War, an end to her loneliness. Maybe she would even find happiness—perhaps she and the general...

She placed the damper on the table lamp and closed her eyes. Until then, she would go on as Mrs. George Peters, would play the game. She must be strong or the doctor would crush her.

***

A fountain of light cascaded into the room as a plump red rooster crowed Jessie out of her slumber and onto the hard floor. She leaped up and scanned the room and breathed a sigh of relief. She was alone. The only sound was Virethia yelling at an old hound that was chasing the chickens. Good, it was still very early. She could get dressed and ride over to the cabin and she and the general could talk about everything.

Jessie bent over and quietly removed her slippers. She lifted the train of her dress and tucked it into the bodice and moved cat-like across the hardwood floor and to the foyer. At the foot of the stairs, she heard the faint cries of a baby. She had no memory of putting her down. She usually left that job for Virethia's daughter Millie—when she could be found. Last night she felt sure she had put the baby to bed before she rode out to see the general. She stopped suddenly. "Oh!" she moaned, her head reeling from the brandy. The clock chimed six times. She must hurry or she would miss her chance to see the general.

The baby's cries grew louder and Jessie called out for Virethia. "Where's that Millie?"

Virethia came running from the kitchen and shrugged her shoulders. "I ain't seen her, Miss Jessie."

"Fine, I'll find her myself!" Jessie said. "But she's in for a whipping when I get my hands on her!" Jessie hurried to the landing of the staircase but the crying stopped, replaced by the creaking of a rocking chair. She tiptoed to the nursery door and crept inside where she readied herself to give Millie a good tongue-lashing.

"Millie," she whispered, her teeth set.

"No, my dear," came a familiar voice.

She jumped back toward the door in one leap. "George?"

"Yes," he said. "Were you expecting someone else?" he asked, grinning slyly. He was sitting like a great bird in the rocking chair as Lucy Mary lay in his arms. "Tell me, Jessie. Do you think she looks at all like me?" He held the baby up and looked her over. "I'm not sure who this child resembles."

Jessie's heart beat in her chest as she struggled to find the right words. "Why, she looks like you, of course." She swallowed hard and tried to steady her trembling knees.

"You may be right," he said with a grin. "*This one* does look a little like me."

### From the Diary of Jessie Peters

*April 13, 1863*

*I awoke this morning to an aching heart. As I sit alone in the parlor I am reminded of a time years ago, sometime after my dear mother had passed on and my poor sweet Papa pulled me aside and said, "Jessie Helen, never love another more than you love yourself. There's danger in it." He told me this more than once—I suppose because he was guilty of that very thing. He had loved my mother more than he should, so that when she died, he did not know how to carry on. I remember how he wandered the halls of our home for those first few weeks after we put her in the ground, and then late at night we watched as he rode off to sit at her grave. I imagined he threw himself across the cold stone and lay there till the morning sun forced him up. For months he repeated this same scene until he caught a terrible chill. He was dead within the year.*

*But his tormented soul did little to discourage my willful heart, and when my time came I followed in his footsteps, falling desperately, madly in love. O, how I hate to recall those sad, sad days, but the memory will not die away. Dear, handsome Luke! If I could have only stopped him— could have taken the gun from his hand. But he would not listen! I tried—O, how I tried—I truly tried! But he met that awful boy at sunrise anyway. And then how dreadful the sight! I remember he was wearing that lovely white shirt I had sewn for him just a month earlier, the one with the delicate stitching on the cuffs. He was so handsome that day. But when they brought him in that morning and laid him in the parlor, his face was ashen; his shirt was marked with a tiny hole where the bullet entered. I must have fainted because I don't remember anything beyond that except that it grew pitch dark outside and I awoke to see his body still lying motionless in the parlor. I was beside myself and thought I would lose my sanity completely. I've often said my heart was buried alongside Luke that day, deep in the cold ground, those beautiful dark eyes gone—forever.*

*I did not think I could love again, but as I sit here reliving my painful past, I feel a longing for the general. I fear I have grown quite fond of him. He is so like my dear, sweet Luke.*

*But enough! I must not think such thoughts lest the past repeat itself.*

*O, how utterly miserable I am! I have tried with all my being to find some moment alone, far away from George. The very sound of his voice sends my skin crawling and the way he takes my arm when we walk out—I could scream! Now I understand what the general means when he laughs at men like George—parlor soldier, he calls them. And he is right. George is soft—not strong jawed and lean like Earl. Still, I suppose I should be happy at least that he was able to sell his cotton last fall. He told me he made a considerable amount of money on the trade and looks to repeat the same next season. We have money now—at least enough to be rather comfortable should hard times befall us. Still, I wish he were back in Arkansas or Memphis—anywhere but Spring Hill.*

*News about Thomas is rather grim and I'm quite despondent over that. I had hoped to hear he was faring better, but it seems his disease has gotten the better of him. George is reluctant to tell me everything. I suppose he thinks I am some naive schoolgirl—but I've known for some time that what ails Thomas is a curse. I'm no fool. George tried to conceal much of the sordid details, but I read between the lines and have painted an awful picture in my mind of his symptoms. (I should like to forget it as soon as I can.)*

*The children are in a fit since George's arrival. They hardly know him, yet they seem overly excited at the new face around the house. Of course George has had his fill of babies and has little desire to dote on them, though they hang about his legs and paw at him. He has been rather annoyed by their attention—which, of course, I find utterly amusing. It serves him right he should endure what I have gone through each and every day since he left last winter. Besides, if they keep it up he may decide to return to Memphis. That is my prayer. Or, should I say, one of many prayers I have right now.*

*Today I have begun to make little Lucy a new dress and although I've not sewn much in years, I'm quite excited to have some distraction from these miserable days with George around. He is sure to drive me insane with his incessant complaining. It's as if he enjoys this daily torture of me. Alexander came in early this afternoon with a fine black mare for the doctor to look over. Seems George has plans to go to Nashville. Good! Perhaps he'll stay there. I hear the Tennessee Legislature may come together soon. If that happens, George will go. He is quite committed to his role in politics. And with George gone—I can finally see my general!*

# CHAPTER 11

# A Fox in the Hen House

*...I came to Nashville on the 22d of April, and was exceedingly mortified on my return home to hear that Van Dorn had visited my house every night by himself during my absence, my wife having no company but her little children...*
—Dr. George Peters, Voluntary Statement

In the Tennessee valley, spring arrives slowly, creeping in and covering the early blooms with a dusting of snow or an unexpected frost. April was often the cruelest of the spring months, with cold showers and a milky sky that lingered until the first days of June. Nature frozen in time. April 1863 was no different except for the added elements of war, of trenches carved into the earth and the persistent smell of black powder and death in the air, miles of countryside ravaged by inexperienced farm boys who pushed on regardless of their losses and dreamed of victories on the field and warm fires back home, a hero's welcome when the War was over. These were the thoughts that haunted Van Dorn's mind as daylight arrived on that frosty April morning, the third April since the fighting began.

The fireplace in the two-room cabin popped and hissed as Milton laid the damp logs across the irons. A thick smoke soon filled the room, running them both onto the small front porch. Van Dorn waved his scarf in front of his face and spat on the frozen ground.

"Hell, Milton," he said through coughs, "if we wanted a campfire we could have come outside." He laughed at the sight of Milton fanning smoke from the cabin with a pair of white pantaloons.

"Where'd you get those?" Van Dorn asked, choking back laughter and smoke all at once. "Don't look to be your size, now do they?"

"Naw, now you know these ain't mine, sir," Milton responded, his head bent toward the ground. "These here is Rose's. She giv'em to me when I left her in Baton Rouge."

The general gave him a curious look. Truth was she had left him, but not before taking what little money he had tied up in a cloth under his mattress. When he confronted her she lied to him. Next day, he threw her belongings in the yard but kept her prized pantaloons thinking she would come back to get them. She never did.

Van Dorn laughed and slapped him on the back. "Don't mind me. I won't tell a soul."

Milton shook his head. "Naw," he stammered. "I ain't lookin' for no woman."

"Well, don't be so quick to say that, now! Every good man needs a good woman!" the general said.

"I reckon so," he laughed, still fanning the smoke. When the cabin was clear, he grabbed a bucket from behind the door. "Gone fetch some water." He opened the door to find Dr. Peters, hand raised to knock. Milton looked back at the general.

"Where is the commanding officer?" Peters asked.

"General Van Dorn's yonder in the cabin, sir," Milton answered.

Peters stared coldly at the crude wooden door. For a moment it appeared he would not move at all, then as suddenly as he had arrived on the place, he threw his hands in the air and yelled. "Well, see that you tie my horse at once!"

"Yassir," Milton replied, his face expressionless. He had heard enough about this Dr. Peters. He wanted nothing to do with him.

Van Dorn now stood in the doorway, bright-eyed and smiling, concealing his shock at the doctor's unannounced visit. "Can I help you?"

Peters removed his hat and held his hand out. "General Van Dorn?" he asked. "I'm Dr. George Peters."

"Well, certainly," Van Dorn said. "Can't thank you enough for your generosity." He led the doctor into the cabin and thanked him for allowing his men to graze their horses in his fields and for the occasional use of the cabin.

Peters nodded. "Don't mention it," he said with a frown. "Do all I can to support the Cause."

"Your home and lands have been invaluable to me," Van Dorn went on. "This cabin, of course, is quite convenient." He cleared his throat and looked at the door. Milton had not returned. "Well, I like to camp near my men when the enemy's close. Can't be too cautious, you know."

They stood in awkward silence for several seconds.

"No, can't be too careful, General," Peters finally replied. He scanned the room; his piercing eyes darted back and forth with great rapidity. "So, you're fixed up rather nicely I see."

"Well, yes," Van Dorn replied. "Thanks to Mrs. Peters. She sent me these furnishings—and your daughter, Clara, I believe it is, brought me several other necessities." His face flushed slightly as he searched for his words. "Pots and pans, and other items, you see."

Peters nodded, his thin mouth pursed tight. "Clara, you say? I had no idea you'd met Clara?" His voice cut the air like a knife.

"Well, yes," Van Dorn replied confidently. "She brought me some warm blankets for these chilly Tennessee spring nights."

Peters looked suspiciously at the general. "Yes," he said coldly. "The Middle Tennessee valley can be brutal. I suppose you're accustomed to a more inviting climate."

The men stood in awkward silence once again. Van Dorn glanced out the window as Milton sauntered back to the porch. Peters was the type of man every soldier hated, the man who stood before the warrior and told him how he ought to go about winning the battle, though he himself would never dream of touching a sword. "Yes, I suppose I am better suited for warmer environs." He bit his lip anxiously awaiting Milton's return. He was tired of the doctor and his questions. "Well," he said hurriedly. "If you'll not be needing anything else, I really must be going. I'm expected in town shortly, you see." He reached out to shake the doctor's hand and moved in the direction of the door. "Remember me kindly to the Peters ladies. And thank you, of course, for your extraordinary generosity." Van Dorn opened the door and waited, but Peters did not move.

"General Van Dorn," Peters said, holding firmly to the general's hand. "If I might have a moment of your time, please. There is one thing I need from you."

Van Dorn's heart pounded in his head. He had not expected any requests from the doctor and had no desire to grant him anything short of a good old-fashioned ass whipping. "Go on," he said as he led the doctor out onto the porch. "I suppose I have a moment."

"I am in need of a pass to Nashville, you see. I have some business I must attend to." Peters reached into his coat pocket and pulled out a piece of paper. He held it out to the general. "If you would be so kind as to repay my generosity," Peters continued. "Here you'll find my papers from General Brannan of the U.S. Army."

Van Dorn eyed him suspiciously. He had heard rumors of the doctor's unorthodox allegiances—two sons and a brother in the Confederate Army yet Peters had pledged an oath to the Union some time back. He was a savvy businessman and was rumored to have traded more cotton in the last twelve months than before the war. George Peters was no friend of the Confederacy. Still, he had better comply. Best keep him happy.

Van Dorn folded the papers and called out for his adjutant, a gangly soldier with reddish brown hair who followed him into the cabin leaving the doctor alone on the porch. Moments later, the two emerged again and Van Dorn handed the pass to the doctor.

"I'm much obliged, General," Dr. Peters said with a crooked smile. "Do let me know if there is anything the Peters family can do for you and your men. Send your requests to me, of course. Mrs. Peters has enough to do than to worry about the Confederate Army."

Van Dorn smiled politely. "Why, of course," he said. "I wouldn't dream of taking advantage of the kind Mrs. Peters."

## From the Diary of Jessie Peters

*I am utterly confounded by this life I live! Every day it seems I am confronted with some sort of trouble—not of my own doing, of course! Just when I have some small ray of sunshine in my life, just when I begin to feel alive again, that dark cloud—better known as George Peters—casts a deadly shadow over me! I declare I hate that man like no other! He does amaze me! I have a good mind to go straight to Jeff Davis myself and tell him that the supposed Confederate George B. Peters is nothing but a common traitor! That would fix him right!*

*Tonight we are to attend a grand affair at Ashwood Hall. I so hope Antoinette Polk is there. Perhaps I can get her alone and tell her my troubles. She is such a good listener and always has a kind word for me, and since it appears George is here to stay, I best find a confidant as soon as possible, for I can't bear to think of spending every waking moment battling that man! Oh, why did he have to come back here? Now it will be all but impossible to see my General—at least it won't be as easy as it has been these last few weeks. If only I could run away from here—far away from this place and from George! I would never return!*

*Well, I suppose I should at least be grateful for tonight's party. All of the Confederate officers are to be there. As God as my witness, I will have that dance with my General—even if it kills me!*

# CHAPTER 12

# A Night at Ashwood Hall

George carried on about the Polk's party until Jessie grew suspicious. He was up to something. She felt sure of it, knew him all too well. Still, Jessie was delighted at the thought of a social affair and dressed in her finest for the party. But as she approached the carriage and saw the smile on George's face, a feeling of dread overcame her. It was all too much! The general—and George—a house full of gossipers all bent on destroying her. She closed her eyes and tried to relax. She must not let them see her nervousness. Oh, what she would give for a drink of brandy!

George sat across from her and spent most of the ride to Columbia in silence, brooding in the corner of the dark carriage. Jessie tugged at her bodice, smoothing the waist and lifting her skirts to keep them off the floor of the carriage. The blue velvet of her dress shimmered against the black silk shawl fastened in the center by a pearl and ruby brooch, her hair held loosely in the back with a single black ribbon. George cast an occasional disapproving glance in her direction. She pulled her shawl tighter to hide the plunging neckline of her dress. But she knew it did not matter. The ladies would talk regardless.

Up ahead, a long train of carriages lurched slowly on the Mt. Pleasant Road as guests arrived at the entrance to Ashwood Hall, the stately mansion of Captain Andrew Polk. From the road Jessie saw Mrs. Polk and her oldest daughter Antoinette greeting guests on the front porch of the home.

"Oh, Antoinette!" Jessie shouted. Antoinette was a heroine in Columbia, a woman ahead of her time, since her daring escapade when the Yankees came to town and she single-handedly saved an entire division of Confederate soldiers by riding with gun in hand across several acres of their estate to warn the troops that Yankees were coming for them. Antoinette was beautiful as well. Jessie admired her greatly.

Guests arrived for another hour until the house was filled to the brim with young and old, soldier and civilian. The parlor resembled a spring garden with young girls in lovely gowns of light pink and lavender, who whispered to each other and giggled as a group of soldiers mustered the courage to ask for a dance. And from the dining room there came the most wonderful smell of smoked ham and venison.

George and Jessie walked arm in arm into the parlor where an orchestra was performing "The Bonny Blue Flag" for the officers in attendance. General Earl Van Dorn was the first to make a toast to the Confederacy, followed immediately by General W. H. Jackson who praised President Davis and General Lee for their strategic plan to secure the Shenandoah Valley. Every glass was raised as the band burst into "Dixie" and every foot took to the floor. While George spoke with an elderly farmer, Jessie joined in the flow of dancers who moved through the parlor like a swarm of bees.

General Van Dorn leaned casually against the wall and smiled as Jessie danced past him. His head was tilted as if studying every movement. Jessie smiled discreetly, and when the band stopped, she moved in the direction of the front parlor.

The general followed and cautiously greeted her with a bow and a light kiss on the hand. "You look ravishing tonight, Mrs. Peters," he whispered.

"Why, you are quite a flirt, aren't you, General Van Dorn," Jessie mumbled, cutting her eyes at a group of old ladies standing nearby. "Mind your voice," she said smiling. "They're watching your every move." She lifted her fan and looked away. "Perhaps you should speak with them first. Satisfy the old bats so they'll leave my name out of their gossip for once."

"Oh, don't mind those dear old ladies," he said with a grin. "They're not so bad. Besides, you should be flattered that they always choose you as their topic of conversation." The general laughed. "They're just jealous that you're getting all the attention."

Jessie laughed and lifted her fan to hide her face. "You are bad!"

By now the room was overflowing with giggling young girls who gathered by the punch table near a small group of unsuspecting fellows. Jessie watched them with scorn. Not so long ago, she was one of them—lovely, full of life and love. Now, she felt a million years old.

"And where has the kind doctor run off to?" General Van Dorn asked teasingly. "Has he left you all alone again?"

"No," Jessie whispered. "Unfortunately, he's still here." She fanned herself and looked away at a middle-aged couple dancing past them as the music played louder. "He's coming through the door there," she said in a panic. "You should go now."

Van Dorn turned his head toward the door, his nostrils fanned out in frustration. "Very well," he said. "I'd lay money he would never say a word to me here. But I'll do as you wish. I expect you'll save me a dance next time, won't you?"

"Go, Earl!" Jessie hissed, though her heart leaped at his playfulness. "Now! He'll get angry if he sees you!" But it was too late. George was glaring at her, his mouth contorted in that familiar scowl.

The general turned away and walked casually toward a group of old ladies. He greeted them each with a kiss on the hand and a courtly bow. Jessie tried to watch both men from the corner of her eye but she found it impossible to take her eyes off George's angry face. She smiled as he approached. "Everyone's dancing," she said cheerfully. "Why don't we join them?"

But, without a word, he took her by the arm and whisked her out the door. She caught the general's eye as they hurried past. "But, George," Jessie said. "What on earth? I don't understand."

"We're leaving," George snapped, moving quickly through the parlor and into the foyer, dragging Jessie behind him. "You'll not embarrass me! At least not in public! You can make your apologies later," he said as he pulled her down the stairs and shoved her into the carriage. "Besides, I've got business in Nashville tomorrow." Then leaning his head out, he shouted to Alexander. "Home! And make it quick!"

Alexander cracked his whip and the horses jerked violently forward. Jessie sat straight against the seat and turned slightly away from George. She glanced back but only for a second. His hatred for her was thick as the heavy night air and sent a chill up her spine. She felt anxious now, like an animal in a trap, locked inside the silent world of George's wrath.

When their carriage cleared the Polk's gate, he turned his back to Jessie and rested in the seat, his hat pulled tightly over his eyes. He was convinced of her guilt now. He had seen it in her eyes.

When they arrived home later that evening, George walked silently to his study and locked himself inside. Jessie slept for a long while on the ride home and now felt dazed and disoriented as she trudged upstairs to the nursery. She lay down on the small bed alongside three year-old William and tried to go back to sleep, but she was too anxious to rest. Her heart pounded in her head as she watched the nursery door. George was sure to barge in at any moment and accuse her of all sorts of nefarious activities: plotting to ruin his good name, intentionally sabotaging his reputation, never bothering to accuse her of any specific offenses but howling her down nonetheless. He would speak in that commanding voice that would shudder most delicate women. But not Jessie. She had learned long ago to pay him no mind.

Still, after his yearlong absence, George was a stranger to her and his anger now seemed very real. She replayed the party in her mind. The general hadn't shown her too much attention. She was sure of it. Perhaps George had heard the rumors about her and the general. Probably that loud-mouthed Mrs. Chisholm—forever spreading lies around town!

Oh! The suspense was too much! She sat up in bed and nervously chewed her fingernail. It was no use! Sleep would never come! She rose quietly from the bed and unlatched the shutters of the nursery window. A light in the stable caught her eye and she jumped back behind the curtain and out of view just as George closed the gate behind him. She struggled to see what he was doing, but a cloudy night sky afforded little light. She squeezed herself tightly as the cool night air sent a chill up her spine. A whimper came from the bed and she remembered. William! He must be cold. She hurried to the bed and pulled the blanket tight over his bare feet and gently rubbed the small of his back until he was once again fast asleep, then she ran back to the window and peered through the break in the curtains. The light in the stable had vanished and George was nowhere to be seen.

***

Dr. Peters stood on the front porch as day broke over the grove of sycamores. The morning air held the distinct scent of burning oak coming from the campfires dotting the back pasture. Alexander approached the lamppost holding tight to the Appaloosa's reins. His head was turned back toward the main gate where a figure walked to and fro in the shadows of the morning sun.

Peters looked questioningly at Alexander. "Who's there?"

"Ain't none of our'n," Alexander answered.

Peters sent Alexander down to the gate and watched as the stranger hung his head and kicked up a cloud of dust before turning toward the house. He followed reluctantly, dragging his feet behind the high-stepping Alexander. Virethia soon joined the doctor and walked down the steps to meet them.

"He got a note!" Alexander hollered as he walked back up the drive.

"A note," the doctor said. "From whom? Who sent you?"

"You's wif the army folks, ain't ya?" Virethia said.

"Yessum, General Van Dorn's man."

"Yep, I knows him," Virethia said confidently. "Seen him down at the cabin." She took the note and started to open it.

Dr. Peters snatched it from her. He opened it and read quietly. "A party?" he asked. "What do you know about a party, Virethia?"

"Well, Miss Jessie, she gone raise money for the hospital," Virethia said. "Like them Polks done."

Dr. Peters frowned and ripped the note. "I know nothing about a party at my home! Who sent this note?"

The man shuffled his feet and looked up at Virethia who had now positioned herself on the step above him. A look of fear shone on his face.

"Go on," she said firmly, "answer Doc Peters."

The man's eyes flew open as if hit by a bolt of lightning, and when he finally spoke, his voice quivered so that he could barely be heard. "The General done sent it—for Miss Peters. He say—"

Dr. Peters turned on the man fiercely. "Tell your master that I will promptly blow his brains out if he ever sends a note to my house again!"

The servant turned and walked quickly down the drive. "Yassir!" he yelled over his shoulder. "Yassir! I tell him!"

Peters watched the man scamper down the drive and for a moment he thought how easy it would be to just shoot him. Maybe that would be message enough for Van Dorn. But that would not do. What he needed was proof, solid undeniable proof that the general was a lecher. With hard evidence, he could exact whatever revenge he saw fit. Death—of course—was the only logical recourse for a man like himself. He turned to Alexander. "Bring my horse round. If the general thinks to play in the hen house, he better watch for the fox."

*From the Diary of Jessie Peters*

*April 22, 1863*

    *I prayed all last night for some peace and it looks as if today my prayers have been answered. George left before sunrise this morning and will be gone at least three days. I would prefer that he never return. He does infuriate me! I don't believe I have ever met a man so bent on causing trouble. Trouble is all I ever get from him. He has watched me for a week now—like a hawk, breathing down my neck, watching every move I make. I just know that Millie has something to do with it. She's one I'd like to get my hands on. And when I get the chance, I plan to send her far away. I honestly think Virethia would thank me—though Millie is her only child. That girl has been nothing short of the Devil since she was born! Yes, I believe she is the root of all my troubles lately though I can't quite put my finger on it. Sometimes when I'm walking about the place, I feel as if she's watching me. But when I approach her, she pretends she's busy washing clothes or beating out a rug. Well, I suppose I should laugh if Dr. Peters has put that girl up to following me. She's certainly had nothing to report since there hasn't been a soldier on the place in the last few days. Alexander says the cavalry rode out of town Wednesday and he heard they had a fight just outside of Nashville. I do hope the general is safe.*

    *With George gone for a few days, I have decided to ride over to Mrs. Perkins home to request help for my party. If I involve the ladies of the church then George cannot possibly complain about my hosting it, though I would not put it past him to act a complete fool regardless. O, what I would give for a flooding rain or some other disaster to detain him in Nashville. He simply hates when I have guests in the house. "They're eating all our food," he says. "They'll drink every drop of brandy on the place!" Well, I made sure to hide a few bottles under the cellar steps. I'll tell him the brandy was a gift and then he can't say a word. I plan to have Mrs. Perkins send over her cook so Virethia will not be burdened with preparing everything. She is always complaining about any gathering I have. What I would give for good help! I swear if we haven't lost control of the Negroes completely.*

*I have just come back from town and was truly shocked that my sister—my favorite sister, I might add—has declined my invitation! She says it is because her stomach has been giving her fits lately, but I do not believe her. I think she is such a ninny at times. The major has corrupted her entirely and I believe I will find myself utterly alone with not one decent family member nearby. If only Alex lived here instead—he's a dear, dear brother and would never treat me so unkindly. Well, I must not feel sorry for myself this afternoon—there simply is no time. So I will pick my feelings up off the floor and go prepare for my party. I'll show my sister what a splendid hostess I am and make her feel awful for missing it.*

# CHAPTER 13

# A PARTY FOR THE CAUSE

*General, as your friend, may I take the liberty of warning you
that your friend, Mrs. Peters, can cause you a lot of trouble.*
—MAJOR MANNING KIMMELL TO GENERAL EARL VAN DORN (APRIL 1863)

**April 27, 1863**

Jessie watched as Alexander loaded the last case of whiskey into the wagon and quickly covered it with a dusty burlap cloth. He had taken it there when Jessie made the decision to hide valuables such as liquor and coffee. The root cellar lay nearly five hundred feet from the house so toting the load was out of the question, and since a wagon filled with anything was always suspicious to the soldiers camped nearby, Alexander loaded at the break of day and covered the cargo with a cloth and an old basket of kindling.

He rounded the back porch and stopped the buggy beside the springhouse. Virethia and Millie sauntered out onto the porch and asked to see what he had in the basket.

"Get on back," Alexander barked, "less'n you wants to pay me sumpin for it." He laughed and slapped his leg.

"I ain't givin' you nuthin', you ol' hound dog," Virethia giggled.

"Depends on what you got in there's to what I might gives ya," Millie said, her smile broad and reassuring.

Virethia smacked the girl hard. "You gits on in de house! Good fer nuthin as yo daddy!"

Millie screamed and sprinted for the door, but Jessie caught her by the arm. "Help your mama bring these things in the house!" Jessie opened the back door and Virethia and Alexander followed her with the boxes of whiskey. "Hide them in there," Jessie said. "Behind those old butter dishes."

They wiped the dust from the bottles and placed them in the ornate sideboard in the dining room. Jessie watched them closely while she rifled through old linens, tossing the tattered ones in a pile on the floor. The room was spacious, but Jessie directed Alexander to pull the chairs from the dining table and place them along the wall to ease the flow of partygoers when the food was served later in the evening. While Jessie and Alexander worked in the dining room, Virethia wiped the buffet with a damp rag and then moved on to the pier mirror in the foyer and polished the base with lemon seed oil. Jessie went behind her when she finished and inspected every piece of furniture by hand.

"Get this rug outside and beat it clean," Jessie said. "I expect a full house this evening."

"I sho hope Doc Peters don't get mad having a party and all," Virethia said. "Don't you hope, Miss Jessie?"

Jessie gave her a hard look. "Dr. Peters has nothing to do with this party," she said angrily. "The ladies of the Episcopal Church are hosting this affair."

Virethia smiled. "Sho," she said with an air of innocence. "Das right. I near forgot it was the church was giving the party. Doc ain't got *no* part in it."

Jessie scowled at her. She would slap her but if she made Virethia mad she'd play dumb as a mule and wouldn't lift a finger. That was the trouble with servants like her—give'em an inch and they'd take the whole farm. Virethia was no fool. Jessie had learned the hard way years ago. You got a whole lot more out of her if you coddled her a little. "You hear too much for your own good, that's for sure!" Jessie forced a smile. "This will be the largest and grandest party of the year. Mind you don't mess it up!"

At half past 4 o'clock, the first buggy rolled up the drive and Millie was ordered to get the door. Jessie checked her face in the mirror one last time and listened intently for voices, but all she heard was the closing of the door and footsteps on the staircase.

"Millie," she called out. "Would you please show our guests in here?"

Millie loped into the room, her hair still messy from all her troubles that day, her dress spotted with dirt and sweat. "Ain't nobody but Miss Clara," she said.

Jessie's mouth flew open. "Well, I had no idea Clara would be here. When was this decided?"

Millie just shrugged and gave Jessie a look, like a tired hound dog. "I don't know nothing, but I bone tired, Miss Jessie—"

"Now, don't you start all that whining, Millie," Jessie warned. "I swear, girl, if you aren't the laziest a body's ever seen."

Jessie went on fluffing the pillows and creasing the puddle drapes. She knew if she turned her head Millie would sneak out the parlor doors and disappear. This was an art she had perfected when she started breaking out at night to meet Jobey, a young black driver who came to Alexander for help fixing wagon wheels. He lived a mile down the road and met Millie halfway on full moon nights until they got caught by his woman just the week before. This woman was mean and more than twice his age. She threatened to kill Millie if she found her anywhere near Jobey again, but that didn't stop the meetings. Millie went right on as if there was no threat whatsoever. Jessie prayed every day that she'd get caught. Nothing was more infuriating than a haughty servant.

Jessie sat down at the piano and tapped lightly on the keys while Virethia stacked cups beside a crystal punch bowl. Moments later the parlor door opened and Clara entered. She was dressed in a light blue silk gown; around her neck was a matching choker and ivory pendant. She looked older, more mature, and walked with a regal air that Jessie had never seen before. For a moment, she doubted her own eyes. This *lady* standing in front of her couldn't possibly be *Clara*.

"Well, don't you look lovely, Clara," Jessie remarked, still focused on the new choker. "Is that a new necklace I see?"

Clara's eyes grew wide and she clasped her hand around the pendant. "Oh, this old thing?" she said. "Why, I've had this for a very long time."

But Jessie saw it in her eyes, the glassy stare of the liar. "I'm quite sure I've never seen it before," Jessie replied, reaching out to touch it.

"Well," Clara said jerking away from Jessie's hand. "You can certainly wear it if you like it that much."

"Perhaps I will," Jessie said coldly, her only desire to take the silly necklace and choke her with it. "I had no idea you would be coming," she said with contempt. "You really should have sent word to me or your father. You know how he hates being disobeyed."

"Why, I've not done a thing wrong!" Clara said with a haughty air. "Besides, I wouldn't dream of missing the party. And since I haven't even seen Father yet, I'm certain he will be happy that I'm home!"

Jessie rolled her eyes. She'd love nothing better than to give her a good smack across her cheek. "We'll just see about that," Jessie hissed. "When your father returns, I will ask him myself if he is fine with his daughter gallivanting around the countryside without permission!"

Clara's mouth shut like a trap and she turned and walked to the window. She watched eagerly as the night sky appeared and the first carriage arrived. The Polk name was prominently displayed on an ornate side placard. "Oh, Antoinette is here!" Clara exclaimed, running to the front door.

Jessie followed behind her, allowing Virethia to go ahead of them and greet the guests. Antoinette Polk looked beautiful in a rose-colored silk gown, low on the shoulders, the skirt sprinkled with tiny buds of mint green. Her hat was a gaudy display of ribbons and tulle. She was accompanied by her cousin, Will Polk, who had just arrived from Bolivar. Jessie greeted them with kisses while Clara bombarded Will with questions about home and her brother Thomas.

"Didn't he see you before he left?" Will asked.

"Well, no," Clara responded. "Father says he took a leave of absence, but he went to Memphis, not here."

"He came through Bolivar, but only briefly. Overnight I think," Will said. "I never saw him but Uncle said he was sick with fevers."

Clara pressed him for details about Thomas but Will refused to elaborate. "I'm sure he's much improved, Clara. Your father looked after him, you know."

"Clara," Jessie complained as she shooed her into the dining room. "Run along now and don't worry everybody so!" Jessie took Antoinette by the arm. "That girl will talk the feathers off a hen! I declare! Now," she said gaily, "you simply must tell me where you got that lovely hat!"

"Oh, Jessie!" Antoinette said. "Why, you're the very picture of fashion! I should be asking for your tailor!"

"Come, then," Jessie said, "we'll both be the envy of the party!" She laughed and stuck her chin in the air. "Shall we?"

The two ladies walked arm in arm through the hallway and into the front parlor where they mingled with several members of the Wounded Soldiers Committee, talking bandages and amputations till Jessie thought she would rather join those soldiers in the grave than listen to another awful description of the wounded. At last, Virethia announced that more guests were arriving and Jessie made a dash for the front door.

"Coming!" Jessie replied. "If you'll excuse me, ladies. I've got guests to greet!"

"Oh, Jessie," Antoinette said, grabbing her arm, and looking desperately around the room. "Just where on earth are you hiding that charming husband of yours?"

"Well," Jessie began, "you know George..."

But she stopped as Clara sprinted past them yelling, "Father! Father! It is you!"

"Well!" Antoinette laughed. "I do believe I've found him!"

George entered the door alongside an elderly couple from Columbia. His face appeared drawn, lines crossed his forehead like thick webs and his eyes were bloodshot and wild. Jessie sighed. George was not happy. She loathed him immediately.

Clara met him at the door with a hug and a kiss. "Oh, I'm so happy to see you!" she exclaimed. "Oh, tell me, Father! How's Thomas? He's going to get better, isn't he?"

"Of course, Clara," Peters said. His tone was disinterested, unemotional. "Don't be silly."

Jessie approached Clara and shoved her aside. She held her hand out to George and said flatly, "Hello, dear. You remember Antoinette Polk?"

Antoinette bent low and curtsied at a smiling George Peters. "Well, of course," he said, his eyes aglow with sudden interest. "It's always a pleasure to spend an evening with a beautiful, charming, female. I do hope the family is well."

"Why, yes," Antoinette said. "They're quite well. And you?"

"Oh, I'm just happy to be back home, Antoinette," the doctor said. "I've hated leaving my dear Jessie alone with war all around."

Jessie took a deep breath and laughed. "Oh, George, dear," she said, rolling her eyes. For a moment she imagined her hate for George poured forth like boiling hot steam. "You are truly a dear, but you'll have to excuse us while I check on our guests." She took Antoinette by the hand again and pulled her along. "Come on, dear. You can help me say hello to everyone!"

Jessie walked proudly, introducing Antoinette to guests, showing her off as if she were a prize animal, and when a young officer asked Antoinette to dance, Jessie interrogated the poor boy till he nearly surrendered on the spot. "Oh, go ahead," Jessie smiled. "Just you watch your manners young man." Antoinette laughed and quickly walked away with the young man while Jessie looked around the room, her heart soaring at the obvious success of her party. Perhaps the gossip wasn't as bad as she thought. By all accounts, the entire town had come out.

The smell of food soon sent the partygoers to the dining room where plates were filled with smoked oysters and slices of pork on hot rolls. A small basket of blackberries sprinkled lightly with sugar sat at the end of the table, a silver spoon rested beside it for serving. Buggy after buggy arrived and within the hour the house was filled with a host of brightly dressed ladies all vying for a dance with one of the dashing Confederate officers who leaned arrogantly against the wall and talked battles and the future of the Confederacy with the prominent men from the community. The Bishop of the Episcopal Church stood watch over the punch bowl, reaching into his coat pocket for a nip of whiskey when no one was looking.

Jessie moved about the parlors and dining room, and chatted happily with her guests, while Rose Dawson sat down at the harp to play. A cheer rose from the parlor, "Long live the Confederacy! Long live General Lee!" And the whole house rang with shouting.

Dr. Peters joined a group of men talking in a corner of the dining room and Jessie took advantage of his absence. She could finally find the general. Major Kimmell had arrived, so she knew Van Dorn couldn't be too far away. The general never went anywhere without him. She walked slowly through the parlor, smiling at guests, searching everywhere. When she reached the large jib windows, she noticed poor Will Polk standing alone, his head hung low. She walked over to him and took his hand. "Why, Will," Jessie said sweetly. "Why on earth are you standing here all alone when there are so many young ladies just dying for a dance with you?"

"Oh, I'm all right, Miss Jessie," he said with a frown. "It's just that I was hoping Clara might introduce me to a few of her friends, but every time I try to talk to her, she runs off to play a song on the piano or dance with some officer."

Jessie raised her eyebrows and giggled. "Really?" she asked smiling. "Our Clara is dancing with soldiers?"

"Well, yes," Will said. "She's dancing right now with General Van Dorn himself. I can't get one minute with her!"

Jessie pushed the poor boy aside almost knocking him to the ground. "She's dancing with the general? Well, isn't that something?" She said as she stormed away.

"Wait! Miss Jessie!" Will called out.

But Jessie never stopped. She raced to the parlor door as a blur of blue silk flew past her. Jessie caught a glimpse of the general out of the corner of her eye. He was dressed in full regalia, a splendid sight. He noticed her and tipped his hat as he passed. Jessie feigned a smile.

When the song ended, Clara ran over to Jessie. "Did you see our dance?" she asked, her eyes as bright as the parlor lamps. "Isn't he handsome? And he asked *me* to dance!"

Jessie rolled her eyes and brushed Clara aside. She was watching the general move across the room to the Bishop and the punch bowl. "Yes, Clara. What did you say?"

"Why, General Van Dorn!" Clara yelled over the noise. "He asked me to dance! Didn't you see us?"

"Yes, I saw," Jessie answered coldly. She had to get rid of Clara. "You should check on Will," she scolded. "He's standing all alone and—well, he seems upset."

Clara cocked her head. "But Will is such an awful bore."

"Just do as I say!" Jessie commanded. "It's only proper! He is your guest, after all!"

Clara shut her mouth quickly and turned to leave. She paused at the door and looked back at Jessie.

"Go on!" Jessie mouthed, pointing in the direction of the dining room. After a moment, Clara lowered her head and left the room.

Jessie made eye contact with the general and he soon walked over with a cup of punch. "And you," he said, his eyes sparkling in the candlelit room, "are looking lovely as ever."

"Well, *thank you*," Jessie snapped. "I'm amazed you noticed."

The general laughed. "Now, Mrs. Peters," he whispered. "I didn't know you were the jealous type."

Jessie tried to ignore him but he grabbed her hand. "Come on!" he said. "Won't you dance with me?" He gave her a sly grin and twirled her around. "That's one of my favorite tunes!"

Jessie wanted to scold him, to warn him not to play games with her, but his charm soon turned her anger to laughter and she smiled. "Very well," she whispered. "But might I warn you—"

"Come on!" the general said, pulling her into the next room. "We better get in line or we'll miss it!"

In the adjacent room, the guests had formed two lines for the Virginia reel. Clara and Will Polk had joined the group of dancers with Clara standing directly across from the general. Jessie watched the line move, her jaw set. When it was her turn, she ran past the poor fellow who was to be her partner and went to the general instead. She held her hand out to him and he looked at her questioningly until the room burst into laughter at the young man standing alone in the center of the circle. The general bowed and Jessie curtsied and off they went.

Dr. Peters appeared at the door of the parlor with his hands in his pockets. His mouth turned down at the corners and a deep furrow had formed in the center of his brow. He glared at the group of dancers as the audience stomped their feet and clapped in time.

"Well, did you see that?" asked an elderly lady standing next to the doctor.

"Pardon?" Peters said. "I didn't hear you?"

"I said," the lady spoke loudly. "Did you see that Jessie Peters and the general?" With the last word, she turned and saw that the man beside her was Dr. Peters. "Oh," she said putting her hand to her lips. "Well, I thought you were someone else!" She laughed, awkwardly and walked quickly toward a group of ladies in the corner of the room.

For a moment, George just stood stone-faced in the doorway. When the song ended, he made his way toward Jessie and General Van Dorn and took her by the hand. "Come with me, Jessie!" he said in a commanding voice. He jerked her by the arm fiercely.

"George!" she said, letting out a squeal. "What on earth—"

He pulled her by the arm until they were in the foyer and then he whirled her around to face him. "Let me remind you," he said in a hoarse, threatening voice. "I am your husband! You will end this party at once!" His voice cracked unnaturally and he tried to clear his throat. The redness in his cheeks had moved to his eyes, giving him the look of a demon. "I will not stand for such embarrassment, Jessie! Why, you're acting like a dog in heat with that Van Dorn!"

"Let me go!" Jessie demanded. But when she pulled away from him, he only gripped her tighter. "You're hurting me, George!"

A movement at the front door startled Dr. Peters and he loosened his grip.

A man was standing at the open door. "Excuse me," the soldier said as he passed quickly.

"Why, Major Kimmell," Jessie said, racing after him.

But the major didn't stop. And as the guests spilled from the parlor, he was soon lost in the sea of men and women. Jessie wheeled around but George had disappeared as well. When at last she found Major Kimmell, he was standing at the piano watching as a smiling Van Dorn accompanied Clara in a lively rendition of "Green, Green Valley." Jessie approached them as the song ended and watched as the major whispered in the general's ear. Jessie struggled to hear but the noise was too much.

But the worried look on the general's face told it all and with a clap of his hands, he gathered up his men. One by one the soldiers stopped at the doorway and thanked Jessie for her hospitality.

When the general reached Jessie, he tipped his hat and winked. "Good evening, Mrs. Peters," he said. "Please extend our thanks to Dr. Peters as well."

Jessie wanted desperately to ask what was wrong, but the general moved quickly toward the front door. The other party guests followed suit, moving slowly past Jessie, until moments later, the entire room was empty.

***

At the end of the front walk, General Van Dorn turned to see a girl standing just out of the lamplight. He couldn't make out the face but he noticed she was holding a lace handkerchief in her right hand. *Clara.*

"General Van Dorn," she whispered from the darkness. "I wanted to thank you for such a lovely time." She started toward him when he waved his hand in the air.

"And I as well," he whispered back. "Care to join me? No sense wasting such a lovely moonlit evening. Why don't you show me around that extraordinary rose garden I keep hearing about?"

Major Kimmell cleared his throat and cracked his whip in the air. "Sir," he said in a commanding voice. "I think it best we leave now."

Van Dorn glared at the major and waved him on. Then turning to Clara, he whispered, "You were saying, Miss Peters?"

Clara looked at her feet and giggled. "Well, I suppose I could show you the garden," she said softly. "If you really want to see it."

The general walked over and took her by the hand. He stumbled a bit and tipped his glass. A splash of punch fell on the toe of Clara's pale slippers and he bent to wipe it up. "I suppose I spent a little too much time talking with your bishop," he laughed. "That man does like good whiskey."

Clara smiled awkwardly while he dabbed at the pink stain on the tip of her slippers. "Terribly sorry," he smiled sheepishly. "I didn't mean to be ungentlemanly." He stumbled a bit as he stood up. "I do hope they aren't ruined. Such a lovely pair of feet—"

"Oh," Clara whispered. "It's quite all right. This old pair of shoes!"

"Very well, then." Van Dorn smiled. "Shall we walk?"

She took his hand and they ventured into the gardens where she showed him row after row of budding roses and gardenias, irises and jonquils. When they reached the stone bench, they sat and talked quietly until the last guest left. He found her to be quite delightful, shy but not awkwardly so, innocent but not unwilling. By the time the clock struck midnight, the two were nowhere in sight.

***

Next morning, Major Kimmell approached General Van Dorn in his headquarters, and closed the door behind him. "May I speak plainly, sir?" Kimmell asked.

"Well, of course, Major."

"General, as your friend, may I take the liberty of warning you that Mrs. Peters can cause you a lot of trouble."

They stood in awkward silence for a moment and then Van Dorn laughed and slapped his knee. "Is this some kind of joke, Major?"

"You may not know this, sir," Kimmell interjected, "but—"

"No," Van Dorn said. "I know that the doctor is no friend to the Confederacy, that he is a traitor and an insanely jealous man. Mrs. Peters, on the other hand, is undoubtedly the smartest woman I have ever met."

Kimmell rubbed his whiskers and paced in front of the general's desk. "But, sir," he said. "At the party, I overheard the doctor say he would not tolerate *you* and *her*—"

Van Dorn put his hand out. "No more," he said in a serious tone. "The Peters ladies are charming—and mysterious." He bit his lower lip and smiled. "But, I assure you Major, I'm no fool." He slapped Kimmell on the back and laughed. "Look man, you and I are simply enjoying good Southern hospitality—not to mention some fine whiskey! How could we be so unkind as to refuse her?"

"Well, no—I only meant that—"

"Good! Then our conversation is over. We have enough work to do fighting the Yankees. We've got a parade in two days and the men have gone soft lately. What do you say we focus our attention on something important, eh?"

"Well, of course, but—" Kimmell said with a frown.

"Very good then. You worry too much. It isn't good for a man to work himself up over nothing. Come now, let's ride to the parade ground and see what those engineers have done today? They've been working so slow, I may just have to send for Polk himself to do the job!"

\*\*\*

Dark clouds moved in later that day and a misting rain began to fall as General Van Dorn left the parade ground. The engineers were still hard at work on the entrenchments, but the general doubted they would be completed in time for inspection the next morning. Frustrated, Van Dorn mounted his horse and rode to the Peters' cabin. He needed some privacy, a place to sit and think. When he arrived at the cabin, he was pleased to see the lot was empty—not a soldier was around. He lit the lamp and sat down at his desk. The latest scouting report indicated a small detachment of Yankee Cavalry moving south of the Harpeth River. He smiled. With the right bait, he could lure the Yankees into the valley and cut them off.

He could capture them. Hell, he might even get a few more rifles for his boys.

He sat quietly studying the stack of maps on his desk, when he heard a faint knock. The door moved slightly, as if pushed open by some rogue wind, and Clara slipped in. The night air followed her, carrying with it her scent of vanilla and jasmine, a warm, moist smell.

She approached his desk and smiled shyly. The general stood and reached toward her, caressing her neck while gliding his hand to rest low on her waist and hip. He leaned forward as she parted her mouth to draw a breath and kissed her. She giggled and he turned her around and stood behind her now. He kissed her neck and slipped his right hand down the front of her blouse, cupping her round breast. He knew he should stop, but his desire won the battle. The sweetest of fruits must be handled with care. He laid her on the bed and pulled her blouse below her shoulders. She whimpered slightly when he raised her skirt and released the buckle of his trousers.

"I'm very glad you changed your mind," he whispered in her ear.

"Oh, General," she replied. "You do love me, don't you?"

Her voice was so childlike that for a moment Van Dorn hesitated.

"Well?" she asked a second time, stroking his cheek lightly. "You do, don't you?"

The touch of her hand brought him back to reality and he lay down beside her. "Of course I do," he whispered. "Of course I do."

*From the Diary of Jessie Peters*

*April 28, 1863*

*A bitter cold rain has set in this morning to match my bitter heart. Why I must be punished for the faults of others I simply will never know. Is it my doings that Clara will not do as she is told and stay at school—that she came unannounced to the party? Is it my fault that George is an unfriendly, cold man who has no love for anyone save those brats of his, who is bitterly jealous of every man around me and seeks to cause me heartache every moment of every day? I ask these questions honestly because I fear I will live under this dark "Peters" cloud for the rest of my days.*

*O, I should take my life today if that is indeed my fate. But not before I take Clara's! That girl makes my blood boil with her lies! To think she would tell George that I requested she attend my party when she knows full well I instructed her to stay in Columbia. I told her plainly that I had no desire to play hostess to any of those sniveling little girls at school—or their mothers. I'll not feed the very vipers who try to ruin me with their gossip! But she came anyway—and what a bold move that was. She's never been so brave before. It makes me wonder what she may be up to, though more than likely, George has her in his employ right alongside Millie, to spy on me and make me miserable. Well, they'll not win. I'll see to it. Let them all attack me at once— I'll not back down!*

*But, perhaps most disconcerting was how Earl acted so cold, like we were complete strangers. Why, he was so inattentive it was as if I did not exist, so preoccupied with Antoinette Polk and that ridiculous Sally Lawson, that he hardly noticed me. And then when Clara sought center stage by offering to play the harp for him—well, I could have slapped her silly! How she smiles and bows her head so shyly when spoken to. Honestly! She's not the innocent child George would have everyone believe. Quite the contrary indeed. I don't trust her at all! I know it was something she said that sent the general and Major Kimmell out the door. I could see it on their faces. But I couldn't say a thing to Earl because George was eyeing me from across the room. I'd like to have thrown the fire poker right between his vicious eyes! Maybe the general heard the fight between me and George—but surely not. I don't recall seeing anyone near when George commenced screaming at me. No, I'll have to give it more thought. I'm simply not sure what got into my general. But I plan to pay him a visit soon. Alexander told me just moments ago that a grand parade is scheduled in the next few days, some celebration for the cavalry's successes these last few weeks. I will make it a point to attend.*

CHAPTER 14

# THOMAS PETERS: A SOLDIER CONVALESCES

**April 1863**
**Council Bend, Arkansas**

Thomas lay in the bed wrapped in an old cotton blanket with yellow faded stripes and cross-stitched edges. It had been his mother's when she first married, had covered her withered body the night she lay in bed, the blanket pulled close to her face until death finally crept through the cotton cloth and took her. He pressed it to his face and breathed in. The scent of lemon and lilac had vanished, replaced by the sweet pungency of laudanum. Now as Thomas lay sick in the same bed, he felt as if death rested on the pillow beside him.

His head was wet with sweat and uncontrollable shivers threatened to shatter his teeth into a million pieces. For most of the day, he pulled the blanket over him and flung it off again. Hot then cold. The fever would linger miserably for a while longer and disappear as quickly as it came. The blisters too. No need for doctors now. Only darkness and the quiet of an empty house would ease the pain.

The shutters of the bedroom windows had been closed and locked down by Jem, a flat-nosed field hand. Jem was working in the house now that it was just the two of them and though he knew nothing about being a proper butler, he moved quickly and had the strength of an ox. With only Thomas in the home, social decorum was not necessary.

Jem tiptoed to the bed and peered down at the covers then turned and left, closing the door quietly behind him. He would go down to the chicken house, Thomas thought, and take a drink from the jug. It was hidden under a loose board in the floor and every night when Jem went down to talk to the chickens, as he said, he would drink until he couldn't feel his fingertips. Thomas liked him. He had a genuine love for the Peters family and had never been known to steal. He could play a decent hand of cards as well. They would have themselves a fine time when the fevers left.

Thomas blinked open one eye and shut it quickly. A candle burning in an iron wall-sconce pierced the darkness and sent a burning pain through his eye and deep into his brain. He must remember to tell Jem about the candles. He couldn't bear the light. He breathed deep again and forced his head down into the worn feather pillow. Outside Jem talked low and persistent. He must have a visitor. He never spoke that many words to man or chicken. The voices continued for a few long moments until Thomas' mind drifted off to another fit-full dream.

In his nightmare he saw cannon fire and bursts of blinding light, the legs of horses and men soaring past his head. He struggled to pull the blanket to his face but couldn't grip it. A voice yelled for him to get up and take cover. But he couldn't move. He was paralyzed, frozen in his dream. More cannon fire rained down on him. Then he saw he was sleeping on the cold ground alongside another soldier, a child, maybe ten or eleven. The boy had no face, just a round hole in the center of his forehead. He pitied him, so young, so innocent. He turned the boy over to help him when suddenly a flock of blackbirds scattered ahead of a great ball of fire. A dark general wearing a gray roundabout jacket barked commands from a horse whose mane glowed red. Then the whole earth shot up under them and both man and horse burst into the gray sky above. The flag of his division flew past him, its edges torn and ragged. Thomas reached to catch it when something gripped his shoulders. He jumped up but couldn't see in the dark room. Fear overtook him as he struggled to scream.

"Mister Thomas," Jem said, shaking him. "Mister Thomas, you come on wake up now. You dreamin' agin."

Thomas forced his eyelids open and squinted. Jem bent down just far enough for his leathery face to be recognizable and Thomas relaxed a bit. Jem patted his arm and pulled the blanket back over him. In a scratchy voice, he whispered, "I'll just go fetch some eggs for supper, now. You gone and rest awhile."

Thomas thought to answer him but his mouth would not cooperate. His cracked, dry lips stuck together like a steel trap. If he could find a little water, just a sip, he felt sure he could rise from that deathbed and shake off this curse. But the door soon slammed and he knew Jem had gone outside. He let himself drift back into his dream, back to the battlefield and the smoke. The bloody boy still lay there, his hand stretched out, and Thomas moved toward him while somewhere in the distance he heard Jem calling, "Shoo! Chickens! Shoo!"

***

Thomas crept out on the veranda at dusk and sat in a small white wooden rocker. He wore a dark gray waistcoat and a pair of checkered wool trousers that belonged to his father. His uniform was too far gone for even a good washing. He would not need it again anyway, not after he secured the surgeon's certificate that would guarantee him the big ticket out. As soon as he was well enough he would cross the river to Memphis. No more treatments, at least not in an army tent.

French pox, he thought, shaking his head. Hell, they had laughed back at Oxford when the infirmary doctor told them what they had. "You'll be over it in no time," he had assured them. But that was a lie. For Thomas the joke had become a curse from the Devil, a series of treatments and infections that now threatened to kill him. This time he was sick enough that he might not make it.

He rocked slowly, resting his head on the upper slat of the chair. A light breeze grazed his skin like a million needles. He gripped his sides, pulling the waistcoat tight against him. Jem hummed somewhere in the house and soon found his way outside where he brought Thomas a nice supper of thinly sliced ham and eggs. He set the tray on the large round table and handed him a crumpled newspaper he got from old man Herring when they came in from Memphis a few weeks past. Thomas held his hand up to shield his eyes. "I can't—not right now," he whispered. "You read it, Jem."

Jem took the paper from his hand and smoothed it out on the table. He grinned wide and licked his lips then poked his chest out and stood straight as a pine tree. Jem was the only black man within a hundred miles who could read. He was more than proud.

He began with the advertisements and spoke in his best Yankee accent, chopping off his usual drawl, over-pronouncing the words till he sounded more like a British butler than a black man from Mississippi. Thomas relaxed in the rocker, taking in the sounds of Jem's voice and the coo of a distant pair of doves. Jem read down one column and on to the next. He used his deep voice for serious news and raised his voice to a girlish pitch for social pieces. He skipped over a few articles and then came across General Van Dorn's name. Thomas stopped him. "Read this one," he said. "Van Dorn's near my Unit."

Jem read the article with a Yankee accent:

"From the *Mobile Register* dated March 22, comes a story of drunkenness, corruption, and licentiousness, all charges laid against Major General Earl Van Dorn of the Rebel army. The people of Mississippi have discarded him and the good people of Tennessee are quickly losing confidence in their military leaders. A correspondent who has traveled about with the General since summer of 1862, relates an incident in the hamlet of Spring Hill between Van Dorn and a buxom young widow of twenty-four. She had congratulated him on his recent successes in battle, and then added: 'General, you are older than I am, but let me give you a little advice—let the women alone until the war is over.'"

Jem chuckled a little at this, but Thomas gave him a stern look. "Anyway," Jem went on, "the General replied, 'My God—Madam! I cannot do that, for it is all I am fighting for. I hate all men, and were it not for the women, I should not fight at all; besides, if I accepted your generous advice, I would not now be speaking to you.'" Jem laughed again, but this time in his hands, feigning a coughing spell.

Thomas frowned and shook his head. "Sounds just like him. Up to no good where the ladies are concerned," he said.

"Ain't nothing bout Miss Jessie," Jem assured him. "Dat's good, right?"

"Don't be so quick," he said. "Sounds just like her." He reached in his pants and pulled out a tiny silver locket. "You see her?" he asked. Tucked inside was a tiny picture of a pretty blonde haired girl. "Now, that's a beautiful girl. And an honest one at that. That's the kind of girl that keeps a man happy."

Jem laughed. "Dat Miss Sallie, ain't it? Bet Old Lady Fentress don't think much a' givin' her up, huh?"

"Her mother likes me very much," Thomas said, looking hurt. "When I get well, I'm going straight home to ask for her hand. Bet I get it too," he said arrogantly.

"All right then," Jem laughed. "You win." He put the paper down and poured a glass of water. "I give'm that letter this morning," he said, handing him the glass. "The one you wrote for your daddy." He reached in the pocket of his coat and pulled out a wrinkled envelope. "And dat man from the ferry. He say give this to you. From Memphis."

Thomas took the letter and turned it over. His father's familiar scroll leaped out at him. This was the first correspondence in a few months, since he had written his father telling him of the rumors running through the camp of Jessie and General Van Dorn. His hope was that his father would listen this time, but he knew that would never happen. His father had become quite practiced in the art of defending Jessie's bad behavior, like that night in Bolivar when he got drunk and broke every piece of crystal in the house, her gift from him on their wedding night. Next day when he saw what he had done and heard she was leaving, he went right into town and bought up every piece of crystal he could. He even took her to New Orleans soon as the first baby came. His father did whatever it took to keep her happy, or at least what he thought would make her happy. But Jessie acted anything but satisfied. Thomas knew the rumors about General Van Dorn were true.

He unfolded the fine parchment. The first lines were as expected—instructions for taking care of himself, questions about the place and Jem. Then he got to the meat. It too was as expected—rife with excuses for Jessie. He skipped much of that and read on to the end. "Good," he said at last. "He's going to Spring Hill. He can see it for himself."

Jem smiled. "All right then." He handed Thomas a spoonful of laudanum and picked up the newspaper. "You don't worry none bout that mess. Worry ain't no good for a sick man."

Jem sat in the chair beside him, and in a melodic drawl he read of General Grant's retreat from a small town in North Mississippi, while Thomas closed his eyes and let the hot numbness fill his veins.

\*\*\*

General Van Dorn lay on the bed in his small room at headquarters. Scouting that day had been exhausting, riding with the 6th Texas, combing the hills between Spring Hill and Thompson's Station for signs of General Granger's movements—a cat and mouse game he had played for going on two weeks now. Van Dorn had become quite savvy at it, had kept the general from advancing south. But he knew Granger's patience had grown thin. It was only a matter of time before the tide would turn.

He held the newspaper up to the lamp and searched for his name. At last he found it. "That son-of-a-bitch Granger," he laughed.

He read the story aloud and smiled. "It's quite difficult to surprise and crush Van Dorn. In the first place, he keeps every road and land and hill-top for miles picketed; the country people are his friends and are always ready to give information." He laughed again. "Ha! A likely excuse, Granger!" He shouted as he stretched and lifted his heavy legs from the bed. "But I suppose he's right. They do love me."

He rose from the bed and dressed quickly, taking a long last minute look in the mirror. His pants were faded, but his waistcoat was new and the finely stitched white shirt sent by his sister Emily distracted from his less savory attire. Tonight, he was invited to Rippavilla for a grand soiree in honor of General Polk who was at home on a brief leave of absence. At the request of Antoinette Polk, General Forrest was to come along as well. He spit in the brass bowl by the bed. Bedford Forrest was one son-of-a-bitch he could live without.

He poured a small glass of brandy and sat at his desk. A stack of newspapers lay on the floor beside his desk and he picked them up one by one, thumbing through them, stopping when a headline caught his eye: "Rebel Skirmish at Thompson's Station." He skimmed the piece. "Nice," he mumbled. Favorable reports were hard to come by. This story was in the Mobile paper. He glanced up and rubbed his whiskers. Carey would no doubt see this one. Better send a note; after all it had been some weeks since he wrote to her. He had sent a letter and some money but both had been returned, undeliverable. Funny, he had just now remembered this. He poured another brandy and took some writing paper from the drawer. There was just enough time for a short note.

> *My Dearest Cary,*
>
> *I wrote to you some time ago by a gentleman who was going to Mobile, and much to my surprise he returned here yesterday and gave me back the letter. He did not go as far as Mobile and did not mail the letter. I regret it, as I enclosed you some money, which I am afraid you needed. I now have another opportunity to send, and hope you will receive it.*
>
> *I fought a battle near here a few days ago and won it. It was a beautiful affair. All in sight in an open plain. I took four regiment prisoners. Have had a rough time, but satisfactory to everybody.*
>
> *I am surrounded continually by a crowd and cannot write. I am well, and stand well with my troops. All cheer and serenade me. Children to change with every change of fortune!*
>
> *Your ever affectionate husband,*
> *Earl*

He placed the money in the envelope as Clement and Major Kimmel came through the door. Van Dorn stood and looked one last time in the mirror, noting the whiteness of his fine new shirt. Weeks had passed since his last decent haircut and his blond hair stuck out in all directions. He pulled his hat down over curls that hung like golden vines at the nape of his neck. The ladies were waiting. With a satisfied smile, he strutted ahead.

# CHAPTER 15

# A PASS FROM THE GENERAL

**May 4, 1863**

George Peters awoke at the break of dawn on that unseasonably chilly Monday and rode his horse out to the cabin. General Van Dorn had slept there the last few nights. He was alone except for the few soldiers standing guard at the far side of the property. Must be a parade today. Perfect time to see for himself.

He got down from his horse and looked cautiously around the yard of the cabin. Satisfied that he wasn't being watched, he walked up the steps and went inside. The small bed was unmade and dirty cups lay scattered across the simple wood table that was now a desk. He picked up a newspaper that had been tossed on the floor and unfolded it. The headline read "Grant's Army Closer to the Mississippi," and underneath that he saw "Pemberton Fearing Great Losses." He flipped through to the next page where a crease in the paper marked another article. He walked to the window and held it up to the light. The fine print read:

"It is reported from a correspondent very close to the Confederate Army that General Van Dorn is indeed the terror of ugly husbands and serious papas. Women of the South better steer clear of the little Dragoon Van Dorn, especially those widows of the Cause who are without the protection of a man..."

Peters looked up from the paper. "Son-of-a-bitch," he mumbled. He hated the war, but not like most who felt sorrow for the loss of life, family, and property. He hated it because of its exclusion of men such as himself, men who were relegated to a different battlefield. And though he beat the Yankees in his own way—by lying—he still felt defeated, like some tragic Shakespearean prince. If he could only get revenge for *this*...

He tossed the paper on the floor and crushed it under his boot. A light shining through the window cast its glow on a basket of flowers, dried up and tossed haphazardly beside a bucket of ashes at the fireplace. He walked over to the crude mantle where a small ivory pendant dangled on a nail. He took it down and looked it over. He had seen it before though when and where he could not recall. Was it Jessie's? The style was rather girlish. Not like Jessie at all. His eyes shot open. "My God!" he muttered, his jaw locked. "It can't be! Not Clara!"

He kicked the basket across the room. "That Bastard!" he yelled. Then without warning, a crashing sound came from the back of the cabin and he dropped to the floor, hunkered down out of sight of the window. Once he caught his breath, he moved on hands and knees to the windowsill and peered out. The sound came again, this time louder. His legs shook with fear. He had given no thought to being caught, what he would say, how he would snake his way out. He waited a moment and looked out again. Alexander's mangy hound emerged from under the washtub that had fallen over on top of him. Peters stood up and shook his head. "Damn dog!" he mumbled. Then he stuffed the pendant in his pocket and hurried out the door.

The yard was still empty though he didn't stop to look this time. His anger pushed him on. He mounted his horse and rode up the driveway and across the pasture until he reached the main road. From here he headed west into town where he was astonished to find the entire Columbia Pike lined with buggies and horses, scores of people, all waiting to see the grand parade of the Cavalry Corps. This general had quite a following.

Peters had no time to spare. He rode around the crowded street and entered the gate. The general's headquarters was just inside the door. He was certainly still there. It was common knowledge that Van Dorn was always the last to arrive on the parade ground, arriving in the fashion of an ancient warrior.

By the time Peters tied his horse, General Van Dorn had emerged from the house and was standing on the steps of the mansion talking with his staff officers. Peters approached the men and tipped his hat. "Pardon, General Van Dorn," he said. "I wonder if I might have a word with you."

Van Dorn gave a quick glance at the doctor and resumed his discussion. When the general finished talking, he waved the soldiers on and turned to face Peters. "Yes, Dr. Peters, what can I do for you? Make it brief, please. As you can see, I'm preparing for an inspection of my Corps."

"Certainly," Peters replied, struggling to conceal his anger. "This will only take a moment. I have business in Shelbyville and would like a pass to leave at once."

Van Dorn nodded casually to his adjutant. "Very well, follow me inside."

They entered the house, the general in the lead, marching loudly through the foyer and into his office. Peters stopped beside a mahogany chair, while the general took his place at his desk and quickly wrote the pass. A small washstand in the corner of the room held a vase of the same flowers he had seen at the cabin. These too were dusty yellow and dried out.

"I see you have taken advantage of the Tennessee springtime to bring a little sunshine to the room." Peters walked to the washstand and touched the dried petals, crumbling them as they dropped into his hand. "Not much life here in the spring unless you search it out."

Van Dorn looked up from his desk with a blank expression. "I'm sorry," he said. "I didn't hear you. You said Shelbyville? Is that right?"

Peters clinched his teeth. "Yes. I *said* it can be hard to find signs of life here in this part of Tennessee, at least not until late spring. I'm sure you're accustomed to much warmer Mississippi seasons."

Van Dorn smiled and gave Peters the pass. "Oh, I find this part of the South to be quite enjoyable. The people here are very accommodating indeed." He looked down at the flowers. "Those were given to me," he said lightly touching the dried petals. "Yes, folks here are quite hospitable indeed."

Peters watched the general closely, his mind racing.

"Now, if you'll excuse me, I must get going or I'll be late," the general said as he rose from his desk. "The natives will grow restless, you know."

"Yes, General Van Dorn," Peters replied. "The natives may grow restless indeed—without a show, that is."

Van Dorn stopped in his tracks and looked at the doctor. "Believe me Dr. Peters," he laughed. "I'm not in the business of putting on shows for anyone. Drilling is a necessary part of combat. My men are the best and I suppose folks like to see them in action."

"Oh," Peters countered quickly. "I meant no disrespect, General. The town speaks highly of the entertainment provided by your drills. They are quite popular."

Van Dorn's smile faded. "If that's all," he said coldly, "I'd best be going now."

"Can't thank you enough, General," Peters said, tipping his hat.

Outside, the drums rolled and a bugle sounded as Peters mounted his horse. Cheers rang out from the crowded streets as the band played "Dixieland." The general would be approaching the parade ground now. Peters laughed aloud and bore his heels into the horse's ribs. Let them hail their hero one last time.

*** 

The road was rutted with dark pools of stagnant water, a remnant of the heavy rains that had fallen the last few weeks. Dr. Peters covered his nose and mouth with a scarf as he rode past the puddles. He held tight to the reins and pulled hard, whipping the horse back and forth across the road, trying desperately to avoid the deeper holes. His horse struggled heroically as the angry doctor increased his pace. He must get to Shelbyville before dark.

General Leonidas Polk's infantry occupied the small town now in an effort to secure the railroad. Peters' brother was quartermaster under Polk, so when he reached the pickets, he dropped his brother's name and was quickly escorted to General Polk's tent. The general was seated at his desk, the light from a small table lamp flickered across his face.

Dr. Peters approached the desk and offered his hand. "General," Peters began. "I'll get straight to the point. Since I arrived at my home, I've heard rumors of General Van Dorn paying ungentlemanly attention to my wife." He paused for the general's reaction but the serious Polk showed no emotion. Peters went on. "Well, I'm here to tell you that I believe General Van Dorn is indeed trying to wreak havoc on my house."

General Polk raised his bushy gray eyebrows. "Go on," he said.

"I have evidence, witnesses," Peters said, his voice rising. "General Van Dorn has been seen at my house, alone with my wife. He's even set up camp on my very property!" Peters' voice cracked. "You know his reputation! Hell, he's all over the newspapers! A scoundrel, I tell you!"

General Polk stood up and rubbed his chin. "I see," he said in a deep voice. "Well, you say you have evidence, witnesses. Just what do you intend to do with this evidence? Van Dorn *is* a general—we *are* at war."

Peters looked dazed. He had no time to consider a course of action. Sure the culprit was a Confederate general, but the insult was too much to be ignored. "Well," he stuttered. "I'll confront him, of course, and demand he admit his guilt! I'll have him declare it in writing," he paused to think. "And I'll have it printed in every paper in the South!"

"Just a minute, doctor!" General Polk shouted. "You can't possibly think you'll get Van Dorn to write such a thing! Why that's absurd."

Peters looked at the ground. His heart beat feverishly. "Then he'll pay with his life!" he roared.

Peter's brother entered the tent and stepped in front of General Polk. "George," he said. "You must be rational, after all—"

Peters paid no attention to his brother's pleading. He turned and walked toward the door of the tent. "I'll not stand by and let that son-of-a-bitch dishonor my name— my family! General or not—I'll not stand for it!"

"George!" his brother called out. "You must listen!"

But Peters flew out the door before they could stop him and galloped away like a demon into hell.

*** 

As the doctor approached home later that evening, he took the path to the cabin instead, his mind set on a private meeting with Van Dorn. He would strike a deal with the general and send Jessie and the children to Bolivar or Memphis, some place out of harm's way.

He passed the bend in the path and crossed the tiny creek behind the cabin when a sudden movement caught his eye. He turned to see a small figure in the shadows, a woman he guessed, wrapped from head to toe in a dark cloak. She crept along for a moment and then sprinted through the soft grass like an animal that senses danger nearby. Peters watched motionless from atop his weary horse and then raced along the creek to a path that ran behind the main house. When he reached Alexander's quarters, he tied his horse and crept to the back porch. When the figure approached, he ducked behind the springhouse.

The cloaked woman went in the house through the back door and moved quickly out of sight. Dr. Peters followed close behind. He had the element of surprise on his side. This time he would catch her. He crept inside and quietly ascended the stairs. To his surprise, he found his bedroom door was partially open. A glimmer of lamplight flickered from the bedside table. He flung the door open and crept in. A soft, steady breathing came from the direction of the bed. Jessie was sound asleep and dressed in nightclothes. His mind raced frantically. Where was the cloak? He searched under the bed and in the corners of the room, but found nothing. Ah! She must have dropped it in the foyer!

He exited the bedroom and started down the stairs when he heard movement in the far bedroom—Clara's room. He crept down the hall and opened the door as Clara was climbing into bed. *A black wool cloak hung on the post.*

He stood there frozen, fighting the urge to storm in and drag her out of the bed. His knees shook, but he managed to stay quiet and out of sight long enough to regain his composure, then he went downstairs and lit the lamp in the front parlor. He pulled out the bottle of brandy he had hidden in the urn beside the piano and poured a tall glass. His hands shook violently as he raised the glass to his lips once, twice, till the bottle was empty.

Then with the patience of a spider, he went into the study and took his pistol from the top drawer of the mahogany desk. Beside the pistol was a soft cloth used for cleaning and in the long drawer of the desk he found several bullets. He took out the cloth and sat in his desk chair. *The general must pay.* By the rooster's first crow, his gun shone like silver on a lake.

*From the Diary of Jessie Peters*

*May 3, 1863*

*I am most unnerved this evening though I'm not sure of the cause. I don't close my eyes longer than a few minutes before I'm wide awake again, so I decided to write a little to calm my mind. Then maybe I can get some rest. I really should be happy with George gone away for a day or two, but my heart tells me to beware—again, I don't know what it is that has me so gloomy. Perhaps it is Clara's presence that keeps me in a fit. She was to have returned to school some days ago but has used everything in her power to stay on longer. I should think George would send her back by the week's end—I can only pray.*

*Poor Lucy Mary has been colicky for nearly two days now and I am quite ready to leap from a bridge! Virethia helps walk her and gives her sugar water but nothing seems to help. Of course, Millie should be here waiting for her to wake but once again she is nowhere to be found. I swear that girl is not worth a dime. I'm sure I will be quite put upon tomorrow should she suffer another bout like today. If only George could do something for the poor child— but he is not so sympathetic to a baby's cries. He says a child is only as tough as his mother will allow. And though I tend to agree with him, I would much rather suffer a spoiled child in years to come than listen to another day of wailing.*

*I had hoped to see my general while George is away but try as I may, I cannot find the man alone. I suppose I will have to ride into town and designate the time and place myself. It is far too bold to think of really doing that—but I must admit I would. I get so awfully bored in this house— and knowing that George will return soon makes me all the more desperate.*

*Well, I think I have at last dulled my head enough that perhaps sleep can come to me now. If the moon were not so bright, I might fall into some deep sleep and in the morning wake to find myself in the general's arms again... That is my prayer.*

# CHAPTER 16

# A DOCTOR'S REVENGE

**May 5, 1863**

Wednesday morning came in on a raincloud, drenching the hard dirt and flooding the tiny porch outside the kitchen.

Virethia cursed as a stream of water flowed under the door, soaking the rug beneath her. She tucked the bottom of her skirt under her apron strings and picked up the platter of hot steamy biscuits, holding it high over her head. Stepping lightly, she pushed the door open and walked up the three steps to the veranda, where she placed the platter on a small table and opened the large wooden door leading into the back hallway. The doctor had returned just before dawn and was asleep in his study. Virethia crept quietly into the study and set the hot coffee and platter of biscuits on the marble table near the settee. She rattled the coffee spoon just loud enough to wake him.

At last he sat up on the settee. "Virethia," he mumbled. "Is that you? Is that coffee I smell?"

"Yassir, and biscuits too, and preserves."

Dr. Peters sat up and rubbed his head. His eyes were blood shot, his face haggard from lack of sleep. Virethia placed a biscuit on a small china plate and spooned out a mound of preserves, but the doctor did not move. "Doc Peters, ain't you gone taste my biscuits?" she asked, pouring the steaming coffee into a cup.

He jumped slightly, mumbling something, and looked up for the first time since Virethia had entered the room.

"Yes, thank you," he whispered as he lifted the cup to his mouth. "Would you see that Alexander brings the carriage around as soon as possible? Tell him to hurry."

"Yessir," Virethia said, turning toward the door. "I go get'em right now." She kept her eyes on him as she made her way across the room. His expression told her something was wrong. She went quickly down to the stable where Alexander was brushing one of the horses and told him what the doctor had said. "Better come on now," she urged. "His face look like trouble for sure."

Alexander grabbed his coat and followed Virethia to the house and into the study where Peters sat staring at the floor, the hot biscuits still untouched.

"What you reckon' done got into him?" Alexander whispered.

Virethia shrugged her shoulders and giggled. "Reckon Miss Jessie done something again."

The sudden clamor of footsteps on the stairs broke the silence and Peters rose from the settee. Jessie entered the room, all smiles, humming a lively tune, until she saw him and stopped suddenly. "Why, George," she stuttered nervously. "When on earth did you return?"

Peters glared at her. If he could only get at her neck, he thought. But he knew he must maintain his composure for now. Clara was his only concern. He brushed by her without a word and started upstairs. "I'm taking Clara back to the school. I should've known better than to leave my daughter in your care."

Jessie's mouth dropped in shock. "Well," she stammered angrily. "What in Heaven's name are you talking about, George Peters?" But the doctor ignored her and continued up the stairs and onto the landing where he slammed into Millie who was carrying a basket of clothes. The girl squealed loudly but still the doctor did not stop.

Jessie motioned for Millie to follow her outside. "Now, go find your mother," she threatened, pointing her finger at Millie. "Somebody's going to tell me just what is going on! Tell it, or I swear to sell you downriver first chance I get!"

Millie dropped the laundry basket and bolted off in the direction of the kitchen. Within seconds she arrived with Virethia and Alexander, both out of breath.

"What done happened?" Virethia asked frantically. "Alexander say something mighty wrong for Doc to act this way."

"I reckon he mad at Miss Clara," Millie giggled. She shuffled her feet and twisted a loose strand of hair nervously. "I mean, I reckon that's why he so mad. You see, he seen'm and I seen'm too last night." She spoke with an air of authority, proudly teasing them with her secret.

Jessie grabbed her mouth and squeezed hard. "Who'd you see? Stop your foolishness and tell me now!"

"I seen Miss Clara," she replied, rubbing her cheeks, her eyes wide. "She was comin' up dis way from the cabin 'round midnight."

Jessie gasped. "You're sure about this? Does Dr. Peters know of this? Don't lie to me, or I promise to stripe you good! You know I'll do it!"

Millie squirmed in Jessie's grip and pulled free, but Virethia's hand landed with a smack on her cheek. "And where was *you*, girl?" Virethia demanded as she grabbed a head full of hair. "How you come to be up and seein' folks at midnight?"

Millie started telling her lie, but Virethia hit her again. "Lawd, what am I gone do with you?"

Jessie grabbed Millie's arm and dragged her into the house. "You'll tell Dr. Peters exactly what you have told me! Do you understand? You'll make it very clear that you've only seen Clara at the cabin. Do you hear me?"

Virethia and Alexander followed close behind but quickly veered into the dining room at the first sound of footsteps on the stairs. Dr. Peters stormed past Jessie and into the study, where Clara was now seated on the settee. He stopped in front of her and looked long and hard at her innocent face. She was no child. Not anymore at least, not after this. Still, he could not wrap his head around what he had seen. *Had Clara been with the general?*

Jessie walked over to the settee and pushed Millie in front of Clara. "Now, tell Dr. Peters what you saw last night!"

Clara broke out in a nervous sweat, wringing her hands anxiously and avoiding eye contact with everyone in the room. Millie told her story, of seeing Clara walking late at night, up the path, coming from the general's cabin.

Peters listened intently. When she had finished, he turned to Clara and in a calm voice said, "Get your things together. We're leaving at once."

Clara tried to speak but she was suddenly overcome with emotion. She covered her face and began to sob loudly.

Dr. Peters started for the settee. In the past, he would have comforted her, would have done anything for her, but now his anger would not allow it. He left her sitting there, head in hands, and stormed out the front door. "Do as I say, Clara! At once!"

Clara started up from the settee, but Jessie pushed her back down. "You aren't going anywhere," she threatened. "Tell me what has happened between you and General Van Dorn! Why were you at the cabin?" Jessie grabbed her shoulders and shook her violently. "Tell me this very instant or I'll see you are sent away—and for good!"

"But, I—" Clara collapsed back against the settee, her voice cracking with emotion. "I can't! It isn't what you think! It's just that—well, he promised me—" Clara freed herself from Jessie's grip and ran across the room to the large wing back chair near the piano.

Jessie chased after her and lunged for the chair. "Stop that crying! Stop it and answer me!"

Without warning, Alexander ran into the room and grabbed Clara before Jessie could get to her. "Come on Miss Clara," he said, lifting her from the chair. "Yer daddy say he'll send yer things along soon. You gots to come on with us now." Alexander grabbed her by the waist as she fell limp, overcome with emotion. "Miss Jessie," he went on, never looking back. "Doc says fer you not to leave the house tills we gets back. He say he means it too."

She laughed and lunged for Clara, grabbing her by the shoulders, wheeling her around with such force that it knocked Alexander into the wall like a fallen oak. "You will look me in the eye! Now! Is this true? Have you been alone with the general?" She slapped Clara's face with all of her might, so hard that small drops of blood formed in the corner of the girl's mouth and dripped onto her white lace collar. Clara whimpered like a wounded animal and cowered to the floor.

Alexander reached down and took Clara's hand. "Please, Miss Jessie. Lemme get her now. Come on, Miss Clara," he said softly, lifting her off the floor and walking her quickly to the door.

Jessie rushed past them and into the foyer, but the sight of the doctor stopped her in her tracks. She backed away and watched in silence as Alexander dragged the sobbing Clara to the waiting carriage.

Peters shoved her into the corner of the seat as Alexander cracked his whip. The carriage lurched violently, throwing rock and dust in its tracks as they raced down the long drive. When they were out of sight of the house, of Jessie, Clara sat upright. "It's not as you think, Father," she said choking back her tears. "I know you are angry, but you must know I love him and I want to marry him! If…" she stammered. "If this awful war would end we could run away and…" She put her head in her hands and cried.

Dr. Peters said nothing. His anger was such that he could find no words to say to her. How could Clara be so naïve? How could she shame herself so? His chest tightened and he took a deep breath. He had always imagined it would be Jessie who sent him to an early grave. But Clara?

"Father," Clara said. "He *is* a good man. I know it."

Peters grabbed her by the shoulders and turned her to face him. "Clara, you must listen to me. The General has a *wife*, a *family*. Why, he's more than twice your age! What *good* man tempts an innocent girl? He's nothing but a liar, Clara! His very actions are *criminal!*" He let her go and threw his hat on the floor of the carriage. "I'll not listen to this nonsense any longer! You will do as I say!"

She turned away from him. "But, Father—"

"You have made trouble for yourself—for the entire Peters family!" He struggled to control his temper. "This is an outrage!"

"But, he loves me, Father!" she wailed. "He told me so!"

Peters took a deep breath and tried to calm his pounding chest. "You have misunderstood the General, my dear. You are naïve, impressionable." He touched her shoulder but she jerked away. "You must listen to me,

Clara. You must come back to reality and stop this nonsense before it's too late."

"But it is too late, Father! It is too late! I *must* marry the General. I *must*! Can't you see that? Father, can't you understand?"

Peters' face grew suddenly pale. It was then he knew, then that he realized the gravity of her words. His worst fears were confirmed. Now, he would settle this matter once and for all. General Van Dorn would pay dearly this time.

### From the Diary of Jessie Peters

*May 6, 1863*

*Today marks the first time in my life that I find myself utterly bewildered. If not for the driving rain I would run screaming into the streets and tear my hair as some tragic figure in a Shakespearean play. How can it be? How could Clara have tricked me so? How did a naïve schoolgirl get the better of Jessie McKissack? I simply refuse to think that my general welcomed any of her advances—no, I'm certain it was Clara's doings! And now she has made trouble for everyone. George will never allow such an insult to pass— no, he will strut about town and talk of morality and devotion as if he possesses even a trace of those virtues. And all the while, the little vixen will lie to herself that the general adored her, that he invited her affections, while I know full well Earl Van Dorn would never care even the slightest for someone like Clara. I hope George delivers her to that school and demands they lock her up and throw away the key! She is a menace!*

*If only I could find a way to get to Earl, but I feel George has set a trap for me at every turn. I dare not leave the house for fear he will accuse me further and will set about to drive the general out of town. He's done so before—and worse. Dr. George Peters, judge and executioner. No, this time I will get the better of George Peters. I will give him nothing to sink his teeth into. Let him stew over his daughter's wickedness—alone. I will have no part of it—I will not take the blame for her actions. He should look to his own past for an explanation—perhaps Clara is rotten to the core, as I've said all along, rotten like her brothers. Whatever the cause, she is no longer welcome in my home and had better think to return to Bolivar, or some place that might take her in with open arms. I care not what George may think; Clara Peters will walk through my door only after they've laid me six feet under the ground. I swear it— on my dear parents' graves!*

# CHAPTER 17

*"Let us cross over the river and rest under the shade of the trees."*

—MAY 2, 1863 - GENERAL STONEWALL JACKSON - DYING FROM AN ACCIDENTAL SHOT BY HIS OWN MEN AT CHANCELLORSVILLE.

**May 7, 1863**
**Captain G. A. Hanson**

Breakfast was served at 7:30 on the morning of May 7, at the Martin Cheairs mansion. The table held fine bone china, and what remained of the crystal goblets had been filled with fresh milk. A glint of sunlight struck blindingly against a silver bowl filled to the brim with hot, steamy biscuits. A red velvet runner spanned the length of the mahogany dining table, and the fine linen napkins were scrubbed white as snow.

The Cheairs mansion seemed renewed with the spirit of days gone by, of bustling servants, houseguests, and parties; spoils of a life deemed gone forever. For now, at least, this feeling was alive in Mrs. Cheairs as she greeted each guest at the main double door with, "Good morning," and "would you please allow Percy to show you to your chair."

Percy, Mr. Cheairs' valet, escorted the men with such regalia that a stranger would have thought the Queen of England was attending. If the outcome of the War were based on that morning's splendor, the South would no doubt be victorious.

General Van Dorn was seated at the head of the oblong table, where he was engaged in a heated conversation with another officer. The controversy involved the recent appointment of a rather unsavory character, a W. O. Williams, as commander of a small unit of cavalry.

"The men have threatened mutiny," Captain Hanson declared, pointing across the table in the direction of Van Dorn. "Williams is not a man of integrity. Ain't nobody going to follow him. You got to get rid of him!"

Van Dorn sensed the vehemence in his voice and rose from his chair. This was gross insubordination and the proud general would not tolerate it. He looked decidedly around the table. Every face held the same shocked expression. "You would do yourself well to retract your command, Captain Hanson. I assure you we'll discuss this matter after breakfast."

"There ain't no time for that, General, sir," Hanson continued, his face flushed red. "These men say they ain't moving from this spot until they get some satisfaction. They ain't following no murderin' traitor like Williams!"

General Van Dorn cleared his throat and looked coldly at Hanson. "Your men will do as expected as soldiers of this Confederacy, just as I have said. I *will* look into this matter. But, you would do yourself well to resign as the messenger of this revolutionary group." Van Dorn glared at Hanson, certain his words would calm the hotheaded soldier.

But that was not to be. Captain Hanson's hatred for Van Dorn was apparent. "Not disrespectin', but you ought to listen, sir. The men ain't taking much more of it. Williams is a scoundrel, and these men think you ought to do something about it. They demand it. As gentlemen, of course, and as Texans."

Van Dorn was furious. His nostrils flared out like a horse at the starting gate. "I see," he said through clinched teeth. "Well, I certainly can respect a Texan, Captain Hanson, but I must remind you again that there is a certain protocol in any army, and you sir have gone well out of those boundaries. Now, take your seat, Captain, and apologize at once to our gracious hostess."

Mrs. Cheairs smiled shyly. "That's quite all right, General Van Dorn. I'm sure Captain Hanson meant no harm."

"Well, that's very kind of you, Mrs. Cheairs," the general said apologetically, "but I will not tolerate ungentlemanly behavior in my army."

The Captain felt the sting of his words immediately, and grabbing his hat, mumbled an apology to Mrs. Cheairs and stormed out the door.

Van Dorn returned to his seat. "My apologies again," he said kindly. "You have my word we will be on our best behavior tomorrow morning." He laughed. "That is, if I make it through this day."

Mrs. Cheairs giggled. "Some days certainly feel that way, don't they? I'm sure you'll fare just fine."

The time was a little after 8:00 a.m.

# CHAPTER 18

# MURDER IN THE MORNING

*"I shot him about eight o'clock in the morning."*
—VOLUNTARY STATEMENT – DR. GEORGE B. PETERS (MAY 7, 1863)

Dr. George Peters paused at the doorway then knocked. He was nervous but confident in his plan. A large black woman named Sundy greeted him. Her skin was greasy and dark as night, and her nappy hair was held in place by a worn-out red rag. It was tied in a knot on the top of her head so that she resembled a woodpecker.

"General Van Dorn, please," the doctor said calmly.

Sundy showed him down the main hallway with a wave of her hand. "Down yonder," she mumbled. "Last door on the right."

A young officer was just leaving and tipped his hat to the doctor as he entered. Peters kept moving, stepping deliberately, and barely missing a fat tabby cat that was curled up at the office door. "Shoo, cat!" he hissed. "Get!"

Peters knocked lightly on the door of the general's office. He waited a moment and then gripped the iron knob. With a shaky hand, he turned it once.

A voice inside the room said, "Come in."

Peters opened the door just enough to slide into the room and quickly shut it. He placed his hands inside his coat pockets, glad for the heavy rains and damp cold that had allowed him to wear his heavy frock coat. He gripped the cold steel briefly then drew his hand out and offered it to the general.

They shook, though Van Dorn seemed hardly aware of his presence. He looked up from his desk only long enough to nod his greeting, and then went immediately back to writing.

A noise from the corner of the room caught the doctor's attention and he turned to see a young soldier standing just behind the door. Major Kimmell, one of Van Dorn's adjutants. Peters remembered meeting him at the party a few nights back. "Good morning," Peters said quietly.

Kimmell only nodded. When the general finished writing, Kimmell took the paper from his hand and left the room. Van Dorn looked up suddenly from his desk as if he had just realized he had a visitor. "Yes," he said. His face was expressionless. "What may I do for you, Dr. Peters?"

Peters approached the desk almost sheepishly. This was most odd. Shouldn't the general be concerned? The father of the young girl— "Yes, General Van Dorn," he stammered. "So sorry to bother you but I must speak with you in private, if I may." Peters removed his hat and cleared his throat, his hands clinging nervously to the velvet trim of his coat.

"Very well," the general replied. "Unusually drab weather, wouldn't you say? I suppose you're accustomed to these endless winter months, but I could use some warmer weather. We'd be well into spring back home. Here, though," he laughed. "Winter drags on forever."

The doctor nodded. "Yes, it does seem cold for May."

A long silence ensued as the two men stared curiously at each other. Outside, a group of soldiers walked quickly by the window, talking in low voices, mumbling complaints about their staff sergeant. Peters watched them as they rounded the back of the house. Their voices soon faded away. "I would like a pass to Nashville, General. Important business. It cannot wait," Peters stated firmly.

"Well, certainly, Dr. Peters, though I must ask the nature of your business," Van Dorn replied with a half-smile.

The doctor stared back, frozen as one in a trance. "It's a family matter," he said coldly. "I've been asked to look in on Mrs. Polk in Nashville. She's a distant cousin of mine, you see."

"I see," Van Dorn repeated, again with a half-cocked smile. "Well, you must send her my regards as well," he said. "She's a fine woman. Rare in these times, wouldn't you agree, doctor?"

Peters forced a smile and nodded. "I suppose you're right."

General Van Dorn reached in the upper right slot of his desk and pulled out a slip of paper. He took a pen from an inkwell sitting precariously close to the edge of the small cherry secretary. He lowered his head and began writing the pass.

Peters stepped in the direction of a washstand that sat in the corner directly behind the General's desk. A crystal pitcher and two small glasses rested on the stand in place of the washbowl. "May I get some water?" he asked, almost in a whisper.

Van Dorn nodded. "Help yourself."

Peters walked slowly, quietly, careful to pick up his heels. When he reached the washstand, he lifted the heavy pitcher and poured a small amount of water into the glass. Then, taking a sip, he set the glass back on the stand and reached inside his coat pocket.

The general folded the pass and started up from his desk.

"Don't make another move," Peters said. He pulled the hammer back and walked closer to the desk. "Now, you son-of-a-bitch. Tell me what you think you're doing with my daughter?"

The general started out of his chair once more and Peters stepped closer. "I'll blow your damned brains out if you move just one muscle! Look straight ahead and keep your hands on the desktop!"

Van Dorn did as he was commanded, though Peters knew by the slight turn of his head that the general was searching for a weapon. A rifle rested in a rack above the mantle and a sword and scabbard stood upright in the corner near the door. The general's gun belt lay across the small bed.

"Now," Peters began. "I would ask you about the rumors involving you and my wife, but to be honest, I'm not the least concerned. Besides, you'll no doubt lie about it. What I want to know is what do you intend to do about my daughter?"

Van Dorn started to turn his head around, but stopped. He took a deep breath. "I certainly hope you are prepared to explain yourself, Dr. Peters. I think it best to consider your words carefully."

"Answer my question! Answer it now or I'll blow your head off! Was my daughter at your cabin?" He inched closer still. "Don't lie to me! I saw her! And *you*!"

"Why you fool!" Van Dorn laughed. "Are you insinuating that I have seduced your daughter?"

Peters' hands shook with rage and his palms were sweating. He lost his grip on the gun and scrambled to get hold of the butt. He steadied his hand. "You'll admit it or I'll blow your brains out! I have witnesses who've seen you —at my house! With my—"

Van Dorn started from his chair. "Why, I'll tear you to pieces!"

Then came a sound like shattered glass. The general's head bent slightly forward and slowly drifted to the right till it rested against the window beside his desk. A puff of smoke appeared above his left ear and a faint stream of blood ran down to the top of his starched white collar.

Peters stood shocked. For a moment he was unsure whether he had truly pulled the trigger. Maybe he had simply dropped the water glass. But a distinct smell of sulfur drifted up and filled his nostrils. A panic spread over him. He tried to take a step but his feet felt like lead. Someone would come soon. With great effort, he made it to the door and ran out into the hallway. *Strange.* His feet felt light as air now, and still gripping the gun in his hand, he moved effortlessly down the empty hallway and out the front door. The familiar gray mare stood waiting at the gate. Not until he cleared the drive did he turn and look back. The two soldiers were still talking in the side yard. They moved their heads slowly in his direction and then toward the porch where Sundy and Laura Beth Cheairs had appeared, their hands covering their mouths. Then with lightning speed, he bolted onto a dirt path that led to the river.

# CHAPTER 19

# THE ESCAPE

*"Dr. Peters shot Van Dorn and left the house by rear with the pistol still in hand, as if going to his own home east."*
—STATEMENT BY MRS. MARTIN CHEAIRS

He shoved the pass into his coat pocket as he hurried out the door. A soldier standing on the west side of the house turned casually in his direction as Peters mounted his horse and galloped away. *Remarkable.* They had not heard. He stuck his boot heels into the horse's side and rode east. When he rode past two men standing alongside a broken-down wagon loaded with sacks of flour, he pulled his hat down low. No one would expect him to go in the direction of his own home. As long as no one recognized him, he would have time to cross the fields leading to the river. Then he would be out of harm's way.

Up ahead a large lake separated his property from the neighbors. He would circle this and come back around to his house. The area was largely untraveled, and he knew his own land well enough to outrun any search parties. He reached the gate to his home in a matter of minutes and found Alexander waiting there holding the reins to an old mare. Surveying the sway-backed creature, he shook his head. Earlier that morning, he sent Alexander to fetch a fresh horse. But this would not do at all. "This is the best you could find?" he asked.

"Yassir," Alexander replied, "ain't another one on the place that ain't ailing."

His horse limped in a circle, sore from the hard ride out.

"That one won't do," Peters said. "You ride that mare out and put the fence rails back up in an hour or so. You hear?"

"Yassir," Alexander said. He tugged at the rope and led the old mare back to the stable.

"And don't talk to anyone," Peters added as he turned his horse in the direction of Davis Ford Road. "You know what to do."

Alexander nodded. "Yassir, I remember."

Peters rode north toward the main road, stopping every few minutes to listen for pursuers. No one was around. Not yet at least. When he reached the Hill Parks Place, he turned and rode in the opposite direction. With luck, he would make the Duck River before night.

He rode frantically until he came upon a narrow road where he paused a moment to study his surroundings. The road was overgrown and he could not recollect it. A sense of panic overwhelmed him. He was lost. Time was running out, and he could not afford to make a mistake, especially one that would land him in the hands of his enemies. He jumped from his horse and surveyed the area on foot. If he could only find the river, then he would be safe.

He walked back to his horse when he heard the faint sound of a man's voice coming from beyond the bend in the road. He panicked and spurred his animal. The horse shot like a bullet into a thicket of ivy and buck vine, ripping his coattail as he struggled to stay atop. The voice grew louder. Peters peaked through the thicket when an old man on a scrawny gray horse came clomping into view. He was talking and laughing. Peters strained to hear, but the thick growth made it impossible. He watched from the thicket. The old man was alone.

Peters slowly got down and walked back onto the road. "Hello, there!" he yelled.

The old man trotted further down the road, his feet nearly dragging the ground as the horse's back swayed with each step.

Peters walked closer and yelled again. "Excuse me, sir!"

Finally the old man stopped and strained his long neck to look behind him. He squinted and shielded his eyes with his hand but took no notice of the doctor.

"Excuse me," Peters yelled. "Over here!"

At last the old man turned his horse around.

"I seem to be lost and need some directions to the Duck River," Peters said in a friendly voice, stretching his hand out as the old man approached.

The old man glared, his steel gray eyes like two ancient pebbles, lifeless and cold. "Name's Buford," he said in a hoarse voice. "Don't reckon I got your name?" He turned his head away and cupped his ear with his hand. "Hearin' ain't so good. Mind you speak up."

Peters stepped closer. Might be one of the Buford's from Spring Hill. If so, he would know him. Better play it safe. "Name's McNeill."

The old man frowned, the corners of his wrinkled mouth hung like folds of a silk curtain. "Don't reckon I know that name round here." He tilted his head to the side and squinted again. "Face looks familiar, though," he mumbled. "Say, you're not one of them vigilante men are ya?"

Peters felt a sudden tightness in his chest. These locals may pose more of a threat than the soldiers. He hadn't planned on fighting the entire population, but he would if it meant certain escape. Peters looked behind him in the adjacent fields. Not a soul was there. Without a word, he drew his pistol from his pocket and pointed it at the old man.

"You listen carefully, old man!" Peters yelled, his hand shaking. "I need to get to the Duck River and I seem to have taken the wrong road."

The old man startled and cocked his head sideways. "Hey, now! You ain't got to point that gun at me!"

Peters shook the pistol at him again. "Which way to the river?" Peters asked. He mounted his horse and approached the old man. "Get going or I'll shoot!"

The old man twisted his face and mumbled something, but the panic on the doctor's face must have convinced him. He finally did as commanded, turned his horse around and trotted slowly ahead.

Peters pointed the gun at the old man and shouted, "Faster! I don't have much time!"

"I don't know what you've done, mister" the old man said calmly. "But I don't want no trouble."

"Just take me to the river," Peters said. "And there won't be any trouble."

The old man picked up his pace to a gallop, eventually cutting through a thicket and into an open field covered with large clumps of hard dirt and deep ruts. The horses stumbled across the pocked earth for some distance when the old mare hit a clump of dirt and fell with a thud to the ground, her front legs crumpling underneath. The old man rolled over the head of the horse and landed in a perfect-seated position on the hard ground.

Peters rode closer and got down from his horse. The old man sat still and watched the mare topple over onto its side. The ancient horse kicked a few times and then thrust its legs out in front.

"Reckon I rode her too hard," the old man said. "Poor old girl."

Peters shook his head in disbelief. He must keep going or Van Dorn's men would certainly catch up. "How far to the river?" he asked in frustration. "Just tell me how to get there, for God's sake!"

The old man bent over and touched the horse's head. "She was a fine mare. I shouldn't a rode her so hard is all."

Peters approached him and held the gun to his head. "Look old man," he said. "You get me to that river or you'll be joining her soon enough!"

The old man glanced up, a look of sheer agony on his ancient face. "Go yonder, past that line of cedars," the old man said. He dropped his head to his chest as one defeated and pointed ahead. "'Bout a hundred yards you'll see a steep bank. You can climb down there to the bridge."

Peters jumped on his horse and raced to the tree line. When he reached the bank, he stopped. He heard the faint sounds of the old man's moans slowly fading away.

***

Peters reached the Duck River Bridge shortly after and went east toward Shelbyville. His brother was there, serving under General Polk. He felt confident they were his allies, would stand behind him since they knew about Van Dorn, about the women. But Peters was no fool. He didn't expect to be a welcome guest in camp. Quite the contrary. Polk was strict military. A civilian shooting a general would never be justified—regardless of the crime. Still, he held out hope that familial ties were stronger than any coda of war.

Peters slowed to a trot about a mile outside of Shelbyville. He scanned both sides of the narrow road, and he saw them up ahead in a heavy thicket. Pickets. Two of them, leaned against a fence post. The drab gray of their uniforms a perfect match for the dried and rotted post. Peters approached slowly and held his pass high in the air. "I have papers," he said calmly.

The soldiers looked at each other and stood from the post in perfect unison. "Yea, papers for what?" asked the scraggly one on the right. He spit at the ground and pointed his rifle at Peters. "Go on, for what?"

"A pass," Peters said. He was nervous now and he was sure it showed. "Dr. George Peters. I'm here to see my brother Major Peters—and General Polk."

The private's expression suddenly changed. "Dr. Peters, you say?"

Peters moved his hand to the pistol in his coat. The soldier seemed decent enough, but he couldn't be too sure.

"Follow me," the picket said as he mounted his horse. They rode into camp a few hundred yards to a large white tent. A small fire smoldered near a gangly soldier who stood smoking a pipe outside the tent door.

"Wait here," the picket directed. He got off his horse and approached the soldier. They talked quietly, each glancing back at the doctor, and then both men disappeared inside the tent. After a few minutes, the picket emerged and motioned for Peters to join them. "In here," he said. His eyes were wide with excitement.

Dr. Peters dismounted and walked slowly toward the tent, hesitating briefly at the door as he glanced back over his shoulder. The picket tied the doctor's horse to a spindly beech tree and remained outside, leaning casually against the trunk of an old oak, while the soldier who had been standing watch took a seat at the entrance. A tall dark-haired officer was seated at a small desk in the back of the tent. Two tables ran along either side of the old desk and were stacked high with papers and folded maps. The only vacant chair held a saddle and a leather crop. The officer made no effort to accommodate the doctor who stood awkwardly in the middle of the mess.

"Dr. Peters?"

"Yes," the doctor replied nervously. "Brother of Major Tom Peters. I must speak with him—or with General Polk. It is a matter of utmost urgency."

The officer rose from his chair. "James Argyle Smith," he said. "Adjutant General to General Polk, and, yes, I'm well aware of your relationship," he said as he moved around the desk. He voice held no inflection, only the monotone exactness of an enemy. "Well, I regret to say but neither is available at this time. In fact, I have been instructed to send you on your way if you were to come by here. I mean, you're being somewhat family to the General, he hated to have to arrest you."

Peters shook his head. "Arrest me?"

"That's right," the lieutenant replied. "Told to arrest you on the spot. But only if you caused trouble or refused to leave."

Peters' face turned a ghostly white. Polk had abandoned him. He had figured as much—but his brother? His own flesh and blood? "Very well," he said, his voice filled with uncertainty. "Well, I'm certain Major Peters will see me. After all, he is my brother."

"Ain't here," the lieutenant answered quickly, his eyes on the flap of the tent. "Left for Chattanooga just this morning."

Dr. Peters shook his head in disbelief. "There must be some mistake," he said weakly. "Why, Tom never mentioned going anywhere." His heart sank at this news. Surely he would remember what they had discussed, would remember to take Clara away and protect her.

"Like I said," the lieutenant interjected. "I've got orders to arrest you on the spot if you don't clear out at once." He folded his arms across his broad chest and planted his feet. "I ain't looking for trouble, Dr. Peters."

The doctor smoothed the brim of his hat and placed it on his head. He moved toward the door of the tent just as the picket reentered.

"See that Dr. Peters gets on his way," Lieutenant Smith said coldly. He stood like a statue at the tent door as Dr. Peters exited with the picket following close behind.

The men trotted casually out of camp, and were soon back at the picket post on the main road. Peters thought to thank the private for his trouble, but he knew that would be a futile gesture. These men hated him. If anything, he might thank them for not putting a bullet in his back.

He rode on in silence toward the orange glow of the sinking sun. Just enough daylight, he thought. With luck he could make another few miles before dark. Now that Polk was no longer an ally, he would need to move quickly. Nashville would be his only hope of escaping. His only sanctuary. The enemy now his only friend. Though he had planned it all along, had understood the reality of his actions, the irony of it all was now too much for even the calculating doctor.

# CHAPTER 20

# INTERVIEW WITH THE MURDERER'S WIFE

Major Kimmell arrived at the Peter's place around 9 o'clock that morning, accompanied by Lieutenant Isaac Ridley, Major Wright Schaumburg, and fifteen members of the 6th Cavalry who surrounded the Peters' home. Jessie watched from her bedroom window as the soldiers positioned themselves and loaded their rifles. Kimmell strolled up the walk, tripping awkwardly over a fat tabby cat stretched out underneath a porch lamp still lit from the previous night. He knocked several times on the door.

"Go see what they want," Jessie ordered Virethia. "And don't let them in until I say."

Virethia sighed and shook her head. "Don't feel right, Miss Jessie," she whined. "Something for sure wrong."

She walked quickly down the stairs as Jessie followed close behind her. When they reached the foyer, Jessie hid behind the parlor door.

Virethia cracked the front door slightly. "Yes?"

"Is Dr. Peters in?" Kimmell asked.

Virethia hesitated and looked over her shoulder at Jessie. "No sir. He ain't home at present."

"Is Mrs. Peters in?" he asked. "I need to speak with her at once. Tell her it's a very urgent matter. Tell her Major Kimmell is here. She'll know me."

"Yassir," Virethia said. She closed the door behind her and whispered to Jessie, "What you want me to say now?"

Jessie stepped away from the door and pulled her cloak tight. She still wore her long silk nightgown, her hair hung loosely at her shoulders. Her hands were shaking as she pulled the cloak together and tied it at the neck. She took a deep breath and motioned for Virethia to open the door.

Kimmell looked at her with surprise and removed his hat. "I apologize for the intrusion, Mrs. Peters," he said in a shaky voice. "I didn't mean to wake you, but—"

"Yes, Major Kimmell," she said as she twisted her hair into a low knot and tied it with a tiny ribbon. "What on earth brings you here at such an hour?" Her voice was edgy and nervous, though she tried to conceal it.

"I have a very urgent matter to discuss," he said. "There's been a terrible—" He stopped himself and turned to look at the other two soldiers standing behind him. They too appeared awkward and uneasy.

She glanced at them and forced a smile then leaned out the door and looked them up and down. "I don't think I've had the pleasure of meeting these gentlemen."

"Major Wright Schaumberg," Kimmell said, pointing to the tall one on his right. "And Lieutenant Isaac Ridley."

"Well," Jessie said, "I would say it is a pleasure to meet you two fine gentlemen, but I might not think so once I get this urgent news you have for me."

The three men looked at each other and Kimmell cleared his throat. "We need to speak with your husband, Mrs. Peters," he said. "Could you tell us where we might find him?"

"Well," she answered. "I don't know. He's out tending his patients, I assume. Why do you ask?" She thought her heart would be out of her chest; still she went on smiling, standing calmly in the doorway.

"Are you certain Dr. Peters is not at home?" Kimmell asked again. "Not on the property anywhere?"

"As I've already told you, Major Kimmell, the Doctor is *not* at home," Jessie answered. "I assure you I know when my husband is at home." She stepped back and defiantly placed her hands on her hips.

Major Kimmell moved closer and leaned in to speak, his voice low and serious. "Not that I doubt your word, Mrs. Peters, and I do apologize for the interruption, but I hope you understand I am ordered to search this property, the house, and all outlying buildings."

"I don't understand, Major," Jessie said. "Why on earth would you search *my* house?"

Major Schaumberg stepped closer and nudged Kimmell. "Major, remember, time is of the essence."

Kimmell cleared his throat again and stood straight. "You see, Mrs. Peters, your husband has just shot General Van Dorn."

Jessie gasped and covered her mouth. She looked at the men and then at Virethia. No one said a word. Her legs grew weak. She grabbed Virethia's skirt and sank onto the brick porch as Virethia held her until she landed safely on the ground.

"I regret bringing this news," Kimmell said, kneeling beside Jessie. "But after your husband shot the general, he rode toward home. We believe he may be here."

"No," Jessie mumbled. "George would never—"

Major Schaumburg knelt beside Kimmell. "There were several witnesses who saw him," he said, pointing to a small man pacing the sidewalk. "Mr. Odil saw Dr. Peters in town earlier this morning and followed him to the general's headquarters. He saw your husband enter the home and watched him come out and leave in a great hurry."

"If I might add," Mr. Odil danced proudly up the stairs and removed his hat. "Mrs. Peters," he said, "that's right! Saw the doctor with the gun in his hand! And it was still smoking at that! And then he raced off in this direction." He paused and caught his breath. "I went right up the stairs and was just about to open the door when, would you believe it, Laura Beth Cheairs came running out screaming at the top of her lungs 'Dr. Peters has shot the general!'"

"That's enough," Lieutenant Rainey said, pulling Odil down the stairs and into the yard.

"It can't be true," Jessie said with a gasp. "Is the general badly hurt?"

Major Schaumburg stepped forward. "We're not at liberty to give out that information, Mrs. Peters. We're very pressed for time, though. I must search the house at once."

"Virethia," she said reaching out for her hand. "Will you help me inside?"

"Mrs. Peters, we must—" Schaumburg began.

"Go on," Jessie mumbled. "Search the house, but you'll not find him here." Jessie got to her feet as Virethia showed the men into the foyer. She followed close behind them, silently praying for George's capture.

Kimmell led a group of soldiers through the house, while Major Schaumburg searched the barns and stable. For nearly an hour, they combed every inch of the Peters' property, even sending a detail down to the creek. When they were fully satisfied the doctor was nowhere in the house, Kimmell thanked Jessie again and ordered the men to mount up.

"Major!" Schaumburg yelled from the gate. "A search party is coming this way!"

Moments later, a large group of soldiers rode into the Peters' yard. A gangly private leaped from his horse and ran up to the major. "Major, sir," he said gasping to catch his breath. "Doc Peters' man was in them fields that run alongside the Cheairs' house. You want to know what we found him doing?"

"What man?" Jessie asked. "Alexander is the only man on this place and he's at the stables there." She stomped down the front steps and stood in front of the private. "What did you say you found him doing? Go on."

Kimmell shook his head and took Jessie by the arm. "I need you to go back inside now, Mrs. Peters. We'll handle this."

"No," Jessie said hotly. "I'll not be ordered around in my own home. This man says he knows something and I want to hear what it is."

Kimmell frowned and let her go. "Very well," he said, glaring at the private. "What did you catch this man doing?"

"Well, if it's okay," the private said. "We stopped this man—Alexander was his name, I think. Well, he was mending some fence rails that were down in the field and we asked him what he was doing on the property. He told us he was just out fixin' the broken fences, so we asked him if he knew about Doc Peters shooting the general and his eyes got big and he said, 'No sir! I ain't helped nobody do nothing!'"

"Are you saying the doctor had prepared an escape route?" Kimmell asked.

"That's exactly what I'm saying!" the private said. "He's still there if you want to ask him yourself."

Jessie gave Virethia a worried look and went inside the house. She quickly gathered her hat and riding crop and returned to the front porch. "I'll go along, Major," Jessie said. "We'll just see about this."

Kimmell gave her a disapproving look then shook his head. "If you insist, Mrs. Peters," he said shaking his head. "But I want you to know I don't think this is a good idea at all. Why, it's just not—"

"But I *do* insist, Major," Jessie scolded.

Kimmell lowered his head and led the group of soldiers with Jessie positioned between him and Schaumburg. They rode down a narrow dirt path that eventually brought them to the cabin on the back of the property. From here they cut through dense woods until they came to a fence that separated the Peters' property from a neighbor's. As they rode the length of the fence, Kimmell pointed out several of the split rails removed and laid aside. Then he motioned for Major Schaumburg. "Look here, Major," he said pointing to the ground. "Hoof prints."

They rode through the opening and onto the adjacent property. The tracks led to another fence that lay about a mile away. A field hand was hard at work replacing the rails on a fence.

"You there!" Kimmell shouted. "Whose property is this? What is your master's name?"

"This here's Peters' land. I belong to Doc Peters," Alexander said. "Uh—Mrs. Peters," he said as Jessie stepped into view and waved her hand in the air.

"What are you doing here? This can't be Peters' land," Major Schaumburg replied.

Kimmell galloped closer. "Answer the question," he said in a demanding voice. "What are you doing here on this land?"

"Jest fixin' the fence here," Alexander replied.

Kimmell drew his revolver and pointed it at the man. "Listen, Dr. Peters just shot General Van Dorn! Now, you tell me what you know about it or I'll blow your head off!"

The man threw his hands up and begged. "Please don't shoot me! I ain't done nothing. I, uh jest did what he tole me to do."

"Major Kimmell!" Jessie shouted. "I demand that you stop this at once!" She dug her heels in the horse's side and bolted toward Alexander. "Come here," she said. "Tell me where the doctor is."

"Go on," Kimmell said, his gun still pointed at the man's head. "Answer the question."

"Well, he done tole me to take down this fence here, and dat's what I done. He tole me to put'em back up when —" He looked at Kimmell and wiped his forehead. "He says to put'em back up after he got the horse I brung him. I never knowed he was gone to shoot nobody."

Kimmell put his gun away and walked closer to him. "Well, do you know where the doctor was going?" he asked, his voice now calm.

Alexander spread his arms out wide. "Far away," he said. "He say he goin' far away. Dat's all I know."

# CHAPTER 21

# A MESSAGE FOR CLARA

*"I knew Peter's daughter, a young girl at school at Columbia Athenaeum. An hour after the murder Capt. Moorman Jackson's adjutant sent for me. He asked if I knew Miss Peters. He gave me a letter with instructions to ride rapidly and deliver to her at once. I rode the 11 miles in 1 ½ hours – saw Miss Peters and delivered the note. You may rest assured I did not tarry. It was to inform her of the killing..."*

—LIEUT. I.N. RAINEY, CSA

Alexander rode over to the general's headquarters later that afternoon and overheard several local men anxiously discussing the search. Word in town was that Dr. Peters was on the loose and anyone who found him was to bring him immediately to headquarters—dead or alive. They all wanted a shot at the doctor, except for a few acquaintances who stayed at home, too afraid to get involved.

"Don't hardly none of'em knows what Doc even looks like," Alexander explained.

Jessie wrung her hands. "Well, he'll certainly not be difficult to find out there in the woods," she said. "Where do you think he was going, Alexander? Did he say anything at all?"

"No'um," he said. "But Capt'n Jackson got a passel out lookin' for him now. He gots men out on the Pike and out in the woods. Says they gone git him and they don't care if he dead or alive when they do."

Jessie frowned and twisted the handkerchief in her hands. "They'll do it too," she mumbled. "They've always hated him."

Alexander shook his head. "I gone keep my eye on it," he said. "Don't you worry none, Miss Jessie."

"You do that, Alexander." Jessie smiled. She knew the truth. Alexander hated George as much as she did. Truth was he probably wished like hell he could be the one to catch him. Still, he was loyal to her and as long as he was on the place she felt safe.

*** 

By late afternoon the carriage pulled up with Clara. Jessie was waiting for her, watching from the parlor window as Clara stepped out into the yard that was now filled with a hundred soldiers and horses. Seemed the entire Confederate Army had gathered, all eager to capture the doctor. But now all heads turned toward the carriage as the doctor's daughter was escorted into the house.

Lieutenant I. N. Rainey entered after Clara and politely tipped his hat to Jessie. "Ma'am," he said looking at the floor. "Lieutenant Sulivane asks that you allow the general's staff to speak with Miss Peters here alone."

Jessie laughed. "Does he honestly believe I will allow those men to speak with my step-daughter alone?"

"Well, ma'am," Rainey stammered. "I ain't saying but that's what the lieutenant intends on doing, you see?"

"Well," Jessie stomped her foot. "I'll not allow it! She can speak to those men in my presence or not at all! You go tell Lieutenant Sulivane I said so!"

Rainey fumbled with the hat in his hands. "I'll just go fetch the lieutenant," he said. "If you ladies will excuse me."

When the lieutenant left the room, Jessie turned to Clara. "Well, what do you have to say for yourself now?" Jessie grabbed Clara's arm and pulled her close. "Answer me!"

"No!" Clara squealed. "It can't be true, Jessie! Tell me it isn't true!"

Jessie shook her hard. "It was *you!* You're the reason the general's dead! And your father—well, he's just as good as dead too!"

Clara slumped to the floor but Jessie refused to loosen her grip. "You'll tell these men what they want to hear!" she said, her face fiery red. "You tell them the truth! It was *you* all along! You *will* take the blame for this! Do you understand?"

The front door opened and Lieutenant Sulivane entered. He was accompanied by Major Schaumburg, Lieutenant Ridley, and Major Tom Peters. A look of shock spread across Jessie's face. "Tom Peters?" she stammered. "What on earth are you doing here?"

Clara jerked away from Jessie and ran toward the man. "Uncle Tom!" she cried, burying her head into his chest. "Oh, I knew Father would not leave me here alone!"

The room fell silent. "Major Peters," Lieutenant Sulivane said at last. "Are you here on behalf of Dr. Peters or has General Polk sent you?"

Major Peters raised his eyebrows. "I'm here on behalf of my brother and his child and I'm taking Clara with me. *Orders of General Polk.*"

Lieutenant Sulivane stepped closer. "You may take her, of course. But not until we have questioned her."

Major Peters shook his head and smiled. "You are mistaken, Lieutenant. Question *her*," he said, pointing to Jessie. "She'll tell you all you need to know."

Jessie drew her hand back to slap the major, but Lieutenant Sulivane caught her by the arm. "You'll apologize to me at once!" Jessie shouted. "And you're not taking Clara anywhere!"

The Major laughed again as a young soldier took Clara by the arm and led her to a waiting carriage. "If you have any questions, Lieutenant," Major Peters said as he followed them out, "send them directly to General Polk. He'll be glad to help in any way."

Jessie stared wide-eyed, speechless as Lieutenant Sulivane took her arm and led her into the parlor. "When we find your husband, he'll pay for what he's done," he said coldly. "You would do yourself good to tell us where he's hiding."

Jessie's eyes were wide. "But, I have no idea where he is! I think you must know General Van Dorn and I—"

Lieutenant Sulivane slammed his fist on the parlor table. "I know what I saw all those weeks!" he shouted.

"This was all a game, wasn't it? A game to trap the general!"

"No! You have it all wrong! You must listen to me!"

"A word of warning, Mrs. Peters," Sulivane said, as he stormed toward the door. "We will get to the bottom of this, and when we do, if we find one shred of evidence that you had a part in this—well, may God have mercy on your soul."

Jessie covered her face and sank low on the settee. "This can't be happening! I tell you! It wasn't me!" she cried.

But Sulivane never looked back. And Jessie soon found herself alone in the dark parlor, her mind racing, her heart beating uncontrollably. She simply must get to her sister's house, or she must send word at least. Susan could do something to stop this madness. She raced for the door, but much to her amazement, she found it had been locked. Fear overtook her. Were they holding her prisoner? Were they—Then it hit her like a bolt of lightning. *Someone must answer for Earl's death and that someone is me.*

George Peters will get his revenge after all.

*From the Diary of Jessie Peters*

*May 7, 1863*

    *Words cannot express the feelings I have tonight as I sit here surrounded by soldiers, alone in my grief. It is evening now, though I'm unsure of the exact time. I've been sequestered in this room since early morning—trapped and held prisoner. And for what, I ask? Am I such a threat to the Confederate Cavalry? I should like to know what these soldiers think to gain by holding me here. And though I have asked, have begged, to be taken to the general, these men continue to ignore me! Even the general's nephew Lieutenant Sulivane has treated me with absolute cruelty. I cannot understand it. Am I suspected of having had a part in this? Certainly not. O, Earl! Surely you live! I cannot bear the thought of you lying there, pale and motionless. If only I could go to you—I would nurse you back to health myself.*

    *The soldiers have moved into the foyer and they laugh and talk as if nothing at all has happened. I wish I could tell them that I hear their whispers, that they should take heed to temper their criticism of me, but each time I speak to them, they stare at me with such hatred that I am afraid now to utter a word. I would like to scream at the top of my lungs—I am no criminal! Yet it is George's Union oath that has them all in an uproar. If I ever get my hands on his neck, I will choke the life out of him! To leave me alone here to be treated like some common Yankee-loving trash!*

    *I've just heard a commotion in the foyer and it pains me to write it in words. The news is out now and my heart is forever broken. The general is gone—my dear, sweet Earl is dead. And though I sit and cry, no one comes to comfort me. I suppose I am to bear this grief alone—perhaps forever. The soldiers are coming and going almost constantly now, tramping through my house as if it were some tavern. I hear them every now and then speak of George and it seems he is still at large. If I could break free of my prison, I would hunt him down and bring him in myself, but it appears he is smarter than the whole Confederate Army.*

    *I am afraid now. There is no doubting the hate in the soldiers' eyes as they walk slowly past the parlor door. I should think their anger stems from frustration over George having evaded capture. Certainly they do not look at me as having been part of it. Still, I fear they will accuse me. I simply must get word to my sister or someone!*

# CHAPTER 22

# FUNERAL FOR A GENERAL

*Headquarters 1st Cavalry Corps.*
*Spring Hill, Tenn., May 7, 1863*
*This Corps, with the exception of those Regiments on picket,*
*will form tomorrow morning at 8, ½ o'clock – adjoining to, and*
*South of Spring Hill; to pay the last sad tribute of respect, to*
*its late commander Maj. Genl. Earl Van Dorn, by witnessing*
*his remains start for the place of interment, at Columbia,*
*Tenn. The commands will move out from their encampments*
*promptly at 15 minutes past 8 o'clock, so as to be upon the*
*designated ground at the precise time.*
    —GENERAL ORDERS No. 2 (BY COMMAND OF BRIG. GEN. W. H. JACKSON)
                          GEO. MOORMAN
                          CAPT. & A. A. GENL.

A blackbird swooped down from the sprawling magnolia tree and circled up again. In his beak was a small red berry ripped from a mass of holly bushes underneath. The landscape on the west side of the Cheairs' home was shielded almost completely by the trunk of the great magnolia, everything else choked beneath an overgrown patch of honeysuckle left to run wild since last summer.

Alexander stopped the carriage behind the bush, out of sight with Jessie slumped in the corner. She was afraid of being seen in town since the latest theory about the general's murder had emerged. Alexander heard it in town the day before—about new evidence, and an accomplice. Van Dorn's staff now believed Dr. Peters had not acted alone.

Jessie closed her eyes and tried to put *his* face out of her mind. She was exhausted from a fitful sleep last night, her mind replaying those final hours with him, his handsome face, now blackened and bruised, his steel gray eyes contorted from the deadly bullet. A member of his staff told Jessie how he lay near death for hours, his implacable spirit refusing to yield itself up until at last his mortality got the better of him. The men admired their general now more than ever.

A young soldier approached the carriage and Jessie shot up in her seat. "That's him!" she whispered.

"Private," Alexander called out. "Private Isaac Boatright?"

"Yes," he said. "I'm Boatright."

"Mrs. Peters would like to speaks to you," Alexander said. He jumped from the seat and opened the carriage door. "She in here."

The private looked around him. "Me? She wants to talk to me?"

"Yassir, won't take long." He motioned for the soldier to step inside the buggy. "In here," he whispered.

The private stood motionless, his eyes narrowed in confusion. "Well, I don't understand," he said nervously looking around him.

Alexander placed his hand on the handle of the buggy door. "The Missus," he whispered. "Miss Peters."

"I don't know why she'd need to speak to me, but, if it'll just be a minute, then I suppose so." He reluctantly stepped inside the buggy while Alexander pushed the door shut.

"Private Boatright?" Jessie whispered, moving out of the dark corner of the carriage. "I believe we met at my party last month." She watched him closely, not sure if he could be trusted. "So good to see you again." She smiled and reached for his hand. "These are such dreadful circumstances we find ourselves in, however. But you seem to be an honest, good soul. I know you will listen to what I have to say. I know you will help me."

"Why, Mrs. Peters," he stammered. "I'm not sure what you're wanting me to do, but I'm most likely not the man for the job." He squirmed in the seat and looked around nervously. "The general's funeral is startin' soon. I really have to go."

"That's exactly why I'm here," she said softly. "I'm sure you've heard the awful lies about me," she said, wiping a ready tear from her eye. "Well, you can't possibly believe them! You can't possibly!" She covered her face with her gloved hands and sobbed loudly, uncontrollably.

He reached over and touched her hand. "Mrs. Peters," the private said. "Please don't cry. You really ought to go on home now. This ain't the place for you. The general's staff may not take lightly to your presence. You understand, don't you?"

There was firmness in his words now, an urgency that frightened Jessie. She was quite fond of the private and had enjoyed his polite, innocent way, but most of all she trusted his instincts. He was afraid—whether of her, or his fellow soldiers, she did not know. But he was afraid. "You know they are all lies," she mumbled. "I cared dearly for the general. I would never harm him. You must believe me. You must help me convince them that I would never hurt him!"

Private Boatright cleared his throat and inched closer to the door. "I really must go now, Mrs. Peters. Please know my heart goes out to you. I know you—"

"I loved the general," she said through sobs. "I would never wish any harm."

"I know," the private said. "You're a real nice lady, but now—well, you must not talk of it. I know you're hurt, but..." He touched her hand gently. "There's a rumor about your husband's loyalties, you know? Folks are saying he's a Yankee lover, a traitor of the worst kind. They're saying his family—you most of all, are traitors too. It ain't safe for you here."

She turned suddenly. "What are you saying, private? Who would dare say such a thing? Why, I'm a true Southern woman!"

"I'm sure you are, ma'am. I'm just saying maybe you should go on home and let it all die down. Ain't there some family you could go stay with for awhile? Maybe in another town?"

Jessie turned angrily away and sat back against the seat. "I have nothing to fear, Private," she said coldly. "I'll pay my respects and *then* I'll go home."

"Well, if you must," he said with a sigh. "Get your man to take you down by the gate yonder. He can pull up beside that live oak and you can see the whole thing from inside the buggy. Best to keep out of sight."

A bugle sounded in the distance and dozens of soldiers marched past. Alexander cracked his whip and moved slowly in the direction of the tree while Jessie watched her neighbors line up along the pike, women and children, old men and young boys, all in Sunday dress. She sank deeper into the carriage seat making sure to keep out of the carriage window.

"Humph!" she mumbled to herself. "I'll show them all a thing or two! They'll not treat me like a common criminal!"

A group of old men huddled near her carriage as the funeral procession moved forward. Jessie listened to them talk about the general, most agreeing he was a gifted soldier, but tales of parties and drinking, unescorted rides with young ladies, a variety of sordid goings on tainted his polished persona and hung over the camp like the stench of a buzzard roost.

"Providence," one old man said. "Divine providence, that's what it is. Says it right there in the Bible."

"I hear tell he got him a young gal too," said another man. "And a wife in Alabama and another in Texas?"

Jessie shook her head. The rumors were bad enough when the general was alive. Now that he was gone, they would hold nothing back. *Poor Earl.* Had he not paid dearly for his faults? What else would they take from him?

Private Boatright mounted his horse and moved past Jessie. He glanced at her and tipped his hat as he rode toward a group of soldiers talking in a circle, their bayonets shining from an early morning's polishing. The private saluted Lieutenant Sulivane and stopped his horse just past the gate. General W. H. Jackson waved him on through, as he took his place in a line of soldiers positioned on the right side of the road. Just ahead of Private Boatright, Jessie saw a four-horse ambulance, its driver in dark attire. A thin pole attached to the front held a small black flag that fluttered gently in the morning breeze, behind it stood the familiar black stallion, riderless with the General's boots facing backward in the stirrups. Inside the hearse sat a metallic coffin, the head of which bore Van Dorn's Mexican sombrero, along the breast laid his gold-hilted sword—a present, he told her late one night, from his once beloved Mississippi.

At half-past eight o'clock, the command was mounted and drawn up on either side of the street. As the hearse passed down the line, the officers and men saluted their dead chieftain with the saber. Extreme silence reigned as the processional continued down the pike. Jessie watched the hearse with a heavy heart. All eyes were moist, especially those of his escort who were of the old army. They adored their general as children do a father. Jessie knew he had loved them as much in return. If only he had been given the chance to prove himself one last time. She dropped her head and cried. Perhaps this *was* all her fault! Maybe she *was* a murderer after all!

The hearse moved toward Columbia and Alexander fell in line behind a host of buggies, their occupants adorned in a various array of mourning dress. They rode in silence, heads down, the slow journey into Columbia, nearly twelve miles to the courthouse where Bishop Otey would perform the last rites. More than a hundred citizens paid their last respects. Private Boatright and the general's bodyguards stood round the coffin as mourners passed, one by one, a few placing a lone flower across the top, others touching the sword lightly as they moved past.

With the Bishop's last prayer, the long line of mourners moved to the side and the general's bodyguards lifted the coffin back onto the hearse. The driver slowly turned the horses' heads toward the Mt. Pleasant Pike and St. John's Church, while the soldiers followed behind, their heads hung low, their faces wrought with heavy sadness.

"You ready to go home now?" Alexander asked. There was gentleness to his voice now, a desire to protect his missus no matter what.

"I—yes, Alexander," Jessie said through tears, her mind muddled with thoughts of George and Clara—and Earl. Oh! How she wished she could take it all back! But, that would never be—not now. He was gone. Dead. At the hands of her own husband. She fell back onto the seat of the carriage. "Oh, why?" she cried as she buried her face in a shawl. "Poor, poor Earl."

"Reckon it's God's will, Miss Jessie," Alexander said softly, as he turned the carriage toward Spring Hill. "Yep, the Good Lord gone giveth, and He sho gone take away."

*From the Diary of Jessie Peters*

*May 9, 1863*

*O, darkest of days indeed. Is my life to be laden with grief, my days shadowed by the darkness of loss and destruction of war? O, Earl! I thought I would lose my wits entirely when I saw your saber laid across that cold coffin, your boots empty in the saddle. My heart grieves so that I fear it may burst if I think on it too much. But I had to see it for myself, and now I know you are gone forever.*

*It seems that is always God's way. Earl, Luke, even my dear mother—all plucked from the vine too soon. And though I miss each of your smiles, I know you are all in a better place. If only those of us left behind could have gone along with you. But that is not to be—no, we are left to suffer through the days and nights of grief and despair. O, Earl! If I only knew the truth—how you truly felt about me. If I could hear just one word, then maybe I would not feel so utterly betrayed. Did you love me? Was it not as I believed? I have asked myself that question till I think my head will burst. I refuse to listen to George's vicious lies. Let Clara tell her vile fantasies, but I will never believe it!*

*You did love me, Earl.*

# CHAPTER 23

# SAFE IN ENEMY LINES

*"I sent details east, and elsewhere to look for Dr. Peters. I later
learned that the detail did not want to catch Peters."*
—General Joe H. Fussell

Peters traveled for hours in the darkness but by
midnight could go no further. Exhaustion overcame him
and he stopped to rest his head against an old oak tree
nestled safely at the end of an open field. This position
offered an excellent vantage point to watch for the soldiers.
He must keep a watchful eye till he was certain he had not
been followed.

The wind blew out of the north and chilled him as he
rested. The unseasonal cold forced him to draw his wool
coat tighter. He longed for a warm fire, would give his left
leg for it but knew the danger in that. He had not gone far
enough to be out of harm's way—not till he crossed the
river would he be safe. *Safe* in enemy territory. A bitter
irony.

For the first time that day, he recalled the morning's
events. He could picture the house, the office door, but he
could not remember the general's face, could not separate
his features from those of the soldier in the side lot, or the
soldier he passed when he entered the house. Yet he had
been face to face with Van Dorn many times. His hair! Yes,
he could see the light curls resting just atop his collar—

and those dark eyes. And his uniform—the white starched collar. Yes! There would be blood on that crisp white shirt now. Not that any of it mattered. He had done it. Had shot General Van Dorn. There was nothing else to say. Funny, he hadn't given much thought to getting caught at the time. Now he wished he had planned more thoroughly. "Self-righteous Polk," he said aloud.

Everything had gone as planned, except for Polk. *A warrant for my arrest*! He laughed aloud. There was a time when Polk would've defended the Peters family without question—even if it meant going against public sentiment. Now the *good bishop* seemed much more concerned with politics than saving souls. He was a hypocrite and a coward.

Peters closed his eyes. That was all in the past now. There would be no going back—not this time. He rubbed his aching head. If he could only sleep. If he could stop his thoughts for a time—just long enough to rest his mind— and his aching body. Oh, how tired he felt. His arms seemed light as a feather, floating at his side as he sat upright against the oak tree.

He rested there for several minutes before finally drifting off to sleep. But sleep was not meant for him, for the crowing of a distant rooster soon awakened him. He jumped to his feet, his revolver in his hand. "What was that?" he said, his legs shaking underneath him. "Who's there?"

He listened closely but the only sound was the chirp of a squirrel high in a pecan tree. He took a deep breath and wiped his forehead. The revolver was still in his hand. It felt cold, unnatural to him, so he quickly put it back in his coat pocket. A dizzy feeling came over him and for a moment he thought he would faint. He sat back down and took several deep breaths. A sense of dread came over him at the thought of falling ill. There was no time for being sick, not now anyway, but then the thought came to him that he had not eaten. "Of course," he mumbled. "I'm starved is all."

He reached in his leather sack. Nothing there except an empty medicine vile and a few pieces of string he used for suturing cuts. He shook his head in disgust. More poor planning.

He got to his feet and scanned the area for berries or nuts, anything edible. A thicket to his left was full of a brownish colored berry though none were ripe yet. He tasted a few but decided it was in the best interest of his bowels to avoid them. Below him were a few old pecans. He culled the half-eaten ones and cracked the others, choking them down. His mouth was dry as the desert, and when he forced himself to swallow, the nuts came up all at once as he coughed and spit them onto the dead grass at his feet. When he could breathe again he went back to his horse where he took out the canteen he had filled when he crossed the Duck River and drank all of it—drained every last drop from the leather pouch. No worries, though. He'd fill it again when he reached the Cumberland. He was sure the river was no more than a mile from there. With great effort, he mounted his horse and rode northeast. Once he crossed the Cumberland River, he would be within the Yankee lines, and from there he would go on into Nashville.

A sense of relief came at last as he rode along the narrow road leading down to the slippery banks of the river. He must be confident, this much he knew. Once he reached enemy lines, he would explain everything to the Yankee commander and reaffirm his support for the Union. No one would doubt his story. After all, Van Dorn had a nasty reputation as a womanizer, a lecher; not to mention, General Granger, who commanded Union forces in Nashville, hated the general. Peters would be greeted with open arms. Hell, he might even get a reward.

When he reached the rocky bank, he heard the roaring of the river, its swift current crashing wildly against the slick Tennessee limestone that lined its banks. This part would be difficult. Still, he must not slow down. Van Dorn's men might catch up if he took much longer. He checked his pocket watch. Time was the enemy now. He looked down the steep cliff at the tricky terrain and studied how best to tackle the jagged limestone and damp, mossy rock. If he moved slowly along the grassy edge, he figured he would not slip. Of course, that would mean leaving his gear strapped to his horse—a scary proposition given the river down below.

A sudden movement in the brush sent him scrambling behind an old pin oak. He listened carefully, and for a moment he thought he heard voices but he couldn't make them out, as the constant crashing of water on the rocky, river bottom drowned out all other sounds. He leaned out over the edge and nearly slipped off the cliff. At last, there it was! A muddy trail leading down to the water. He pulled himself back up and rested on the ground for a moment. The trail was nearly perpendicular at the top but tapered off to a slight slope midway down. He could make it if he walked his horse down the difficult part. The rest should be easy.

He pulled his horse toward the trail, but the sound of the violent water spooked the animal and he stopped cold like a stubborn mule. For several minutes he would not budge. Peters decided to ride him to the bank and ease down to the water. With luck this would work. He jumped in the saddle and kicked the horse's ribs. The horse bolted toward the bank and slid several feet as Peters fought desperately to hold on. Making a slight turn to the right, the horse hit a slick spot on the bank, then slid on its hind legs, crashing into a large boulder that marked the entrance to the trail. Peters pulled back the reins and the horse stepped away from the edge.

When the frightened animal had calmed, he led him down the trail to the raging waters. The current was swift, maybe too much for a horse and rider, but Peters had no intention of pulling the horse across, not in this frigid water and not against such a strong current. He scanned the river until he found a shallow area. Then he plunged the horse into the water and drove his heels into its sides. Grabbing the horse's knotty mane, he fought desperately to stay atop and out of the frigid waters. He must not get wet. At least a full day of travel lay ahead of him, which meant no time to stop and dry his clothes.

He positioned his legs high in his saddle and moved through the water with ease until a cold wave splashed up and soaked his thighs. He jerked from the chill of the water and gripped the saddle tighter. Then without warning the

horse lost its footing and rolled over, plunging them both
headfirst into the crisp current. Peters grew frantic as he
and the horse fought the deadly waters. He would drown if
he got hung up, so he let go of the reins and tried pushing
the horse away from him, but the swift waters only lifted
them up and sent them soaring down the river.

"Hello, there!" a voice drifted down into the raging
water.

But Peters was moving too fast. He struggled to see who
was there, but the current dragged him back under.

The voice yelled again from somewhere across the river,
"You there! Hold on to your horse! I'm coming out!"

Peters grappled for the reins but his hand hit the end of
a stirrup instead. A wave lapped over his head and down
he went again, choking on the mud and debris that washed
over his face. He was sure he had breathed his last.

Then the voice again: "Get the rope! I'll pull you out!"

Peters struggled against the weight of the water and the
animal until at last he surfaced just as the heavy rope
landed on his head with the force of a hammer. He caught
the end of it and let go of the stirrup. The horse drifted
away, swept down river, rolling and tumbling like a log in
the water.

Peters awoke face down on a sandy bank. He coughed
hard and a stream of warm water ran out the side of his
mouth. He tried to turn his head but he could not make
himself move, his arms and legs were weightless as air. A
stinging sensation ran across his skin like the prick of a
million needles and he felt his body float up and away. He
felt sure his time had come.

"Hey, mister!" came a muffled voice.

He felt a hand on his shoulder and soon found himself
face up on the sandy bank. His eyes were coated in wet
sand, his ears roared like a seashell on the bottom of some
ocean. More sounds came, but the roaring only worsened.
He lay there blind and deaf, paralyzed on the cold sand,
until with one thunderous cough, warm liquid ran from his
ears and he could suddenly hear again.

"Come on, mister! You all right?"

Peters lifted his dead hand to his eyes and wiped some
of the sand away. He blinked until he could just see a

blurred figure before him. A soldier! He was certain of this though he could not tell if he was a Yank or not. In one hand the soldier held the other end of a rope, in the other was a rifle.

"Damn near killed yourself, mister," the soldier said with a slight giggle. "Ain't nobody ever told you not to cross a river that ain't still?"

Peters wiped his eyes and held his hand out.

"Private Altho Lum," he said, lifting Peters from the ground. "United States Army."

Peters shook the water from his sleeves and wiped his hand on his wet pants. "Dr. George Peters, here. I'm *very* happy to see you."

Private Lum smiled congenially. "Hate to bother you after you near drowned, but I got to see some papers. What you doing 'round here?"

Peters reached in his pocket and felt around for the papers but they were not there. Then he remembered the leather pouch strapped across his body. He reached in and was surprised to find the paper was only damp. "Remarkable," he said as he nervously dug through the pouch.

"Yeah, it is," the private replied, "I ain't got nothing'll keep dry."

Peters handed the paper to him. "I need to see your commanding officer, then I can answer any questions you may have."

Lum shut one eye and twisted his mouth around. "Well, well," he said. He spoke slowly, deliberately. "This pass here says you was going to Shelbyville. You're a long way off track."

Peters frowned. He had no time to waste on the powerless. "As I have said, I will answer your questions as soon as I see your commander."

Lum's face straightened out. "All right, then," he said, pointing his rifle toward the bank of the river. "We'll just see. Right up yonder."

Peters stood and went ahead of the private. His clothes were heavy from the soaking and he felt as if he might collapse under the weight. They walked a half-mile until they arrived at the campsite, which was nothing but a few tattered tents and several dirty soldiers. General Granger was their commanding officer, but he was nowhere in sight. "Where exactly is this Granger," Peters asked.

"He ain't here just now," one of the soldiers replied. "Reckon you tell us just what you're doin' crossing that river."

Peters looked around at all the faces. This was the perfect audience. He told them first and foremost he was loyal to the Union. And when he had their undivided attention, he told them the rest—about the murder, how he had committed the crime single-handedly, and how he had eluded the entire Confederate Army for nearly two days. The soldiers listened with eager faces. He could tell they liked the sound of a dead Confederate general.

"You ain't lying, right? Granger ain't a man for foolishness," one soldier said.

"Naw, he ain't," another shouted as he spit over his shoulder.

"Hang him!" yelled a gangly soldier from the rear of a tent. "He's a lyin' reb!"

But Private Lum stepped up. "Now, wait a damn minute!" he yelled. "Let's check it out and see! Hell, we might have ourselves a hero here!"

"Yea, and if it ain't true, then we'll hang the son-of-a-bitch!" the cook yelled.

A few low-ranking officers conferred for a while and finally settled on a plan. They would send a rider to General Granger's headquarters, a young soldier about sixteen, their fastest rider. In the meantime, they would set about making a fine noose—just in case the doctor was lying. A couple of burly soldiers were ordered to stand guard over Peters.

The guards were nice enough, and when they asked for details, Peters felt compelled to oblige. Besides, it may be to his benefit to tell his side of the story. So he told them about Jessie and the general—the rumors, and how he eventually caught Van Dorn red-handed in his own home! He rambled on about other alleged affairs involving the general and even went so far as to throw in a few lewd details, though they were utter fabrications. Within the hour, he had the guards hooked. Soon after, the entire

camp circled round the doctor and listened with wide eyes
to his tawdry tales.

"I'd do the same if a man so much as touched my
Sarah!" the cook yelled back. "Shoot that son-of-a-bitch
right between the eyes! Wouldn't bother my conscience one
bit!"

The whole lot agreed. When the crime involved a man's
wife, then killing was justified—the only honorable thing to
do. *Hell, honor was all a man had.*

Peters breathed a sigh of relief. He had won them over.

When the fire died out, the men dragged themselves
back to their tents, puffed up with newfound pride, self-
proclaimed gentlemen now, eager to pass judgment on any
man who dared challenge the bond between husband and
wife. And best of all, they sang the doctor's praises. He was
a hero to the Union—a hero to all good and decent men.

Peters leaned back against the tree and placed his pack
under his head. If he had his way, he'd be in Nashville by
now, not sitting on some cold hillside. But the warm
reception he had received at the hands of the enemy was
well worth the pain. If he could convince these roughnecks,
then he could win over just about any court in the land.
Besides, no self-respecting man in the country would
publicly condone lechery. He closed his eyes. If only he
could convince the judge without any mention of Clara...

Next morning the young soldier returned from
headquarters and verified Peters' story. General Van Dorn
*was indeed* dead, and from all accounts, the doctor had been
honest about the shooting—his story seemed plausible.

"You're a famous man," Lum said. "Granger's happy as
a pig in slop! Says you done the Union Army a fine service
killing ol' Buck Van Dorn. Says he thought about killing
the son-of-a-bitch hisself but didn't never have the chance!
Wants you right away." He laughed and slapped Peters'
back. "You're a hero, man!"

***

Lum and Peters arrived in Nashville on the 12th of May,
five days after the murder. Union Colonel Truesdale
ordered Dr. Peters held at the Nashville headquarters until

he could return from Murfreesboro and question him about
the murder. Rumors were rampant, Truesdale explained in
his order, and the circumstances surrounding the events of
May 7 were clouded by miscommunication and blatant lies.
Dr. Peters would be questioned thoroughly. After all, a
general was dead—Rebel or not.

From the moment of his arrival, Dr. Peters enjoyed the
spoils of a hero's homecoming. The Yankees showered him
with gratitude for killing the notorious Van Dorn. It was a
timely death for Union forces, the perfect disruption in the
Rebel cavalry's recent run. With Van Dorn gone, the only
force remaining was Forrest. For this, the soldiers thanked
Dr. Peters profusely.

Colonel Truesdale arrived in Nashville at the Office of
Army Police around 10:00 a.m. on the morning of May 23.
The examining room had been prepared earlier that
morning and Peters had been brought in by two young
privates who now stood guard in the doorway. Truesdale
sent for his adjutant, a youthful lieutenant with a patchy
black beard, who brought in paper and pen and sat across
from Peters at a long oak table. The doctor was given
instructions to give a brief sketch of his life and a detailed
account of the events of May 7. He smiled and appeared at
ease, even confident in the presence of his captors as the
interrogation began. The time was 10:13.

"I was born in the State of North Carolina, and raised in
Murray County, Tennessee, where I now reside. I have
practiced medicine twenty-three years in Bolivar,
Hardeman County, Tennessee. I was State Senator from
the Twenty-First Senatorial District of Tennessee in the
years 1859-60-61. For some years past I have been
planting in Philips County, Arkansas, where I have been
constantly during the last twelve months. After the Federal
troops reached Helena, Arkansas, and had possession of
the Mississippi River to that point, I went to Memphis and
took the oath of allegiance to the United States
Government. This was in the summer of 1862. After that
time I dealt in cotton and carried supplies to my neighbors
by consent of the military authorities there commanding,
and never went beyond the Federal lines until recently. I
have in my possession safeguards from Rear-Admiral

Porter, commanding gunboat flotilla, and Major-General U. S. Grant, commanding Department of Mississippi, for the protection of my property. About the 4th day of April, 1863, I came to Memphis and obtained a pass to go to Bolivar, Tennessee, at which place I received a pass from General Brannan, commanding post, to pass out of the Federal lines, my intention being to go to Spring Hill, Murray county, where my wife and family were staying. I arrived at my home on the 12th of April, and was alarmed at the distressing rumors that prevailed in the neighborhood in relation to the attentions paid by General Van Dorn to my wife. I was soon convinced of his intentional guilt, although a doubt still lingered on my mind as to the guilt of my wife. After witnessing many incidents too numerous and unpleasant to relate, and which confirmed the guilt of General Van Dorn, on one occasion, when a servant brought a note to my home, I distinctly told him I would blow his brains out if he ever entered the premises again, and to tell his whiskey-headed master, General Van Dorn, that I would blow his brains out, or any of his staff that stepped their foot inside of the lawn, and I wanted them to distinctly understand it. My wife did not hear this order."

Colonel Truesdale rubbed his chin. "Let me get this straight," he said coldly. "You threatened General Van Dorn once before the actual murder occurred?"

The room was silent. Then Peters took a sip of water, cleared his throat, and continued his narrative:

"That is correct, sir. Notwithstanding all this, I came to Nashville on the 22nd of April, and was exceedingly mortified on my return home to hear that Van Dorn had visited my house every night by himself during my absence, my wife having no company but her little children. I then determined to catch the villain at his tricks: so feigned a trip to Shelbyville, but really did not leave the premises. The second night after my supposed and pretended absence, I came upon the creature, about half-past two o'clock at night, where I expected to find him."

Peters stopped. His face felt hot, his shirt was drenched in sweat. He had merely *seen* the general, had only *seen*

Clara. His actions could seem rash, even unwarranted. But he could not, would not incriminate Clara. *And so he lied*:

"The general readily acknowledged my right to kill him, and I fully intended to do so—gave him a few moments to make certain declarations—in which he intended to exonerate my wife from dishonor and to inculpate himself completely—and, upon his agreeing to make certain acknowledgements over his own signature, I agreed to give his life to his wife and children. He readily, upon the honor as a soldier, accepted the proposition, but stated that he cared but little for his wife. I then ordered him off, and we parted about three o'clock. Next day, being sick in bed, I was unable to call upon him as agreed upon between us; but the second morning, after having recovered my health sufficiently, I called upon him and notified him that I was ready to receive that written acknowledgement—when he attempted to evade it by springing a discussion as to its propriety. I unhesitatingly told him I would give him one half-hour, and further told him that he knew what the consequence would be in case of a refusal to comply. I then went up through the village to communicate to a friend these facts, inasmuch as no one else was privy to them. At the expiration of the time, I returned to Van Dorn's headquarters, and found him engaged in writing. He stopped and read to me what he had written. The first proposition was written out in accordance with the previous interview; the second was a misrepresentation and lie; the remaining two he utterly refused to comply with."

Peters rose from his chair and removed his jacket. His face burned hot and his hands shook. He took a deep breath and continued, his gaze fixed on Truesdale who sat motionless in a chair across the room.

"I then denounced him for his bad faith; and he in reply said it would injure the cause, the service, and his reputation for that thing to be made public. I answered, 'You did not think so thirty hours ago, when your life was in my hands: you were then ready to promise anything. Now you think I am in your power, and you will do nothing; but, sir, if you don't comply with my demands I will instantly blow your brains out.' He replied, scowling,

'You damned cowardly dog! Take that door, or I will kick you out of it.' I immediately drew my pistol, aiming to shoot him in the forehead, when, by a convulsive movement of his head, he received the shot in the left side of his head just above the ear, killing him instantly."

Colonel Truesdale stood and raised his hand. "Then you admit to single-handedly shooting Major General Earl Van Dorn on the morning of May 7?"

Peters nodded and spoke calmly. "I picked up the scroll he had written, for evidence. I then went to Shelbyville to surrender myself to General Polk, believing they would not arrest me. Finding out, however, that they intended arresting and incarcerating me, I came around by McMinnville, thence by Gallatin to Nashville, within the Federal lines."

The adjutant finished writing and shuffled back through the statement. He looked curiously at the last few paragraphs and then asked, "Now, Dr. Peters, you say here you were standing behind him when you shot the general. Where exactly was Van Dorn? And was this in the a.m. or p.m.?"

Peters glanced up and started to speak. He could not remember, his only thought had been that he must shoot straight. Nothing else had seemed important at the time except killing him. "Yes," he said. "I shot him about eight o'clock in the morning. General Van Dorn was still seated at his desk."

The adjutant scratched the words on the paper. Colonel Truesdale took the statement from the adjutant and read it aloud while Peters sat motionless, eager to reach the end of this inquisition.

When Truesdale finished, he smiled slyly and asked, "Tell me again, Dr. Peters, how would you describe your relationship with General Van Dorn? Were you at all friendly, or was that just your wife?"

Peters began, flushing red in anger. "Now, let me remind you—"

"No, Dr. Peters," Trusdale leaned over the table. "Let me remind *you* that we are in charge of these proceedings. You'll answer every question or I'll have you locked up. Now, tell me how it is you have two sons and a brother fighting for the South, and a wife who is an obvious supporter, yet you are no friend to the Confederacy."

The words cut completely. How could he explain his opposing views and still sound trustworthy? It seemed as damning as the act of murder itself. Traitor, they would call him.

"I have interests in medicine and planting—"

"I'm certain you do," Truesdale interrupted. "I'm certain your interests have nothing to do with loyalty to country."

Peters looked sheepishly around the room. He felt like a fool. Truesdale had won.

The adjutant leaned in and asked softly, "Your allegiance?"

Peters continued. "Yes, it is as I have already stated. When I arrived at Spring Hill, Van Dorn immediately had me paroled. So when I reached Nashville a few days back, having left my certificate of having taken the oath of allegiance in Memphis, I renewed the oath and gave security."

The adjutant stopped writing and looked up at Truesdale. "Any more questions, sir?"

Truesdale paused. "No, I suppose that's enough. Have him sign it."

Peters rose from his chair and followed the adjutant into an adjoining chamber where he was told to wait until Truesdale conferred with the other officers on a course of action. He had not told them where he planned to go. At the time, it seemed unimportant. But now, with the possibility of parole, he had to make it clear—he would not be going south, even if they demanded it.

A short time later, he was ordered back into the interrogation room where Colonel Truesdale stood at the head of the table and read the paper aloud. "We find Dr. George B. Peters justified in the killing of General Earl Van Dorn, CSA, and thus release him." The colonel paused a moment and then shoved the paper in front of him. "Sign here."

"Am I free to go, then?" Peters asked after signing.

"We're arranging a room for you tonight, Dr. Peters," the adjutant said, walking him to the door. "The judge insists you depart from the city in the morning. Not sure where you plan to go, but you can't stay here. If you'll follow me, please."

The adjutant led Peters out onto the street and in the direction of a line of hotels, the first of which was a small three-story brick structure on the adjacent street.

The adjutant stopped out front and held his hand up to wait. "I'll handle this," he said. "You wait out here. Ain't many places eager to house a murdering man."

Peters sat down to wait on a small wooden bench outside the hotel. A full moon was just rising in the Nashville sky, casting an orange glow across the gray buildings ahead. On either side of the vacant street sat empty houses, some with boarded windows from the recent skirmish. A deep sense of loneliness crept over him like the shadow of the approaching night. Everything had happened so quickly—there had been no time to think clearly, to see the big picture. And now as reality sunk in he realized being vilified by the Union court was almost insignificant. Now he would face the grim possibility of death at the hands of his own countrymen—his own South. Like them, he had acted rash, foolishly, had given no thought to his own mortality. But he knew the cold truth. He had been given no choice. He must accept things as they are and must find a way to win.

His thoughts soon turned to Arthur and Thomas, to earlier days in Bolivar, when he and Eva first married, back when there was only hope and pleasure. Now all was lost. His reputation, his marriage, even his children would pay. *And all for Jessie.* All for a woman who did not love him. He slammed his fist hard on the wooden bench. If he could only hate her.

The adjutant returned in a matter of minutes. "Ain't no room in the hotel, but I found a boarding house with an extra space. If you'll follow me you can lay your head down in a short few minutes."

Peters rose from the bench and fell in behind the adjutant. His legs felt heavy as lead, his head was swimming from lack of sleep and even less food, still he dragged himself the two blocks to Ben Weller's boarding house on Clay Street. It was a large house, clean and well kept, quite different from many of the homes in the area.

Once again, Peters waited outside until the adjutant emerged with a stout middle-aged man.

"Mr. John Brownlow," he said. "Allow me to introduce Dr. George Peters. He's had a little trouble, you see—"

"I'm well aware of Dr. Peters' unfortunate ordeal," Brownlow said. He smiled and stuck his hand out. "I'd personally like to commend you on a job well-done. The actions of a true gentlemen and family man, I'd say."

Peters was taken aback. He had heard of this Brownlow. His reputation was that of a hard dealing businessman, ruthless to a point, yet here he was eager to help him. Some deep sense warned him to beware.

"Good then," the adjutant said as he turned to leave. "I'll just be on my way. The Union Army thanks you again, Mr. Brownlow, for your kind assistance."

"Much obliged," he said as the adjutant hurried down the sidewalk. "Well, I'm not much for company," he said to Peters. "But seeing your awkward position at present. Well, I suppose I'm the man to help."

Peters followed him inside the house and down a long hallway. They stopped at the last room on the right and Brownlow opened the door. On one wall was a great fireplace and in the corner of the room there stood a half-tester bed covered in patchwork quilts. Two long windows on the opposite wall stood open, their faded silk drapes blowing gently in the evening air.

Brownlow walked in and removed his muddy boots. He stripped off his pants and sat on the side of the bed. "Been a long day," he said, crawling into bed and stretching out the full length of the frame. "Tomorrow's bound to be even longer. No sense waiting up for it."

"No sense at all," Peters replied, removing his hat and coat. He was exhausted, his bones stiff from the stress of the hearing. He sat in a small wingback chair positioned between the two giant windows. "Aren't you here to protect me?" he asked weakly.

Brownlow jumped a little at the sound of his voice and sat up angrily in bed. "I'm sorry. Did you say something?"

"Why, I asked if you meant to protect me," Peters said matter-of-factly. "They'll hunt me down, you know."

Brownlow laughed and sat up. "Now, Dr. Peters, you aren't afraid of me are you?"

"Of course not," Peters said. "It's Van Dorn's staff. That's all. A soldier told me they were looking for me and vowed to catch me. And I'll tell you right now, they don't intend on talking to me when they catch up with me. If you know what I mean."

"Well," Brownlow replied. "They won't get you here, at least not tonight." He laughed. "Relax won't you?"

Peters got up from the chair and walked toward the open window. "I don't think you understand," he said nervously looking out the windows. He removed the pistol from his coat pocket. "They have vowed to kill me on sight. Can't let my guard down for a moment."

Brownlow got out of bed. "Shut that window or we're catch our death for sure! And, why don't you put that gun away? I don't much like having an armed man in bed with me."

But Peters held tight to his gun. "I'd feel better holding on to it," he said, returning to his chair. "You go on back to bed now. I'll not bother you one bit. I simply can't sleep knowing they could be out there right now. I'm sure you understand."

Brownlow frowned. "Well, I don't like the idea much. Mind you point the barrel down. I'd like to see tomorrow myself."

## From the Diary of Jessie Peters

*May 14, 1863*

*Alexander has just returned from town and brought with him the latest newspaper. It seems George has been located, taken in by the Yankee army, and subsequently interrogated. If only I could have been there—I would have asked a few questions of my own.*

*And, just as I would have expected, my fine husband has filled their ears with nothing but lies! Oh, the very nerve to say he caught the general at our home and threatened to kill him. Who would ever believe a Confederate General would run from a country doctor! And to make matters worse, George says he cannot tell all there is to tell and will not disclose the main reason for his actions until he is allowed to do so in a court of law. Well, he's certainly slandered my name in every newspaper—why then, I ask, has he allowed me to bear the blame if my supposed indiscretions are not the true cause for his actions? I should like to hear his answer for that one!*

*I suppose he is still trying to convince the authorities that General Van Dorn attacked Clara—pshaw! Where's the proof? I say let them interrogate Clara herself. Let them call her in and pick over her words with a fine tooth comb. She'll fold instantly and their lie will be out, then George will be forced to admit his sweet Clara is not so sweet, and that he actually killed the general in a jealous rage because he is a weak and petty man. He may still get away with it, but at least he will be forced to admit the truth.*

*I have thought about it a great deal and have decided I will write a letter to General Forrest asking him to interview Clara himself. He likes me a great deal and will certainly assist me or pass my letter on to the proper officials. The courts will know the truth whether I am vindicated or not. George Peters will not ruin my reputation without paying dearly for it!*

# CHAPTER 24

# BROWNLOW AND PETERS

*"You ask me to tell you the conduct of the man. He acted like a crazy man."*
—JOHN B. BROWNLOW

It was near midnight when Brownlow convinced Dr. Peters to come to bed. The windows had been shut since nightfall, but the curtains were left open, so Peters would have a clear view of the yard. A small gas burner remained lit in the room as well. All at Peter's request. Van Dorn's cavalry would certainly hunt him down and kill him, though Brownlow tried to convince him otherwise. It was no use, though; the doctor took his loaded pistol to bed and lay back with his eyes wide open, alert to every flicker of light or shadow on the wall.

"If I might ask," Brownlow said politely. "What makes you think the general's men are after you? Would Confederate soldiers really hunt you in enemy territory? Wouldn't it be more logical for them to get you when you're on their ground?"

Peters got out of bed and reached into his brown leather satchel hanging on the bedpost. He unfolded the paper. "It's right here in the *Mobile Register*, May 15, 1863. Read it yourself, if you don't believe me."

Brownlow took the paper from him and sat up against the ornate cherry headboard. He put on his glasses, moved the candle by the bedside table, and read the following aloud: "We the undersigned, members of the late Gen. Van Dorn's staff, having seen with pain and regret the various rumors afloat in the public press, in relation to the circumstances attending that officer's death, deem it our duty to make a plain statement of the facts in the case.

"Gen. Van Dorn was shot in his own room, at Spring Hill, Tenn., by a citizen of the neighborhood. He was shot in the back of the head, while engaged in writing at his table, and entirely unconscious of any meditated hostility on the part of the man who had been left in the room with him apparently in friendly conversation, scarce fifteen minutes previously, by Maj. Kimmel. Neither Gen. Van Dorn nor ourselves were suspicious in the slightest degree of enmity in the mind of the assassin, or we would certainly not have left them alone together, nor would Gen. Van Dorn have been shot, as we found him five minutes later sitting in his chair, with his back towards his enemy.

"There had been friendly visits between them up to the very date of the unfortunate occurrence.

"Gen. Van Dorn had never seen the daughter of his murderer but once." Brownlow paused a moment and looked at the doctor, but Peters sat silently staring at the window. After a moment, he continued, "While his acquaintance with the wife was such as to convince us, his staff officers, who had every opportunity of knowing, that there was no improper intimacy between them; and for our own part, we are led to believe that there were other and darker motives, from the fact that the assassin had taken the oath of allegiance to the United States Government, while in Nashville two weeks previously—as we are informed by refugees from that city—that he had remarked in Columbia, a short time before, 'that he had lost his land and negroes in Arkansas, but he thought he would shortly do something which would get them back'; and finally, that having beforehand torn down fences and prepared relays of horses, he made his escape across the country direct to the enemy's lines.

"Such is the simple history of the affair, and we trust that in bare justice to the memory of a gallant soldier, the papers that have given publicity to the false rumors above alluded to—rumors alike injurious to the living and to the dead—will give place in their columns to this vindication of his name. Signed M. H. Kimmel, Maj. and A. A. G., W. C. Schaumburg, A. A. G.,

"Clement Sulivane, Aide-de-Camp, R. Shoemaker, Aide-de-Camp."

Peters made no reply. He stood up and shuffled to the window, where he bent low and gently pulled the curtain back. "There you have it," he said, squinting and wiping his glasses. "They've declared my actions criminal. I'm as good as dead."

Brownlow put down the paper and wiped his brow. "Well, threat or not, I'd be much obliged if you would put that gun down and close your eyes. You're safe here."

Peters looked at him and shook his head. "No thank you. I'm not ready to die just yet."

"Well, you could put it down close by, you know?" Brownlow pleaded. "Close enough to grab it in case you're right. You won't be much good to yourself if you're dead tired."

Peters thought about what his roommate had said. He was right. He must keep up his strength. Why, they'd catch him with one hand if he went on like this. "Very well then," he said. "I suppose you're right. I'm going to need all the strength I have if I'm to win this one." He set his pistol on the bedside table and lay back on his pillow. After a moment or two, he resumed staring out the dark window, reluctant to let his guard down. Van Dorn's men would come after him as long as he was within their reach, and now that several days had passed, they were surely closer to finding him. He simply must get to St. Louis—to Clara.

Or maybe Texas? He hadn't decided where he should go, but he knew it must be far away. He closed his eyes and turned on his side. What if Van Dorn's men pressed on? What if he was forced to leave the South forever? The Confederate Army would banish him! He would be exiled, an outcast...

He could not abandon his sons, yet he knew they were better off with him gone. Van Dorn's men would never let go of their desire for revenge. Thomas and Arthur would only suffer with him around. Yes, it was best that he leave the South for now, but there was still George, Jr., and the other children to think of. If he left them with Jessie—why, the very thought sent him into a rage. He threw back the covers and lay there in a sweat.

Brownlow snored peacefully, and Peters finally drifted to sleep, though only briefly, for he was soon startled awake. He shot up in bed, and rubbed his blurry eyes and strained to listen. Were those voices he heard? Yes, he was sure of it! There were men outside! He reached for his glasses and stared out the window though the pitch darkness offered no view. His thoughts were running wild in his head but he knew instinctively that he must be ready for whatever lay ahead, must defend himself at all costs. He moved his hand slowly across the table till he felt the revolver, and taking it, leaped from the bed. His hand was damp with sweat. He worked frantically to grip the gun but his finger slipped and *boom*! He fired. The piercing sound echoed through the room like a cannon blast.

"What was that?" Brownlow yelled. He jumped from the bed and threw himself on the hard floor. "Who in hell is shooting?"

"The window!" Peters yelled. "At the window, there!"

Brownlow jumped to his feet and hid behind the bedpost. From this vantage point, the glow from the gas burner provided just enough light to see through the window and into the dark yard. "There's no one out there," he whispered. "Nothing!" He crawled to the window and rubbed the glass. "You shot a hole through the damned thing!" Brownlow snarled. "What in hell's name are you doing?"

Dr. Peters turned toward the window with his pistol now aimed directly at Brownlow.

"Don't point that gun at me!" he said. "You're insane, man!"

Peters glared through the dark window; the gun shook violently in his hand. "Did you see him? He's out there! He shot at me through the window!" Peters stood against the wall, frozen from fear.

"I said put that damned gun down, now!" Brownlow growled. He stretched up and peered out the window. "Ain't a soul out there, I tell you! There was only *one* shot! And that was from *your* gun!"

Peters would not believe it. "I know what I saw," the doctor said in a shaky voice. "I have excellent vision. I know what I saw, I tell you!"

Brownlow moved a little toward the chair and Peters jumped. "I'm just going to sit," Brownlow said slowly. "Now, if you'll give me the gun, I'll put it back on the bed stand for you."

"No!" Peters replied. "They've vowed to kill me! I must be ready for them!"

"There's no one out there!" Brownlow screamed. "Now, give me that gun before you kill one of us!"

Peters stared out the window at the phantom assassins he believed lurked in the yard. His eyes were wild, crazy with excitement and fear. "I had no choice. My wife is a very attractive woman, and very friendly, perhaps too friendly at times. And then my daughter, Clara—" He covered his face with his hands and shook violently. "Well, she had nothing to do with any of it, I tell you! I did what I had to do," Peters said, looking up at last. "I have no regrets. I would blow his brains out all over again if I had to!"

He waited for a response but Brownlow said nothing. "I need a pass to St. Louis, you see," Peters went on. "But Colonel Truesdale refused me. You must help me! You have connections in the city, don't you?"

"Yes, of course I do," Brownlow said with an air of uncertainty. "But I don't understand—"

"It's my daughter Clara," Peters said. "She's all alone there, and—" He rubbed his sweaty palm against his pants leg and pointed the gun at the window. "You get me the pass. Then I'll give you the gun."

"My father has connections, of course," Brownlow said calmly. "He can get you a pass to St. Louis. I'll see him at first light." He reached slowly out to take the gun from Peters. "You have my word. Just hand me the gun."

Peters focused his bloodshot eyes on Brownlow. Spit had pooled in the corners of his dry mouth. "I think you are an honest man," he finally said, licking his parched lips. "But, let me warn you. If you double cross me—"

"My word is good here," Brownlow said in serious tone. "Just give me the gun."

Peters handed him the gun and sank slowly into the chair. Daylight would come in an hour. The days of no rest were finally taking a toll on him. He nodded off a few times and eventually fell sound asleep.

He was awakened at sunrise by the slamming of the bedroom door. Brownlow stood fully dressed in the doorway, a piece of paper in his hand. "Here is your pass to St. Louis." He walked to the bedside table and picked up the pistol. "I'll just hold onto this till you're ready to leave."

Peters cleared his throat. "Very well," he said sheepishly. "My sincerest apologies if I frightened you last night. It's just that—"

"No need for apologies," Brownlow said. "I'm no man to judge another. Let's just get you on that train to St. Louis."

Peters got dressed quickly and pulled his coat over his shoulders. "I'm much obliged, Mr. Brownlow," he said calmly. "The truth will come out soon and—then, the world will know General Van Dorn left me with no choice."

"I'm sure it will," Brownlow said with a curious smile. "In due time—the truth will rear its ugly head. It always does."

# CHAPTER 25

# A Funeral for a General

*"As we watched the immense procession of soldiers, the hearse drawn by six white horses, its gorgeous array of white and black plumes, that bore the grand casket in which the dead hero lay, we thought with sorrow of the handsome face still in death and the heart-broken wife thus cruelly widowed."*

—Eyewitness account of Van Dorn's funeral

Jessie held the paper closer to the lamp and read the headline: *Private Funeral for General Earl Van Dorn, CSA.*

She closed her eyes. Her stomach rolled; a wave of nausea rose up to her throat and she bent over. She refused to believe he was dead. Earl dead? The entire affair was to her as unreal as the War itself—just an ugly nightmare. She wanted desperately to believe she had nothing to do with his death, that it was George's irrational mind and Clara's selfish actions that put her handsome general in the grave. But at times like this, when she was alone, she wasn't sure of anything. Perhaps Lieutenant Sulivane was right. She heard him say it that night in her house. "Jessie Peters was a temptress, a black widow. She led the general into a viper's den."

They could say what they wished, but she would tell herself the truth every day, as long as it took to convince her heart she was right. George shot the general over *Clara.*

Jessie held the paper to the lamp again. The article was short, from the *Mobile Register*. Such a simple piece and not enough for a general, she thought. She read it through once, and then, as if it might reach the heavens, she read aloud once more for Earl: "After lying in state in Columbia, the remains of General Van Dorn were conveyed by members of his staff and a guard of honor to Rose Hill, the lovely home of his wife's family in Alabama, and there deposited beneath the sighing pines of that State. His little daughter Olivia was the chief mourner visible at his bier, the wife being too much prostrated by grief to leave her room. The general was laid to rest about forty yards from the house, and the exquisite little Olivia, weeping and clinging to the staff officer's hand as she walked to the grave. Based on an account by a high ranking member of the late general's staff, the poor girl was the most charming child at twelve years of age ever before seen."

She laid the paper on the marble table and walked to the bedroom window. A soft morning breeze blew against her face. The silk curtains rustled, breaking the eerie silence of the room. She shuddered and drew her shawl tightly around her shoulders. The sun shone magnificently in the early morning sky, yet the world seemed oddly dark. Jessie began to cry. Her heart felt tight in her chest and she sank to the floor and wrapped herself in the billowing drapes. The fresh spring air, the brilliant sky, even the singing birds were a lie, a pretense meant to trick the grieving soul into smiling again. For now she could not be fooled by it, could not let the past go as if it had never happened. She closed her eyes and let her mind drift back to happier times, to gay parties, and the sweet sounds of music and laughter, dancing, and handsome soldiers in gray coats, a time far in the distant past, gone forever...

*From the Diary of Jessie Peters*

*May 18, 1863*
 *I have no words for my feelings of loss tonight. Poor, poor Earl. I have just read news of his burial in Alabama— of all places. Indeed! He spoke once of his loveless marriage and given Mrs. Van Dorn's absence at his funeral, I can see full well what he meant. Such an unkind, unworthy farewell for a man so full of charm. Goodnight sweet prince.*

\*\*\*

On a bench in the Nashville depot, Dr. Peters sat waiting for the evening train to St. Louis. Atop his head was a brown wool fedora, his coat was an unusual mossy green. His hair was cut short at the neck and his face was clean-shaven. By all appearances, he was an Irish immigrant, a stranger in the land. He opened the *Nashville Daily Union* and read the headlines, scanning each column until he finally found what he was looking for—or rather what he was hoping he would not find. Van Dorn's burial in Alabama was the only mention. For the first time in days, Peters' name was nowhere to be found. The notorious general left behind a grief-stricken wife and children—the details of his death were omitted. Was the Confederate Army ashamed? Or was this omission for the sake of his family?

A whistle blew and a barrage of people, women carrying babies, old men walking on canes, even a group of wounded soldiers, bandaged from head to toe, stampeded the loading platform as the train barreled into the station. A young man in a cropped jacket and knee britches stood on a box near the whistle and called out, "All passengers for St. Louis please prepare to board!"

Dr. Peters rose from the bench and folded the paper. He pulled the fedora over his brow and turned up the collar of his waistcoat. With his head lowered, he joined the line at the base of the platform, pushing his way to the center of the mob. When the conductor took his ticket, Peters looked at the ground, pretending to drop his bag. The conductor passed him by and Peters boarded the train. He was never noticed and slipped with ease into the last car where he sat beside a pretty young girl accompanied by a nanny. He sank into the corner of the seat and listened to the nanny's sweet voice as she sang to the sleepy child, rocking her slowly as the train left the station.

# CHAPTER 26

# ST. LOUIS

**June 1863**

Clara stretched her legs and repositioned herself in the carriage. She had insisted on going to meet her father who was to arrive that morning. A cold rain had fallen steadily, making the ride from the train station very uncomfortable in the tiny carriage. The wool shawl her Uncle Tom Peters had given her to place over her legs was nearly soaked through, so she bundled it into a pile and laid it on the floor of the carriage.

The driver turned in his seat and glanced at her. He was a burly black man with gray hair and a long gray beard, and large white teeth like a horse.

"Miserable day, isn't it, Henry?" Dr. Peters asked as he settled himself in the carriage.

"Yassir," Henry said. "It sho is that."

The train whistle blew and Clara jumped in her seat. Dr. Peters put his arm around her and pulled her close to him. "Don't worry so," he said reassuringly. "I'm here now. We'll be fine in St. Louis."

"But father," she replied. "You don't know anything for sure. Why, the general's men could be right in front of us and we wouldn't even know!"

"You must trust me, Clara," he said taking her hand in his. "We're safe here. I've arranged for your protection. You must believe me."

"But," she began. "What about the child?"

Dr. Peters slammed his fist against the hard carriage seat. "You must never speak of it! Do you understand? This has all been a bad dream, Clara! When your time comes, we will take care of everything and put it behind us, forever!"

Clara blinked back a tear and sat up in the seat. The rain had stopped for the moment though distant thunder warned of more to come. Henry stepped down and walked to the front of a long line of carriages.

"Clara, you must be rational," Peters said. "You cannot possibly think—"

But Clara was no longer listening as she stared out the window of the carriage. "Look, father." She pointed to a young woman standing at the platform, her two young children clinging to her skirt. Two burly men slid open the heavy train car door. Inside were several soldiers, all in full military dress, who bent over all at once and in perfect unison, lifted a wooden box into the air. The young woman walked closer to the open door and covered her face with a white handkerchief. The soldiers carried the box slowly down the steps and onto the platform. They placed the box on the ground at the young woman's feet and handed her what appeared to be a uniform and boots. The children pulled at her skirt, their innocent voices echoing, "Papa! Where is papa?" But the young woman never spoke. She took the children's hands and followed close behind the soldiers as they lifted the box again and placed it in the back of a rough wooden cart. A boy around twelve-years-old came out of the station and helped the young woman into the wagon. Then he took his place in the driver's seat, cracked the whip, and drove the old cart out of the yard and onto the muddy road.

Clara turned away and wiped her eyes. "Poor young girl. Already a widow, and those little children now fatherless. Oh, father! What have I done?" She covered her face with her gloved hands as the tears streamed down her cheeks. "I am to blame for everything!"

Peters put his arms around her. "There, there," he whispered. "That simply isn't true, Clara. You're a child yourself, dear. This is not your fault."

"And you, Father," she said, sobbing loudly. "You've committed an unforgivable sin, and all because of me!"

Peters grabbed her by the shoulders and turned her to face him. "Clara, you mustn't say such things! You must never think any of this was our doing! You were the victim of an evil man, and I did what I had to do. God knows that, Clara! God knows that!"

But Clara only sobbed harder, an uncontrollable, gut-wrenching cry, as they rode out of the station and onto the streets of St. Louis.

\*\*\*

Their carriage arrived at the home of Trusten Polk within the hour. Polk was on the run, fighting to stay one step ahead of the Missouri Unionists who now wanted his head. But his wife Elizabeth had stayed behind, stubbornly refusing to leave her home.

Henry helped the doctor carry the sleeping Clara into the house and Elizabeth led them down the hallway and into a tiny room filled with trunks and mounds of paper—Trusten's papers she explained. She pulled the covers back as Henry and Dr. Peters lay Clara in a small bed in the corner of the room.

"Is Clara not well?" Elizabeth asked.

"Exhausted," Peters replied. "Exhausted from the trip is all."

"They want us out of here," Elizabeth whispered. "I'm afraid they may come any day."

"Who?" Peters asked. "Surely there are some good people of Missouri who still stand behind you? My God, Elizabeth, Trusten was once their Governor."

"Oh, that's no matter to them now. The good folks are gone from here. All that's left are cold-hearted Yankees hell bent on ridding the state of any semblance of the South—mainly anyone who bears the Polk name."

She turned up the lamp and Peters saw the deep lines at the corners of her once bright eyes. A large crevice had formed in the middle of her forehead. It seemed the War had affected everyone, even the beautiful Elizabeth.

"You know," she said. "We are the last Polks in St. Louis. Everyone else has been driven out." She turned to Peters and shook her head. "To think our very neighbors would turn against us is simply unimaginable. They've even accused Mary and Anna of espionage and aiding the enemy! The very idea! My own daughters!"

"But Trusten won't allow it," Peters said. "Certainly he won't take such abuse."

"Trusten fears they will arrest us if we don't leave soon," she said, her voice now angry. "We leave for Arkansas first thing in the morning. Trusten went ahead of us to make sure the house was still standing. It's just a nightmare, George!" She turned away from him and began to cry.

Peters put his arm around her. "Elizabeth," he said. "Don't worry. I promise to keep you safe until you're ready to leave. But you must be honest with me about Clara. Is St. Louis where we should be? Is this school you spoke of a safe place for her?"

She took out a small lace handkerchief and dried her eyes. "Yes, it's the best place for her right now. I sent my own girls there, you know. The nuns are good souls." Clara stirred in the bed and Elizabeth motioned toward the door. "Let's let her rest now."

They walked out and closed the door behind them. Henry had gone into the parlor and was busy rolling one of the rugs they intended taking with them. The remainder of their furniture they would leave behind in the boarded-up house until their return. This was the first time Peters had truly understood the gravity of the situation. The Polks were leaving St. Louis, perhaps for good. He wondered now if coming there had been a wise decision. They simply had no alternative. Tennessee was no longer safe.

"I plan to take Clara to the school in the morning. Will you come along with us?"

"Yes," Mrs. Polk replied. "I'd be happy to ride out with you and introduce you to the sisters. They'll be so happy to have a girl like Clara."

Peters smiled awkwardly. He had not wanted to discuss the murder or Van Dorn or anything about the last few weeks, but he had to know the truth. "Are you sure," he asked hesitantly, "that they'll want her with all that has happened?" He had hoped to avoid the conversation, but now it was out. The Polks held a firm hatred for Jessie, so Peters felt confident they were on his side. They would blame Jessie for involving Clara in her sordid affairs, this he knew for certain. But he was still unsure how they felt about the murder. He waited patiently for her answer.

"I have spoken with Sister Maria, and she is more than happy to have Clara as a student. They are not in the business of judging, George," she said reassuringly.

Peters sighed with relief. "That's wonderful news, Elizabeth." He reached for her hand, but she drew back.

"George," she began. "Is it true about Jessie? What was said in the papers?"

Peters looked away with a pained expression. "Yes, Elizabeth, it is true," he said with a sigh. "I did what I had to do—what any decent man would do."

Elizabeth cocked her head and raised her eyebrows. "Then Clara was not harmed? The papers spoke of misconduct between the general and Jessie—but there was mention of the daughter. And Trusten—well, he sent word awhile back that—"

Peters looked at the ground. He had no intentions of going into everything, had never even considered telling Elizabeth or any other family member for that matter. Only if necessary, if the pregnancy proved viable. When Clara's condition could no longer be hidden, then and only then had he any plans of revealing the truth. "Well, there was some—uh, Elizabeth," he said in a low voice, "It is true that the general's affections were not just for Jessie."

Elizabeth gasped and covered her mouth with her handkerchief. "No, George," she said. "Tell me she wasn't—"

Peters closed the parlor door. "No, nothing as bad as—" He struggled to find the words. He simply could not say it, not now. "Even I don't know everything. Not yet at least." He took her hand. "Elizabeth, I need your word that you will keep this to yourself. For Clara's sake, you understand."

"Of course I will, George," she answered.

"My only concern is for her safety right now," he said. "I'm a wanted man, Elizabeth. Clara is not safe with me.

But at the convent—well, are you certain she'll be completely welcome?"

"Rest easy," Elizabeth said. "The sisters will take good care of Clara." She patted his hand gently. "Don't you worry. The young are resilient. In time she'll forget any of this ever happened. In time, we'll all forget."

He mustered a smile and tried to hide his nervousness. He hated lying to Elizabeth, but he had no choice. His biggest worry now was how to best handle Jessie. He had hoped to bring her and the children here as well. The guilt of leaving them in Tennessee had become quite unbearable, but he was certain Elizabeth would want no part of that—no part of the vile Jessie Peters. Elizabeth loathed her, as did all of the Polks, had hated her since the first affair occurred, had begged him to let Jessie go. But he refused to leave her, and soon after Jessie was expecting the first child. Then, after the second one came along, Peters said he could not possibly divorce her, would not lower himself to desert a wife and young children. So, he busied himself with his medical practice and ran for public office. Once he was elected to the House of Representatives and was away most of the time, Jessie seemed happy. It had been the perfect arrangement, or so he thought. Now with everything that had transpired, he knew Jessie would never be welcome. He would handle Clara first.

"I know you'll help me protect Clara. And for that you are dear to my heart," he replied. "I truly hope Clara—well, that all of us get through this, Elizabeth."

The door opened suddenly and Clara stood before them, her dark eyes were bloodshot and swollen. "I heard you talking, Father. Where am I going? What school?"

Elizabeth walked over to Clara and kissed her on the cheek. "Clara, dear. It's the best school in all the state. My girls attended there. Why, all of the best families, both North and South, send their daughters there."

Utter despair shone in her face. "I didn't think I would be here that long, Father," she said weakly. "Do you think it's a good idea? Do you think they know about—" She stopped suddenly.

Sensing the tension, Elizabeth turned to go. "I'll go make us some tea," she said leaving. "I'll let you two have some time to talk it over."

When the door closed behind her, Peters grabbed Clara by the shoulders and sat her on the piano bench. "You must listen, Clara. The sisters are happy to have you, happy to help. It's best this way, dear—for now."

"I see," Clara said, looking at the floor. "And what about—" She bit her lip and looked at him, her once bright eyes were clouded with tears. "Oh, Father!" she cried. "Won't they know soon?"

"Clara," Peters whispered. "We'll deal with that *if* and when it is necessary. Until then, you will do as I've said. You must remain here."

"And what if there is a child? Do I leave then?" she asked.

Peters fell silent. He looked into her eyes and knew she would not accept his answer—not now. He would have to wait until it was all over, then he could make arrangements as he saw fit. "In time, dear. All in due time. One day, this will all be just a bad dream."

### From the Diary of Jessie Peters

*June 21, 1863*

*I have just received a letter from George—quite unexpectedly, I might add. The letter offers no clues as to his location, only that he is safe and out of the South. I suppose he is in St. Louis where he sent Clara. At no time does he offer any explanation for the accusations he made against me—at no time does he beg forgiveness for ruining my good name. He should stay there forever. And Clara— well, she is the reason for all of this in the first place. He says that Clara is despondent as any victim would be and has taken up with the Catholics. I'm not at all surprised that she would find comfort among a sect of people who believe a quick confession and a handful of "Hail Mary's" will cleanse the soul. O, the devil is at work here! How long will George continue to listen to her vicious lies while I suffer at the hands of every gossip in the country? If I could get my hands on Clara, I'd string her up myself! That's the only justice for her!*

*I would have burned George's letter right away but I had to keep reading when I saw Thomas' name. I am quite saddened by this news. It seems the poor boy is worse than before and may not live through the summer. I must admit I have a soft spot for Tom. He's so like myself, having lost his dear mother so young. He is a handsome fellow too with a very agreeable charm that would work quite well for him if he could only shake this sickness. I will say a prayer for his full recovery, and then I will pray that when he does get well that he chooses to live far away from George and Clara.*

# CHAPTER 27

# AWOL

**Fall, 1863**

Jem brought the newspaper in and laid it on the small table beside Thomas' bed. "This a new one," he announced proudly. "Took a long time to git it."

Thomas smiled. "Good work, Jem. I can always depend on you."

Since early August, they had been isolated there at the plantation, cut off from the rest of the world except for an occasional deserter lost in the swampy bayou. On the last visit to Memphis, the doctors told Thomas he seemed to be improving and sent him home to rest. Per Dr. Peters' request, they agreed to travel to Council Bend once or twice a month to bring an ointment or perform a treatment. They were always friendly, but Thomas knew they only tended him for the money. His father was paying them plenty. The kind doctors couldn't afford to say no.

Thomas turned over in bed and picked up the paper. The date at the top read September 15, 1863, just two weeks earlier. He was pleased at this since he had heard nothing substantial about the fighting since Vicksburg fell in July. This had crushed him. Had he been well enough, he'd have shot General Grant himself—right between the eyes. And when news of Gettysburg came, Thomas wondered if he might ever get the chance to fight again. He wasn't sure why, but something still burned in him, urged him on to battle, though he didn't thirst for glory like so many. He guessed the longing to fight stemmed from his sickness and the guilt he felt at being absent from his unit, or maybe it sprung from the gaping hole in his pride. Whatever the cause, he wished he could feel like all the other men who had chosen to stay out of the War—men like his father. They felt no remorse.

Thomas opened the notebook in which he kept a log of Union troop movements and scribbled the battles on a crude map he had drawn. From his calculations, the Yankees could win if they took the railroad towns in Tennessee and Alabama. This would cut off the Confederate supply line for good and the War would be over. Hell, maybe that would be the best thing for all of them.

He picked up another newspaper and thumbed through the war news. "Damned lying bastards," he grumbled, spitting on the floor. Newspapers told nothing more than embellished reports of Yankee successes and bands of Southern infidels. He never believed any of the stories, unless the correspondent used statistics from official army reports, and even those tended to be inflated. He had been away from the fighting so long now that he could only imagine the bloody battles and miserable nights in camp. Still, he read all he could, in a desperate search for news of his division. They were in the vicinity of Chattanooga, this much he knew, but he had heard nothing significant in weeks. When he reached the last page of the paper, he mumbled again, "Nothing in here either. Guess Polk's laying low."

He closed his eyes and laid the paper back down on the bed. *Absent without leave.* Those words burned his tongue like poison. The guilt of deserting had proven more painful than the syphilis that wrecked his body, but he had not the strength to ask for mercy. Dying was preferable to the explanations he would be forced to serve up in a court martial hearing—if he was given such a luxury. Deserters weren't treated kindly. *But he had not deserted.* He was sick, a victim of a wretched disease. If only he could make himself believe that.

Jem pulled back the curtains and poured a glass of water. "Might drink sumpin, now," he said, his big hands spread out across the lip of the glass.

The bright October sun blanketed the dingy room and Thomas covered his eyes. He preferred the darkness since the last attack of fever and chills came on. He had only seen daylight once in nearly three weeks. Thomas took the glass, but his weak and shaky hands caused him to spill most of it. He sipped what little was left in the glass and closed his eyes again.

Nine months had passed since he left his Company back in Shelbyville, Tennessee. He made his way first to Memphis, but Yankee occupation there forced him to hole up in the townhome of an old Bolivar family friend while he received treatment from a group of local doctors. His prognosis was not good then, though the doctors said little about it. He must keep his spirits up, they told him. But his body ached with the fevers that came on every few weeks and his skin had become so sensitive that he could not bear the slightest touch. When the doctors informed him they had done all they could, he left for Arkansas. *Time,* they said. *Time is the only remedy—if you can be cured.* That was April, a few short weeks before his father had killed a Confederate general. He had to remind himself of this when their friends called them all traitors, Yankee lovers. His father had not lied. Killing Van Dorn had been his only option.

Jem took his seat on a long cherry wood bench at the foot of the bed. "I'm listening," he said, slapping his knee. "Ain't you gone read?"

Thomas smiled at him. Jem loved hearing about the crazy generals and their bad decisions on the battlefield. He and Jem would sit and talk for hours about strategies they would have used if they were in charge. Thomas enjoyed their little game as much as Jem did; without this, he had no connection to the War at all. Thomas blinked and tried to focus on the words again. A thin film had formed over the right eye and he rubbed it till it felt raw.

Jem pulled a small table over and brought the lamp closer. "Now," he said, "this here oughten to help you see."

"Yes," Thomas replied, turning the page. "This'll do fine."

He started on page two and read through to the last line of the last page. Nothing substantial in this paper, unless bad news was what you wanted. It seemed the Yankees were winning in every corner of the Confederacy. If winter would only come, then maybe the men could rest, and when the New Year came, they could rally for a big win in Virginia or Georgia. By that time he hoped to be well enough to join up with his unit, if they still wanted him.

Jem got up and opened the window. He stood looking out as a cool breeze blew across his shiny face and across the bed, rustling the paper as Thomas lay back against the ornate headboard, a pillow doubled over and stuck behind his neck. They were listening to Jem's old hound as he barked at something in the front yard when a knock sounded at the front door.

Jem squinted his eyes and cocked his head. "Humm," he said softly. "Wonder who dat is? You 'spectin' somebody?"

"No, you?" Thomas' head was pounding again so he closed his eyes and pulled the blanket over his face to shut out the light from the window. "Well, go see who it is."

Jem walked to the foyer and opened the front door. Thomas moved the pillow just enough to hear the familiar voice of Maxey Davenport, an ornery old man who owned a thousand acres of Crittendon County. He was so greedy it was said he would cheat the devil if he could own a piece of hell. Dr. Peters loved the old man.

Soon, Jem entered the bedroom with Maxey Davenport close behind. "Says he gots a letter for you. Says I can't gives it to you." Jem turned and gave old Maxey a scowl. "Says he gotta do it hisself."

Thomas rose up on his elbows and rubbed his eyes into focus. "A letter? Who's it from?"

The old man approached the bed and leaned down to look at Thomas. "That's right," he said. "A soldier, name was Falconer I believe it was. He rode over on the ferry with me and when we struck up a conversation about the war, he mentioned he missed his home a great deal. Well, I said to him 'where you from boy?' and he said 'from Bolivar, Tennessee.' Then I told him I knew another soldier from that area. When I said your name, well he almost jumped off the ferry. Said he had a letter for you that he hadn't been able to deliver. So, I told him I'd bring it out to you since you lived right down the way from my place." He fingered the letter in his calloused hand. "And so here I am, a man of my word."

Thomas lifted himself to sit straight against the headboard again and held out his hand, but the old man did not move. He just stood there, his eyes darting side to side. Thomas gave him a hard look and moved himself to the side of the bed. "Well," Thomas said, his voice weak but serious. "You gonna give it to me, or do you want something for your trouble."

The old man didn't budge. "No, young man, I don't want nothing for my troubles, unless you want to give me the truth. Is it like they say, that you're hiding out so your own unit don't gun you down? Hidin' like your daddy?" He chuckled under his breath.

Thomas was wide awake now, his heart pounding in his chest. "What'd you say?" He looked at the table and the shelf on the wall. Where was the pistol? Then he remembered. He left his back in Memphis. There had been little time to send for his belongings.

"Some folks say there's a nice reward for Doc Peters," he said rubbing his chin. He wore a sidepiece strung low on his outer leg, and it was common knowledge he carried a knife in his right boot.

Thomas threw one leg over the bed. He was unsteady, a little dizzy, but his instincts told him he better at least appear to be well enough to defend himself. Davenport was old. It would be difficult for him to draw quickly. Still, the old man had spunk, and Thomas knew he must not let his guard down for one moment. The only possible weapon in the room was the poker leaning against the fireplace. He would have to strike hard and fast. He moved toward it, but his arms still felt heavy as lead. A movement by the open window caught his eye and he looked up as Jem gave him a slight nod. Thomas nodded in return. Jem would take care of this one.

Davenport was standing firm as an oak, the letter clinched in his large wrinkled hand, when Jem pounced on him with the iron poker. He held it high above the old man's head.

"Now, you tell your boy here to put that thing down!" Davenport cowered beneath the towering Jem. "I ain't aiming to fight nobody, just wanted to know is all. Ain't a man got a right to know who his neighbors really are?"

Thomas clinched his teeth. "My father had no choice. He was forced to protect the honor of his home!"

Jem took another step toward the old man and raised the poker as if to strike.

"Tell your boy here to back off," he said. "I ain't looking for trouble." Jem backed up and Davenport tossed the letter on the bed. "You'd be wise to listen. It ain't smart sneaking around like you got something to hide. Folks is curious about who's living in their own backyards." He turned toward the door. "Best tell your daddy to steer clear of folks around here."

Thomas watched the old man walk out the door. Jem followed seconds behind him and locked the front door as Thomas watched out the window until the Davenport buggy was clear of the drive. When Jem returned to the bedroom, Thomas was reading the letter. "Says I better send surgeon's certificates or something to explain my absence."

Jem shook his head. "Means we got to go on back to Memphis then, don't it?"

"Says I might want to consider transferring to another unit when I return. The boys don't want to fight alongside me." Thomas tossed the letter on the bed. The verdict was in. The Confederate Army had cast him aside. He lay back against the pillow. Maybe he would be better off dead.

Jem leaned over the bed and whispered, "Mista Tom."

Thomas opened one eye and stared blankly at Jem.

"I can go fetch them doctors in Memphis and bring'em over here."

Thomas raised his eyebrows in thought. The trip across the river would set him back, just like last time, and he would go through all of it again, the sleepless nights of fevers, the agonizing pain that not even laudanum could touch. The breeze coming in the window had picked back up and brought with it the smell of sweet olive blooms. Thomas breathed deep, the scent of his mother, of life years ago, before Jessie and the War. He must get better. He did not want to die like this. "All right, then," he said. "I'll write a letter asking them to come to Council Bend." He rubbed his forehead. "They'll want payment up front, you know."

Jem nodded and shook his head. "Yassir, they'll want they money. Reckon where we can find some?"

Thomas got out of bed and went to his writing desk. He rifled through the drawers but only found ten dollars—Confederate dollars. "This won't do," he said pacing the floor in front of the open window.

"I can fetch Doc Peters," Jem said with a smile.

Thomas stopped his pacing and sat down at the desk. He must at least try to get that surgeon's certificate if only for the peace of mind that *someone* in the Confederate Army knew the truth about him. "The ferry goes out again at dusk," Thomas said. "You can take a letter to Memphis and then ride down to Coahoma. Father should be there by now."

Jem smiled at him. "Sho, don't you worry none. I'll take care of it. You can trust ol' Jem."

Thomas tucked the letter in his brown leather satchel and handed it to Jem. Then he dragged his heavy legs back to the comfort of the bed and the cool quilt. He listened as Jem saddled his horse and galloped away toward the river. The trip would take four days at best. For the first time since his mother was laid in the ground, Thomas felt utterly alone, deserted by all who knew him, loved by none. He pulled the blanket over his face and melted into the pillow. From somewhere in the distance he thought he heard the faint coo of a dove. At times like these, death seemed a welcome visitor.

## From the Diary of Jessie Peters

*October 1863*

*Received a letter from Marsh Polk this morning and was so happy to find at least a few old friends still care about my welfare. Poor fellow—this war has taken his leg (and his spine)—figuratively speaking. That Eva treats him horribly to say the least. Why he puts up with it is beyond my understanding. I know if I were a man, I would never be treated so poorly by a woman—especially one like Eva. Perhaps she should be reminded that she is the lucky one in that marriage. Had Marsh not come along, I dare say ugly Eva would still be sitting in her parlor with her head in a book. Of all the Polk men, he is the most handsome one. If I had Marsh, I would handle him quite differently indeed.*

*Though Marsh's letter was welcome relief from my loneliness, it was nonetheless very disheartening, and I find myself once again in a state of anxiety. So much has happened lately that I fear the end of the War might come as early as tomorrow. I pray that is not to be since the South has suffered so many losses that I don't see how we could possibly be victorious at present. Surely our boys will regain their strength and forge ahead. I pray for this every day. And as if that were not enough dark and gloomy news, Marsh went on to say that Thomas has failed to secure proper leave from the army and will subsequently be charged with desertion. O, how my heart does break for the poor boy. It seems trouble follows him wherever he goes. Of course, I have written Marsh that I will go to him myself if need be, though I doubt it would be wise for me to travel into Memphis at present. Nevertheless, I will do all I can to help Thomas—even if he is a Peters.*

*Perhaps most troubling, were Marsh's questions concerning Clara. I must admit I'm a bit confused by them. He asked of her <u>condition</u> and I fear what he may mean by that word. Certainly I am wrong, but I do plan to write to Elizabeth Polk. She will certainly answer any questions I may have, even if she cares little for me. I cannot imagine George would keep me in the dark if Clara is indeed in that way. Why, certainly he does not think he can hide a thing such as that. I should ruin her with it if it is true! I will tell* *the world how she tricked a Confederate General and led him to his death. O, I pray I was not so blind as that! Earl, speak to me! Give me some sign! Tell me that I was not a fool!*

# CHAPTER 28

# THOMAS RESIGNS

*Army of Tenn.*
*Oct. 23, 1863*
*No board is necessary. This officer is absent without leave. He*
*can be gotten rid of by Genl. order No. 15 current series.*
    —BY COMMAND OF GENERAL BRAGG, KINLOCH FALCONER, A. A. GENL.

The Arthur place was a sprawling plantation in Coahoma County, Mississippi, situated in the middle of the lush delta farmland. Pidge Arthur had written her uncle George weeks earlier, begging him to come see her. She was alone on the place with her small children and her sister Beck. Though he hated to leave Thomas alone in Council Bend, the Texas Cavalry had made another threat against his life and he had no choice but to stay on the move. He had been in Coahoma now for a little over ten days, but in that short period of time the Confederate Cavalry had moved into northeastern Mississippi and he knew he would have to move yet again. He lived in constant fear of the Texans and for good reason. They were known to be men of their words, always following through on a threat.

As soon as he was alerted that a visitor was coming, Peters rode down to the bend in the road about a mile from the house. Jem was waiting there, flashing a broad smile, and talking incessantly about how he was sure thankful to see a familiar face. The War had changed things so, he felt like he was in another country. He told Peters about the letter from Captain Scott. Without a surgeon's certificate, Thomas would face court-martial.

Jem carried the brown satchel and walked to the porch. He sat down on the bottom step and put a plug of tobacco in his cheek.

"Is it Thomas?" Pidge Arthur asked in a weak voice. She stood on the top step and looked down at him, her hand covering her mouth in anticipation of his answer.

"Yessum," Jem replied, "but it ain't like you think. He's needin' to git a letter from them Memphis doctors and they ain't wantin' to give us one, dat's all."

"Then he is no worse?"

"I can't rightly say, but Doc Peters' gots to come talk wif the Memphis doctors and git the letter. They's trying to give'em a court-martial if he don't come on back. Says he's gots to have a letter to prove he ain't well enough, then they'll leave him be."

Peters sighed. He had begged Thomas to resign his position in early spring when the symptoms came back in late February; instead, he requested only a month's leave. Thomas never returned. "Marsh Polk sent word a week ago that Captain Scott had reported him absent without leave. Charges are inevitable."

"What can you do, Uncle George?" Pidge asked.

Peters walked to the edge of the porch and stood quietly. It was risky for him to be seen in Memphis, but he had to do something. "I must get that certificate," he said. "We'd better get going if we're to make the city by dark."

\*\*\*

By early afternoon, they were on the road heading north into Memphis. A glassy-eyed Jem slid off the back of his mare twice before they cleared the drive. He had been awake going on a full day now and could barely keep his eyes open. Peters rode ahead, nervously watching every movement in the brush and every rider who passed them on the road.

They reached Memphis late in the evening and went directly to the red brick building on Monroe Street. The lanterns cast an eerie orange glow across the porch so that

Jem looked the color of melted chocolate when he stood in the shadows of the flickering light.

Dr. Peters knocked on the large black door. The brick townhome was an unusual deep red color and was positioned between two large white wooden structures, giving it a striking appearance on the dull gray street. To the right of the door was a wooden placard that read *Taylor and Williams, Medical Doctors*. It swung back and forth in the gentle breeze blowing in from the Mississippi River. After a few minutes, Dr. Peters knocked again. A skinny black woman peeked through the transom. She was dressed in all black with a white wrap tied around her head.

She opened the door just enough to see and asked in a squeaky voice, "If you needin' Doc, he busy with guests at present."

"Well," Peters said. He pushed gently on the door till he could just see inside. "As a matter of fact, I do. I need a surgeon's certificate for my son. He was a patient of Dr. Williams."

She grunted under her breath and closed the door, leaving him alone on the porch. A whistle came from below as a one-legged man called his dog, a mangy, emaciated animal that shook when it walked. He cursed the dog and poked at his ribs with his walking stick as he ascended the steps. "Beg pardon," he said as he passed Peters on the steps. The man entered the house and slammed the door with his cane.

Dr. Peters shook his head in disbelief. He was not one for waiting and knocked on the door with all his might. The skinny black woman reappeared. This time she wore a red wrap on her head and her skirts were layered in red silk. Inside the house, several men and women dressed in evening attire, milled about as the sound of a piano and harp drifted through the adjacent parlor and into the quiet street.

Peters peeked inside. "Dr. George Peters," he said, removing his hat. "As I said earlier, I'd like to see Dr. Williams, or Dr. Taylor, please."

"He's inside with his compny," she replied with a scowl. "But, you can come on in while I git him."

Peters stepped inside and the skinny woman closed the door and disappeared down the hall. A group of men emerged soon after and greeted Dr. Peters in the foyer. They apologized for the wait and asked that he follow them into the study.

"What can we do for you, Dr. Peters?" Dr. Williams asked.

"Is your son in need of recuperation time, or is his plan to resign altogether?" a young doctor asked. "Seems like most are resigning lately. Can't take the thought of defeat."

The room grew silent. "He is ill," Peters said. "My son is no coward."

The elder Dr. Taylor spoke up quickly, changing the subject to his new supply of Scotch whiskey and directing the company of men to the sideboard where he poured a glass for each of them. He shuffled through his desk until he found papers detailing Thomas' treatment. "This seems to be what we're looking for. Now, if each of you would kindly read the diagnosis."

The doctors added the necessary information as Dr. Peters gave them details of Thomas' current condition. Then, one by one they signed the bottom of the letter. "Here," Dr. Williams said, handing the letter to Peters. "This should be sufficient."

Peters took the letter and held out his hand. "I am forever indebted, sir. I will see to it you are well compensated."

The men followed Peters to the door where he thanked them again and apologized for his haste. Time is of the essence, he explained. Jem stood up when the door opened and followed Peters down the stairs and onto the long brick walk. When they reached the end of the dusty Memphis street, Peters stopped under the lamplight and read the letter:

*Memphis, Tenn.*
*October 24, 1863*
*We the undersigned practicing physicians of the city of Memphis certify on honor that Lieut. Thomas Peters formerly of Scott's Battery, Army of Tenn., a young man 21 years of age called on us this day to consult us*

*relative to the state of his health. He has been laboring under intermittent fever for several months past, at this time occurring daily. His health is likewise suffering from disease of the genital system requiring medical treatment and probably a surgical operation. In view of the actual condition of his health, and the intense mental anxiety under which he labors, we are of opinion that he should be relieved of duty by resignation, or by furlough, until his health can be restored.*

*M. Taylor, M .D.*

*Albert Taylor, M. D.*

*John Williams, M. D.*

This would do, Peters thought, as he stuffed the letter in his bag. Now to the Goyosa Hotel, a popular Memphis establishment and a favorite among the soldiers. He was sure to find a courier willing to deliver a message to M. T. Polk, who was rumored to be in Meridian. Polk could write a statement attesting to Thomas' condition. A surgeon's certificate and a personal note from Polk himself would certainly satisfy the Confederate Army.

When they arrived at the Goyosa, Jem took the horses to the livery stable while Peters mingled with the patrons in the hotel lobby, casually inquiring of any man needing to make a dollar. After an hour or so, he found a courier willing to ride to Meridian and back.

"Be glad to do it," the young man said. "But, it'll cost ya. Ain't exactly a joy ride, ya know?"

"I'll pay," Peters said firmly. "Half now and the other half when you make it back with the letter."

The young man frowned and kicked a clod of dirt from his boot. "I don't much like doing business with a stranger," he said at last. "But, I reckon I ain't got much choice in the matter."

"Good, then," Peters said handing him the money. "Deliver this to Lieutenant Colonel Polk, and to no one else. Do you understand? My man Jem will be here to get the letter when you return. You can ask for him at the livery stable."

When the courier left, Peters gave Jem final instructions. "When the letter arrives, take it at once to the station and give it to old man Banks. Tell him there's good pay for him if he brings it out to Coahoma."

"Yassir," Jem said.

"When you get that done, head back to Council Bend. I don't like leaving Thomas alone for too long," Peters said as he mounted his horse. "Tell him not to worry. He'll be a civilian again in no time."

# CHAPTER 29

# THE CAPTURE OF DR. GEORGE PETERS

Next evening, Peters left for Coahoma. He traveled through the backcountry; hat pulled low, a drab wool coat across his shoulders, and arrived after a few days of rough riding. Having eluded Van Dorn's men for nearly six months now, he was more confident than ever. If he could just get an honorable discharge for Thomas, then he could rest. The only remaining obstacle was Clara.

"Tell me, Uncle," Pidge Arthur asked as she ran to meet him on the front steps. "How is Thomas? Will they release him from the army?"

"Thomas will recover," he said. "We'll all feel better if Marsh can help with the discharge." He held tight to the banister of the front porch steps and crept to the top. Fatigue and emotional distress had taken hold of him. He needed rest but there simply was no time. "I'm riding to Mound City on Monday to handle some business. From there I'm going back to St. Louis. I'm taking Thomas with me. I believe he'll fare better in the Missouri climate. And then there's Clara, of course."

Pidge hesitated. "Will Clara remain at the Catholic school? Or will they allow such—"

"Clara is," he stuttered. "Well, she's faring well enough." He sighed heavily and sat down on the top step of the porch, dropping down hard as one burdened with a heavy load. He lowered his head.

Pidge sat beside him and put her hand on his coat sleeve. "Clara will be just fine," she said. "She's a strong girl. When this is all over, she can come back home and go on with her life. No one need know a thing other than she went away for her own safety."

He put his arm around her. "You're a blessing, Pidge. I don't know what I'd do without your undying love and support. Family's all a man has in this world."

"You're so right, Uncle George," she said helping him up. "Family will always be with you, though friends may change as the wind."

"Yes, I suppose you're right." He tightened his jaw as the sadness crept up his face. "A man's family *is* worth more than any worldly treasure."

"Come on, Uncle," she said lifting him by the arm. "You're surely tired from the ride. Come inside and rest. There's someone else here to see you." She tugged on his sleeve until he finally stood up and reluctantly followed her.

"Uncle George!" Beck exclaimed as they entered the parlor. She stood on her toes and kissed his cheek. "I'm so happy you're well." She reached into the pocket of her gingham skirt and pulled out two crumpled envelopes. "Letters for you," she said, placing them on the marble game table in the center of the parlor. "Mr. Banks brought them out this morning." She leaned in and whispered, "He says you owe him a pretty penny for his troubles." She giggled. "I do think that man's the devil himself!"

Peters looked at the first envelope. In the upper left corner was the highly recognizable scroll of Marsh Polk. He put his hand on his heart. "Thank God," he whispered. When this War was over, he would remember friends like Polk. He took a seat by the large front window and read the letter.

> *Respectfully forwarded:*
> *I know unofficially the condition of Lieut. Peters. His health is ruined & he is now in Arkansas unable to move. I have no doubt he has sent forward certificates but they have not reached us. If he can be relieved from duty—honorably it would be better for him & when the*

*Board is convened I respectfully request that evidence of his gallantry in the field & his strict and cheerful attention to his duties be considered. I deem it proper to state that my knowledge of his condition is derived from my former home in West Tennessee & was sent out from there by our cavalry men in a letter earnestly calling my attention to his condition & asking me to have him released from the service so that his relatives can get him home to nurse him. From my own knowledge of his condition, I am sure he will never recover & it would be proper to have him at least die at home, and he will not consent to return unless he is honorably relieved.*
    *M. T. Polk, Lt. Col. Polk's Corp*

Pidge came back into the parlor with a tray of hot tea and buttered biscuits. She placed the tray of biscuits in the center of the marble table and brought a cup of tea to her uncle. "Drink this," she said, smiling. "And eat a bite. You'll feel better if you do."

"Thank you," Peters said, sipping the warm tea. He drank slowly, letting the bittersweet flavor linger on his tongue. "I'll just be a moment. I have a bit more to read." He smiled at them and took up the second letter. The handwriting was familiar but the left corner was empty. It was addressed simply *Dr. George Peters.* He tore the envelope and the scent of lilac emerged from within the folded paper. Jessie! He got up and walked to the window, turning his back to his nieces. He was not ready for any questions, not now, not with all of the unanswered questions with Clara and Thomas. Nothing in his life was clear.

"A game of hearts will cheer us all," Pidge said as she arranged a deck of cards on the table. "What do you say, Uncle George? Will you join us in a quick game? It'll make the time go faster. We could all use a little fun, don't you think!"

Peters turned and waved his hand. "Yes, of course. Just give me a few more minutes and I'll join you." A feeling of suspense overwhelmed him. He unfolded the letter and held it in the light. The delicate scroll wound like ivy across the paper. He could see her, sitting to write at the small cherry desk in the parlor, her pen poised to shape each poisonous word.

>*Dr. Peters,*
>
>*Let me first say that I am most appalled at your treatment of me. I am your wife, after all, yet you dare to treat me as a common harlot. You do amaze me! And mark my words—you will pay—one day, whether it is on earth or in Hell, but you will pay.*
>
>*You should know that I was quite relieved to read of your escape. After all, you cannot suffer as I do if you are dead, and oh, how I wish you to suffer. Not that I wish you any physical harm, but knowing you must pay for your sins, I just assume it will be easier on Judgment Day if you pay a little as you go. Still, no manner of revenge can ever equal the pain and suffering you have caused me—the betrayal, the lies! You must know by now that I will not stand by and accept the blame for your crime. I know the truth, George. As I've said before, the children shall bear the sins of the father... May God have mercy on Clara's soul.*
>
>*I have heard that you plan to remain in St. Louis permanently, and I hope that is true. I do not wish to hear from you or see your face—ever again. Above all else, I cannot forgive, and I will never forget. As for myself, well I plan to go on as if you never existed. Lucy Mary and William will remain in my care, as for little George, Jr.—well, I think it's wise that he remains in Bolivar for now. I will retain ownership of my land and home here in Spring Hill, and you may do as you wish with all other properties. A sufficient amount of money will be necessary for me to survive. You may forward it care of my sister Mrs. Nathaniel Cheairs at Rippavilla.*
>
>*Jessie*

He folded the letter and stuffed it inside his coat pocket. How he wished she were dead in that grave with the general! He may tell himself he had really never loved Jessie, still he couldn't help feeling hurt. A thousand thoughts ran through his brain—hatred, fear, jealousy, and rage... He stared out the window. Was this to be his life from now on? On the run, paranoid, despised? The evening sky cast a pall over the delta landscape, a heavy darkness that lay across his soul like the weight of winter, of loss, of death.

Beck brought out a tray with four small glasses and a decanter of brandy and placed it on the round marble table beside the piano. She poured drinks for everyone and sat at the piano with Pidge, who tapped out a repertoire of lively tunes. Peters tried to look happy and took his seat at the card table.

"How about a game of two-card Monte?" Pidge asked coming to sit beside him. "Uncle George, won't you play?" She gently patted his hand. "You just seem so awfully sad is all."

"Oh, come now! Such a fuss! I'm not all that bad, am I?" Peters asked. "Of course I can play a hand. But first, how about another glass of brandy, dear?" He pushed his glass to the edge of the table.

Beck jumped from the piano bench. "Uncle," she said in a sweet voice. "You really must cheer up. Remember, the Lord never gives a man more than he can bear." She walked to the sideboard and reached for the brandy decanter. "We would all do well to remember those words," she said gripping the neck of the decanter. "Why, just the other day—oh my!" She screamed and pointed at the window. "Look! Someone's out there!"

Peters bolted to the window and peered out. The lamplight was just enough to reveal a soldier dressed in gray with a long rifle in his hand. "I see him," Peters said, edging out of sight. "Get back."

Pidge jumped up at once and ran to the corner of the parlor where a gun sat propped against the sideboard. "Uncle George!" she yelled as she shouldered the shotgun. "You will be careful, won't you?"

Peters checked his holsters. Were both pistols loaded? He would have to take his chances. He approached the door and slid one pistol into his right hand, holding it just behind his right hip as he slowly opened the front door.

The soldier had just made his way up the steps and removed his hat. "Beg pardon, sir," he said, holding out his hand. "Lieutenant Dan Alley, here."

Peters didn't move. One hand was on the doorknob, the other still holding the pistol. "Yes," Peters said nervously. "What is it?"

"We're with Company G, under command of General W. H. Jackson. We're scouting out homes in the area where a few of our men might get a night's rest. We won't bother you for more than a bed or two." Suddenly another soldier emerged from the dark yard and joined Lieutenant Alley on the porch.

Pidge stepped forward and gently pushed Peters out of the door. "We have a house full, as you can see." She smiled and motioned around the room. "But I'm sure we can put up a few men in the cabin out back. Won't you come in?" She opened the door wide and motioned for the men to come inside. They were hesitant until Pidge insisted they come in from the chilly night air. "It's not good to be out in the weather all the time, especially when there's a warm fire just inside." She led the soldiers into the parlor. "I'll just gather up some blankets. You wait here. It'll just take me a few minutes," she said, disappearing down the hallway.

"Much obliged, ma'am," Lieutenant Alley said. He kicked the other soldier who took his hat off and mumbled something.

Beck smiled at the men and returned to her chair. She picked up her cards and motioned for Peters to join her. "Uncle George," she said, "come sit back down. We'll just see who wins this time!" She took his hand and giggled. "I'll take two cards, please."

Peters returned to his chair and pretended to play the card game. How did Jackson's men end up out here? He was sure they would recognize him if he gave them the chance, so he turned his back to them and held his cards high in the air. "Go on," he said teasingly. "It's your turn, Beck."

"Oh, Uncle George!" she said. "You're surely going to let me win, aren't you?" She giggled again.

The soldiers had been whispering in the corner of the parlor when Lieutenant Alley suddenly spoke up. "Could we trouble you for a cup of water, ma'am?"

"Why, certainly," Beck answered. She smiled sweetly and walked to the sideboard where she poured two glasses of water and took them to the waiting soldiers.

Lieutenant Alley thanked her and whispered something to his companion. "If you'll excuse us, we're going back and let our commanding officer know we've found a place for the night. Much obliged, ma'am." He placed his hat on his head and turned to the door.

"Wait!" Pidge yelled as she came back in the room. "I've got some blankets and things. I think this will be sufficient." She placed the heavy patchwork quilts on the settee in the foyer.

"Thanks again, ma'am," Lieutenant Alley said as he opened the door. "We'll be back before too long. If it's all right with you, ma'am, I'll just get those blankets when we return."

"Well, certainly," Pidge said. "We're happy to help."

Peters watched the soldiers until they were out of sight and then he returned to the card game. "Always makes me a bit nervous when soldiers come around," he said gulping the glass of brandy. "Can't be too careful. Loyalty for Van Dorn runs deep—I'm just a murdering civilian to them."

"Why, that's absurd!" Beck said in her usual stern voice. "You had *no* choice but to take care of business. Even Van Dorn's own men knew the truth!"

Peters nodded and smiled. She was wrong. The Texas Cavalry wanted him dead, *not* alive. And for all he knew, so did every other soldier in the Confederate army.

"Well, let's not think bad thoughts tonight," Pidge said dealing a hand of cards. "Let's just be thankful we are together."

"Yes," Beck said. "Let's do just that!" She took her place at the piano and tapped out a light-hearted version of "God Save the South," and followed that with a lively rendition of "The Bonnie Blue Flag."

Pidge sang loudly and danced a circle around Peters until he conceded and joined her. For the first time in weeks, he felt at ease as he let the music carry him back to the happy days of years past, back when his children were young and trouble had not yet found him. But as always, the reverie was short lived when a knock sounded at the front door. The soldiers were back. Instinctively, Peters jumped out of sight.

Pidge let go of her uncle's hand and walked quickly to the foyer. "Well, that was a fast trip," she said as she opened the door. "You're just in time. We're just about to sing 'The Yellow Rose of Texas'."

Instinctively, Peters had taken cover, positioning himself behind the parlor door and watched through the opening as five more soldiers entered and posted themselves casually against the arched doorway leading into the parlor. Peters counted them as they came through the door. Did all of these men plan to stay in the cabin? In one bed? He studied their faces. They didn't appear suspicious. Maybe this was a customary hardship of the soldier. Suppose anything beat sleeping on the cold ground.

"Well, don't let me stop you," Alley said. "By all means, play."

Peters watched him carefully. His demeanor seemed different, his voice tense.

Beck returned to the piano and began to play while Pidge and Ann sang along. The soldiers smiled and clapped in tune as they trickled into the parlor, one by one.

Peters walked casually to the window, watching the soldiers closely, trying to hide his nervousness. They seemed interested in nothing but spending a nice evening in the company of his nieces. Maybe he was just paranoid. He walked to the sideboard to pour another glass of brandy, unstrapped his holster and placed the pistols on a velvet settee in the corner of the room.

When the music stopped, without warning, a dark-haired soldier stepped forward and held his rifle out. "George Peters?" he said. "I don't think we've had the pleasure of meeting. Name's Boster, Sergeant Boster, of the 6th Texas Cavalry. *General Van Dorn's* cavalry." He pointed the rifle at Peter's chest. "Don't make a move. You're under arrest."

The room grew suddenly quiet. Beck's hands were frozen on the piano keys. Pidge let out a gasp and collapsed back on the bench beside her sister.

Peters calmly set his glass down and turned on his heels to face them. He tried to appear unmoved, confident,

but he was suddenly unsure of himself. He could try for
the rifle in the corner of the room, but what if they did
shoot him, and in front of his nieces?

"Stop right there!" Sergeant Boster said. "Don't make a
move or I'll shoot!" He motioned for the others and the
group surrounded Peters while Boster walked over to the
settee and picked up the doctor's holster. Inside were two
polished Smith and Wesson revolvers. "I'll just hold on to
these awhile," he said.

"Why, this is an outrage!" Peters yelled. "Where's that
lieutenant? The one who was here earlier."

"Back at camp," one of the soldiers answered. "He's
sending word to Meridian as we speak." His excitement
was awkward, almost comical. "Got ourselves a murderer!
Yessir!"

"Well," Peters said, his voice shaking in anger. "I
demand to see your commander at once."

The soldiers started laughing, "Yea, boys. We got ourselves a wanted man."

"It isn't right," Peters said. "I demand answers! On what
grounds am I being arrested?"

The soldiers laughed again but Boster held his hand up
and silenced them. "You know damned well why," he said.
He held the pistols in the air and looked them over
carefully. "Is this the one you used to kill the general?"

Peters slammed his fist into the settee. He must not let
them see his fear. "I demand to see your commander at
once!"

The soldiers moved in and pointed the tips of their rifles
at his shoulders then a bearded private shoved the tip of
his rifle under Peters' chin. "Ain't none of us supposed to
let you out of our sight. You'll see somebody when we got a
mind to let you. So, you best keep it down or we might just
have to put a bullet 'tween your eyes."

"We can send our man," Pidge said, leaping from the
piano bench. "If you'll just put those guns down. We can
send Willie for your lieutenant and then we can straighten
out this whole misunderstanding."

Sergeant Boster smiled. "All right, then. Send your
man, if that's what you want to do. We're camped down by
the creek just outside of town." Boster laughed and

smacked Peters playfully on the back. "You ain't gettin' any royal treatment from the lieutenant, if that's what you're thinking. Hell, he'll want first shot at you soon as he gets word."

Peters looked away. Better keep quiet, especially around these men. Their eyes were hungry, and he knew any explanation he offered would fall on deaf ears. Oh, they had orders to guard him and bring him in alive, but he knew the truth. They'd shoot him the second nobody was looking.

Willie was brought up from the barn and Boster gave him his instructions. "Tell the pickets you're bringing a message for Lieutenant Alley, and tell'em it's from me. And don't do nothing funny. They won't mind shootin' you. Hell, they might just shoot you for fun!"

Willie looked pleadingly at Peters. "Reckon I ought to go, Doc?"

"You have to," Peters said. "They won't shoot you if you do as you're told. Take the message and return as fast as you can."

"Yassir," Willie said, dragging himself out the door. "But, I don't likes it one bit."

When Willie was out the door and his shuffling, reluctant footsteps had faded, Peters seated himself at the small desk in the corner. He must be smart. There was no time for fear. He must handle this situation with precise care. His very life depended on it.

The soldiers stood awkwardly around Peters, staring at him, then pretending to guard him, then staring him down again, until they grew tired and laid out in various places around the parlor, on the rugs, on the settee, one even sat on the piano bench and tried his hand at tapping out what sounded like a hymn. Some talked quietly, trying hard to stay awake, while a toothless old soldier took a liking to Pidge and sat smiling at her, wringing his dirty hands like a young boy at his first dance.

For the remainder of the night, Peters scribbled feverishly at the desk. First, he penned a brief declaration of his innocence, which he would give to Sergeant Boster, and then he wrote a short letter to M. T. Polk, a plea for help which he folded and secretly slipped into Pidge's hand when she brought him a cup of warm tea.

In the early morning hours, Willie returned with Lieutenant Alley. "Dr. George Peters," the lieutenant said with an authoritative air. "You are under arrest for the murder of General Earl Van Dorn and are hereby ordered at once to the headquarters of General W. H. Jackson in Jackson, Mississippi."

Peters turned to his nieces who started to cry. "Don't worry," he whispered. "Remember Marsh. He's in Meridian." He pointed to Pidge's apron where she had tucked the note he gave her. "He'll know what to do."

"But Uncle George," Beck cried. "What will they do to you?"

"Don't worry," Peters answered. "I'll be fine. Soon the whole army will know the truth."

The lieutenant took Peters by the arm and led him out the door. "Get going, Doc. You can tell it to the judge."

# CHAPTER 30

# PETERS AND THE TEXAS CAVALRY

*Meridian, November 13, 1863*
*General Seddon,*
   *Our cavalry has arrested and sent in the murderer of Major-General Van Dorn, a citizen. What course can be taken? There are no courts for us in Tennessee.*
                                        —GENL J. E. JOHNSTON

By mid-morning, the rain came down in sheets like a million sharp knives, the chilly November wind driving the cold drops through their thin cotton coats. The soldiers pulled their hats low and wound strips of old wool blankets around their faces and necks to shield them from the biting cold rain. The weather was unusually harsh for November, but they had to push on if they were to make Jackson, Mississippi, and General Jackson's headquarters.

Peters rode in silence, nervously watching his captors' every move as they trudged through the muddy Mississippi delta. If his letter got to Marsh Polk in time, then he might just make it out alive. This was his only hope. "Marsh Polk will be awaiting my arrival," Peters reminded the soldiers. "I think it would be in your best interest to deliver me to headquarters in one piece."

"Sounds like a threat, Peters," Sergeant Boster replied. "I wouldn't be threatening nobody, if I was you. Anything can happen out here in the middle of a war." He cut his eyes at Peters. "Your money and your name ain't worth a plug nickel to the Confederate Army."

The soldiers all laughed. "I'd give a month's pay to put a bullet in him myself," one man shouted from the rear of the line.

Lieutenant Dan Alley dropped back and rode alongside Peters and soon began to make small talk with the doctor. But Peters was reluctant to speak. They would trick him into saying something, would twist his words. He would give them nothing.

"Folks say you ain't a supporter," Alley said. "That you ain't nothing but a traitor—and maybe even a Yankee spy."

"Well, that is a *lie.*" Peters snapped. "I support the Confederacy! I have two sons fighting for you, for God's sake!"

"But what of *your* allegiance, huh?" Alley asked. He turned to face Peters. "Is it a lie you signed a Yankee oath? Swore to be faithful to murderin' Yankee scum!"

Peters looked away. No use trying to explain his actions. Men like Alley had no idea what it meant to lose money and land. Most of them had nothing to begin with. They just wanted to fight the Yankees, the negro-loving, pasty-skin, cur dog Yankees. They wanted their war and they got it. Damn them all!

Lieutenant Alley remained still, waiting for his answer. "Well?" He spit over his shoulder. "Are you a damn Yankee-lover or not?"

"I signed an oath out of necessity!" Peters shot back. "Why, hundreds of Southerners have been forced to do so. My allegiance had nothing to do with General Van Dorn. He got what he deserved! If you were any kind of decent man, you'd admit I was right to kill him! You'd have done the same! Have him do to your wives and daughters what he—"

The soldiers in the front of the line stopped abruptly and turned around as Peters' voice echoed down the narrow dirt road. One man yelled back, "Shut that man up! Or I'll come back there and shoot him myself!"

Lieutenant Alley grimaced and dropped behind the doctor. "You just stay quiet. You'll have your chance to talk soon enough."

Peters shook his head. They were all fools. The whole army knew about Van Dorn's womanizing. Yet his fate was likely sealed. He must be cautious. They would kill him if they had the chance and he had just given them one. He had to find a way to make them listen, to make them walk in his shoes. "It's my wife, you see," he began apologetically. The soldiers turned and looked at him, their eyes like wolves. "It could have been any man and I would have done the same thing. On my honor!"

"Go on, then," Alley said, pulling his horse back to a trot. "Tell us about that wife of yours." He smiled and waved at the other men to gather round. Several stopped and circled around Peters. "Reckon you tell us all about that pretty Mrs. Peters. I hear she's a real looker." The whole line broke out in laughter.

Peters shook with rage, his hands felt lifeless from the long ride but he knew he must not show any weakness. They would surely have him then. Besides, who were these bastards to ask him such a question, to insult a man of his stature? Why, it was too much to bear. He looked away and took a deep breath. "That's a personal matter, gentlemen. But since the matter does involve one of your own, I'm sure you expect an explanation." He set his jaw and gripped the saddle hard. Must not let them see his shaking hands. "I understand. And seeing how I am a man of integrity, it is only fitting that I oblige you. Let me first say that it was common knowledge around our little town that your general was quite familiar with my wife. He was seen alone with her on numerous occasions, taking buggy rides, visiting my home. Any man knows, that's a breeding ground for trouble —at least, any man with integrity and class. Well, I am sure as gentlemen you don't want to hear it all."

"Yeah we do!" yelled a young soldier from the rear of the line. "Tell us all about it! We ain't had no woman or heard about no woman in a coon's age! Make him tell it, Lieutenant!"

Others yelled throughout the line, begged to hear the sordid details, what he saw, what that wife of his looked like. Wasn't she a pretty, young thing? Peters was caught. Surrounded by hungry faces waiting to hear the dirty truth.

"Tell us and maybe we'll let her do us some favors in trade for your head!" a young soldier hollered.

Peters looked at Lieutenant Alley for support. Alley was a Texan, but he had a decent way about him and seemed a gentleman, one who would not allow such behavior in his men.

"All right then, Dr. Peters," Alley laughed. "Go on and tell us why you *had* to kill *our* General. The boys say they want to hear it all! Why don't you just tell it?"

"Why, you know yourself!" Peters said, glaring at the lieutenant. He had sorely misjudged him. "You certainly don't want me to tell—"

"Oh, yeah we do!" Alley shockingly replied. "We ain't worried about the general's ways, we already know he had an eye for the ladies. Only problem is, it was your wife who chased after the general, your wife who got him caught in your web. Reckon you tell us what that wife wanted with the general? Huh?" Laughter broke out down the line. "Go on," he insisted.

"If he don't talk, let's cut off his ears!" the men yelled.

Peters was suddenly dizzy, his head was spinning from the laughter and the smell of wet horses; the stench of unbathed bodies and filthy uniforms permeated his skin. He reeled in his saddle but caught himself just before he hit ground.

Lieutenant Alley held up his hand to quiet the men. "Shhh," he said. "Let the doctor tell us the *truth* and maybe we'll take him in without a scratch."

Peters stared out at the mob of grimy faces, their eyes ravenous. His heart beat so loud it drowned out their voices. He was sure the men all heard it, smelled his fear. "My wife is a good deal younger than me," he said nervously. "And she had been alone for some long months when the army arrived."

The men waited like children at Christmas, their brows furrowed in suspense, their jaws set.

Peters cleared his throat. "And she is a rather beautiful woman, very young, very willful."

"Sounds like a wildcat!" a soldier yelled. "I like 'em like that!"

The soldiers laughed again and Lieutenant Alley waved his hand to quiet them. "Cut it out!" he yelled. "Let the doctor tell his story. Hell, he might give you something to dream on tonight!"

Peters was furious. He shook his head in disbelief and turned suddenly toward Lieutenant Alley. "I'll not tolerate such talk, I tell you!"

"Oh, yea you will!" Alley said. "Just keep talking."

But his patience had worn thin. They could shoot him if they liked, but he would not yield to their base insults. "I've told you all I am going to tell you. If you want more, well you'll just have to—" All eyes grew wide with anticipation and the soldiers leaned toward Peters. "You must understand," he said. "She was angry with me and thought to hurt me." He stopped and clamped his mouth. He could not say it. All eyes were locked on him, all ears waited for the rest of the story. "But it was the general! It was Van Dorn—not my wife! It wasn't her doing! He forced himself in her bedroom!"

A soldier yelled from somewhere within the sea of uniforms, "And then what?" Then a roar of laughter followed, rising like waves in a choppy sea.

Peters threw his fist up in anger. "My wife was—is vulnerable!" His voice was shaking uncontrollably now. "And your General took advantage of that! He went to my house at all hours of the night and saw my wife! And she was alone there, with no one save the little children! And my daughter Clara!" He darted his head around as the dirty, laughing faces of the soldiers converged on him all at once. "My daughter Clara—she was there too," he went on, a pained look on his face, "and your general was *no* gentleman!"

The laughter ceased. "Ain't nobody said General Van Dorn messed with no daughter," came a voice from somewhere in the swirling crowd of scornful faces.

Peters wiped his brow and fanned himself. He felt weak and clammy, his eyes lost focus as the sunlight coming through the trees suddenly disappeared, replaced by an eerie green darkness. For a second, he felt the saddle move under him and he tightened his grip. "Jessie," he said, "and Clara, and all those damn soldiers on the place—" He spoke, though he had no sense of it. His body felt like a puppet on a string, controlled by some great hand.

The soldiers watched silently as Peters swayed in the saddle, words tumbling from his mouth. "I caught him that first time in the middle of the night. It was raining and I came in the house and there he was—sitting in the parlor. And she was practically in his lap." Peters pointed as if he was back in that room, standing face to face with the general. "Well, he jumped to his feet and grabbed his hat. But I came toward him and he bolted toward the door. I yelled for him to stop but he ran out. My pistol was in my hand by now, I believe." He paused a moment and tilted his head as if recalling a dream. "Yes, I remember now. I followed him onto the porch and watched him scramble for a hiding spot. I yelled for him to come out and when he didn't, I grabbed him by the hair and pulled him out myself!" His voice grew louder still. "Come out or I'll blow your brains out!' I told him!"

"That's a goddamned lie!" yelled a burly soldier in a brown felt hat. "I ain't heard that before. Ain't nobody ever said nothing like that to Buck Van Dorn. At least ain't no man ever lived to tell it! I guarantee that!"

But Peters was back in the parlor now, back at the moment he knew he would have to kill. He rambled on like a crazy man, spitting the words out like balls of fire on the tip of his tongue. "He was drunk and when I reached under the porch to grab him, he moaned and begged me to let him go. He said he had a wife and children back home— that he had no intentions of losing them." He swayed in the saddle once again. Sweat dripped from his brow and burned his eyes, but he couldn't stop. "But I saw him, I tell you! With my wife and my daughter—my Clara." He stopped as if shocked back to reality. "No," he mumbled. But his strength was gone. His eyes rolled back and he slid sideways out of his saddle and onto the muddy ground below. He fell in slow motion, his legs like molasses, his hands unable to catch him.

The soldiers watched unmoved as he slid off and hit the hard ground with a thud. "Help him up," Lieutenant Alley said. "That's enough." But no one moved. A young soldier, the newest member of the Texas corps, got off his horse and walked over to the crumpled body. The boy looked to be about eleven and wore a Confederate uniform several sizes too large. A rope held his britches in place and his soiled white shirt was ragged at the bottom. He tapped on Peters' shoulder a few times.

At last he came to and sat up, dazed and pale. "Thank you, son," he whispered, his voice barely audible.

"Ain't no bother, mister," the young boy replied. "Reckon I ought to be kind to you since they're surely gonna hang you when we get to Jackson."

## From the Diary of Jessie Peters

*November 24, 1863*

*I was quite shocked this morning when I received a note from my sister Susan. She was feeling a bit under the weather and did not come to visit but instead sent word by her man that George has been captured. She was unusually upset and begged that I contact General Polk to help at once. I don't know why she cares so much—indeed! She's never liked George any more than I have. I suppose she still thinks to keep me married and out of her hair. Well, I say to the devil with all of them! I have no desire to help George even the slightest. Since he has seen fit to desert me and the children; he is not worthy of my sympathies. It's only justice, I say.*

# CHAPTER 31

# A MURDERER SET FREE

*Dr. Peters, who killed Van Dorn, has been captured by rebels at his plantation in Mississippi; said he had been desirous of getting back to Dixie and stand trial.*
—NASHVILLE DAILY UNION, 2 DECEMBER 1863.

After arriving in the burned out capitol city of Jackson, Mississippi, the detail received word from General Seddon for the Texans to take Dr. Peters to Meridian, Mississippi. Two weeks had passed since that fateful night at his niece's plantation, and now in these last days of November, Peters would finally be given his day in court. William Kilpatrick, a successful lawyer-turned military judge, was to preside over the hearing. He was a Mississippian, a friend of the Confederacy. His reputation as a fair and honest man preceded him. Ironically, he had been a staunch critic of General Van Dorn during the Vicksburg Campaign—a fact that offered Peters a glimmer of hope.

Peters had heard nothing from Marsh Polk but he refused to give up hope. Somehow the powerful Polk family would come through for him. They had been there in the past. He had no doubt they would do so again.

A young soldier on guard at the courthouse came for Dr. Peters around 8:00 that morning. He tripped over the basket sitting just outside the door and cursed loudly. Inside was a cold biscuit with a slice of ham—the doctor's breakfast. The soldier filled a rusty tin cup with black coffee and handed it to the doctor.

"Drink up," he said smiling. "They're ready for you."

Peters gave him a quizzical look. "Now?" he asked. "But I have no lawyer present."

"Don't know nothing 'bout that," the soldier replied. "All's I know is they said bring you to the courthouse."

"Well, that was not the way I was told we were going to do this," Peters snapped. "I was explicitly told we would—"

"Ain't no need to tell me. Save that for the folks waiting on you. I ain't got nothing to do with running the court." He spit on the floor near the doctor's feet. "Besides, I wouldn't make too much fuss if I was you. I don't reckon there's too many folks give a good damn what you say." The soldier laughed.

Peters dug out a biscuit and tossed the basket on the floor at the soldier's feet. The biscuit was cold but he ate it anyway and threw the ham to the hound dog stretched out in the hallway of the boarding house. The dog belonged to the lady who owned the place. "Devil doctor," she called him and gave him such awful looks when she brought his supper each night that he felt sure she meant to poison him. When she brought breakfast that morning, she stopped and laughed. "Your time done come Yankee lover!"

Peters smiled as the dog licked up the slice of ham and swallowed it whole. He almost wished he had time yet to watch the old hound die. He put on his jacket and smoothed out his trousers. His clothes were dusty and wrinkled, but after the first few days he became unconcerned about appearances—staying alive was his only objective. He picked up his crumpled hat and worked the creases till they were straight again then placed it lightly on his head. Time to face the executioner.

The stately courthouse was quickly filling with locals curious to see the "cuckolded doctor." They pointed and whispered as Peters and the young soldier marched across the wide dirt street and onto the brick sidewalk. The front door was guarded by two old men in Confederate uniforms who looked like two stone statues. The young soldier saluted them when he started up the steps and the two old men returned the gesture, though they moved so slowly that Peters and the soldier were forced to stop momentarily until they had completed the salute.

"Morning, sonny boy," the old guard said. "And who have you got here?"

"This here is Dr. George Peters." The young soldier threw his shoulders back and raised his head in the air as he spoke. "Killer of General Earl Van Dorn of the CSA."

The old man stared at the soldier. "Who'd ya say?"

The soldier leaned in and whispered to them, and then as if struck by lightning, they said in unison, "Oh, well now. Is that right?"

"Yessir, this here is the very killer hisself." The soldier beamed with pride as he led the doctor into the foyer and up the stairs to the judge's chambers. Peters scanned the rooms as they passed. Still no Marsh Polk. He sighed and shook his head. This was not good at all.

The soldier ushered him into the chamber and walked Peters to a table with two chairs. "Sit here," he said.

"George," a familiar voice called.

Peters scanned the room in every direction when he noticed a gaunt figure standing near the judge's chair. "Marsh!" Peters said, gasping with relief. His appearance was so shockingly changed that the doctor had not recognized him at first. "Man, it's good to see you! I thought you might never come! That I would be—"

"Keep quiet!" a voice boomed from behind a wood partition in the far corner of the room. "Quiet in the courtroom!"

Marsh Polk joined him at a small table in the corner of the room. "You don't look so good," he said. "Have they treated you badly? You let me know and I'll see something is done about it. You have my word."

"No worse than I would've expected," Peters answered. "Just get me out of here. That's the only justice I want."

"Yes, exactly," Polk replied. He brought out a notebook and turned to a clean page. "Tell me George, what would you have me say in your defense? And make it good. These men mean business. I don't think I have to tell you that."

"Why, my defense is the truth, of course," Peters said, trying desperately to look away as Polk repositioned his leg, an oddly unnatural-looking stick of wood.

"Yes," Polk replied, "and what is the *truth*?"

Polk had served early on in the war as a military court judge and knew full well the procedures of the court. Peters had such hopes that they would pull it off, but Polk seemed detached, jittery.

"I don't understand, Marsh," Peters said. "Well, I felt sure Eva had told you. She knows everything."

Polk looked down at the table. "Eva?" he asked with a hint of sadness. "What would Eva tell me? I haven't been home—uh, haven't seen her since my accident, you know?"

"I see," Peters replied. Eva Polk was a cold wife. Folks in Bolivar pitied Marsh Polk—everyone except Peters who figured any man who put up with a difficult woman got exactly what he deserved. She demanded perfection and Marsh Polk could never measure up. Now that he was half a man, he would surely disappoint. "But, now you are faring well enough, I see."

"Well as can be, I suppose," Polk said as he reached down to rub the leg of his trousers. "Some days it feels like my leg is still there, like I don't have this awkward wooden appendage."

Peters smiled reassuringly. "It's not so bad, Marsh. May as well accept it. The faster you get accustomed to it, the better off you'll be. At least you are alive, agree?"

"Yea, I suppose you're right." Polk talked slowly, as if pondering the very words. "I might get used to it one day, to having a piece of me gone. But Eva, well I'm not sure she's got it in her, you know?"

Peters tried desperately to appear sympathetic, but the truth was the leg was gone, and he saw no use in pining over it. Marsh was too soft, that's all there was to say. That part worried him. Perhaps he wasn't the best choice for his defense. "I'm sure in time she will adjust," Peters went on. "But as I was saying, I was sure she told you about the letter—Clara's letter. She wrote to Eva awhile back about, uh." He stopped and looked over his shoulder, still whispering though the closest man was seated halfway across the room. "Her condition." There—he said it.

Polk tilted his head and raised an eyebrow. "No, George, I don't know anything about a letter."

Peters leaned in closer to Polk. "About her condition, Marsh. About the general—"

Polk's eyes grew wide. "I had only heard rumors, but I never believed any of it. Surely, you don't mean that—"

Peters grabbed his hand in desperation. "You must tell them for me, Marsh. They will believe you. Your name carries much weight in the army."

Polk shook his head. "I'm not the one to speak."

"But, you have to tell them this!" Peters demanded. "They'll hang me, Marsh. If I don't give them this."

Polk grabbed his shoulder and pulled him closer. "What are you saying, George? That it *wasn't* Jessie? Are you saying it was General Van Dorn and *Clara*?"

"Yes," Peters whispered. "That's exactly what I'm saying."

"But, George!" Polk jumped up, nearly toppling his chair. "Do you have proof? I mean, are you planning to make a public statement—about Clara?"

Peters grabbed Polk by the sleeve and pulled him back down to his chair. "That's exactly what I don't want. That's why *you* are going to present the facts as such based on *your* good name alone. I will give them a written statement and they will give me their word as gentlemen to protect my daughter's reputation."

"But you can't possibly think they'll take me on my word alone."

"My daughter was an innocent victim!" Peters exclaimed, his lips quivering. "She will not be hurt more by the very system meant to protect her!"

All heads turned toward Peters.

Polk tore a blank page from his notebook. "We better hurry," he said. "Write your statement—tell them *everything*. I'll have them read it before we convene."

One of the old guards entered the room and changed into a black jacket. He introduced himself as the court clerk and then left the room again. Moments later he reentered, this time he was leading a man in a long black robe. The old clerk banged a gavel on the table and cleared his throat. "Court will now come to order. The honorable Judge William Kilpatrick, presiding."

"Lieutenant Polk," Judge Kilpatrick said. "To what do we owe the honor of your presence today?"

Polk approached Kilpatrick and shook his hand. "Good to see you, sir," Polk began. "On behalf of Dr. George Peters, the accused, I submit the following statement from the defendant." Polk leaned in and whispered. "We respectfully ask that you read this statement quietly. It contains some very delicate personal information as you may well imagine."

Judge Kilpatrick looked at Polk and laughed. "Well, what have you got up your sleeve on this one, Lieutenant Polk?"

Polk returned the smile. He liked Kilpatrick, respected him as a fellow Confederate. "Nothing but the truth, Your Honor. We only ask that you read the statement and consider the facts as such. I say again, facts. I am vouching for them personally, on my honor."

Kilpatrick eyed him suspiciously then took the paper and reached for his glasses. He read for a moment and then set the paper on the table. "Come with me, Lieutenant." Polk followed the judge into the anteroom.

While Peters waited alone at the table, he leaned back to hear what the officers in the rear of the room were saying. Peter's heart was beating wildly. What if he refused to believe it—what if this Kilpatrick wanted revenge as the others? This may be the end.

When the two emerged from the anteroom, Judge Kilpatrick called Peters to the table. "If your statement is true, Dr. Peters, and I have no reason to doubt the word of Lieutenant Polk, I have no recourse but to release you." His beady eyes narrowed as if searching for the truth in the doctor's face. "The delicacy of this case is such that your statement will remain sealed for the time being. But let me just say, Dr. Peters, I think it's in your best interest to get on out of Dixie. Some folks might not agree with my decision."

Peters' heart was near bursting. He shook the judge's hand wildly. "I can't thank you enough, sir. I knew you were an honest man."

Kilpatrick smirked. "Don't be so quick, Peters. It ain't over yet. Just make sure you're headed out of town by dark. I can't guarantee your safety if you hang around."

The old clerk stood and slammed the gavel one last time and Peters was released. Marsh Polk escorted him out of the courthouse and back to his room where he gathered his belongings quickly, eager to leave as soon as possible.

"I can't thank you enough, Marsh," Peters said as they stood outside waiting for the carriage. "The Polks and Peters go back a long way. I never forget a friend. If you should ever need anything."

Polk frowned and looked at the crutch shoved under his arm. "I don't think there's much you can do for me, George. But, hell, maybe they'll at least call me a hero. Who knows, right?"

Peters shook his head. "Maybe they will, Marsh."

Polk seemed suddenly embarrassed. "I apologize, George. I don't know what's got into me. Guess I'm feeling a bit sorry for myself." He blushed at his own revelation. "Enough about me. Tell me, what will you do now? Where will you go?"

"St. Louis," Peters said. "For Clara, you know. Maybe soon she can put this nightmare behind her. Maybe in time *we'll* all put it behind us." Peters tried to look convincing but he knew his fear showed.

"What about Jessie..." Polk asked hesitantly. "Will she go?"

Peters put his hand up. "I can't say. I may never—"

"I understand," Polk said. "I didn't mean to pry."

Peters smiled and shook his hand. "Not at all. Best wishes to you, Marsh. I am truly indebted to you."

Tomorrow he would be in St. Louis. Maybe then he could think more clearly. For now he had no answers, had no plan, but to keep Clara hidden and safe. He only hoped she would listen to reason when the time came. She must never see the child. That much he had decided. That was the only way. She must leave the past far behind her. Forever.

### From the Diary of Jessie Peters

*January 10, 1864*

*After months of silence, George has written me at last, though I wish he had never put pen to paper since what he told me has broken my heart entirely. Clara will bring her bastard child into the world a short time from now! I can no longer deny the past now that living, breathing proof will soon exist that my general was not as I believed. It is an awful reality that I'm loath to accept as yet.*

*I find it quite peculiar that George has waited so many months to write to me and even more peculiar that he would dare ask me to bring the children and join him in St. Louis. He claims the general's men are still hunting him and that we should leave Spring Hill for our safety. I think it more likely for his protection than ours. Perhaps he believes he is safer if we are present. I personally believe none of it. I think he is alone in his misery and cannot take it another day. George was never one for handling situations, especially where Clara is concerned. I believe he is perhaps one of the weakest men I have ever known. He may beg night and day, but I'll not lift one finger to help either of them. As far as I'm concerned, both George and Clara equally betrayed me. Let them suffer for their sins—alone.*

*10 p.m. – I had an unexpected visit from General Forrest and three members of his staff earlier this evening. We had a very agreeable time though I had little information to share. General Forrest is quite charming and handsome, as is his adjutant Major Strange. They have promised to stop by again when they are back this way as they are off tomorrow for the eastern part of the state. I hope they return soon—I feel much safer with soldiers near.*

# CHAPTER 32

# MEDORA WHARTON PETERS

**January 26, 1864**

"Give it to me," he said. "Wrap it in that thick blanket. There's no time to talk now."

Annelle did as he said and handed him the bundle. "I think you should consider Clara, Dr. Peters," she begged. "It isn't right."

He tucked the bundle inside his heavy coat and opened the bedroom door. "You will *never* speak of this night. Do you understand?"

"Of course," Annelle said in a frightened voice. "You have my word. I only—"

Dr. Peters silenced her with a finger to his mouth. He carried the bundle out the back door of the house and ducked down behind the sweet olive bush. A black carriage moved slowly toward him, its driver cursing as he struggled against the bitter January wind. He stopped just under the shadow of the full moon. The street was empty except for the small black carriage. Peters hurried from his hiding place. The driver looked nervously around and climbed down.

"Cold night," the driver said, clutching the neck of his dark wool coat as he climbed down from the seat. He looked behind him and then stepped onto the sidewalk. "You Dr. George Peters?"

A sudden wave of paranoia swept over him and he stopped under the shadow of a large cedar tree. "Where's Mrs. Berry? I was told to expect a Mrs. Berry."

"Yes," the man replied. "She's right there in the buggy." He moved closer to Peters and held out his hand. "Watkins," the man replied. "I'll assume you're Dr. Peter. Glad to meet you. I'm from over at St. Ann's Orphanage."

Peters shook his head. "Yes," he said, nervously clinging to the bundle in his arms. "And did you say this Mrs. Berry is in the buggy?"

"Yes," a woman's voice called out from inside the carriage. She opened the door and a strip of light from the full moon shone across her face. She was younger than he thought, maybe forty.

"You must take it now," Peters said anxiously. "I must hurry back."

Mrs. Berry scowled at him and motioned to the driver. "Very well," she said. "Put it in the basket."

The driver held out a round willow basket and Peters quickly placed the child inside.

"Did the mother of the child—" A sudden gust of wind blew up and Mrs. Berry pulled her head back inside the carriage. "Was it as you expected? Did she not make it?"

The wind came again and Peters shook violently. "She didn't," he lied.

"So sorry to hear that," her voice cut off. "Poor girl."

"Yes," he said, and for a moment he believed it too. *What a shame.*

"And the father?"

"Dead."

"I see." She tilted her head questioningly. "When is it you plan to settle things, Dr. Peters?" Mrs. Berry asked, suddenly cold. "You do plan to provide for the child, don't you?"

"Yes, of course. I'm sure you understand—this is a very precarious situation." A light in the foyer caught his eye and he grew anxious. What if Clara heard? "I must get back at once! I'll come speak with you in a few days. Until then, you have the facilities to handle it yourself. It will be worth your while, Mrs. Berry. That I can promise you."

She shook her head. "At St. Anne's, our only interest is in the child, Dr. Peters."

"I'm certain it is," Peters replied half-heartedly, remembering the dollar amount agreed on. He walked nervously away from the carriage and started back to the house, looking nervously over his shoulder until he reached the porch where the lamplight flickered in the bitter wind. The dancing light startled him and he jumped in fright.

"Is there a name?" Mrs. Berry called out, her words echoing in the chilly night air.

Peters stopped in his tracks. She must not attract attention. "Please, we must not make noise."

"But, the child," she continued. "Does it have a name?"

He struggled to think clearly. It must have a name. But what would that be? It simply couldn't be Peters.

"No," he said weakly. "The child is—"

"Very well," she interrupted. "We will call the child Peters, then."

"But—" He started to speak but Watkins cracked the whip and turned the buggy around. Within seconds the black carriage was out of sight, lost in the shadows of the night.

He sat on the step and hung his head. The wind whistled in the quiet street and for a moment he thought he heard voices, Jessie's voice. *The children shall inherit the sins of the father...* Her words pierced his conscience like the jagged edge of a sword.

"Dr. Peters?"

He jerked suddenly and turned toward the voice. Annelle was standing in the doorway, her hand on the rosary that hung from her neck. Her face glowed eerily in the flickering light as she spoke. "You must come in now. You'll catch your death of cold."

He got up and went quietly inside. Annelle led him into the study where a fire still burned in the large brick fireplace. "Warm yourself here," she said. "I'll go see about Clara."

He stared at the flickering flames until he drifted off, lulled to sleep by the crackling of the wood and the howling January wind that beat against the windows. He slept fitfully, drifting in and out of consciousness, dreaming he was perched atop a black horse galloping swiftly down O'Fallon Street. At the large iron gates of St. Ann's Orphanage, he was greeted by a group of smiling nuns who waved to him as he passed. Then he rode on through a picturesque meadow and over rolling hills until he reached a bridge. Standing by the wooden rail was a beautiful girl with a baby in her arms. It was *Clara!* "God forgive you, Father," she said as she dropped the baby into the raging waters below.

He awoke suddenly to the sounds of the shutters beating against the glass pane. For a moment he heard the voice again, *God forgive you...* He listened carefully for footsteps but the only sound was the steady howling of the wind. The room was icy cold now and he shivered slightly. He threw more wood into the fire and poked at it until the damp logs lit at last. And when the fire was roaring nicely, he sat awake in the chair—he dared not sleep—and stared at the flames till morning broke through.

*From the Diary of Jessie Peters*

*February 15, 1864*

    *I received a letter from Bishop Quintard this morning. I am quite pleased that Thomas is faring much better. He has even joined in the fighting again as the army was in Meridian and he reenlisted in a newly formed artillery division. The Bishop says he spoke highly of Marsh Polk and his Uncle Tom Peters as having had much influence in his reenlistment. Seems his previous desertion has been forgiven, though they did strip him of his Lieutenant title. Still he sounds quite content to be a soldier again. The Bishop found it odd that he spoke nothing of his father or Clara, though he did mention George, Jr., and Arthur. I suppose George intends to keep all of us in the dark regarding Clara, and well he might since he has her tucked away in St. Louis. The child must surely be here by now though I've yet to hear one word about her "condition."*

    *I sat down to write Thomas this afternoon but was interrupted by an unexpected visit from my sister and her children. I've no idea why she came out in this dreary weather. Perhaps boredom has at last gotten the better of her. I'm surprised she's held out this long with only her young children and two or three Negroes on the place. I know I would have gone stark mad if I had been unable to leave this dreadful town this past winter. My brother's home may be removed from the bustle of the city, but at least I was able to attend two grand parties during my stay. But my sister prefers living in the strict formality that is such a part of the Cheairs family heritage. One day she will see the error of her ways—one day when she is old and gray and can't remember the last time her blood turned hot or her heart skipped a beat. As for me—well, I will just say I'm quite happy that my veins are filled with the warm blood of youth and my heart still has a sense of its own. Without it—I say life is not worth the living.*

# CHAPTER 33

**Okalona, Mississippi**
**1864**

Picket duty for Thomas meant pacing off the twenty steps to a fencerow, where he would stop just before a pool of stagnant water, turn and head back to the same spot. He had seen no action since he showed up in camp ten days ago, but there was hope yet. Forrest had skirmished over near Meridian and rumor was the Yanks were sending fresh troops.

He smiled for the first time in a long while. Months earlier death seemed inevitable, but he had refused to give up. He told Marsh Polk he would not resign, not before he died, but they sent the letter off anyway, and about the time they accepted his resignation he began to improve. Within a month he was well again and marched right over to Meridian and joined back up. He was a private again, his rank stripped from him. But he didn't even mind. His pride cared nothing for rank. Now he could hold his head up like a respectable Southerner.

He tried to forget what they called him—a coward, a traitor's son—all out of the mouths of his own company, men he called friends. Still, he was happy to be back in the army. Those months at Council Bend had been to him like death itself. With only Jem to talk to, he had grown deeply depressed, at times even hopeless. Now he had a fellow or two with whom he could pass the long nights in camp. For this alone he was grateful.

But the women—well, maybe they were who he missed most, set up a little way beyond the soldier's camp, so close you could smell the cheap oil and even cheaper whiskey. He had smelled it before, the scent that left a man powerless. He had gone like the other young boys at the university, wide-eyed and innocent, marching as lambs to slaughter toward the sweet voices, sirens with lavender-soaked hair. Rachel was her name, the one he chose, the one who took care to leave her mark on him. By the time he came down with the first symptom, she was gone. Run off to the next town. He had often wondered if she had died, or better yet, if some other poor fellow had been lucky enough to catch up with her and slit her throat? It would serve her right.

He leaned against the fence post. The sergeant chose him for watch that night and he was ready and eager for anything to come his way, something he might shoot at or capture and take in. That was all he cared for when it came to soldiering. Not much of a profession otherwise. All the drilling and marching seemed a waste of time to him. He was in it to kill Yanks. That was all.

A light flashed far down the line of canvas tents and Thomas squinted till he could just make out the silhouettes of two scrawny figures. They were coming his way. One stopped halfway and bent over. A hard, dry cough had gotten the best of him and he struggled to keep upright on the path. The damp cold had given the chills to most of the men. A few seemed near death. Thomas watched and waited and shoved his hands in his pocket, his gun leaned up against his leg. He wasn't about to shake hands. At the fence row, the sick one started coughing again. Thomas kept still as they approached.

"Peters?"

"That's right," Thomas replied. "Here to relieve me?"

"Yeah, reckon so," the sick one answered, holding out his hand. "Name's Ralston, Private Ben Ralston. This here's my cousin Lou."

Thomas nodded at the men. He brought one hand out of his pocket and picked up his gun. "Both of you doing duty?" Thomas asked.

"Naw," the sick one said, "just me. Lou's here in case I come down with a coughin' spell. A few days ago I passed clean out."

"That's right," the cousin replied. "I done my duty a few days back. But I can't go and leave ol' Ben in a bad way."

He smiled. Thomas thought he recognized him. His crooked mouth and short dark beard were familiar. Somewhere in his past—before all of this.

"Where're you boys from?" Thomas asked.

"Arkansas," they answered in unison, "'round Pine Bluff. How 'bout you?"

"I'm from Bolivar, Tennessee, but my family has a place around Council Bend. Name's Peters."

Lou cocked his head, a big gapped-tooth smile spread across his face. "Hey, Ben," he said, poking him with his elbow. "Reckon he's one of them Peters that kilt ol' Buck?"

Thomas didn't move.

"Naw," Ben said with a grin. "He ain't apt to show his face 'round here." A coughing spell came over him and he had to sit down by the fence.

"We's just fooling ya," Lou said. "Just fooling with ya's all."

Thomas forced a smile. "Yeah, pretty good one." He gave them a casual wave. "Best be getting on now."

Lou laughed again. "Alright then," he said with a smile. "Reckon you better."

Thomas felt his cheeks grow hot with anger, but he knew he could do nothing, not with these men who'd like nothing more than to put a knife in his back. He walked back in the direction of his tent and tried to put it out of his mind. A few campfires still burned along the path and he listened to the men talking as he passed. The older ones talked of home and their sweethearts, while the young ones lied about battles they had never seen and bravery they could only imagine. But Thomas did not stop to talk. He was worried now. Worried if Lou and his sick cousin were fooling him or not. Maybe they did know who he was. If so, they would eventually run him off.

He walked on toward the small brown tent that was again his home and went inside. He pulled the flap down tight. Tomorrow they would move southeast to Selma, and then perhaps toward the Carolinas, and Virginia. General Lee would never give up. There was hope in that. All he wanted was time. Time to reclaim his honor. Time to repair all that had been taken from him. And when the damned war was over, he could go home just like the rest of them.

He would ask Sallie to marry him—would tell her how he had redeemed himself. He felt sure then she would have him.

He took his lantern and laid it beside the bundle of old blankets that served as his bed and dug out some writing paper and a pencil from his pack. Nearly six months had passed since he had written to Sallie. He had all but given up when she stopped writing him sometime last winter. He figured she had heard about him—had listened to the vile gossip around Bolivar. But he made up his mind to write to her anyway, to never give up hope again. He was better than all the boys back home. Sallie knew it—had even told him so once. This time he would tell her how he felt. This time he would make her his own.

## From the Diary of Jessie Peters

*April 1865*

*After so many tragic losses, it appears the proud Confederacy will lay down arms and bow at the feet of the tyrannical Yankees. Though a bitter loss, I remain firm in my belief that the War was not in vain. Loss was inevitable though difficult to bear indeed. So many lives ruined, our beloved South forever changed—still we had no choice but to cling to our cherished Southern way, to fight to the death for this life of grandeur and wealth. And though I shall loathe the Yankees till my last dying day, I feel much more hatred for my neighbors who turned their backs on the Confederacy. Let the free Negroes do as they please, just so long as they do it in the North. As for the Yankee sympathizers—I say they should be banished from the sacred Southern soil forever! Let them join their filthy Yankee brethren! There, I've said it. I feel the same for Dr. Peters—let him pay for his past discretions. I will look to the future and will do everything in my power to maintain my self-respect, my lands, and what little money I have left.*

*With so many of our gallant men and boys gone, it has become quite obvious to me that Southern women must prepare themselves to run their own homes since they may be the only capable bodies around. My sisters are quite capable of running their own homes, yet they lack the courage to deal as a man would, to make demands in matters of business and not be taken for a fool. I am quite ready to take on the challenge and hope and pray every day that Dr. Peters never returns so that I may remain in control of my house and farm. I have made a vow to stay strong and not give into feelings of helplessness that may come from time to time, but to relish every moment of my newfound freedom! To everything there is a season...*

*A sad bit of news comes out of Bolivar this evening. I received a letter from George's sister Susan Peters and it seems Thomas had thought to return to his hometown sweetheart and make a life for himself there, but sadly Sallie Fentress has promised her hand to Jerome Hill! (Quite a handsome fellow, I might add!) Susan says Thomas looks well, though he has fallen off a great deal since the early days of the War, has lost his muscular frame and that mass of curls perched atop his head. I think we have all lost something since the start of the war. Oh, poor Thomas! I do hate to hear that boy will be let down yet again. I mean, was it not enough that he should be cursed with sickness these last few years? Was it not enough that he should have endured this awful War only to throw his hands up and surrender? He may be one of George's but I can't help but feel sorrow for his situation. I suppose I have a soft spot for him since he is the only one of those children who ever gave me any respect. For that, I shall say an extra prayer for him.*

*Nearly two months have passed since I wrote to Susan, but I am still happy that she felt the need to reply. She is a rare find indeed in the Peters family and one whom I most adore. She had very little to say in regard to my questions about Clara and I feel certain she has answers. She thinks to hide the truth just as George does, but I fear they will be unable to do that now that the War is over. I dare say the good folks of St. Louis will eventually tell all. But George has kept Clara well hidden; I must admit that, though nothing can stay a secret forever. I really can't imagine what George has planned for the girl unless he intends to bring her back home as if nothing ever happened. I wouldn't put it past him to do just that. George has a way of recreating the past and making people believe it—though this time may prove a bit tricky, with the child and all—just a small bit of damning evidence. But that must be George's plan exactly. Susan's silence tells me all I need to know.*

*I have been thinking quite a bit lately about going to see Alexander. Holly Springs is such a nice town and the good folks there have always treated me with such kindness. I simply cannot stand it here another day. I'm so saddened by news of our surrender—loss seems all around me. Perhaps a month or two with Alexander would cheer me up and give me some hope for the future—besides, I have no desire to lay eyes on George and I fear he may come this way since the War has ended. It would be just like him to walk right up and take over my place and act as if nothing ever happened. Well, I should hope he would be smarter than that. I will not relinquish my property for all the money in the world! Let him stay in Council Bend or take up his old residence in Bolivar—I couldn't care less just as long as he leaves me with my inheritance, and if he dares to try to take my land and money, I will sell my soul to the Devil himself to keep him from it!*

# CHAPTER 34

## Bolivar, Tennessee
## April 1865

Dr. Peters sat quietly in the large dining room of Polk Place. On the long mahogany table, the candles still flickered in their silver holders. The night was unusually dark, a moonless April evening, quiet and lonely. A feeling of desperation permeated the damp spring air and his soul. Now he must live with it, all of it—the sin, the regret, the agony. Alone.

News of Lee's surrender hit hard in the small town of Bolivar. Somber faces gathered on porches, at the depot, and in small shops in town expressing their disbelief. Every citizen who could walk came down to hear the news. They stood motionless on the steps of the courthouse as Reverend Gray read aloud from a Memphis newspaper brought in on the last train. They listened with stone-faces until the words sunk in, then one by one they trudged back to their homes, their heads in their hands, weeping openly, asking each other had it been in vain. *It had not. Their Cause had been just, necessary.*

That the South had lost was without question. That the North had won was a point of contention. As the last weeks of spring rolled by, Yankee newspapers busied themselves printing concocted stories of Southerners and their regrets at having risen up against the mighty United States of America, while Southern papers wrote of regret at having lost the most worthy cause ever attempted by man. Most folks in Bolivar agreed the uprising failed, though they would not yet say they wished to rejoin the Union. But that was in the past now. The Confederacy was no more.

But not at Polk Place where Dr. Peters sat brooding his own losses, stubbornly convicted to the old ways, determined to resume life as it had been five Aprils ago. Yet he knew that would not be. Everything had changed, even his own family was unrecognizable to him now, lost forever —all but the children back in Spring Hill. Still, they offered him little comfort. Besides, he had abandoned them—they were Jessie's children now.

He followed Clara into the study and watched as she thumbed through some old leather-bound books. Her custom had been to read the Polk's family Bible or a worn copy of the *Poems of Percy Bysshe Shelley.* On those days when she would offer up a smile, she opened to her favorite poem and read it aloud. But when the darkness covered her face, she read quietly from the Gospel of John. Clara lifted the large black Bible and sat down. Dr. Peters frowned. Perhaps she was lost forever, her soul tucked deep inside the stone walls of the convent. He cleared his throat, but she paid him no attention. "Clara," he said. "I'm leaving for Memphis tomorrow. Won't you join me? See some old friends, perhaps?"

She hesitated, looking at him with that same blank expression. "I suppose that would be nice," she said at last. "I should like to see Mrs. Joy in particular. Yes," she continued, looking away as if she were traveling there already. "I suppose."

Peters smiled. "Wonderful, then," he said softly, taking her hand. "Soon, my dear, this will all be a bad dream. Time heals all wounds, you know. You do believe me, don't you?"

She looked at the floor and shuffled her feet. Her tiny silk slippers gave her the appearance of being much younger than her age yet she had lately begun to wear her hair pinned up in old maid fashion. Her cheeks had lost their color altogether and the sparkle had faded from her eyes.

"You must be strong, Clara. You must believe in who you are—a Peters—and we Peters are resilient, brave." He lifted her chin and studied her dull eyes. "Like the Phoenix," he said with a firmness he had previously reserved for his sons, "we shall rise up from the ashes and resume our place in society. All of this will be but a distant memory."

She blinked back a tear and turned away from him. "It's not society that concerns me, Father. Society cannot forgive me." And like an apparition, she disappeared through the parlor door.

Peters stood in silence. Pangs of guilt pervaded his spirit though he tried to push them out of his mind. He must stay focused, in control. For several days now, he had received death threats from various members of Van Dorn's cavalry, and he knew he must get Clara away from here. Must force her to let the past go. If not, he feared he would lose her forever.

## From the Diary of Jessie Peters

*August 18, 1865*

*At last I have received word from George's cousin Miriam that the whole lot of them—George and his brood—are all in Bolivar and staying no less at Polk Place. Well, I do hope they're faring well—and well they should since not one of them has a care in the world while I sit here in Spring Hill, forced to endure all manner of contemptuous looks from my neighbors. Miriam says Clara has come home from her Catholic school and joined the mighty Polk family in their stately home. But, fancy this—not one word of the bastard child! Am I to believe the family knows nothing? Pshaw! The very idea! I should think the Peters' clan smarter than that. Have they given the child away? (I can only imagine the devilish scheme George has devised to cover this grand accident.) Well, they may play pretend with the good folks of Bolivar, but God knows how black their hearts are.*

*Personally, I care nothing for Clara and her sin except to protest her life of leisure. It is an abomination that she should walk around unscathed, without so much as a blot on her reputation, while I suffer injustice in my very home! And Thomas! Even he has chosen to abandon me as I've not received one letter or kind gesture from him in over a year. George has poisoned their minds against me. Well, two may play at this game—George had best beware! In time, the chickens always come home to roost!*

*I was most surprised this afternoon by an unexpected visit from my sister Lucy and would enjoy more visits from her if she would not bring her sour-faced sister-in-law along. I declare that Anne Parham is a complete prude. How she sits with her hands folded in her lap as if she were afraid of touching something—and sitting upright in her chair like her spine would snap if she were not straight as a board. I suppose I should be thankful I had visitors at least—even if they were not in the least inspirational. Some days I feel as if I might die of outright boredom right here in this parlor.*

CHAPTER 35

# TROUBLE ACROSS THE RIVER

**November 1865**

When they made it to Memphis, Peters arranged to leave Clara there, safe with old Bolivar family friends Levi Joy and Pitser Miller. Thomas left too, for the tiny town of Coffeeville in north central Mississippi, where arrangements had been made for him to study law under the distinguished General Ed Walthall. With his children out of harm's way, Peters could hide out and take on the Texans alone—if they found him.

He arrived in Council Bend and found Jem there, alone and looking after the place as if it were his own. For the first few days, Peters holed himself up inside the house, barely sleeping, keeping watch day and night. But after a few weeks passed, he relaxed, felt better about being there.

Early one morning he took a ferry to Memphis and checked on Clara. He saw little change in her demeanor. Mrs. Joy told him to be patient. In time Clara would come back to herself. But it was Thomas who shocked Peters the most. For the first time in months, he seemed cheerful and confident, by all indications he was wholly well again. They should plant in the spring and pray for a bumper crop, he suggested. Peters agreed. Like the rest of the plantations along the Mississippi River, a good season was the only way to survive the Reconstruction. But the floods from last year had sloughed off more than a third of the rich delta soil, leaving a hole that cut right down the middle of his property. What he needed was additional land, the most logical of which was a farm owned by James Lusby—nearly 500 acres of some of the richest dirt in Arkansas.

"The bank is soon taking the Lusby farm," Peters told his neighbor and good friend William Berry, who owned a thousand acres on the edge of Lee County. "I think I may buy it. It would certainly boost my harvest."

"Why don't you buy some other piece," Berry said frowning. "Did you forget? Lusby made it clear he'd shoot you if he ever got the chance. He ain't one for lying either."

Dr. Peters smiled. "That's exactly why I'm going to buy that land," he said. "Lusby's a coward. He doesn't have it in him. Besides, he's lost nearly everything. The son of a bitch couldn't pay the bank even if he wanted to."

A few days later, Peters rode the thirty miles to the Arkansas State Bank building in Marion, Arkansas. The bank president had arranged to sell the Lusby land at public auction, and the doctor was first in line. James Lusby holed up in the tiny back room of the bank building where he argued vehemently for the right to keep his property. The Lusby family had been in Arkansas nearly fifty years and had yet to lose a farm. But he was two years in arrears and the taxes were due again. Dr. Peters made his offer.

"Look, Peters," Lusby growled. "You ain't taking my land!"

But Dr. Peters smiled calmly and placed both hands on the table. "The debt must be paid or the land is mine. You know well—"

Lusby suddenly leaped from the table and threw his chair against the back wall. A bank officer hurried over. "Gentlemen," he began. "Let's just sit back down and talk this over. There's no reason for a fight."

But Lusby shoved him out of the way. "I ain't letting my land go that easy, Peters. If you want it, it'll cost you."

Dr. Peters stood up and held his hand out to Mr. Williams. "You've got my money. I'll assume we have a deal. I'm sure Mr. Lusby will come to his senses shortly."

"Why, you son-of-a-bitch!" Lusby yelled. "I should've killed you when I had the chance back in Hardeman County! You ain't nothing but a crook! And that wife of yours—well, she ain't worth half what you think she is!" He put his hat on his head and walked to the door. "And trust me, I know Jessie better than you do."

Peters slammed his fist on the table. "You'll pay for that!" he yelled. "You bastard! I own you!"

But Lusby turned and bolted from the room. The bank officer followed him into the lobby but soon lost him in a sea of customers standing in line. When he returned to the room, Peters was still seated at the table, his head in his hands, his mind wrapped around a past he wanted to forget. Was it five years? Or six? Had the years flown by that quickly? He had almost forgotten, and had it not been for Lusby, he may well have put the dirty memory to rest forever. But now it was back, alive again, and he remembered all of it—the filthy talk, the vile rumors of Jessie's lone visits to the plantation at Council Bend and Mr. Lusby's generous attention to her needs. Peters confronted him but he vehemently denied any wrongdoing. In the end, Lusby got the last laugh. Peters was made to look like a fool, a jealous old man.

The officer cleared his throat nervously. "Dr. Peters," he said. "Are you still interested in purchasing the Lusby farm? I understand if you may need—"

Peters looked up from the table and slammed his fist down hard. "Hell yes! Go on with it! I plan to buy every last inch of Lusby land in the state of Arkansas!"

When the paperwork was complete, the two shook hands and the officer led Dr. Peters into the bank lobby where John Carmack, a business associate of Peters, stood waiting. Carmack was in a panic. He had just seen James Lusby coming back down Main Street moments before. He suggested Peters leave at once. "He's going to be trouble this time," Carmack insisted.

Peters was angry. His first instinct was to walk out of that bank and put a bullet in Lusby's head. But he had to agree. He had better leave right away or risk some public scene. The papers would catch wind of it and the whole state would know where the infamous George Peters was.

He decided it would be wise to leave at once, so he walked the two blocks to the livery stable. An old Negro man came out to assist him and as he was in the process of renting a hack, Lusby appeared out of nowhere and struck Peters with a cane. The blow sent him instantly to the ground. He struggled to regain control and somehow pulled himself up and knocked the weapon from Lusby's hand.

"You'll pay, Peters," Lusby yelled. "You'll pay for what you've done to me! I'm ruined! Ruined! You can have your whore wife, you son-of-a-bitch, but you'll not take my land!" Lusby drew a Derringer from his coat pocket and fired once at Peters' head.

The bullet missed the doctor but whizzed directly over the head of a Negro stable boy who had poked his head out from behind one of the stalls. The boy ran wildly into the street. "They shootin'!" he hollered. "They tryin' to kill me!"

Lusby stepped closer and aimed once again at the doctor's head, but Peters was ready for him and kicked the gun from his grip. Lusby leaped on top of him and the two punched wildly at each other, rolling on the dirt floor of the stables At last, Peters made it to his feet and reached in his pocket. His pistol was not there—but he kept searching till he hit something cold. *His penknife.* Peters lifted his head just as Lusby lunged at him, and with one hard thrust, he stabbed the blade into his assailant's neck. A stream of bright red blood poured from the wound and soaked the ground at Peters' feet.

John Carmack came running toward the stable as Peters stumbled into the street. "I've been attacked!" Peters yelled. "The man's trying to kill me, I tell you!"

"George!" Carmack called out. "Are you shot?"

Peters' shirt was soaked with blood. He felt his chest. "No, I think I'm all right. But Lusby—he had it coming I tell you! He tried to kill me!"

A surgeon named Maddox ran over to see about Lusby's wound. "Carry him to the tailor's shop!" he yelled. He ran alongside, his finger covering the gushing hole.

Peters watched as they carried the bleeding man across the street. "I've killed him!" he said in a panic. "I know it!"

"Stay here," Carmack said. "I'll go check. Then we have to get you out of here!" He ran across the street to the tailor's shop and quickly returned. *The windpipe was severed. The wound was mortal. The man would not live to morning.*

Peters gasped. "What should I do? It was self-defense, I tell you!"

"Turn yourself in," he advised. "You have eye witnesses. They will attest to everything, the attack, the gunshots. Lusby acted like a madman!"

Peters stood staring out the stable door. "Why, I ask you? How did this happen? I've brought trouble on myself again."

\*\*\*

By evening, word had spread through Marion that Dr. Peters, the murderer of Confederate General Van Dorn, had struck again. This time he had sliced the throat of a fellow Arkansan, an upstanding farmer with a family and several hundred acres. And this time the people were not so quick to believe the notorious Peters. Sensing trouble might be brewing in town, the magistrate advised Peters to leave at once on condition that he return first thing in the morning for a hearing. This would allow time to see if the poor injured man would survive his wounds, then the court would make a decision whether a crime had been committed, or if it had been as Peters said—an act of self-defense.

\*\*\*

Dr. Peters arrived at Mrs. Joy's house late in the evening. He was astonished to find Clara sitting in the parlor with a room full of callers—nearly ten in all. She appeared radiant, happy. He pulled Mrs. Joy aside. "Does she know anything?"

"No," Mrs. Joy answered. "We've made sure to keep her in the house today. She knows nothing. When do you plan to tell her?"

"I don't want her to know just yet," Peters said. "She seems so happy. I know she'll take it hard. She blames herself you know—for everything." He walked to the window and rubbed his forehead. A feeling of hopelessness came over him. "I'm afraid I may lose her for good."

Mrs. Joy put her arm around him. "No, Dr. Peters," she said softly. "It's not like that. She'll understand you had no choice. You did what you had to do, for goodness sake."

"I don't know," he said rubbing his hands together nervously. "She believes she's somehow cursed the family."

"But, she can't really think such," Mrs. Joy said.

Peters frowned. "I'm afraid she does."

"Why don't you wait and tell her tomorrow—after you are exonerated."

"Yes, of course," he said. "The matter will be over then and Clara will have nothing to worry herself about." He spoke with confidence though in his heart he knew the truth. This time he would lose Clara for good.

\*\*\*

The next morning, Dr. Peters left for the courthouse in Marion. Levi Joy had sent word to Judge Scruggs, a well-respected lawyer in Memphis, to accompany them and to serve as a character witness and legal counsel if needed. The weighty names worked as planned, and once the surgeon testified Lusby would live, Peters was released.

By late afternoon the men returned to Memphis, and Peters rode out to the Joy's. He was surprised to find Clara waiting for him in the foyer. Her trunk was packed and standing in the corner. The blue silk gown she had worn the previous day had been replaced with a gray cotton day dress. Her hair was tied up in a knot, tucked neatly inside a matching bonnet.

"Did he live?" Clara asked.

"Yes," Peters said. He approached Clara but she stepped away from him. "This had nothing to do with—"

"Please, Father," she said in a strange voice. "I know you only want to make me feel better, but I know the truth now." She turned to the door. "I'm going back to St. Louis. I don't belong here. Not anymore."

\*\*\*

Thomas arrived in Memphis later that same day but could do nothing to convince Clara to stay. He stormed into the parlor and approached the doctor. "This must stop!" he yelled. "We can't run for the rest of our lives!"

Dr. Peters closed the parlor doors. "Keep it down! Someone will hear you! Have you lost your mind?"

"Lusby's Texas Cavalry," Thomas said, throwing his hat on the mahogany sideboard. "He was cavalry! He didn't shoot at you over some land! Can't you see?"

Dr. Peters' mouth dropped open. "Are you sure of this?"

"I'm certain of this," Thomas said. "He wanted you dead."

"But, what about Lusby—and Jessie?" Peters stammered. "Surely you remember."

"Of course I remember." Thomas smirked. "The whole damned state of Arkansas remembers it."

"Then what makes you think this has anything to do with Van Dorn?"

"Can't you see it, Father? Whatever the reason, we can't deny the relationship between Lusby and Van Dorn. To do that would be naïve."

Thomas turned quickly away, but Peters recognized the dark circles, the sallow cheeks. He had seen it countless times, yellow fever, typhoid, the ravaged body in those final days. "You're not well, son."

"I'm fine," Thomas replied coldly. "Just a minor relapse—nothing to worry about." He walked to the window and stared out at the vacant yard. "I've written a letter to Major Schaumburg. He was Lusby's commanding officer. I knew him to be a decent fellow. I told him we're ready to settle this once and for all." He turned to face his father. Tears had welled in his eyes. "You must face a judge," he said angrily. "It must end! Your name must be cleared for good!"

"And you think this will end it?" Peters laughed. "You think this will satisfy Van Dorn's men? A slap on the wrist from their old commander?"

Thomas stomped angrily toward the door. "The war is over! They may think to get revenge for the dead bastard but they'll have to kill me first!"

Peters caught him by the arm and pulled him back. "Don't be a fool, Thomas!" he yelled. "You'll stir up a hornet's nest! I tell you Van Dorn's men had nothing to do with this!"

"That's a lie and you know it!" Thomas snapped. "I'm sick to death of it all! That damned war—" He dropped to his knees. "My name, my reputation, is all but gone! I can't live like this!"

Peters bent over and showed his teeth like a rabid dog. His first instinct had been to kick him, but he held back. Thomas was weak. "You sound like a woman!" Peters bellowed. "Get up from there! You can't change the past! Don't be a fool!"

"Our own neighbors hate us. The Peters name is ruined!"

"Have you gone mad, boy?" Peters asked scornfully. "That doesn't matter! What matters is that we're still ahead! We're wealthier now than before the War! Doesn't that make you happy? You have a fine life ahead of you, fine friends."

"You don't understand," Thomas said. "It's not about the money!" He turned away but Peters saw the tears streaming down his cheeks. "Friends—Hah!" he yelled. "I have none! Hell, even the women have turned against me! Sallie Fentress won't even look at me now!" He grabbed the arm of the chair and pulled himself up. He pointed at his father. "And all because of your damned whore wife!"

Peters slapped him hard. "Blame whomever you wish," he said scornfully. "But for God's sake, hold your head up and carry yourself like a man!"

Thomas fell back to the floor and cried like a baby. There was nothing left in him, no fight, no courage, not even the will to live. When he regained enough strength to lift himself from the floor, he walked out the door, out into the warm Memphis night. Peters called after him, pleaded with him to listen to reason, but he never looked back.

## From the Diary of Jessie Peters

*September 7, 1865*

*I was quite pleased to hear from my dear brother this morning and will leave first thing for Holly Springs. I'm absolutely beside myself with expectation. O, to once again have pleasant evenings and lively conversation. Why, I'm positively giddy! I would much prefer to go alone, but Virethia will come along to help me with the children and that should suffice. Perhaps this is just what I need to lighten my heavy mood.*

*Have heard not one word from George and have decidedly given up on his offering to help my situation. He obviously feels no responsibility toward his wife and children save to send a few hundred dollars to my brother on occasion. I would greatly enjoy a few minutes alone with him so I might tell him exactly what I think of him! My sister Lucy alluded to his absence when she visited last month and made me feel quite guilty—of what, though, I haven't the foggiest idea. I will never say a word about the general to any of them. Let the gossiping hens tell their own tall tales. I'll not give them one crumb of truth!*

*I began packing my trunk this evening and will leave early tomorrow morning for Holly Springs. I haven't traveled in so many months I'm not sure I remember how. The children are quite excited as well—I only pray they are quiet and well-behaved while we are there or we will not be asked to return. My poor sister-in-law cannot take the noise, or so Alexander says. He would like me to believe she's not quite recovered from the loss of the baby, but I think she's just one of those females with a delicate constitution—to put it lightly. Eliza has always seemed to me a bit addled, though I should never let on that I think such. Why, it would break poor Alexander's heart if he thought his favorite sister had such a lowly opinion of his wife.*

*I am up early this morning and eagerly await my carriage to take us to the depot. I dare not travel with my diary and so leave you here till my return.*

*Au revoir mon amis!*

# CHAPTER 36

# WHEN IN APRIL

The letter arrived the third day in April. Delivered first to Memphis, and then to Coffeeville where Thomas had recently completed his studies under General Walthall. He opened the tattered envelope and sat down in the light of the parlor window. The letter read simply:

*Cambridge, Maryland*
*March 12th, 1866*
*Thos. M. Peters, Esq.,*
*Sir:*

*My friend Maj. Wright C. Schaumburg of New York City has this day put me in possession of a letter of date of Feb. 23d addressed by you to him, and from circumstances which I will at once state, without the slightest reference to any action of his, I deem it my duty to write to you.*

*You will pardon my interfering in this matter when I inform you that I was a nephew of the late Gen. Van Dorn, that I was an officer upon his Staff at the time of his murder, that it was I who drew up the statement of facts concerning that murder which you are pleased to term "an infamous card" and which I signed along with other gentlemen whose integrity you know, if you know anything, is beyond suspicion. I therefore suggest that if you have ought to complain of in connection with that affair it will be with more propriety that you address yourself to me.*

*In relation to your intimation that the Courts of the country are open and that Dr. Peters is ready and willing to abide his trial, I have to inform you that the propriety of a prosecution has been discussed by the family of Gen. Van Dorn and only given up or postponed, as you will by a knowledge of the fact, as well known to you as to us, that in the present political state of Tennessee, when every office from high to low is filled by the bitter enemies of the Confederate Army, any attempt to bring Dr. Peters to trial for the murder of a Confederate Officer of high rank would be worse than useless, a mere farce when we remember that every Confederate soldier's life was forfeited by the very law under which it is proposed to try a man for shooting one. It is to this state of affairs that Dr. Peters owes his escape thus far from the penalty of his crime. It may prove unwise in you to persist in agitating matters which, having yielded to force of circumstances we have consented to lay at rest. Having no feeling of vengeance in the matter, we are content to leave my Uncle's assassin to the pangs of his own conscience.*

*Having said this much it is almost unnecessary to say further that I have never even heard before of the absurd rumor you mention that we (the officers of Van Dorn's Staff) have pledged ourselves to slay your father. We are not assassins, and I think I can speak for the rest at the same time that I speak for myself when I state that, having escaped us at the moment of his crime, such a design against him as you inquire into has never been entertained for a moment.*

*I have no desire to hurt your feelings unnecessarily, you being a perfect stranger to me of whose existence even I was not aware before the receipt of this letter, but I feel called on to speak plainly and courteously in regard to a most serious matter. You have unnecessarily revived old memories and have yourself to thank if you, perforce, hear the truth. It is not unnatural that a young man, as I judge you to be, should feel keenly any allusions to so delicate and distressing a tragedy in which your father was a principal active and the ladies of your family were concerned (by public rumor) but that you may understand these things once for all, I will state the cause that led to the publication of the card alluded to above. You will find what I state here also recapitulated in a letter to Col. Marsh Polk, written about the 25th of May, 1863.*

*It was bruited about in a number of newspapers that Dr. Peters had shot Gen. Van Dorn for criminal connection with his wife and daughter, and to put a stop to the foul slander, one who was familiar with all the circumstances and knew the falsehood of the report, determined to publish over my signature a brief statement of the real facts and of my views in relation to them. This we did and I think we succeeded, at least I heard nothing more of the thing afterwards. The facts as we stated them in relation to the murder and its surroundings were true and can be substantiated before a court of justice, and I take the liberty of suggesting that it is unmanly and ungenerous, without you are prepared to contravene it by proof, to call that statement "infamous" in letters to men 2000 miles off, whom you well know you would not dare thus address face to face. The precedent circumstances I should think it madness in you to endeavor to establish in contradiction to our card—the immediate circumstances attending the murder (Dr. Peters last visit, the shooting, &c.) are stated by us on our honor as soldiers and gentlemen and it would be foolish in you, who knew nothing about it, to gainsay them and the reports concerning his visits to Nashville, &c. we spoke of as reports which prevailed at the time we believed them, but whether they were actually true or not we would not pretend to assert.*

*Thus, Sir, I have given you succinctly what had been to me a painful review of some of the circumstances attending the unfortunate transaction which occasioned your letter to Maj. Schaumburg and mine to you. If well advised you will not seek further to kindle and inflame old recollections, but in all events I must insist that it is I who am mainly concerned in this affair and not Maj. Schaumburg. I have therefore to request that if you will persist in pursuing this correspondence, you will address yourself to me and not to him.*

*I am very respectfully Your obedient servant,*
*Clement Sulivane*

He tossed the letter on the table and walked to the sideboard. *Bastards.* He was no fool. The bottle of laudanum was nearly gone. Now he would have to take the coach into the city. Pitser Miller knew the druggist—he could get whatever he needed. Tomorrow he would make his plans. They would not beat him—not this time.

*\*\*\**

## April 8, 1866

Thomas paced the floor in his room at Pitser Miller's dry goods store. The tiny bed in the corner resembled the cots in the army hospital, and he could suffer lying on it for only an hour at a time before he had to walk the stiffness out of his aching legs.

He stood before the washstand and splashed the dust from his face. He glanced at the mirror but he did not recognize his reflection. There was the small scar on his left cheek, but even that was odd, blood red against his gray skin. He seemed old now—his skin like the cracked bark of an ancient oak. Yet he was not even twenty-three. He ran his fingers through his hair. The dead strands fell like puffs of cotton to the rug beneath him.

He checked the brown bottle in the drawer by the bed. The laudanum was half gone and he had yet to find a doctor he liked well enough in Memphis. Doctors were all alike. They were quick to diagnose but offered little hope of a remedy. He took a swig and stuffed the bottle deep in the bag beside his bed. Maybe he could make it a few more days. He would have to take it easy, keep to himself. When supper was ready, he would eat and return to his room. Besides, the store would be filled tonight and the noisy dining room would only set his head to throbbing again. Better to avoid them altogether.

The clock chimed five times as he rounded the corner of the storeroom. Sam greeted him with a glass of whiskey. Sam was one of the few remaining servants and Thomas liked him almost as much as he liked Jem.

He took the whiskey from Sam, drank it down, and reached in his pocket. The letter was still there, still gnawing at his pride. He seated himself at the table near the window. From there, he had an excellent view of the entrance to Miller's store and could easily slip away and retire upstairs the moment familiar faces arrived.

He looked at the envelope and stared in amazement at the name in the upper left corner. *Clement Sulivane, Esq.* He smiled. At least he had gotten their attention. *Three pages, and from the nephew himself.* He unfolded the paper and read it again.

The sky grew darker outside as evening approached and he turned up the lamp above his table. Sam brought out another whiskey and his wife followed shortly with a small loaf of hot bread and a bowl of honey butter. But Thomas never looked up. He read to the end of the letter and then read it again, taking in every word, hoping to glean from it some truth about the affair.

*The General and the daughter...* He could hardly read the words without going into a fitful rage. He was sure Van Dorn's men knew the truth, was sure they had covered up every shred of evidence that convicted him. But still the question lingered in his mind. He knew only what he had been told—and that had not been much. There was Jessie, and Clara, and neither was at fault. They were victims of an opportunist, preyed upon by a sadistic flatterer. These were the words of his father, and he believed some of it. Jessie was the pursuer; that was her way. As for Clara, he had no way of knowing exactly what happened, what promises were made. For now he could only speculate, and with Clara's silence he had little hope of ever knowing the truth. Maybe none of it mattered now that the war was over. He tried to convince himself this was true. But the past inevitably showed up to remind him—the dead *would* be avenged.

He placed the letter on the table and stood up to stretch his legs. Through the large front windows he noticed a young couple holding hands under the glow of the streetlights. Her blonde hair shone bright against the man's long black coat as he held her tightly and helped her into a waiting carriage. Thomas looked away and shut his eyes. He had not thought of Sallie in weeks, had tried desperately to erase the memory of her face, but now everything about her came flooding into his mind. He had not loved her so much as he imagined he did. It was the insult he supposed, the slap in the face to his ego that kept him in knots about her. Or maybe he *had* loved her. To admit that was admitting defeat, and that was something he would never do.

He watched the couple and thought of that last night in Bolivar. Sallie smiled at him—he did remember that much. And Jerome Hill! Yes, he was there, too. But he could not recall why Sallie had cried. He was drunk—and he yelled at her! His memory was coming back to him now. Jerome Hill! Yes, he hit Jerome! And then he ran into the woods as Sallie yelled at him to come back! But he didn't go back. He ran and ran until he collapsed on the banks of the frozen creek just below their house. And the rain that night! If not for the whiskey he would have died. Sallie's brother found him that next morning lying face down in a small ravine.

Thomas could just see Frank Fentress' face staring down at him, his dear, lifelong friend. "Leave here," he had said. "You're crazy, Tom. Sallie doesn't want you. Can't you see that?" That had hurt him the most—maybe more than anything else in the world.

A loud voice echoed in the street and he snapped back to reality. The lovers were no longer there. Probably on their way to some secret rendezvous. He closed his eyes. His head was spinning from the laudanum and he felt a hot sweat creeping up his neck. He gripped the edge of the dining table but it was no use—he was too weak. He slipped from his chair and sank down on the floor. If he could just get outside where the cool breeze blew off the river...

"Tom!"

He heard the voice but he could not move; his eyes shut tight as if in eternal sleep. Then the voice came again, "Tom!" and he knew it was Mr. Miller who picked him up and set him back in his chair. "Tom! Are you sick?"

Thomas lay back in the chair and rested his head against the brick walls of the dining room. He was sweating profusely and an uncontrollable nausea rose in his throat. "Help me outside," he begged.

Mr. Miller helped him to the small porch outside. The night air was crisp and a damp breeze blew in off the dark Mississippi. He lifted his head till the cool air hit his face. Within seconds the sick feeling subsided and he opened his eyes. On the corner just below the store's entrance, a group of young men stood talking and laughing. A few of their voices were familiar but they were too far out of the lamp light for him to see their faces. He wiped his mouth with his coat sleeve and pushed himself up onto the bottom step. By now, the group of men had made their way to the front of the store. They walked past him and went inside. He watched as a few of them glanced back over their shoulders. If only he could stand—he would fight them all.

Mr. Miller helped him to his feet and brushed the dirt from his pants and coat. "Can you walk now?" he asked.

"Yea," Thomas groaned. "Get me to my room."

The door was heavy with a large brass pull that resembled an old prison lock. It took two men to hold it open while Sam helped drag Thomas back inside. The stairs went up to a second-floor landing and Thomas stopped there to rest as he held onto Sam's strong, thick arm. Mr. Miller joined the group of young men in the dining room and greeted them with his usual "Hallo boys!" while Thomas sat down on the landing and strained to hear their conversation. But all he could hear was the clink of glasses as the drinks were being served.

"Come on, now," Sam pleaded. "Best getcha in the bed."

Thomas did not move. Their voices were familiar—but he wasn't quite sure who they were. He cupped his hand around his ear and listened, their words like a broken string on a violin, a nail on a windowpane.

"Sallie and Jerome... a wedding Thursday night." *Yes*, he heard it. He was certain of it. And then again, "Lucky fellow, that Jerome!"

"You think Tom knows?"

"Shhh!" someone hissed. "You're drunk man! He'll hear you!"

"Tom didn't really think she'd marry him, did he? Why, the man's insane!"

"Oughta count his blessings old lady Fentress didn't have him thrown in jail! He tried to kill the whole lot of'em!"

By now Thomas was bent over so far that he slipped from the step. Sam picked him up and carried him to the top of the stairs. The bedroom door was open and Sam dragged him inside and laid him with a thud on the small cot-like bed. A damp cold air blew in from the open window and a thick river stench now permeated the bedclothes. Sam walked over and pulled the window shut and drew the heavy curtains tight. "Lay back now and rest, Mr. Thomas," Sam urged. "I'll fetch some fresh water up."

Thomas turned over in the bed. His voice sounded muffled, small like that of a child. "She did it! She married him!"

Sam shook his head. "They's others, Mr. Thomas. Don't worry your head none 'bout that gal."

But the tears fell like rain as he lay back and closed his eyes. Hopelessness overwhelmed him and a sharp pain shot through his brain like tiny knives whittling slowly at his sanity. He pulled the damp blanket over his legs and buried his head deep in the pillow. The laudanum was in the drawer by the bed but he no longer had the strength to lift his head.

"Please, Sam." He moaned. "Can you get my bottle?"

Sam went to the table and pulled out the drawer and felt around until he felt the glass bottle. He could tell at once that it was nearly empty. "Better get some more when mornin' come, Mr. Tom." He laid the bottle on the bed beside him and walked out.

Thomas pulled out the cork and drank till the bottle was empty. Soon the light in his eyes faded and numbness overtook him. His pale lips turned slightly upward, the hint of a smile. He dreamed he was flying high over the old Bolivar home, past the Polk cemetery where his mother lay sleeping in the cold ground. From somewhere in the distant night, he heard his mother's voice, singing sweetly, his head resting against her warm chest, the rocking chair moving to his favorite tune...

*When the snow is on the ground,*
*Little Robin redbreast grieves.*
*For no berries can be found,*
*And on the trees there are no leaves.*
*The air is cold, the worms are his,*
*For this poor bird what can be done?*
*We'll strew him here some crumbs of bread,*
*And then he'll live till the snow is gone...*

## From the Diary of Jessie Peters

*April 1866*

*At last I am happy to be back in Spring Hill. I thought I would never say that in a million years. Alexander's home is quite comfortable and Holly Springs has a delightfully active society, but that wife of his—ugh! I simply could not bear her another moment. She is as cold and sniveling as ever. I declare, someday she will run my poor brother screaming into the night! I pray each day now that he allows her to go on to Texas or any place where she might sing and play the piano—and frolic with those intellectual types for whom she whines incessantly. If only she could have given my poor brother a child, then he wouldn't be so awfully alone, as I don't envision his marrying another—ever.*

*These first days back have been rather uneventful, but I simply had to come home. I only wish I could have brought the good folks of Coldwater with me. And the Davises and Finlays as well. They are so much more enjoyable than anyone here at home—not judgmental in the least. In fact, they welcome a little controversy—Luke Finlay says it enlivens the place a great deal. (Of course, he's a handsome snake in the grass himself!)*

*This afternoon I rode into town to pay my sisters a visit but Lucy was in bed with a headache and Susan was away at her sister-in-laws' home. Sometimes I believe it is not meant that I have any contact with my family—I'm beginning to feel as if they don't want to see the children or me. I have asked myself many times why they would feel such, how they could possibly want to hurt my feelings. Why, it's been months since my sisters have laid eyes on Lucy or William, and they never bothered to inquire about us while we were in Holly Springs. Virethia has told me several times that I ought to call on them myself—and well, now that I have done just that, I believe we have our answer. I think now I would like to join Alexander in Holly Springs. He has more than enough room for me and the children, and I am so well-liked and popular there that I should think my days would never be boring. If only Alexander would send that wife of his to stay here at my place. She's bound to leave their home anyway, or at least that is what seems to be her plan. Eliza's certainly better suited for this prudish Spring Hill society. I'm certain my dear sisters would love poor, weak Eliza just as George always did. Not for me, though! Posh! It is a pity that everyone feels the need to mistreat me so. But, I am strong and I will win in the end. In time, they will be begging me back.*

# CHAPTER 37

*April 9, 1866*
*The poor unfortunate young man lay weltering in his blood.*
*The vital spark had fled, and the soul returned to the God*
*who gave it.*
                                                          —DIARY OF JOHN H. BILLS

Thomas sat motionless on the window seat, perched like a stone gargoyle on some ancient castle. The shrill horn of a riverboat blew in from the Mississippi River and floated with the morning fog across the dark water and into the thick city air. Wagon wheels churned holes in the muddy streets and young boys with stacks of the *Memphis Avalanche*, hot off the presses, called out in voices that echoed through the alleys of Second Street. The smell of hot coffee drifted up from the storeroom as the great clock in the hallway chimed the hour. Thomas listened as Sam made his way up the stairs to the second floor. He imagined he carried a tray with a cup of hot coffee and warm biscuits soaked in honey. Sam would bring it to him and they would laugh at the sound of Viola as she wrung a chicken's neck in the coop out back. He smiled. He had to go now or they would stop him.

He listened as Sam laid the tray on the table in the room below. Thomas imagined every move old Sam would make. He would reach over and find an empty bed, the crumpled pieces of paper and the small brown journal. He was fond of Sam, would've done more for him, but it was out of his hands now. Fate would settle everything.

Thomas turned up the flame of the lamp and walked the remaining few steps to the attic.

Moments later, Sam called out. "Who's up there?"

Thomas stopped and waited. Better move slowly now. His heavy boots would make noise.

"That you, Mister Tom?" Sam asked.

Thomas crept up the remaining steps and slipped through the doorway. A slant of light streamed in from the tiny window and radiated across cobwebs and through the rafters to an empty corner of the room. Perfect. He lay out the shawl and took the gun from his belt.

"Mr. Thomas?" Sam whispered. "That you?"

Thomas stepped out of the darkness and saluted the intruder. "Lieutenant Peters, sir."

Sam cleared his throat and walked slowly toward the slant of light. "Sho," he said. "I know who you is, but it's a might cold up here. Best you get on back downstairs where it's warm and all."

"No time for that," Thomas said. He drank the contents of the bottle and tossed it onto a pile of lumber. A sense of calmness came over him and he staggered to the window. The morning light fell on his shaking left hand and the shiny metal of the pistol.

"You got a gun there, Mr. Thomas?" Sam asked. "Come on now and put that down. I'll fetch you some hot coffee." He turned to leave the room. Better fetch Mr. Miller.

"I cannot," Thomas whispered. "I'm sorry, Sam." He knelt to the floor and lay back on the silk shawl. Then came a moan, a low, sorrowful moan, and a sound like the blast of cannon. Then all was silent.

*** 

It was late afternoon when Dr. Peters arrived. A crowd had gathered in the street outside Pitser Miller's store while the usual patrons milled around the entrance, waiting to hear the gossip. Peters looked straight ahead and walked through the crowd.

Pitser Miller met him at the door of his store and led him upstairs to the attic. "George," he said. "I don't know what to say—I just can't understand it." Miller lowered his head.

Peters reached out and took his hand. "Please don't, Pitser. None of us understands it. None of us knows why Thomas would—" He turned away and choked back his tears. "It—uh, it was all too much for him. Too much. If I had only known then maybe..."

Miller paused on the last step and pointed straight ahead to the attic room. "In there, George," he said in a sorrowful voice.

At the top of the stairs, Peters paused and took a deep breath and then went into the tiny room. Sam was there, leaning over the body, his hands by his side. Peters walked in and stood beside him. Thomas' fixed eyes were a lifeless blue; a stream of blood congealed along the side of his face, having poured from the hole behind his ear. It was stagnant and thick like the waters of the Mississippi. His right hand gripped the cold pistol; his left hand held his Bible. His tall black boots were polished to a brilliant shine. And he wore a clean white shirt under the gray jacket, the uniform of the late CSA. Beneath his head lay a shawl, edged in a delicate fringe and meticulously arranged, the once spotless fabric now spattered with drops of crimson and black. The shawl had been a gift from Clara. Tucked inside the Bible were three letters, scratched out and barely legible.

"Dr. George Peters?" a man asked.

"Yes," Peters answered. He never looked the man in the face, never knew to whom he spoke. His gaze was fixed on the scene before him: the body, the blood, and that unmistakable smell of death that permeates the skin of the living.

"Dr. Caldwell." The man held his hand out. "Coroner for the City of Memphis."

But Peters was not listening; he was busy studying every last detail: the white shawl, the bloodstained floor beneath a tuft of curly hair, Thomas' hair. *Soft as lamb's wool*, his mother had said. Peters bent closer to the body and touched the small black hole on the side of Thomas' head.

At the end of two hours, Dr. Erskine wrote four words in his book—*Death by pistol shot.* The coroner's young apprentice looked over the body and gathered the evidence as Peters stood nearby. A pistol, three letters, a blood-spattered Bible. The witnesses were few and had little to add. Thomas was distressed, Pitser Miller observed, but showed no more distemper than was normal in young men from time to time. The clerks talked about his mood and agreed that he grew more melancholy as the evening wore on, though no one knew exactly what had upset him.

Dr. Peters listened as several young men were interviewed. What did they know about the deceased? Had the unfortunate fellow said anything prior to taking his life?

"It was that stepmother," one fellow said as he moved toward the stairs. "Real piece of work, I hear. And then his daddy killed Van Dorn."

Peters started after him but Pitser Miller held him back. "Leave it alone. They don't mean anything by it. It's just what they've heard—they're *boys* is all."

Peters nodded his head and sat back down watching in disbelief as two broad-shouldered Negroes lifted Thomas off the floor and onto the small bed. They wrapped the body in a large sheet, twisting and folding until only the face remained uncovered.

Dr. Erskine approached Peters and tapped him lightly on the shoulder. "Dr. Peters, if you'll sign here, please," he said quietly. "Says you've identified the deceased as one Thomas McNeal Peters, male, twenty-three years of age. The cause of death is stated as a self-inflicted gunshot wound to the head. Died at approximately 10 a.m. this morning, April 9, 1866."

"Yes," Peters mumbled. He was confused and for a moment he forgot where he was. "I'm sorry, but what did you say?"

Dr. Erskine stepped closer. "Just sign here," he said handing him a pen. "Says you're the father of the deceased."

Peters took the pen and signed his name.

"Very sorry for your loss, Dr. Peters," Dr. Erskine said. He then handed Peters the evidence—the gun, the Bible, the letters, and the now bloody shawl, all placed neatly inside a brown cloth sack. "My deepest condolences to your family."

Dr. Peters walked out the door of the tiny room and stopped in the hallway. As he started down the stairs, a reporter from the *Memphis Avalanche* yelled out to him, "Can I ask you a few questions, Dr. Peters?"

Peters clutched the brown bag and hurried down the stairs past the reporter. He thought to disappear, to run as far as he could, until the world as he knew it was vanished forever. But he knew that could not be. His was a world of pain and lies—an ugly, unforgiving world. Thomas had escaped—but Peters knew he would not be so lucky.

He pulled his jacket tight. The night was cool and damp and an evening fog floated in from the river, coating every inch of the city with an oppressive film. He walked slowly, through the dark Memphis streets, his thoughts wandering back to the years before the War, back when his life seemed blessed beyond his wildest dreams. Now all was lost. When he reached Union Avenue, he turned and walked to the riverbank. He paused under a streetlamp and took out the letters. He opened the first: *Dear Father...*

*From the Diary of Jessie Peters*

*April 10, 1866*
   *Today marks yet another dark day in my life as I have received the most dreadful news! I wish I could retire to bed and awake tomorrow as if it had all been a bad dream. How horrible to think—Thomas is dead! Dear, sweet Thomas. O, the power of human despair! I suppose I should be thankful that dear, sweet Will Polk felt the least compelled to bring me the news since George obviously had no intentions of telling me the first thing. I think sometimes the Polk family has more goodness in them than any other I know. God only knows the torment poor Will would endure if the kind folks of Bolivar knew he visited me—the infamous Jessie Peters! I swear I hate George and every last one of those Bolivar hypocrites more with each passing day! Still, I cared a great deal for Thomas and I refuse to let their despicable humors hinder my grieving. That poor boy has suffered so.*
   *I truly believed Thomas would come out of this nightmare whole, but I suppose he simply did not have the strength. If I only knew what happened, what had changed to make him feel so utterly hopeless to take his own life. Will told me about Sallie Fentress—I suppose he really did love her after all.*
   *The funeral is to take place on Thursday and I have prepared to leave first thing in the morning. Will begged me to stay here, warned me I would not receive a warm welcome if I were to go, but I couldn't care less about those people. Let them hate me all they want!*
   She unfolded the thin paper and laid it across the folds of her diary. The article in *The Memphis Avalanche* read as follows:

*Distressing Case of Suicide*
   *Yesterday afternoon, Thomas Peters, son of Dr. Peters of this State committed suicide by shooting himself through the head with a pistol. The circumstances connected with this unfortunate and sad affair are as follows.*
   *Mr. Peters passed through our city, a week ago, on his way to his father's plantation below the city. His friends*

state that he looked unusually well while in Memphis and no signs were discovered of any intention to commit an act that heaps distress upon a doting father, and deprives society of one of its bright ornaments. On his return from the plantation Sunday night, he seemed cheerful as usual and still presented no indication of anything unusual in his feelings.

A few hours before his death, he was in the store of Pitser Miller on Second Street where he slept the night before, and gentlemen who were with him, say that he was in a pleasant humor, and his mood as agreeable as was the habit of this companionable young gentleman. A short while previous to the shooting, he went upstairs into the sleeping room, placed his shawl carefully on the floor, arranged a pillow, polished his boots carefully, combed his hair, dressed himself complete in an artillery uniform of the late C.S.A. in whose ranks he was a commissioned officer, buttoned his coat to the chin, laid himself down, and deliberately placing a pistol with the muzzle behind the ear, fired.

His appearance after death warrants us in these statements. He must have died without a struggle, as after the report of the pistol, some gentlemen rushed upstairs and the flesh was still quivering. There was very little blood upon the pillow, and the shawl was not disturbed.

He had written three letters, two to his parents, and the other to someone whose name we did not learn. Thos. Peters was a promising young man. Previous to his death he was studying law with General Walthall of Coffeeville, Miss., and bid fair to take an honorable position in the social world; but with an organization too sensitive to combat the cruel decree of fate—it seems so in this case; too keenly alive to the woes of others, the gallant and the true, the talented and generous has, by his own hand, deprived himself of an existence whose burdens were too heavy for his sensitive nature to bear. Every heart knoweth its own sorrow and what the lacerated heart of this noble fellow was called up to bear, is known only to his God.

# CHAPTER 38

# LAST RITES AND THE PAST RETURNS

When the mourners had gone at last, Dr. Peters sat alone in the parlor of McNeal Place holding tightly to the letters Thomas left behind. Three in all—each with its own message, each intended to close a chapter in a short, tortured life. But Dr. Peters had not shared them, had failed to follow through on his dead son's final request, and now he felt sure his guilty conscience would take him to the grave as well. He had told Clara the letters were gone. And when she begged him to tell her what Thomas had said, he lied and told her "Your brother asked for forgiveness, for salvation for his soul."

But Clara had only frowned. "I fear he cannot have it," she cried. "He is lost forever." She kissed Peters on the cheek. "Perhaps we are all lost."

He read the letter one last time. All was lost indeed, at least that is how it seemed. His eldest son now dead, his daughter drawn to the dreary chambers of a convent. He stoked the dying fire. *For the first time, I say you are a fool,* Thomas had written. *For the sake of the others, you must do what is right.* Peters stared at the flames. *Do what is right.* Now he knew what he must do. With tears in his eyes, he held the letter to his heart one last time, and then one by one, he tossed the pages into the fire and watched until the last spark died away.

At first light, he boarded the train to Memphis, and when he arrived in the city, he took the ferry across the river to Arkansas and to the Phillips County courthouse. The clerk brought out a large leather-bound book. In the center, stamped in gold, were the words *Petitions for Divorce.* On the lines below his name, Peters wrote the following: "I was deserted by my wife on May 7, 1863," and then pushed the book back across the counter.

The clerk read the entry and cleared his throat. "Is that all you wish to say?" he asked. "Nothing more?"

Peters glared at the man. "Nothing more," he replied coldly.

Sensing his anger, the clerk left the matter alone. He stamped the lower corner of the page and closed the book. "Very well, then," he said, a hint of irritation in his voice. "Good day, Dr. Peters."

Without a word, the doctor turned and left the courthouse. That much was done. He had fulfilled one of the requests in Thomas' letter. He had denounced Jessie's actions in the public forum, had told the world that George Peters was a man after all, a man to be respected and even feared. Perhaps the Van Dorn embarrassment would one day disappear and the Peters name would be restored— just as Thomas had written. For now, Peters felt no relief. His heart was heavy as he rode out of the city. He did not stop until he had reached the swampy bayou of Council Bend, his home now—far from Jessie and the past.

*From the Diary of Jessie Peters*

*April 14, 1866*

    *Have just returned from Bolivar this evening and was greeted by my sister Eleanor and her husband Uncle Spivey. They are dear to me indeed. (I'm glad now that they inherited the family home. Let Susan and Lucy and their greedy husbands complain till the heavens rain gold but I'll not pity them in the least!) Eleanor and dear Uncle all but showered me with love and kindness this evening and for that I am most grateful as I fear I too would fall into despair if left alone. Uncle was particularly outraged at the insults heaped upon me at Thomas' funeral. Eleanor was utterly speechless when I told her how George and those Bolivar people shunned me, refusing to even acknowledge my presence. I was mortified that so-called civilized people would behave so horribly at such a sacred affair as a funeral. And now I find myself greeted with another slap in the face. A petition for Divorce!*

    *I may be forced to forgive George when my time comes to stand before our dear Lord—but I have made a promise that while I'm alive and walking this earth, I shall never forget.*

# CHAPTER 39

# A TWIST OF THE VEIL

**June 20, 1868**

They moved slowly, methodically, a serpentine train of white veils, through the halls of the convent and into the sanctuary, down the narrow aisle and past the sparsely filled wooden pews. Faint sighs emitted from the congregation as the solemn spectacle floated by. Dr. Peters turned as Clara passed; her face held the glow of the blushing bride. *Such a lovely girl.* Yet it no longer mattered —beauty held little value in the walls of the convent.

The priest knelt at the prie-dieu and all heads bowed as he began the ceremony of the Novitiate, but Peters could not hear his words, his only thought was the loss of his daughter. Today marked Clara's twentieth birthday, an age at which most young women moved from girlhood into the realm of wife and mother. But not Clara—the stone walls of the church would be her home, the silent world of prayer would fill her days.

When the ceremony ended, Dr. Peters found Clara in the sea of girls and pulled her aside. He kissed her on the forehead. "Clara, you must be certain of this. Is there nothing I can say to make you change your mind?"

Clara smiled at him, her dark almond eyes as bright and cheery as in the days before the War. She took his hand. "This is where I belong, Father."

Peters felt a sudden wave of sadness rising in his throat. So much had happened that he had lost track of time, could not recall when Clara had gone from a little girl to the young lady standing before him. "Very well, Clara," he said weakly. "But if ever—"

She pressed her finger to his lips. "Please, Father," she whispered. "I know."

Then taking his hand, they walked to the quaint rose garden on the east side of the chapel and sat together on the stone bench. A statue of the Virgin Mary stood watch in the center of a mass of yellow roses.

"I've arranged everything with the Mother Superior. If you should need anything—"

"Oh, Father," she said. "I know you only mean to help, but I'm fine—really."

The church bell rang and the nuns began assembling inside the chapel. "Evening mass," she said. "I must go now."

Dr. Peters kissed her one last time and walked her to the door of the chapel. His mind searched frantically for the words he might say to make her come with him, but he could not find them.

Clara stopped at the door and turned to face him. "Father," she said in a serious tone. "You must listen to me. The soul is the most precious part of us. You must not forget that." Tears welled in her eyes; her voice was now small and childlike from emotion. "Father—about the children. You must not abandon them. It is a mortal sin. They need you, Father. Just as I did. And Jessie—"

He cocked his head in confusion at the sound of her name. "What are you saying, Clara? You can't mean—"

Clara wiped her eyes and smiled reassuringly. "God will direct you if you let him, Father," she said as she walked through the chapel door. "There is time enough to make amends. Time enough to save your soul." The bell rang again in the tower above as Clara waved goodbye. "Do what is right, Father," she said as she disappeared in the sea of black robes.

Dr. Peters stood on the stone steps and watched her go. For a moment, he imagined she would come back out again and tell him she had changed her mind—but the only person to emerge was a nun dressed in the habit of St. Anne's Asylum. Peters stepped aside as she moved past him. She was followed by a group of orphans, marching like ducks in a row. The last in the long line of children was four year-old Medora, her olive skin and dark, doe-like eyes, a mirror image of Clara. She smiled at the doctor as she passed.

In the carriage ride to the St. Louis station, Dr. Peters made his decision, or rather he came to the only logical conclusion possible. Clara and Thomas were gone, but Clara was right—there was still William and Lucy. What if they did need him... perhaps he could redeem himself after all. He approached the desk and handed the attendant his ticket. "I would like to change my destination, please," he said. "I'll be going to Thompson's Station, Tennessee."

"Thompson's Station, you say?" the attendant asked. "Alright, but it'll be awhile. Ain't another train till morning."

"That will do," Peters said. "I can wait." He purchased the ticket and took his seat on a bench inside the station.

He was exhausted and wanted sleep more than anything, but he could not stop thinking of what Clara had said. Could she be right? Could he reconcile the past? Nearly two years had passed since he last saw Jessie. It was a few months after the divorce had been granted and he had stopped in to see the children. She had pushed him away with her usual haughtiness, even demanded he leave. He tried his best to explain the reasons for his actions, the reason he had to file for divorce, the reason for the words on the petition, tried to console her with every excuse he could find, but she would not listen. *You have betrayed me,* she told him. And when he left that day, he was sure he would never lay eyes on Jessie or the children again. Now he had made another promise, only this time it was a promise to Clara, one that he must fulfill. Surely there was a way to win Jessie back, to convince her that she needed him after all. Then it hit him. The one thing he could give her that she did not have, the one thing that truly made her happy—money.

\*\*\*

Peters slept on a bench in the station till early the next morning when he was awakened by the sounds of a young newspaper boy selling his papers. "Gityer morning news," he cried out in a squeaky voice.

"Here, boy," Peters said, giving him a nickel and taking the folded paper. He stretched his arms high over his head. His body was stiff and ached from the hard bench.

"Thank you, sir," the boy said, grabbing the nickel with his dirty hands and then darting off between rows of benches to an elderly man in the corner.

He watched the young boy skip from one person to the next and thought of his own boys when they were young. Thomas with his good looks and sharp wit, Arthur with his penchant for trouble.

The station was coming alive now with the chatter of morning travelers, so Peters took his paper and moved to the far corner of the station where the old man now slept soundly. He thumbed through each section, stopping suddenly on the society page. Just as he had requested. There, in bold print, and written by the Mother Superior, was the following article:

*Only a Woman's Heart:*
*The Saddest Story of the Cruelest of Wars*
*The most startling and tragic occurrence of the late war—not even excepting the wholesale slaughter of human beings in battle—was the killing of General Earl Van Dorn, of the Cavalry Department in the Confederate Army, by Dr. Peters, at one time a Senator in the Tennessee Legislature. The tragedy occurred at Spring Hill, a short time previous to the battle of Murfreesboro. The sad details of that affair, and circumstances which led to it, are too familiar to our readers to render repetition of them necessary here. The recollection of the sad story is revived by a paragraph going the rounds of the press to the effect that a daughter of Dr. Peters, young, accomplished, and beautiful, had arrived in St. Louis, where she was about to enter a convent and take the veil. The St. Louis Times of the 21st, alluding to her arrival in that city and the contemplated devotion of herself to the church, says, feelingly, that 'every calamity that war may beget has befallen her family, kindred, fortune and home. The residence in which she dwelt from childhood was in the path of a destroying army that swept wide districts with*

*unsparing desolation. Every species of property was destroyed, and she and an only brother beggared, and fated to encounter even greater calamities, wandering among strangers.*

*The mother, a weaker woman than the daughter, accustomed to ease, flattery and every pleasure that wealth could buy, yielded, never criminally, to the flattery of an army officer, and overstepped rules of decorum prescribed by the social habits of the South. The father wreaked terrible vengeance upon him who destroyed the delights of his poverty—stricken home, and while the people approved the deed there was bitterness insufferable in the cup of grief pressed to the lips of the faultless daughter.*

*The brother bore accumulated misfortunes, unsustained by that divine faith which never fails to give consolation and strength. His sorrows made him insane, and in moody madness he dragged out a miserable existence. Life at length became insufferable, and in an evil hour he put a period to his own existence. The sister lived to soothe a father's sorrows, and lighten anguish that almost dethroned his reason. She was divinely inspired. Her soft, sweet voice never lost its tenderness, and its very tones were silvery with hope, that beamed from her lustrous eyes. She was a divinity, to guard him in the midst of adversity—*

> *Bright as that, oh! too transcendent vision*
> *When heart meets heart in dreams Elysian.*
> *Sweet as the memory of buried love;*
> *Pure as the prayer that childhood wafts above—*

*The daughter, who reached St. Louis a few days since from a Southern city, has sought repose in the bosom of the holy Catholic Church. During the week, she will assume the vows of a sisterhood famed the world over for those charities which this daughter of the South has learned so well how to practice within the precincts of her own unfortunate household. We are induced to write this simple recital of her misfortunes that a sad chapter of personal history might find a place in the memories of men.*

He folded the paper neatly and got up from the bench. Such an elaborate announcement—he truly had not expected it. But the Mother Superior had kept her word—

the article was indeed sympathetic. That was all he had asked. Think of Clara, he had told her. Maybe this was a sign that better days lay ahead. Perhaps his new plan would work.

A train whistle blew and Dr. Peters tucked the paper inside his black leather bag. When the attendant took his ticket, he took his seat among the noisy travelers. In a matter of days he would be back in Spring Hill, back with Jessie.

## From the Diary of Jessie Peters

*June 23, 1868*

*I awoke this morning to find none other than George Peters hovering above my bed like some great bird. He has fallen off a great deal since I last saw him, his face so pale and gaunt that for a moment I thought he might be a corpse. But then he spoke and I knew I would not be so lucky. He was alive—and in the flesh and blood right there in front of me. Of course, when I caught sight of him my first instinct was to scream at the top of my lungs. I frightened him so that he nearly jumped out the bedroom window! The sight of his hands waving and his mouth agape sent me into convulsive laughter. I don't think I've ever seen a funnier spectacle in all my days! How he begged and whined. I think the man is positively insane. Did he think I would pity him? Is that what he would have me do? Pshaw! To feel sorrow for a man who has only himself to blame? I should think not.*

*So, when he at last finished his ridiculous pleadings, I told him to take the door, never to return. Indeed! But instead he dropped to the floor and taking my skirt in his hands, he blubbered like a baby. "You must understand," he wailed. "I had no choice but to divorce you. My reputation was at stake. How was I to provide for my family if my good name was ruined?" How he went on and on till I thought my poor head would burst.*

*But I let him talk, nonetheless. I suppose I wanted to hear his excuses, wanted to hear him beg for my forgiveness. And though he was quite convincing at times, I refused to fall prey to it. I know who he truly is. He is a liar and a cheat who thinks to have his cake and eat it too, but I've got news for him—he will Never get such a luxury from me! Not in a million years will that man ever get the better of Jessie McKissack—never again! And I just laughed and kicked him away, but still he came back for more, groveling at my feet, showering me with promises. And suddenly, it dawned on me—George Peters was courting me! Ha! The very idea! To court me, the discarded wife! I knew there must be a catch, so I asked him just what he was up to.*

*Just what did he want from me? Had he lost his property? Had his friends and family deserted him?*

*He just shook his head and looked at his feet and in the meekest manner said, "Oh, Jessie—how can you say such things when you know that I had no choice? Don't you know that I love you?" Then, just when I thought I could not be more surprised, he got on bended knee and asked for my forgiveness. "What will it take for me to make it up to you?" he pleaded.*

*Well, at last he got my attention. I explained that I had no desire whatsoever to have him live with me—money would be sufficient. "You hurt me deeply when you left me to suffer public humiliation while you ran around hiding your precious Clara! Why should I even forgive you? I think that is sufficient enough!" I said.*

*"But what of the poor children? Will you not consider reconciliation? For their sake?" he asked. But I just laughed and shook my head.*

*Still, he pressed on, begging, pleading. He finally left around midnight but declared he would return next morning as he was staying the evening at Major Cheairs'. I feel quite sure the major and my sister have something to do with all of this. I can't imagine George planned any of it himself. Anyway, I suppose I must give his offer some consideration. That is the least I can do; after all, my children do call him Father—not to mention, he's become quite well-to-do since the War ended. At least that is what I am told. He is adept at making money—I'll grant him that much.*

*But let this be known—if I should ever reconcile with him, it will be out of necessity and nothing else. Never will I love the man! And as for my forgiveness—well, he will pay dearly for that. Redemption costs a pretty penny!*

# CHAPTER 40

# BEGINNING AGAIN

**August 1868**

Jessie smiled with delight as the mahogany trunk was loaded into the carriage. Inside was her new ensemble—a potpourri of silks and velvets, furs and lace trimmings, her wedding gift, George had said, her payment for becoming Mrs. George Peters, again.

"Come give Mother a kiss," Jessie called out to the children who were jumping from the steps of the carriage, bouncing around the yard as if Christmas had come early.

"But why do you have to go?" Lucy asked, her doe eyes filled with giant tears. "I don't want to stay here without you."

"Now, you stop that crying," Jessie teased, as she lifted Lucy from the porch steps and hugged her tightly. "I'll not be away too long this time," she whispered. "You be a big girl and do as Virethia tells you. Won't you do that for me?"

"Oh, Mother," Lucy cried. "Won't you take me with you?"

"Now, there, there, sweetheart," she said, stroking her long golden curls. "You know that Papa and I are going to New Orleans. Now, you be my helper and help take care of your brother while I'm away, and I promise to bring you a china doll of your very own—one with angel hair just like you."

Lucy giggled with delight and hugged her mother's neck. "Oh, Mother! Will you really? And a pretty dress too?"

"Absolutely," Jessie said. "Now, let's have one more kiss then I must go." She pecked her cheek and quickly set the girl back onto the porch. The thrill of traveling again, of eating fine meals and seeing new faces far outweighed her guilty conscience.

"Come, dear," Dr. Peters said, as he emerged from the carriage house. "We must make the depot by 2:00 or risk waiting on another train."

The children followed close behind and jumped inside the carriage before Peters could stop them. "You, Lucy and William!" he scolded. "Get out of the carriage at once!"

"Oh, Papa," William whined. "Won't you take us with you?"

Without a word, Peters grabbed him by the waist of his britches and set him on the grass. "You'll do as I say. Do you understand? I'll not have this foolishness."

"Oh, George," Jessie pleaded, giving the boy a hug. "You are too cruel indeed. Why, how will they grow to love you if you are such a devil to them?"

Peters gave her a scowl and climbed inside the carriage. "You overindulge them, spoil them, and they will only grow up to ruin you," he said.

For the first time since their reunion, the thought suddenly struck her that perhaps her intuition was right— George would never change, could never make her truly happy. She had pushed the thought aside at first, would not allow herself to consider anything but her future security and the security of her children. After all, the land and the houses were all that was left. Who would work the land if she had no husband? Who would protect her and the children now that the dirty carpetbaggers and vile Yankee officers had taken over every inch of the sacred South? Why, it was simple. She had no choice but to marry George again. Together, he had said, they would overcome the events of the past and take back what was rightly theirs. But now she knew. When George had shown up that day in June, proclaimed his undying love, had begged for her forgiveness and cried that he could not go on living without her and Lucy and William, she had believed him. At least she had wanted to believe him. Now she was certain he had fooled her again. Now that he had the house and the land again, he was back to the same old George he had always been—all money and power. But, no matter, she concluded. He might own every inch of land that was rightfully hers, but he would never have her heart. She would live as she pleased, would find her happiness wherever she liked, and she would let George provide the means to do just that. This arrangement more than satisfied her.

She climbed inside the carriage and waved out the tiny window as they moved slowly down the long dusty driveway. The rolling green fields and patches of wildflowers were a testament to the world's resiliency and gave Jessie a renewed sense of hope. She took a deep breath and closed her eyes. If not for the scars etched on her heart, she could easily lose herself in the soft summer breezes, could forget the last five years. But she understood all too well the danger in forgetting. That is something she would never do. Those who forgot the past were doomed to repeat it. She was much too smart for that.

The trip to the train depot took them through the heart of Spring Hill. The wounded little town was once again teeming with life. Buggies were lined along the main street, where men in suits stood talking and laughing, while the ladies casually bought things like coffee and sugar, items that were prize possessions not a few years before. Now life seemed normal again, as normal as it could be after suffering the loss of so much. Even Dr. Peters seemed uplifted by the sight and smiled at Jessie as they made their way down the long street and onto Columbia Pike. As soon as they were out of sight, he went back to his usual brooding, but Jessie did not mind. The quiet was a welcome change to the noisy world of children and servants, and it gave her time to think about this trip—this honeymoon, as George called it. She had always loved New Orleans and now that she was no longer poor, she was more than excited at the thought of Magazine Street and the Roosevelt Hotel.

When they arrived at the station, the attendant called for two broad-shouldered boys to assist in loading the massive mahogany trunk. Jessie smiled proudly. She could hardly wait to show off her beautiful attire, to watch every lady in New Orleans seethe with envy.

"Come along," George said, pushing his way through the sea of strange faces. He hated crowds now more than ever, partly because he disliked most people, the other because he still feared Van Dorn's Cavalry. He supposed he would always feel this way.

Jessie followed alongside him, mesmerized by the noise and bustling activity, eager to rejoin the society that had so cruelly tossed her aside during the War. When they reached the ramp and a waiting attendant, Dr. Peters made his usual request—a private apartment in the front of the passenger train. Jessie smiled at the attendant as he tipped his hat and helped her up the steps. He led them down a long, narrow hallway to the main compartment where he pointed to a door on the left. This was the finest they had, at least on the L & N, he explained.

Jessie went in first and tossed her pearl-trimmed satchel on the wooden bench that ran along the right side, from the door to the window. The dark décor gave the room a stuffy, dismal feeling, so she asked the attendant to open the curtains a little. "How am I to know if this is the finest room or not if I can't even see my hand in front of my face?" She giggled at her own words.

"Well, of course, Mrs. Peters," he replied with a smile. "Let me take care of that for you."

Jessie watched him as he moved to the window and pulled on the long cord on the side of the thick velvet curtain. He was handsome with dark, wavy hair and gray eyes. With his thick arms and trim waist, he cut quite a figure in his blue coat and crisp white shirt. Jessie liked him at once.

"Will there be anything else?" the attendant asked. "Anything at all?" He noticed her watching him and inched closer. His eyes were wide and bright, his voice suggestive.

Jessie felt it at once—that flutter in her chest, the heat rising up her neck. She looked at George who had put his bag on a small valet in the corner and had already reclined on the plush settee. Soon, he would nod off to sleep.

"I'm sure I will think of something," she replied, fluttering her long lashes and twisting a small strand of hair between her slender fingers. "I'll be sure to ask for you, uh," she stopped abruptly. "I don't think I caught your name."

"It's John, ma'am," he said, tipping his hat. "John Murphy."

"Very well, John," Jessie said sweetly. "I'll let you know if I think of anything else I need. Anything at all you say?" She asked, turning toward the water basin in the rear of the compartment.

"Anything at all," he answered, a hint of delight in his voice. "I'll be just down the hallway there." By now his cheeks were hot; his forehead was beaded with sweat.

Jessie glanced over her shoulder and gave him an approving wink as he closed the door behind him. She would wash her face and hands and freshen up a bit. The carriage ride had been quite a dusty affair and she simply detested the gritty feeling on her skin. Besides, this would give George just enough time to be good and asleep. Better safe than sorry she had always said.

By the end of hour, George was snoring, his hat pulled low over his eyes, his breathing deep and steady. Jessie pinched some color into her cheeks, smoothed her bodice and fluffed the layers of her silk dress. Her heart was beating out of her chest, thrilled at the very thought of living again. She quietly opened the door and slipped down the long hallway to the dining car where scores of travelers sat eating, laughing and talking, happy couples, entire families, the ornately decorated compartment filled to capacity. Jessie relished in the vast possibilities that lay before her.

She scanned the room until she saw him at last. His eyes were much brighter than before, his face all the more handsome. She approached him and leaned in to whisper. "Now that I think of it, John. There is *one* thing you could do for me." Then, licking her lips slightly, she brushed the side of his leg with her hand. "Why don't we go some place private where we might discuss it further."

The attendant wiped the sweat from his brow, his confused expression now replaced with a look of sheer delight. "Well, of course, Mrs. Peters," he said, his words spilling out in one long breath of excitement. "I know a nice quiet place down the hall here. We can discuss it for as long as you like." Then, taking her arm in his, he escorted her down the dark hallway, stopping only when he was certain they were out of sight.

\*\*\*

The train moved slowly through the dark Tennessee night as George Peters suffered a fitful sleep. He could not recall the last time he slept through the night, nor could he recall a night without the dream. Tonight had been no different, except that this time he had almost welcomed the apparition, had felt a sense of peace when it presented itself.

The figure had first visited him at Ben Weller's Boarding House in Nashville, the night after he shot the general. A spectacle always in the same form: the silhouette of a man in the uniform of the CSA, standing like a statue in the doorway, his outstretched hand holding a bloody shirt, in the other hand, a small, shiny object. Peters would often scream out, but this time he had sensed no threat, had felt no terror at all, just an overwhelming sadness, a feeling of utter despair came over him. He had reached out for Jessie in hopes of making the vision pass, but had decided not to wake her, opting instead to sit up until daylight would save him. And it was at first light that he finally understood the truth about everything, about Jessie, as he watched her sneak quietly into the room. He remained still and watched her lie down at the opposite end of the long bench, settling in as if she'd been asleep the whole while. He had no desire to confront her, to ask her where she had been, or with whom she'd spent the last few hours. Now he understood. This was his debt to pay, his penance, his redemption. He would no longer fight it.

When the train reached New Orleans, Jessie bolted upright and stretched her arms high above her. A brilliant sun enveloped her as she drew the curtains back and stood staring out the window as the train crept to the station. She was beautiful, radiant—and she was Mrs. George Peters again. *Mrs. George Peters,* he thought. Delightful. Even if she was not entirely his.

Jessie moved to the window and fanned herself. "Oh, George! Just look at them! Look at all the people! I do love this city!" She grabbed a comb from her silk case and began smoothing her tussled chestnut hair. Her dress was a bit wrinkled, but it would do for now. She would change into the red silk at dinner. She giggled aloud at the thought of its scandalously low neckline.

Peters rose slowly from the settee. His back ached and his knees were weak and stiff, but he no longer resented the signs of aging, not like he did years before when he fought Father Time with all his might, resisted the natural process of aging so that he might enjoy his youthful bride. Now he embraced a new role. Power and wealth would be his avatar.

After breakfast, he planned to see the new Cotton Exchange on Carondelet Street. Thoughts of the fall crop had consumed him lately, much like it had all the other farmers in the South. His land must produce more this year; it was all he had left, perhaps all he had ever really had. The War had taught him that. Gone were the days of ease and luxury for most Southerners, but not for the Peters family. He refused to be like the others, refused to be defeated. This was a new time, and he planned to embrace every last bit of it. He would not be naïve like so many.

As the train came to a stop, the handsome attendant appeared again in the doorway. His smile was full of guilt, his eyes a testament to his night's activities. "Pardon my intrusion, Dr. Peters, but I was wondering if I might help you and Mrs. Peters to your carriage."

Jessie turned from the mirror where she stood fanning herself, her cheeks a faint red though the room was pleasantly cool.

Peters glanced at her eager face. "Why, certainly," he said to the attendant. "Why don't you see that my wife gets to our hotel—the Roosevelt? I have a little business to tend to." He then smiled endearingly at Jessie. "I'm sure you won't mind, will you, Mrs. Peters?"

Jessie's eyes grew wide, though she tried to conceal her excitement. "Well, if you must, Dr. Peters," she complained, her talent for dissembling alive and well again. "I suppose I can manage without you." She scooped up the train of her skirt and strutted toward the attendant. "Shall we?"

Outside, the New Orleans sky shone a brilliant blue as a warm breeze blew in from the river. Peters watched with resignation as Jessie and the attendant climbed into a waiting carriage. With the crack of a whip she was gone again, just as he had imagined she would be, lost in her own desires and passions. When the carriage was out of his sight, deep in the narrow streets of the Garden District, he started his long walk toward the river. He would do whatever necessary to protect his name, to keep the Peters family whole. *Secrets*, he thought. *So many secrets...*

### THE END

# AFTERWORD

## George and Jessie Peters

Dr. George Peters remarried Jessie Peters on July 9, 1868, at the Methodist church in Bowling Green, Kentucky. Reverend Thomas Bottomly conducted the private ceremony. According to the *Bowling Green Democrat*, dated July 17, 1868, "The marriage was to be kept strictly secret, lest Dr. Peters' daughter should execute her threat to take the black veil at a convent, to which she retired soon after the war, and is only made public now because of her return to society." Of course, several newspapers had already reported that Clara in fact entered the convent around the week of June 20, 1868, a mere two weeks before her father remarried Jessie. The reason behind this misinformation remains unclear, but it would seem likely that Dr. Peters and Jessie solemnized their marriage in the state of Kentucky for the privacy it afforded, doing everything in their power to keep their reunion out of the limelight.

Dr. and Mrs. Peters spent the next few years between Council Bend, Arkansas, and Jessie's home in Spring Hill, Tennessee. In October 1872, they sold the Spring Hill property and lived exclusively in Arkansas until Dr. Peters purchased the Memphis home in 1874, shortly after the death of their eldest daughter, twelve year-old Lucy Mary.

George Peters, Jr., the youngest son of Dr. Peters and his wife Evalina, was a prominent attorney in Memphis who eventually became Attorney General for the state of Tennessee. Another son, James Arthur, who served in the Confederate Navy, inherited the Council Bend plantation

*Photo of Jessie McKissack Peters when she is in her 70's.*
*Courtesy of Rippavilla Plantation, Spring Hill, Tennessee.*

and farmed there until taking his own life in 1891, thus becoming the second of Peters' sons to commit suicide.

George and Jessie's remarriage in 1868 resulted in the birth of a daughter, Kate Chalmers, in December 1871, and a son, Robert E. Lee, in March 1876. These children were no doubt welcome blessings for George and Jessie, after the death of young Lucy, and later in 1885, when their firstborn son William suffered an untimely death as well. With their pre-War children in the grave, all that remained of the past was Medora.

By all accounts, the doctor and his wife lived relatively quiet, yet separate lives for the remainder of their married years. Dr. Peters maintained his residence on one of his

*Dr. George Peters. Photo was obtained by Nate
Lenow from a descendant of Medora Peters Lenow.*

Arkansas plantations, as evidenced by his election to the
Arkansas House of Representatives in 1885, while Jessie
must have been content with life in the city of Memphis.

Their obvious marital disharmony is perhaps most
apparent at the time of Dr. Peters' death in April 1889. His
obituary states that he was nursed at the home of his
*daughter* Medora Lenow until his death on April 29.
Ironically, the funeral was held at Medora's home as well.
It was reported by members of the Peters family that on the
day of the funeral, Jessie complained terribly about
wearing mourning clothes, casually stating, "Well, I never
cared much for George, but I guess I owe him this much."

Afterward, she donned her black dress and took her place as the grieving widow.

Medora's position within the Peters family is perhaps the most compelling argument for her parentage. Her role as caregiver to Dr. Peters, along with the subsequent lands bequeathed to her in his will, indicate a genuine affection between Medora and the doctor—an affection that would be highly unlikely if Medora was indeed the bastard child of Earl Van Dorn and Jessie Peters. But if Medora was in fact the *granddaughter* of George Peters, then their relationship seems much more plausible.

Jessie lived the remainder of her life as a modern, independent woman, separate from her husband for the majority of their marriage, in charge of the Memphis home and children; so it is not surprising that her last will and testament stipulates that "The share of any devisee or legatee under this will who may be a female shall be to her sole, separate, and exclusive use, free from debts, contracts, obligations, or marital rights of any husband they may ever have." Jessie Peters was indeed a woman ahead of her time.

Though Jessie is reported to have revealed the truth about the Van Dorn affair to a few family members, she never publically denounced the long held belief that she was the general's paramour. Perhaps she kept the family secret out of respect for Clara—or maybe she maintained her silence as personal penance for her own sins. Whatever her motive may have been, Jessie Peters took the truth to her grave on July 16, 1921.

George and Jessie Peters are buried beside each other in Elmwood Cemetery in Memphis, Tennessee. After years of vandalism, their defaced headstones were removed. Their graves remain unmarked to this day.

## Clara Peters
## (Sister Mary Paula Peters)

According to church records, Clara Peters first came to the Visitation Monastery in St. Louis as a student of the academy. Her name appears in the January 1864 account book; though no further official records exist of her attendance during the years before the War. However, her presence at the academy is noted in a few letters and diaries of close family friends from her hometown of Bolivar, Tennessee. These personal accounts provide very candid observations of Clara's behavior during the years immediately following the death of General Van Dorn. The diary of one such family friend describes Clara as one suffering under great mental strain, a tortured soul who spent her days in silent anguish, returning often to the quiet refuge of the St. Louis convent until June of 1868 when she settled there permanently.

Clara Peters took the name of Sister Mary Paula in December 1868, and served for nearly fifty years in the capacity of Choir Sister at the Visitation Monastery in St. Louis. Throughout her years there, she was a beloved teacher at the Visitation Academy and a highly respected sister within the church. A history, written at her death on November 30, 1917, states: "Sister was our very own. Over fifty years ago the young Clara, daughter of Dr. and Mrs. George Peters, nee McNeal, came to us from her home in Bolivar, Tenn., then endangered by the Civil War. She was a fervent Protestant, upright and intelligent. The holy influence of the convent school told on her pure soul. She wondered at the virtue of the Sisters; then she questioned. Faith came; and though to embrace it entailed great sacrifices, the noble girl never hesitated. We who know how she loved her faith and her vocation thank God for her fidelity to His grace."

Clara Peters is buried in an unmarked grave at the Calvary Cemetery in St. Louis, Missouri. It is unclear whether the church ever knew the truth about Clara's past.

*Copy of photograph of Sister Mary Paula Peters (Clara
Peters) obtained by Nate Lenow from Archivist at the
Visitation Academy, Sister M. Louise Gordon. Mr. Lenow
also observed and photographed a similar photo of Sister
Mary Paula Peters in Memphis, Tennessee, on August 11,
1989, in the possession of a descendant of Medora Peters
Lenow.*

*Copy of scrapbook page of Clara Peters as a young girl. Copy of photo obtained by Nate Lenow from archivist at Visitation Academy, Sister M. Louise Gordon (Clara Peters pictured bottom center and below.)*

## Medora Wharton Peters

Medora Wharton Peters spent several years as a student of the Visitation Academy in St. Louis, where Clara Peters served as choir sister. According to monastery archivist Lisa Chassaing, Medora was known as the sister of Clara Peters during her years there. She graduated from the academy in June of 1879, at the age of sixteen. Upon leaving St. Louis, she moved to Arkansas and assumed a place within the Peters family for the first time, as she appears in an 1880 census as the daughter of George and Jessie Peters. Medora's absence in previous census records gives credence to the local legend in Spring Hill, Tennessee, that a Peters' child born during the war years spent her early life in the care of a convent.

Medora most likely went to live with George and Jessie out of necessity alone; since she had no plans of becoming a nun, she would have left the Visitation Academy upon graduation. Still, she remained with the Peters family until October 1884, when she married Henry J. Lenow, son of a prominent Memphis businessman. Over the course of their forty-year marriage, Medora and Henry had thirteen children. Perhaps the absence of a family during her formative years fueled her desire to have such a large number of children.

Medora and her children remained in Memphis and stayed in touch with Jessie, or "Grand" as the grandchildren called her. Although Jessie and Medora maintained their public relationship as mother and daughter throughout their lives, little is known of their true affections for each other. Was their relationship mere pretense, or did they in fact share a common bond? Medora's presence as an heir in Jessie's will seems to indicate there was at least some affection between the two.

As for Medora and Clara, neither of them ever publically acknowledged their relationship as mother and daughter, nor did any member of the Peters or Lenow families.

Perhaps the most compelling piece of evidence proving that Medora's parentage is indeed questionable can be

*Medora Peters Lenow's tombstone in Elmwood Cemetery in Memphis, Tennessee. Medora was born on January 26, 1864, yet the date of birth on this stone is incorrectly listed as January 26, 1865. Photo in possession of author.*

found in her death certificate dated October 26, 1931. Medora's youngest daughter was living with her at the time of her death and was asked to complete the death certificate. In the space provided for the deceased's parents, her daughter left it blank, writing instead the words "Don't Know," a bizarre act considering Medora was buried the next day alongside George and Jessie in the Peters' plot at Elmwood Cemetery in Memphis, Tennessee.

Was this nothing more than an innocent oversight, the actions of a grieving daughter? Or was this an attempt to conceal the true identities of Medora's parents?

Then, sometime in the late 1980's, in an obvious effort to permanently remove the stigma of the Van Dorn affair, a member of the Peters-Lenow family had a new stone placed at the Memphis cemetery to mark Medora's grave. The birth date cut into the new marble stone—January 26, 1865—exactly one year later than Medora's true date of birth, a date that would preclude Van Dorn as her father. A false monument erected to bury the truth of one murderous affair in the darkest days of the Civil War.

*This photo is of Jessie and her children when she is in her 70's. The children are, from left to right: Medora, Kate, and Robert E. Lee. Photo courtesy of the Jill K. Garrett Collection, Tennessee State Archives and History.*

*Thomas McNeal Peters was a student at the University of Mississippi in 1861 before joining the Confederate Army. Photo from the Class book of 1861, printed with permission from the Archives and Special Collections, University of Mississippi Libraries.*

*Ladies (believed to be the McKissack sisters) on the front porch of the McKissack home on Main Street in Spring Hill. Photo in possession of the Spring Hill Public Library (Courtesy of Helen Dark).*

*The Martin Cheairs mansion known as Ferguson Hall in Spring Hill, Tennessee, the site of General Earl Van Dorn's headquarters in the spring of 1863. On May 7, 1863, Dr. George B. Peters entered the home and shot and killed the general in his downstairs office.*

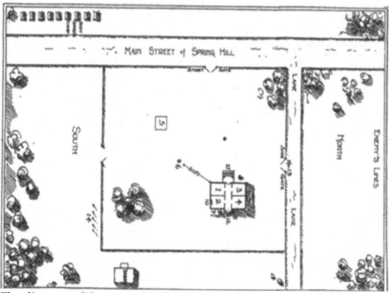

*The diagram of the grounds of the Martin Cheairs home as it appeared in* A Soldier's Honor *(1902), a memoir written by Emily Van Dorn Miller, General Van Dorn's sister. The diagram shows the location of the staff officers at the time of Van Dorn's murder, as well as other important landmarks surrounding the home.*

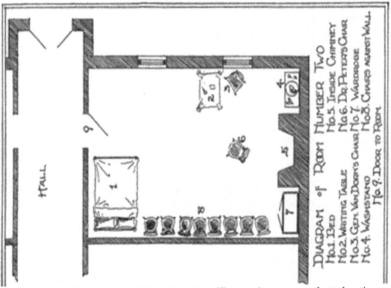

*A diagram of the General Van Dorn's office as it appeared at the time of his murder, also included in* A Soldier's Honor (1902).

# A NOTE FROM NATE LENOW

On March 15, 2010, I received a letter from Bridget Smith regarding my family and the Peters—Van Dorn affair. I had begun researching the story in 1989, but the pace of my life had forced me to put aside my work. Now that there was someone else with the same interest, I was determined to see it through. We were both on the verge of correcting a footnote in history, and we decided that together we could get there.

I came across the story of the doctor and General Van Dorn strictly by accident. I had heard the story in our family of how the doctor shot the general, but was not especially interested in it until I met with two distant cousins one August afternoon in 1989. We were all very interested in our family genealogy and decided to meet at their home in Memphis, Tennessee to discuss it. While sharing our research, my elder cousin, the matriarch of the home, stopped abruptly and changed the topic to the murder of Van Dorn.

What she proceeded to tell me was the *real* story. I did not question her credibility, as she had lived in Memphis in the same home with her grandmother Jessie Peters, the doctor's wife, until Jessie's death. Her own mother was of course a central character to the story. She then really got my interest when she produced a rare photograph of Clara, the daughter of the Dr. Peters from a previous marriage. Clara had become a Sister at a Monastery in St. Louis several years after the death of General Van Dorn.

The Matriarch chose not to tell me the whole story, yet she had told me enough and I began my search. I later realized that she had been entrusted with this incredible secret, yet within the secret was a great injustice that had to be corrected. Perhaps it was her intent that this secret was revealed to me as I left their house that day. While sitting in my car I reflected on what I had just observed and it suddenly came to me that the way the Matriarch had talked of and held the photograph of Clara with such a respect and pride, that she was not simply some distant relative. Clara was her grandmother.

Clara's life was full of great tragedy, yet she chose to excel in her circumstances and lived a life as an unknown heroine to the world, respected and revered by all who knew her.

NL

# BIBLIOGRAPHY

The bulk of the research for this book was derived from primary sources. I relied on diaries and letters, official military correspondences, and newspaper articles as the basis for my story. As for the motives of the persons involved in the murder of the general, and the actions of the Peters family years later, I based my theory on a careful study of related writings and family histories. Though not a complete bibliography, the following resources were invaluable to me throughout my years of research:

Lisa Chassaing, archivist for the Convent of the Visitation Archives. Special thanks for her assistance in obtaining various records of the Visitation Academy and the Convent of the Visitation in St. Louis, Missouri.

Branch, Mary Polk. *Memoirs of a Southern Woman* (1911)

Carter, Arthur B. *The Tarnished Cavalier: Major General Earl Van Dorn C.S.A. (1999)*

Clinton, Catherine. *The Plantation Mistress (1982)*

*Diary of John H. Bills* (Bolivar-Hardeman County Tennessee Public Library)

East, Charles, ed. *Sarah Morgan: The Civil War Diary of a Southern Woman* (1991)

Fitch, John. *Annals of the Army of the Cumberland:1861-1863 (1864)*

Fowler, William Ewing. *Stories and Legends of Maury County, Tennessee* (1937)

Garrett, Jill K. *Hither and Yon* (The Maury County Historical Society, 1999)

Hartje, Robert G. *Van Dorn: The Life and Times of a Confederate General (1967)*

Miller, Emily Van Dorn. *A Soldier's Honor: With Reminiscences of Major-General Earl Van Dorn* (1902)

McAlexander, Hubert H. *Strawberry Plains Audubon Center: Four Centuries of a Mississippi Landscape* (2008)

Rose, Victor. *Ross Texas Brigade (1881)*

Shea, William L. and Earl J. Hess. *Battle of Pea Ridge: Civil War Campaign in the West (1992)*

Smith, Frank H. *History of Maury County Tennessee* (Notes) Compiled by the Maury County Historical Society (1969)

The following manuscripts in the Tennessee State Library and Archives Manuscript Collections:

*Cheairs-Hughes Family Papers* (1636-1967)

Figuers Collection, Addition (1830-1964)

*Will Hicks Jackson Papers* (1766-1978)

*Jill Knight Garrett Collection* (1800-1969)

*Talbott-Fentress Manuscript Collection* (1817-1953)

*Van Dorn Battle Flag, 1862*

The Van Dorn battle flag was carried by the Army of the West under the command of General Earl Van Dorn. The flag was officially issued between June and September 1862 but may have been used as early as March 1862.